Surprise Me!

Surprise Me!

Nancy
Goodman

Diversion Books
A Division of Diversion Publishing Corp.
80 Fifth Avenue, Suite 1101
New York, New York 10011
www.DiversionBooks.com

First Diversion Books edition March 2012.

ISBN: 978-1-938120-05-3

1 3 5 7 9 10 8 6 4 2

ACKNOWLEDGMENTS

To Lani, Sam, Alex, and Scott; to my mom, to Phyllis and my DAD (capitalized for being so big in my life). To Mikey, of course. My family is my home and my heart.

Many thanks to Bob Sievewright for introducing me to Melissa Giovagnoli. The woman who looked at my dusty cluster of manuscripts and ventures, tagged this book and said, "That's the one." And even more so, I thank you for making me believe that in the world of connecting and building, there is a place for me.

To my friends who not only read the pages, but offered solid advice:

Linda Blumenthal, Denyse Goodman, Shanna Guthman, Andi Kaplan, Marci Malter, Cindy Meister, Linda Moore, Terri Olian, Abby Ross, Ruthe Schwartz, Larry Stern. Special thanks to Mark Greenberg.

To those kind talents who became part of my team:

Julie Clark, Graham Lee Giovagnoli, Tara Lynn Price, Nicholas J. Rizzio, Diane Tyrrel, Josh Studzinski, and many thanks to Janet Goldstein.

And finally, a heartfelt tribute to those who played a role in my heart, which blew puffs of real life to the story...

Thank you

CHAPTER 1

Genie heard her cell phone ring just as the light turned green. Crossing the street, she reached in her purse and felt for the zippered pocket. That special place she kept the phone so she always knew where to find it. Why was it never there! Second ring, third ring, the race against the forth ring to voicemail.

"Hello!"

Steven's voice: "Where *are* you?"

"There was a huge pile up on the highway and then I got stuck behind a…"

Steven interrupted. "Just tell me what you're wearing. I need to tell the Finches so they'll recognize you."

"Gray suit."

"*Oh* God. Don't tell me you're wearing that awful thing that screams, 'Why wasn't *I* born Chanel!'"

"Ha ha Steven, very funny."

"Hold on, Gene. I'm going to call them from the other line."

Genie was now walking so fast, with such large and stretching strides, it felt like she was doing Pilates on a treadmill. She wondered if the sweat from her face was enough to wreck a cell phone. She wiped the phone on her sleeve, put it back up to her ear, and used her free hand to dig through her oversized fake Prada bag, which was hanging on her shoulder for dear life as though it knew it was slipping close to the edge.

Steven came back to the call. "Where are you now?"

"Just walking up to the building." Genie took a swipe of her L'oreal Never Fail Lipstick. "I think I see them walking in. Short couple, gray hair, she's wearing a navy blue..."

"Yep, that's them. Don't forget, you're *Amanda*."

"I know Steven, I've rehearsed the..."

Just then, Genie's heel got caught in a sidewalk crack causing her to catapult forward. Like it was jumping from the sinking Titanic, her handbag flew from her shoulder, spewing most of its contents. Her *not* fake Coach wallet hit the pavement, spilling credit cards and old receipts, while two quarters performed like choreographed partners on Dancing with the Stars.

Genie's hands were on the sidewalk, butt pointed up toward the sky. She didn't dare look up to see who was watching. Gently, she came to her knees and reached for the phone, which had skated just a tad out of reach. Groaning and swearing, she grabbed it and put it back to her ear, wondering if Steven was okay in there.

"Steven?"

"Yes, Genie."

"I *FELL!* Damn it, these stilettos! And the *suit*. How do people move in these things!"

Steven was silent.

"Stop laughing, Steven. It's not funny!" Genie began gathering the items and stuffing them back in her purse. Steven wasn't talking which she knew to be a confirmation of the laugh.

"You're so unconcerned! I could have broken my ankle!"

"You also could have been adopted by Michael Jackson and named Blanket."

Genie rolled her eyes. She clumsily picked herself up, smoothed out her skirt, placed her handbag back on her shoulder and removed the strands of hair from her mouth.

"Ok, I'm walking up to the Finches now." Genie ended the call, slipped the phone in her purse, and approached her awaiting clients.

"Mr. and Mrs. Finch?"

The elderly couple turned toward Genie and smiled. And didn't everyone? Despite her klutzy tendencies, limited retail budget, and a couple added pounds from the weekend, Genie had a warm appeal, a girl-next-door kind of pretty, and a smile that walked in before she did.

"Hello. I'm Amanda Burns. So nice to meet you."

Mr. and Mrs. Finch reached their hands out to Genie. They were about the same height, both gray, but quite adorable. Genie had seen pictures of them, but in person they seemed so... *connected.* So Genie, the "high-end real estate maverick" began her appointed performance. In heels that surely would kill her. In a skirt she surely would rip.

"Are you two ready to go up and take a look see?"

The Finches nodded. Genie led them to the bank of elevators. Once inside, Genie inserted a key and pressed the top button marked Penthouse. Then, she spoke in the most formal voice she could muster. "The architect who designed this unit had a vision. He wanted you to walk in the door and experience the unexpected. There's an actual term that describes this. It's called *procession.* As you move through the space in an orderly fashion, there will be elements of surprise."

Mrs. Finch laughed politely. "Nothing surprises us anymore. We've seen it all!"

Oh, how Genie loved her job! "Well, Mrs. Finch, I'm in the business of surprises."

Mr. Finch said, "With all due respect, Ms. Burns, I've had many surprises in real estate deals and none of them have been anything to celebrate."

Genie would have been offended, had she been who she said she was.

"Mr. Finch, I guess surprises in general are a bit of a crap shoot. They may be blueprints for disaster, or dreams that step off a page. But what you're about to see is most definitely the latter."

Mrs. Finch chimed in. "Well how about fifty years together? These days that's quite a surprise."

Genie couldn't have scripted this better. "Really! Married fifty years? What an accomplishment!"

Mrs. Finch gloated. "And actually, we think the kids are planning something."

"*Really?* What do you think the kids are up to?"

"Oh, we're quite sure it's a surprise party. Saturday night. There have been some slip-ups."

Genie smiled. She knew the slip-ups. She had planted them. "So is this Penthouse your empty nester's dream?"

Just then the elevator stopped. A workman and three more people got in and pressed floors. In the back of her mind she knew Steven was waiting impatiently.

Mr. Finch answered Genie's question. "Well, we've been looking for about a year. We haven't found anything that we've fallen in love with. And frankly, what you describe doesn't seem like it fits our style. We like more traditional layouts."

"Well, Mr. Finch. The more conventional layouts are certainly lovely. But let me ask you a question..." The door opened, the workman stepped out, and the door closed again, "...looking back on your fifty years together, would you say that your best memories were the ones you expected? Or the ones that were a surprise?"

Mr. Finch smiled. Genie felt like she just witnessed his memory button on rewind. "Ms. Burns. You ask smart questions. My wife is... *not* the conventional layout."

Genie laughed. "What was the best surprise of all?"

"When she said yes."

"To marrying you?"

"To trusting me."

Genie suddenly felt a pang. Whatever it was, she loved these two people. She spoke to Mrs. Finch. "What was *your* biggest surprise?"

Mrs. Finch looked at her husband. "That he never gave up trying. He never stopped loving me. I wake up surprised every day."

Genie stared at them. "Well, you two do seem perfect."

The Finches laughed abruptly in unison. Now Genie was surprised.

"You're not?"

Mr. Finch spoke boldly. "My wife is a pain in the ass."

Genie laughed and Mrs. Finch nodded. "I can be a bit long in the feelings department!"

Mr. Finch said jokingly, "*Long?* Her feelings come like a fleet of stretch limos lined up on Oscar night. *Dressed to kill.*"

Genie laughed and Mrs. Finch nodded again. "This is true. But for the sake of the environment, and our marriage, I've gone Hybrid. I've switched from feeling blue to green."

Genie was riveted. "Was it love at first sight?"

Mr. Finch gloated. "As a matter of fact, it was. I knew at the end of our first date that I would end up with her. But oh boy, was I tested!"

The elevator stopped again, and the door opened and closed.

"So what's the secret to your marriage?"

Mrs. Finch smiled. "Choosing the better view." Genie had a questioning look and Mrs. Finch continued. "It's like living in a home with a beautiful front and backyard, but some not so pretty views from the sides. You walk by them every so often. You see them and know they're there. But it's not where you place the sofa."

Genie smiled and nodded. She understood the message. She wished they had more time to chat, but the elevator stopped and opened onto a large marble foyer. A chandelier dipped from a high ceiling trimmed with magnificent crown molding. Ahead, ten-foot high double doors were closed, and Genie put her hand on the handle. She looked at the Finches with excitement, adoration, and the most heartfelt anticipation of the moment that was seconds away.

"Mr. and Mrs. Finch. In honor of your fifty-years together. Are you ready?"

They both looked at Genie and nodded. Genie opened the door.

"We're ready. But don't get your hopes up. We don't like sur—"

"*SURPRISE!*" The word boomed from eighty-seven family members and friends. The Finches stood frozen in the doorway. They were so stunned that they looked back at Genie as if to confirm they were in the right place. She nodded warmly with tears in her eyes.

The Penthouse real estate agent Maggie had certainly taken a chance, encouraging her clients to open their home for something of this nature. She'd told Genie she was crazy to even suggest an eighty-seven person "showing." Genie watched as the Finches were swallowed up by arms, hugs, and stories. After screams and tears; laughs and embraces; food, memories, and wine, the Finches bought the view.

CHAPTER 2

Genie woke up in a sweat. She looked over toward the chair. It was empty. Not more than a second ago he was sitting right there talking to her, laughing with her... what had they thought was so funny? And what about that story he told her? Now she couldn't remember.

It was the oddest feeling to see her dad again. It *had* to be him. The coincidence was too uncanny. First of all, twenty-one years to the day. What's the likelihood of that? But far more bizarre was the *cough*. She wouldn't have remembered that when he laughed hard, it sounded like happy congestion. Kind of like a giggle hack.

The last time Genie saw her dad alive she was nine years old, groggy and foggy, buried underneath her covers. This early wake up was part of their ritual on the Mondays he left for the airport. Her bedroom was always a bit dark on these mornings, since the sun wouldn't be stretching its rays for at least another hour.

After the kiss and stroke to her hair would come her weekly allowance. He pulled out his money clip, thumbed two dollars, and placed the folded bills on her nightstand. Never did he lay them down flat. They were placed in a tented position.

It was the third week in March. Genie and her friends were walking home from school. Since it was the beginning of the week, and their allowances hadn't been spent, they could stop at Bob's Mart for a snack. Just one block shy of that corner, they heard a car screech behind them. It was Aunt Dotty, and Genie could tell something pretty bad had happened.

Aunt Dotty lived a colorful life, no doubt. Whatever this was about, however, it was way worse than the break-ups with bad boyfriends, getting fired, or being evicted from apartments that were simply too nice for someone who was capable of being hired for a well paid position, but not of keeping the job.

Aunt Dotty called out harshly through the passenger window. "Genie, you need to get in the car!"

Genie felt an immediate ache in her stomach.

"*Now!*"

She turned back toward her friends. She motioned for them to go ahead and she got in the front seat with her aunt, who refused to look at her.

"Genie, I don't know how to tell you this." Dotty grabbed a tissue and wiped her eyes and nose.

"You don't know how to tell me *what?*" Genie looked straight at her aunt.

"Your daddy's been in a terrible accident."

Genie's stomach had been correct. And the pain knob just turned to the right. She spoke with panic. "A car accident? Is he in the hospital? When can I see him?"

Aunt Dotty didn't answer. Genie argued her silence.

"Daddy wasn't in an accident! He called from the airport before I left for school. He's on an airplane to New York. He told me he'd call me tonight!"

Dotty was crying so hard that Genie could barely understand her words.

"He *was* on the airplane, Genie. The plane..."

Genie froze. She couldn't feel anything except for her stomach. Words formed inside her head but all of the exits were closed.

"Genie, do you understand what I'm saying?"

Genie didn't respond.

"Genie, listen to me." Finally her aunt was looking at her, but Genie turned away. "This is a terrible, terrible thing. You are a big girl and now you're going to have to be even bigger. Your mommy is very sad. She is in her room sleeping. We need to help her by being very strong. We need to take care of her now."

Not one tear rolled down Genie's cheek. No flashes or pictures came into her mind. She didn't feel fear or panic. It felt like she had been unplugged from her body. She couldn't feel the other part and didn't know where it had gone. All she could feel was the car in motion as it traced the familiar route home.

They drove past Genie's friends as they walked into Bob's Mart. She turned her head to watch them. If they stayed in her vision long enough, maybe she could become them again. She could go back to being the Genie she was, just five minutes ago.

Suddenly, she remembered. She reached inside her pocket and pulled out the folded dollars. Right about now, she would have been handing one over to pay for her candy bar. A dollar that meant nothing before, and could be given away without thought, was now the last thing he gave her.

The girls disappeared inside the store, living the same day they woke up to. Genie slowly turned her head back. She watched withered tissues piling up as they were discarded in her aunt's purse. She knew, as if she had already seen it, that the mahogany table next to her mom's bed was in the exact same condition. Soggy white puffs of a life that was over, catching the bad days to come.

• • •

Now, twenty-one years later, unlike a memory that's distant and removed, this felt warm and familiar. His laugh was too fresh and precise in detail. If Genie hadn't heard him today, she wouldn't have remembered. So why did he wait so long to come back? *And what was he trying to tell her?* Genie rolled over on her stomach and buried her head in her pillow. Within seconds she was fast asleep. The sight of her dad would be forgotten by morning because whatever he had come back to say, Genie wasn't ready to hear it.

CHAPTER 3

Genie reached across the nightstand, hoping for some good news. Maybe she hadn't overslept and it just happened to be a bright morning. Maybe her inner clock was so precise that she had woken up all by herself. She turned the alarm clock to face her. "*Damn!*"

How she hated the negotiations that always followed the mishap of waking up late. Morning routines are a science. It's where Karma meets vanity. The abandonment of any step can bring disastrous results to the day. At best it can mess with your looks. In extreme cases, it can kill you.

It may be necessary to skip the shower, but make-up and hair aren't electives. And then, of course, there's the bed. Whenever Genie left with an unmade bed, she was afraid something bad would happen. There would be some sort of accident. And whoever was left to sort through her place would walk into a mess. "Oh, *this* is how she left her apartment?"

Genie flung back the covers. She flipped her legs across the bed and felt for her fuzzy slippers. She hobbled into the bathroom and checked herself out in the mirror. Half of her hair was in a high ponytail with bangs tiptoeing just past her nose. She tucked them behind her ear, brushed her teeth, and began making major decisions.

Genie was a firm believer that your hair *is* your make-up. But when you're short on time, hair is a great place to make the cut. Figuratively speaking that is. So here would be the plan. Hair goes up in a messy bun. Steven will tease, but who cares? Brand new sweater offsets dirty hair. This buys time for one made bed, one outfit change (in case she feels fat), and one stop at Starbucks.

Within thirty minutes, Genie was placing her order. "A tall Soy Steamer, extra hot with extra foam, and a coffee of the day."

As she waited at the register, Genie looked at the couple ahead of her. She did this often in the presence of couples, perhaps because she had no real belief that she'd ever be lucky enough to *be* part of one. Steven was her partner, that was it. Danny was her friend, that was that. So Genie stood behind these two people, studying the nuances of their body language.

Genie guessed them to be about her age, late twenties or early thirties. No wedding rings. What really caught her attention, however, were the woman's fingers lightly holding on to the bottom of her boyfriend's shirt. He leaned into her. *This* couple was the real thing.

Genie imagined the rest of their day together. The phone calls they'd make to check in with each other. The plans coming up in their week. Arguments they would have and get over. This one shared Starbucks moment was better than all the shares of Starbucks to Genie. This was the kind of "holdings" she longed for, touching the bottom of a boyfriend's shirt.

Genie had certainly survived her share of unsuccessful fix-ups. In most cases, she would sit across from a guy who seemed nice enough, but she didn't feel any attraction. She questioned herself and challenged her shallow nature. She reasoned through the lack of chemistry, could she trade it for stability? She would be kind and open, believing maybe she could do it. But when it came to trying to *kiss* them? *Ew.*

The guilt she felt at her lack of interest caused Genie to overcompensate in friendliness. *These* were egos to stroke, accompanied by a rejection that was so buried in situational lies that the guy would walk away feeling *better!*

A few of the guys she met were charming and seemingly good catches. She felt a *definite* attraction, *yay!* Until, that is, she found out that their attentive, charismatic natures weren't inspired by their feelings for Genie. They were inspired by egos that needed the constant strokes of lots and lots of women. Or, as Genie had witnessed with her friend Lori, some guys had rejection techniques that weren't exactly ego-friendly. For all of these reasons, Genie kept a distance from men.

Just as Genie was about to pay for her frothy morning start, she felt a slight tug to the back of her sweater. Kind of a pull with a twist. She turned to see what she was caught on. And that's when she heard a voice.

"You overpaid, don't you think?"

One quick glance was about all it took. The price tag from her brand new sweater was with the tan-armed and dangerous. But Genie knew the five signs of impending disaster when it came to men and their weapons. One was over-confidence. Two was charm. Three was an outgoing nature. Four was a quick wit. And five was anyone who was not only gorgeous, but knew she'd overpaid for that sweater.

In order to fend off the approaching danger, her system went into battle. Her brain cells instant messaged the butterflies in her stomach. The butterflies flew straight to her gut intuition, which sent a red alert to her heart. *Danger, danger! Cease all fire! Abort launch into attraction!* If only she had washed her hair. *That's ok. Dirty and tough, all the better to beat you, my dear.*

Genie looked into his brown eyes. She refused to be taken in by the sexy stubble of yesterday's shave. No way would she succumb to the blondish brown waves or the tan that looked happenstance. What a *manipulative* backdrop just to highlight the ever so perfect white smile. This wasn't a man. This was an R.V. on civilian soil!

Genie smiled politely as she plucked the ticket from his hand. "Thank you, but obviously you don't know Burberry."

"I don't. But I think I saw his cousin this morning."

"And who would that be?"

"Dingleberry?"

The employee at the register laughed. Genie rolled her eyes with a smirk. She paid for her drink and without looking back, headed to the condiments stand. She took a few packets of sweetener for "now." She stuffed a few in her pocket for later. When she was finished stirring, she put the lid on her cup. Then casually, innocently, she grabbed a few more packets and dropped them into her purse.

Suddenly, the voice again, "Now you've *underpaid,* don't you think?"

This guy was country boy-like in his charm and it made him positively deadly. Genie knew better than to fall for it; she had met this man-brand before. She was clearly dealing with an ego that was so inflated, a man who was so used to woman falling all over him; and Genie refused to be number whatever.

"*I'm* sorry. There must be people around here who need a price check. I'm just not one of them."

"Well, price checking is only one of my great assets."

Genie's mind began scrolling down what had to be a long list of his assets. Heavenly ones, she was sure. But she had to stay strong, not just for herself. This was for all womankind!

"I believe you're more of a *pain* in the asset."

"Oh, you're so wrong. Everybody likes me."

"Really!"

"Ok, name one thing you don't like about me."

Genie couldn't resist the fun. "Ok, I'll name two."

"Awesome. Lay it on me, Girl."

"Fine. Number one, you have no class. And two, you have no taste."

He put on a face of celebrating shock. "Are you kidding? I have impeccable class and taste! That's why I didn't want you walking around with a blueberry tag."

Genie laughed.*"Burberry."*

"What*ever.*"

Though his chemistry warfare was lethal, Genie's defense team was just too well trained. The enemy was a persistent one though, as he moved in for the kill.

"Ok, we can say our goodbyes and I will get out of your hair. But speaking of your hair... I have just one question, do you mind?"

"Go right ahead!"

"That thing on the back of your head." He motioned a swirl with his pointer finger. "Is it a bun or a hairy crab?"

It took every bit of restraint not to laugh. Not to play along and attempt to get him to ask her out on a date. So she could experience his long list of assets and get dumped in less than a week.

"Oh! You do image consulting as well?"

"Well, I just wanted to know who did your hair, that's all. I'm guessing Cuisinart."

Genie stared at him. He raised an eyebrow, claiming innocence. It was this very look that left Genie with no doubt in her mind. Regard him as a gapers block; something to look at and quickly move on.

She grabbed one more handful of sweetener packets and tucked them in his jacket pocket.

"Those are for you. I like the fake stuff to sweeten my drinks. In my life, I'm looking for real." She smiled and walked out the door.

CHAPTER 4

Surprise Enterprise was on the second floor of a vintage building walk-up. While it hosted many high-end clients, the office was warm and inviting. Twelve-foot ceilings with antique chandeliers boasted open-air elegance, while the deliciously overstuffed chairs and sofa begged you to sit down, bond as one, and never leave them again. When Genie walked in with an extra coffee, she set it in front of her partner Steven, who was doing what he did best.

"Well, Mrs. Ford," he was saying, "Surprise Enterprise *is* pricey. That's because we aren't just event planners. We tell prospective clients to think of their event, not as a party, but a plot with a surprise twist at the end. We literally write the script from the story you give us about the person. The surprise has to reflect who they are, and where they are in their lives. And of course, what they're celebrating."

Genie spoke as soon as he hung up. "Did we get the job?"

"Maybe." Steven looked up at Genie. When she turned to walk to her desk, he noticed her hair. Predictably, he couldn't resist. "Genes."

She turned and looked at him. He pointed toward her head and twirled his finger. "What do you call that thing, other than a mistake?"

Genie rolled her eyes. "It's called a messy bun, Steven."

"So, all you need is a messy shirt and then you've got an outfit!"

Genie shot him a look and they smiled at each other sarcastically.

"Hey, Gene." He lifted his cup. "Thanks for the coffee."

The first time Genie Burns had laid eyes on Steven Jastrome it was at the Mayor's daughter's surprise party. He had been brought in as the caterer, as he did all of the Mayor's affairs. Steven had heard about Genie and her event planning business before meeting her. He had the idea that they should joint venture and he brought it up casually after the party.

Business aside, Genie immediately thought she'd arrived at Fairy Tale Central. It would go something like this. Steven entered in, right on page one, tall, dark, and handsome. Page two, she would partner with him and off-the-charts chemistry would build. They would fight their feelings, as all great loves do, until finally they'd have to give in.

Of course, they would fall madly in love. They would get married in a glorious wedding, and have kids who would man the phone lines. They would chase each other around the desk and their love would never grow old. Their kids would take over the business. Genie and Steven would die at old age, *one day apart.*

Genie would go first, of course, and Steven would be so lost without her that his heart would stop just to find her. In honor of their love, the way they met, and the business they had built together, the kids would throw a surprise funeral. Their shared casket would have overstuffed pillows with chenille throws covering their feet. The business would go on forever and ever, surprising people with love worldwide. *The End.*

Steven had *clearly* not gotten the memo. As a matter of fact, as far as Genie was concerned, somebody up there had a bad sense of humor when it came to passing out genetics that determined gender attractions. *Same* gender attractions. She hadn't meant *fairy* tale! Nonetheless, fate had handed her a trusted friend and the partner of the century.

"That's cute, Steven. And you're welcome for the coffee. By the way, who was the prospect on the phone?"

"This lady named Melanie Ford wants to have a big surprise party for her husband Tom. He's a truck driver. Problem is, her budget is really low. I don't see how we can do it."

"Hey, I know Melanie Ford. Isn't she the one who adopted a little boy with autism? There was an article about her in the paper a while back."

"Yep. That's her. But she's got maybe five hundred bucks total. We can't do a surprise, rentals, a location, and food for that. There's no way."

Genie sat quietly. She was remembering the article and what she read about this woman.

"Steven, I'd really like to help her."

"Genie, please don't go there. It's not fair to the paying customers. And it's not even professional." Before the words were out of his mouth, Genie picked up the phone and looked up the Caller I.D. to redial the last incoming call.

"Genie, what are you doing?"

"I know a way we can help her within her budget. Does he own his truck?"

"Does he own his own truck? How *negligent* of me. I need to start asking clients if they rent or lease their autos. Use AT&T or Verizon. Use roll on, speed stick, or spray..."

"Stop, Steven! I'm saying we can hire *him*... to do deliveries to a party."

"*What* party? Oh, gotcha! I need to ask if they're Republicans or Democrats."

Genie laughed. "He can make the delivery to the Sutton's party next month. It's perfect and it actually helps us out! I've been looking for someone to transport a cow." Genie looked innocently at Steven, whose mouth was now hanging open. She continued anyway. "Maybe a goat and a pig too, depending on availability."

Steven rubbed his temple. "Genie, could you please move from the part of your brain that makes sense to you and use the part that the rest of the world understands?"

"Ok, Steven. We hire Tom to make the delivery that I would have paid someone else to do. Since the Sutton's party is an over-the-top, money is no object kind of gig, we can piggyback Melanie's party on to their set up. That makes it affordable for Melanie." Steven raised his eyebrows in question.

"Steven, it won't cost the Suttons any extra money and we still go with the original plan. David Sutton and his wife get a flat tire on the way to their weekend home in the country, their cell phones are *mysteriously* lost and they get picked up by the fake farmer who takes him back to his fake farmhouse to call the fake tow truck... David gets surprised in the barn we rented, *right?*" Steven didn't respond.

"So *after* that party is over, instead of taking everything down, we keep it up for Tom. We get him to his *own* party by having *him* do the pick up!" Genie could see that Steven's intrigue was piqued and that got her excited. She continued. "I know it will be late, but the guests will just know that's the deal. We've gotten people up in the middle of the night before. We use the same rentals, serve light breakfast food since nobody's hungry at that time of night, and we're well within her budget."

Genie looked at Steven, who now looked utterly exhausted. Genie knew that face. He loved the idea! She took out her nail file, looked down at her hand, and filed those babies with pride. This was the only place she was smart, but she milked it like a rented cow.

Steven spoke with surrender. "Ok, that's actually brilliant. So how can such a brilliant mind be so incredibly stupid?"

Genie paused. She looked up from her nails. "I'm not sure. But I'm thinking maybe it's the same way a nice man can be such a prick?"

"What I mean is that you're not willing to travel. You need to get over your fears, Gene. We could go national and you know it."

Genie was defensive. "Steven, I started this company with the intention of keeping it local. You signed on knowing that, ok? I hate when you pressure me."

"Genie, you had a small business then. It's grown and you're holding us back."

Genie knew he was right. Her tone was one of defeat. "Ok, Steven, we can do out of town parties. I'll do everything from here and then we'll just staff them."

"Gene, come on. You're never going to step on an airplane? You'll hold yourself back for the rest of your life because of an incident in your past?"

"It has nothing to do with that incident. I could fly if I wanted to. I just don't need anything more that what I have here."

"That's bullshit, Genie. You are afraid to fly."

"I'm *not.* I just like land. I like when what's below me isn't moving. It's personal taste."

"Personal taste my ass!"

They raised their eyebrows at each other. The pun hovered over them like smog that's so common it's not even worth discussing.

"Genie, why are surprises for everyone but you?"

"I hate surprises."

Steven laughed. "What a hypocrite!"

"I am not! You don't have to love donuts to open a donut shop!"

"That's not the point. That's not a decision based on fear. With you and travel, we're talking irrational fear. People travel every day and nothing bad happens to them."

"Oh yeah? I know lots of people who would never work in a donut shop because they're afraid of donuts."

Steven looked at Genie with a smug smile.

"Tell me you really didn't just say that."

"That's right, Steven. Afraid of donuts. Afraid of cookies. Afraid of potato chips. They can't be around them. But, and correct me if I'm wrong, I don't recall any recent headlines about donuts actually killing anyone. No reports of cookies holding up banks and taking people hostage. No stories of potato chips attacking kids on playgrounds. But everyone's afraid of food and nobody thinks that's strange. I, on the other hand, choose not to fly, and that's an irrational fear?" And with a confident twist of fun she added, "I can be around surprises even if I don't choose to eat them."

"You know, Genes, you actually sounded intelligent there for a minute. I got kind of freaked out listening to you, like maybe you really have been smart all this time and I just totally missed it. Then the real you came out again. I'm so fricking relieved!"

With deliberate motions, for great affect, Genie opened her desk drawer, pulled out a Snickers Bar, opened the wrapper, and slowly, every so gingerly, took a bite.

"Mmmm. Deeeelicious. I'm not scared of it at all. Which is amazing because do you know how this Snickers Bar got its name?"

Steven knew this would be good. "How did the Snickers Bar get its name, Gene?"

"It held up a bank at gunpoint, took hostages, threatened them all with weight gain, and *snickered*."

Steven refused to reward her by laughing. "Ok, Genes. You play it safe. But you're missing out on a ton of business. You know one day I'll have to leave you because of it."

Genie felt her stomach drop. This wasn't funny anymore.

"What do you mean you'd leave me? We're partners!"

"And business partners typically partner to make money. Not *not* make money. If the business can't grow because one of the partners is a baby, then that partner might have to plan surprise potties on her own. Pun intended."

"Steven, I so resent that comment! I'm not a baby. I have a way of life that works for me. And without me, your idea of a surprise party would be having everyone come out of the closet. Pun intended!"

"And without me, you'd have no income because you'd feel too guilty to charge anyone."

Genie felt like a little girl with a lemonade stand, reprimanded for giving free refills.

Steven paused and softened. "Genes. A staff can't do what you do."

"So what good does leaving me do you? I hate that you make that an option."

Steven was quiet. He looked at Genie with a face of compassion. "It's not an option, ok? But I grew up and spent my whole life with people who held me back, either by not believing in me, or not believing in themselves. I don't want to live that way anymore. We have something here that's really unique."

"Ok, Steven. I need time though, ok? Let me take baby steps. I can't do an airplane yet. But I won't shoot down the possibility anymore. I'm really going to try."

"That's my girl. That's all anyone can ask."

CHAPTER 5

Never shop for groceries on an empty stomach. Words to live by. Unless of course, it's an upscale market, known for the best free samples. Genie had already eyed hummus with pita bread, squash stuffed ravioli, pecan raisin bread, goat cheese flatbread and sushi. Man, would they lose money on her.

Genie looked at the sushi but wasn't sure what it was. She decided to ask the woman behind the display table.

"Excuse me, what's in this one?"

Genie heard a deep and familiar voice behind her. "It's *crab,* isn't it? I wonder if they serve it with *buns.*"

Holy shit! Genie felt like someone had injected her with Red Bull concentrate. She turned around to face him, trying to sound casual.

"Well, hello there."

"Hello to *you.*"

Genie smiled. Her mind was racing. What now? *Cantaloupe.* The perfect destination.

"Really nice running into you." Genie turned away and headed toward the produce section. She felt out of breath and shaky, which made it very difficult to concentrate on the ripeness of the melons. Then, the voice again.

"You still don't like me, do you?"

"Oh, I…"

"That's a problem."

She felt words come out of her mouth, as if she were a doll with a "push-to-talk" button.

"Why?"

"Well, I just made reservations." He looked at her with flirtation.

"For what?"

"For dinner."

"For who?"

"For us."

Genie looked at him with a curious smile.

"For *us?*"

"Yep. Aisle seven." Genie had no idea what was happening but it was amazingly fun.

"What's aisle seven?"

"The aisle between six and eight."

Genie laughed. "You made reservations for dinner in aisle seven?"

"Yep. Free samples. Guess what they are?"

"If it's free, who cares?"

He smiled. "*Crab cakes.*"

Genie laughed. "Very funny. But I have rules."

He looked at her in fun. "What are your rules?"

"Never accept a date without at least two days notice. And don't accept dates for free food."

"Well, I have rules too."

"Oh yeah? What are they?"

"Never date a girl who has rules."

Genie's smile was way too big, and she knew it. But she couldn't tone it down. Her defense team put their heads on their desks, banging them in utter frustration.

"Hmmm. Well, I guess we'd both be breaking rules then, huh?"

The enemy smiled. "I won't tell if you don't."

Genie held out her hand. "I'm Genie."

"Hi Genie. I'm Jeff."

"Well Jeff, which is the getaway cart? Yours or mine?"

"We'll take my cart. It's got four wheel drive."

CHAPTER 6

As though she were auditioning to be a judge on Top Chef, with exaggerated flair Genie grabbed a toothpick and placed the sample crab cake in her mouth. As though he was auditioning for Fear Factor, with the most serious expression, Jeff analyzed the sample. Genie looked at him in fun.

"Jeff, you don't have to worry. The crab is dead."

Still looking at the crab cake with suspicion he spoke slowly. "I know. I'm looking for onions."

Genie couldn't help but laugh. "Are you allergic?"

He answered quickly, "Phobic." Jeff popped the sample into his mouth. He began chewing. Suddenly his face turned into something that Genie immediately recognized as a sudden need for a napkin. She grabbed one off the table, giggled, and handed it to him. Jeff quickly took the napkin, put it up to his lips, and emptied the contents of his mouth.

Genie found it hysterically funny. Laughing, she said, "Are you ok?"

Jeff was horrified. "Acccchhhh! Oh my God!"

Genie was hysterical. "Jeff, are you one of those guys who has strange aversions to food?"

He wiped his mouth with the napkin, trying to regain composure. "No. I have normal aversions to strange food. *Acccchhhh!*"

Genie was laughing so hard her stomach hurt. For such a good-looking guy, he was actually kind of a dweeb. And she found it reassuring.

Jeff, now mostly recovered except for watering eyes, looked at Genie. "So, you come here often?"

They both looked at each other and cracked up.

"Yes I do," she took another napkin and wiped his chin, "Met my first four husbands here."

"And what happened to them?" He wiped his mouth again. "Died from eating bad samples?"

"Well, yes. One did. The other was involved in a terrible cart crash. One went to check out, and *checked out*... if you know what I mean. And the other one is still alive."

Jeff smiled with flirtation. "And where is he, might I ask?"

"He works over in meats."

Jeff nodded. "So what happened between the two of you?"

Genie was matter of fact. "I worked in dairy."

"So what's the problem with that?"

"I'm Jewish. You can't mix milk and meat."

Jeff laughed. He looked at Genie in fun. "Oh, so irreconcilable differences."

Genie couldn't understand why she felt warmth toward this man. Maybe it was the small piece of a breadcrumb on the corner of his mouth. They looked at each other as though they were following a memorized script. That was what was so fun about this; the words just fell into place.

Jeff spoke again. "Well, I'm about to break up with someone too."

Genie raised her eyebrows. *"Really."* She smiled. "You're gonna bag her, huh?"

"Yep."

"Paper or plastic?"

"Paper. I always break up green."

Genie laughed. Their eyes met in recognition of the obvious intrigue they both shared. There was a pause in the conversation.

"So Genie, what would you say to a meal with menus?"

"You mean like a date?"

"Yeah, but just lunch. I save dinners for the girls who like me."

Genie smiled. "So if I never end up liking you we still do lunches?"

"Why would you want to be with someone you don't like?"

Genie was flippant. "It's fun!"

Jeff was more serious. "It's a copout."

"How is it a copout?"

"Keeps you from falling in love with me."

Genie felt like someone had socked her in the gut, but in a way that felt good. "That's *your* copout."

"How is that a copout?"

"Keeps you from seeing the part of yourself I don't like."

Their eyes met for the duel. There was a smile and a fascination. Genie looked away, about to say something. When she didn't, he laughed.

Genie had to know. "What are you laughing at?"

"That expression on your face. There was a whole story behind it. I just have a feeling that if that look was translated into words, I'd be in for a seven hour story."

"Jeff, I don't have any stories that short."

They held a flirtatious glance. He spoke with warmth and humor.

"Ok. I'm in. Lunch at Finder's Keepers. You free on Wednesday?"

"Yep I am. Noon?"

"A nooner it is..." he paused, "...you need a lift back to your cart?"

"Sure!" Genie stood on the end of his cart. Jeff pushed her fast, and swerved as she screamed and giggled.

As she approached her parked cart, she playfully fished around her purse for her keys. She took them out, turned to her cart, and turned back to look at Jeff.

"Well, thank you for a wonderful time. I'd invite you in but you'd crush my melons."

"I'd invite you in but you'd squash my salami."

They giggled. They gleamed. They parted.

CHAPTER 7

Genie had barely entered the front door when the phone rang. "Hello?"

"Hey Genes, how about a pizza, a DVD, and some great sex for just a few hours? I've got a date after that."

Genie laughed. "Do the pizza and movie with me, and save the rest for your date."

"How 'bout I do the pizza and movie with the date, and do the rest with you?"

"You know if it's a choice between sex and food, I'll always go for the food."

Danny laughed. "I'll be over in half an hour." Genie hung up and went into her bedroom. Her apartment was similar to her office; whites, soft colors, and woods. Between the living room, spare bedroom–which was really her home office–and her bedroom, there was a total of twenty-seven pillows. From duvets and comforters to sofas and chairs, Genie lived in a small palace of poof.

She grabbed her favorite sweats. They were actually Danny's, pale blue and baggy, and the minute Genie had seen them she had insisted he give them to her. She put on a white tank undershirt and her big floppy socks; hair in a ponytail. A girl dressed for only safe options.

Danny and Genie had met in their freshman year of college when he'd dated Genie's roommate, Jamie. Genie hadn't pursued or allowed any attraction to him since she didn't want that kind of trouble with girlfriends. By the time Jamie had moved on to another crush, Danny and Genie's status as friends had been set.

In their senior year, Genie helped him pick out furniture for his apartment. Often, she shopped for him. Danny put together Genie's sound system and fixed things when they needed repair. They walked to classes together, met at the library, and talked on the phone almost daily.

One night they were strolling home from a party that offered a dangerous substance mix; Genie's boyfriend had *substantially* broken up with her and Danny had been *substantially* drinking. This put them somewhere around a 0.8, walking under the influence. They had ended up at Genie's apartment, in bed. In the morning when they woke up, Genie had a flash of feeling that this was meant to be. She felt a deeper love for Danny. It was the one she already had, enhanced by another connection. She couldn't believe that she was suddenly lined up to have it all.

As they were lying in bed, Genie looked over to him and spoke.

"Danny, can you believe it?"

"No, I can't believe it. I just can't believe it," Danny whispered. "Believe *what?*"

Genie slapped him on the chest. How could he be so cavalier and not connected?

"Be serious, Danny! How do you feel about last night?"

Danny stretched and yawned. "I feel great!"

Genie had a frustrated tone. "I mean this changes things a bit, don't you think?"

"I guess it does."

"Dan, what does this *mean?* We're still friends? We're a couple? *What?*"

"Whatever you want, Gene. You're the one who puts in the order. I'm the one who picks it up."

"Danny! Don't you have an opinion?"

"Yeah. I've got sixty-nine opinions! Want to..."

Genie recoiled in disgust. This was so incredibly *off.* "Ok, Dan. This was obviously a mistake."

"Genie, relax." He put his hand on the back of her shoulder. "I was just kidding."

"You're making me feel dirty, Danny!"

"I'm sorry."

Genie felt somewhat relieved when Danny put his arms more fully around her.

"Genes, I would never want you to feel dirty. Let's take a shower and get you cleaned up."

That was it. Genie got up, got dressed, refused to look at him and went home. Neither of them called each other for two weeks. It took Genie a lot to call him, and when she did, she acted as though nothing had happened. It seemed the only way to save the friendship, which she couldn't bear to lose. She knew Danny wouldn't mention it if she didn't, and she was right in that assumption. The night wasn't mentioned again.

• • •

Eight years later, pizza box in hand, Danny rang the bell. Genie opened the door. Food being first on her mind, she peeked inside the box. "Ooooh, what kind?"

Danny whined, "The half horrible kind."

Genie cooed, "You got half without cheese for *me?*" She gave him a hug and a kiss on the cheek. "Thank you!"

Genie went to the kitchen to bring out paper plates and napkins. Danny sat on the sofa and Genie sat on the floor. She opened the box and began slicing the pizza.

"So Gene, you still thinking about him?"

She licked her fingers. "Who?"

"Mr. Aisle Be Watching You."

Genie laughed. "Yeah, and Dan, I don't know why but this guy just scares me. I mean there's nothing scary about him at all. But I shake every time I'm around him."

"Maybe you're just cold!"

Genie laughed as she put a slice on a plate and handed it to Danny. Before it even hit the plate, she took a huge bite of her slice with total love and passion.

With a full mouth of pizza, she said: "You know, Dan. I'm so comfortable with you. I never shake. Why can't I have that with other guys?"

Danny looked at Genie. She already had sauce on her face.

"So Genes, I don't get it. What are you so afraid of?"

"I can't put my finger on it. I guess I'm afraid I'll get hurt."

"Why, is he a jerk?"

"No. I mean I don't know if he is."

"So, why not go for a guy who won't hurt you?"

"The only ones who can't hurt you are the ones you don't fall in love with!"

"Well, don't let yourself get attached. Not until you know you can trust him."

"You're the only man I trust; you and Steven. That's it."

Danny laughed. "Why do you trust us?"

"You're both really good people. And neither of you reject me."

Danny laughed. "Genie, you're not in a *relationship* with us. Rejection is a mathematical improbability."

Genie smiled with certainty. "Yep. *I like that.*"

"And Steven is gay!"

Genie nodded. "Even better! He rejects my *kind.* It's a politically correct rejection!"

Danny's expression became more serious. He paused before he spoke. "Genie, I know we never talked about it, but that night..."

Genie felt her stomach drop. "Danny, we don't need to..."

"I need to say this. That night and the next morning, I was insensitive. I hurt you and I'm sorry."

Genie was quiet, not sure how to respond.

"Genes, I think I was scared. I didn't want to lose our friendship but I wasn't sure what I felt. I made jokes because I didn't know what to say. And afterwards, when we weren't talking, I didn't know how to deal with it. I'm really sorry."

Genie's eyes welled up as he continued.

"And I appreciate that you brought us back together and didn't hold it against me. If I had to do it all over, I'd handle it differently."

"What do you mean?"

"I would have moved forward with the relationship. I would've given us a chance."

Genie was dumbfounded. "Dan, why didn't you say that before? I mean why wait until now?"

Danny smiled. "I don't know."

Genie looked at Danny. His eyes were warm and sincere. She walked up to him and gave him a hug. She felt something inside, but it didn't wear a nametag. There were no definitions that came to mind. What she did know, now more than ever, was that she loved him.

CHAPTER 8

It would be the last Halloween they would spend together, though neither of them knew it. It was a Saturday, and Genie had woken up to find a package on her dresser. It was wrapped in black paper with a huge orange bow. She opened it up to see a sparkly fairy princess costume, complete with the crown, wand, and gloves.

Since then, there wasn't a Halloween that went by that Genie didn't think about that day. Walking down the street, loot bag in one hand, her father holding the other. She could never quite recall his voice, but her mind read the day like a script.

"You know why we named you Genie?"

"Why?"

"You were supposed to be named Lila. But you popped out so fast it was like magic. We knew you must have had special powers. So we decided to name you Genie."

Genie could remember her answer. "Daddy, magic isn't real."

Her father had stopped and looked at her with such a serious face that she thought she might actually get punished.

"Genie, not only is magic real. It's *everything*. Only a few people on earth are selected for the position of spreading magic, you see? And you are one of them."

Genie felt like she had just been handed a job at an age when she shouldn't be working.

"How does someone spread magic?"

"You're the Genie. I guess you'll figure it out."

Twenty-one years later, Genie opened the door of her apartment, candy bowl in hand.

"Trick or Treat!" A little girl, about ten years old, was dressed up as a... *Genie.*

"Oh my Goodness!"

The little girl smiled but wasn't sure why this woman wasn't handing over the goods. Genie stared at her, and then snapped into local time zone.

"I just love your costume!" Genie held out her hand. "I'm Genie."

The little girl looked confused. "No, *I'm* a genie!"

"My *name* is Genie!"

"It is?"

"Yep!"

The little girl shook Genie's hand, paused and shrugged as if to say, *that's really nice and all but let's get to the candy.* "Oh. Cool. Trick or Treat!"

Genie laughed and held out the bowl. This was a full faced, adorable girl with long brown hair that peaked out from her genie hat. Her makeup was heavy and bright.

"What's your name?" Genie asked.

"Casey. And last year I dressed up as Batman."

Genie laughed in amazement. "When I was little I had a Batman glass, a Batman toothbrush, and Batman dreams every night!"

Genie had apparently found the one topic that rivaled Casey's sweet tooth. "I have the backpack and the sleeping bag!"

"Oh, lucky you!" Genie laughed with affection. "Do you live around here, Sweetie?"

"I live upstairs. We just moved here."

"Oh wow! Do you have sisters and brothers?"

"Nope. Just me."

"What are your parents' names? Maybe I know them."

Casey was matter of fact. "I don't have parents. I live with my grandma."

Genie's heart took a dive. "Oh, I'm so sorry." Casey shrugged. Genie recognized that response from her own emotional trick or treat bag. "You know, I lost my dad when I was about your age."

"You did?"

"I did."

"How did he die?"

Genie always detested explaining this because it carried an element of shock. She wished he could have died from a heart attack so his death wouldn't feed other people's wide-eyed fascination.

"Plane crash."

"Whoa."

They looked at each other and despite the age difference it felt like a shared respect. Genie smiled, took the bowl of candy and offered it to Casey. She watched her fish through the assortment. Genie decided which candy she thought Casey would choose. It was her way of testing out the fateful connections. Genie concentrated on the selection. *Pick the Nestle Crunch!* She just loved when things like that happened. She *believed* in them.

Casey was having a hard time deciding. Finally, she grabbed a bag of Skittles. Casey looked up at Genie, who smiled through her disappointment.

"Well, Miss Casey. Will you come down and visit me sometime?"

Casey perked up. "Sure! Do you have any kids?"

"Nope."

"Do you have any pets?"

"Nope."

"Do you have any toys?"

Genie smiled. "Nope."

"What *do* you have?"

Genie kneeled down directly in front of Casey. She tapped the little girl's chin with affection and spoke to her with a smile.

"I'm not sure. But I have a feeling it's going to surprise us both."

Just as Genie was about to close the door, Casey spoke. "Hey Genie, can I have one more piece of candy for my grandma?"

"Of course!"

Without hesitation, Casey grabbled the Nestle Crunch Bar and skipped off down the hall.

CHAPTER 9

The office phone rang at the end of a long and rather stressful day. As it rang a second time, Steven and Genie looked at each other. She told him with a look there was no way she was about to answer, but Steven was the responsible partner.

"Surprise Enterprise, Steven speaking, may I help you?" Within five seconds, he hung up the phone. Like it bit him.

Genie laughed. "Who was that?"

"My mother."

"How could you tell?"

"I know the sound she makes before she speaks."

"What sound is that?"

"The Prevent."

Genie was incredulous. Not just because of what Steven had said, but how serious he was when he said it.

"The *Prevent?* What's that?"

"Pre-vent. It's the sigh before the venting and bitching."

Genie laughed. "Doesn't she know you're hanging up on her?"

"Probably. But she can't prove it since I don't give her a chance to talk. If I let her talk, I can't hang up. That's why I don't wait."

"Why don't you just look at the Caller I.D and not pick up at all?"

Steven sighed with a roll of the eyes. "My mother may be annoying, Genie, but she's not stupid. She never calls from her own phone."

"So you never talk to her at all?"

"I see her once a month. But no in between contact."

Genie's mouth was open. "Why not? That's so rude!"

"She has it coming." Steven had the face of tempered anger. Genie was unsure of how to react. Suddenly, she felt the need to be careful.

"Why, Steven? What did she do?"

"She just let it be known in small ways that being gay wasn't something that happens in '*our family*'."

"What kind of small ways?"

"She stopped making efforts to see me. Before that, she was on my ass all the time to get together, or come home. And that fucking sigh. She never did that before. It's the sigh of her pain that her son isn't married with kids."

Genie felt resentment toward anyone who wouldn't appreciate who he was. But she knew pity was the wrong way to go.

"Hey Steven, there's still time to make it right, you know. You could marry me, we could have cute little babies, and she'll watch them when we go on vacation."

"Vacation where? Across the street? Genes, five days of being married to you would only remind me why I'm gay in the first place."

"Oh Steven, what could be better than living with me?"

"Uh, let's see. Watching paint dry? Doing autopsies on road kill?"

"*Really*," she said with light-hearted sarcasm. "The truth is, you probably became gay only because you believed you could never find anyone as good as me. Now that you have, you're just afraid I'll reject you."

"I'm actually afraid you wouldn't."

"Ok, fine. I've never been attracted to you anyway. So why not make yourself useful and find a way to get the Seven Eleven on Hazel to consent to a surprise party in their store. Amanda Hardy says her husband goes there every night, for some reason. I thought that's where we should have the surprise."

"Yeah, well she would have a surprise alright. When she finds out her husband is not at the Seven Eleven every night!"

"No way! How do you know?"

"Genie, everyone knows."

"Hmm. We could add new meaning to the term 'catered affair'!"

Steven, who was thumbing through bills, missed the remark. Too bad, Genie thought. She hated for a good one like that to go to waste.

"Genie, why is there a $250 charge on the Visa from the gas station? Stocking up on gum?"

Damn! She had prayed the amount of that bill would be overlooked. She began furiously shuffling papers on her desk. She spoke with purposeful distraction.

"Oh, I had a little accident." She got up quickly to get a file.

Steven looked up. "What kind of accident could you have with gas?"

"Well, it wasn't exactly the gas. It was the hose. Man, are these files disorganized!"

Steven looked at Genie with a smug and inquisitive expression. He spoke slowly. "You *broke* it?"

"Kind of."

"How, may I ask, do you break a hose?"

Genie was matter of fact, giving this a chance to pass off as normal. "You know, it broke as I was pulling away, actually. Have you spoken to Pat lately? She never got her refund from Tony's Bistro. And I think..."

"If you were pulling away, then how did you know it was broken?"

"I was tipped off by the sound."

"The sound of the gas pouring out?"

"Not exactly. You know Tony's has been exceptionally unresponsive lately in terms of returning calls, have you noticed?" Genie looked at Steven right in the face.

"I haven't noticed. So what sound did you hear?"

"Flapping. I actually heard that Mario might be quitting."

"The hose was *flapping?*"

"Yes, Steven. It was flapping against my car."

"How could it flap against your car if you were pulling away?" Steven perked up in disbelief. "Genie, did you actually drive off with the pump still in your car?"

"Steven, I was on a stressful call. It was a mistake anyone could make. I simply forgot..."

Steven was hysterical. "Genie, you pulled it out of the tank? Nobody does that!"

"Whatever. I'm very busy. Stop talking."

With a loving smirk, Steven paid the Visa bill.

CHAPTER 10

Finder's Keepers was a casual, woody kind of cafe. As Genie walked in, her heart started to pound against her chest. She felt sweat in the middle of her back and at the bottom of her bra. As she looked around, she saw Jeff waving her over. She approached him as though she was *so* rushed, *so* late, and *so* not phased by him.

"Sorry if I'm late!"

Jeff was *so* not phased by how not phased she was. "Oh, you weren't late. I just got here a little early."

Genie spoke with a fun sarcastic tone. "Did you think I wouldn't show?"

"No, I knew you'd show. Thought you'd be a little late, though."

Genie felt like she was talking to Batman trying to pretend he was just Bruce Wayne.

"Haven't you ever been stood up?" she asked.

"Nope."

Flippantly. "Well, there's always a first." Genie smiled devilishly.

"Well, if I *had* stood you up, what would you do?"

"I guess I'd call Bubbles and have lunch with him."

"Who the heck is Bubbles?"

"He's my partner."

"What's his real name?"

"Bert."

"So, what do you guys do? Work for Bazooka?"

Jeff smiled. "We're doctors."

Genie wore an expression of admiring surprise. "Where did he get the name Bubbles?"

"You don't want to know."

She laughed. "Yes I do."

"When we were all in high school, his folks had a swimming pool. We'd all be in the pool and there were always a bunch of…"

Genie rolled her eyes…"Bubbles around him. Ok, I get it."

"I told you that you didn't want to know! Guess what his wife's name is?"

"Lafarta?"

Jeff laughed. "Her name is Brenda. But everyone calls her Babbles."

"Ok, I'm afraid to ask. What does Babbles do?"

Jeff paused. He smiled. "She blows Bubbles!"

With that, Genie threw her head back, laughing. Jeff smiled confidently.

"Genie, you want an iced tea?"

Still laughing. "I hate iced tea."

"Would you like coffee?"

"Stains my teeth."

Jeff was laughing. "Can you find anything wrong with Coke? Diet Coke?"

"Makes me hiccup."

He smiled with adoration. "You're not an easy person, are you?"

"Nope."

"But you're worth the trouble, right?"

Genie shrugged. "Not really."

Jeff kept the smile up. "So why would anyone want to be with you?"

"I never said they would."

Jeff was clearly intrigued. "You don't think very highly of yourself, do you?"

"Oh I do. I like me just fine. Everybody loves me!"

"Then you're *not* trouble."

"Well to some people I'm not trouble. It depends on their level of tolerance, I guess."

Jeff looked at Genie with such deep interest she thought she might slide off the chair.

"Tolerance of what?"

Genie paused. "Do you drink milk?"

Jeff laughed, trying to keep up with her. "Yeah, I dip my Oreos in it."

"Does it upset your stomach? Give you gas?"

Jeff laughed. "Nope. Milk doesn't give me gas."

"Well, if you were lactose intolerant it would."

Jeff paused. "Oh, I get it. You're milk."

"Yep. Served hot, warm, and cold, depending on what you do with me."

Jeff laughed. "So, for some you're milk with temperature changes. No big deal. But for someone who's Genie intolerant, you're five hours on the toilet."

"Exactly. A genuine pain in the ass."

Before Jeff could react, the couple seated next to them stole his attention. Their voices were becoming louder and louder. It was clear they were in a heated argument and Genie and Jeff found themselves staring. Suddenly, the man stood up. The woman quietly asked him to sit down. He ignored her and headed for the door.

The woman seemed as though she was trying to hold back tears. Genie and Jeff looked at each other without speaking. Suddenly, the woman stood up, grabbed the check, and walked to the front of the restaurant. Genie spoke quietly.

"I can't believe he walked out on her like that."

"How do you know she didn't deserve it?"

"I don't think anyone deserves to be left in a restaurant. If he came in with her, he should have left with her."

"Why would anyone want to sit with someone and argue?"

"I'm not saying anyone would *want* to. But in an argument, both people think they're right, right?" Jeff shrugged and nodded. "So at the very least he should suggest that they leave the restaurant together. To leave her there is awful."

Jeff laughed. "How do you know she isn't a relentless bitch and he left because he couldn't take it anymore?"

"I heard her tone of voice and it wasn't bitchy. She was upset."

"Yeah? Jeff laughed. "Well, I heard her tone and thought to myself if I were him, I'd get up and leave."

Genie looked at Jeff incredulously. "You're kidding, right?"

"I'm dead serious. If a woman talked to me like that, I would tell her that when she was ready to be civil, we could discuss it like two adults."

Genie smiled but it was mixed with contempt. She spoke carefully.

"It sounded to me like they were *both* engaged in the same tone. And I didn't see her get up and leave *him*."

Jeff smiled sweetly. "Here's my mantra. Don't let the argument happen in the first place. Give each other the benefit of the doubt. That's the better way and then nobody has to leave."

Genie looked at Jeff. Was he arrogant or *confident?* Had she judged him on his looks *backwards?* Just because he had the nerve to be sexy did it automatically make him a bad guy?

"Hey, Jeff?"

He leaned toward the middle of the table and stared directly in her eyes. "Can I help you?"

"Yes." She spoke in a playful tone. "Don't you dare leave me in a restaurant, ok?"

Jeff's eyes were direct and warm. "Don't you dare drive me away, ok?"

He stayed fixed on the gaze. Genie felt that gaze in all sorts of places that gazes aren't supposed to go. She smiled warmly looking back at him. "I'm sure I'll drive you away. But I won't mean anything by it."

Jeff laughed. He reached across and touched her face with one finger. Her whole body reacted to that incredibly simple gesture. As Jeff looked over the menu, Genie felt a frightened but thrilling sensation. It was quiet and knowing. It was an acknowledgment that came from her core. It was unlike anything she'd felt before and she wasn't sure why she'd feel it now, in this moment, for this man she barely knew. But she knew this to be her truth. She wanted more.

CHAPTER 11

Genie and her mom had survived two years of their family of three, minus one. Birthdays and holidays were celebrated as though they were required subjects at school. Traditions, Genie learned the hard way, weren't about the large picture. They were in the small details. The napkin her dad tucked in his shirt to carve the Thanksgiving turkey. The way he sang out of tune. The relatives would chant, "Jimmy, don't quit your day job!" The house was full of his missing sounds, but his weren't the only ones missing.

The mother Genie had before her dad's death was not the mother she had today. Laughter wasn't a part of their interactions anymore. Doing things together felt empty. Jennifer didn't even look the same. It always seemed to Genie that she had lost two strong parents, and gained a weak imposter.

One particular day, however, Genie came home from school to find Jennifer on the phone—*laughing.* Her beautiful smile, the shape of her face, and the sound of her voice had come back. It was like losing all your valuables in a burglary, learning to get by without them, then suddenly coming home one day to find each item had been returned.

Genie continued to watch her mom on the phone. She couldn't wait to run up to her and share this celebration. This meant they would bake pies again, they would run errands together. She wouldn't have to shop with Aunt Dotty because her mom was too tired to go. She knew her mom would probably cry from having been gone so long. *It's ok, Mommy. I know how sad you've been but now the bad part is over.*

Finally, Jennifer ended the phone call. For a moment, she was very still. Genie watched her take a deep breath, leaning the back of her chair against the wall, and resting her head against it. Genie thought she looked so peaceful, almost as if she was dreaming.

"Mommy?" Jennifer turned in surprise. Her face lit up and she reached her arms out.

"Oh Genie, I'm so glad you're home! Come here and give me a hug."

Genie ran up to her mother and rested her head on her chest. She couldn't even remember the last time she had done that. She could smell her mom's skin and her hair, and feel her hands stroke her back.

"Oh Sweetie, I have wonderful news for you."

Genie didn't ask. Nothing could be better than this.

"You're going to meet someone very special. He's made me very happy and I know you're just going to love him."

Genie's arms and legs stiffened as though they prepared her to take a hit. She couldn't speak; her face felt stiff, and suddenly her body felt heavy. Jennifer gently lifted Genie's head from her shoulder, kissed the top of Genie's head on her way to the cabinet where she got a glass, opened the freezer, reached for some ice cubes and walked to the sink for water.

"Genie, go get ready because he'll be here in an hour to pick us up. Wear that pretty purple dress, ok?"

As Jennifer walked toward her bedroom, Genie listened to the ice cubes rock back and forth, hitting the sides of the glass. The sound faded as she moved further away. Genie sat frozen in her chair listening to the freezer make ice. It was the body double for a connection.

CHAPTER 12

A good girl follows directions. Genie put on her purple dress to look nice for mommy's new friend. Then a good girl vents. Genie took a pair of scissors, made a cut in her curtains, and tore them until they were shreds. She put on her socks, buckled her shoes, and waited for her mother to call her.

"Genie, are you ready?" Genie didn't answer. She walked out of her bedroom and planted herself on the sofa in the living room.

Jennifer walked out wearing a bright blue skirt with a soft, furry white sweater. "Do I look pretty?" she asked.

Genie looked at her mother and didn't know what to say. At no time during the last year had she ever dressed like this. She had barely even combed her hair. Now this guy comes along and suddenly she's Madonna. The doorbell rang.

"I'll get it!" Jennifer ran to the front door like a manicured poodle. Genie heard soft voices, a muffled laugh, and she heard a couple of kisses. Then they appeared in front of her. "Genie, I would like you to meet Gregg. Gregg, this is my beautiful Genie."

"Genie, it's nice to meet you." He reached toward her with a package of flowers. "I hope you like daisies. I brought these for your room."

Just as Genie was about to choke up a nice girl *thank you,* Jennifer interrupted.

"Oh Gregg, Genie's curtains are full of white daisies! Sweetie, what do you say?"

Genie knew what she wanted to say. Instead, she simply thanked him.

An hour later, as they sat at the table of an Italian restaurant, Jennifer and Gregg exchanged affectionate glances. They included Genie in the conversation but it didn't help. The only thing that made her feel better was the warm bread on the table. She thought back to her mom's closed bedroom door. As bad as that had been, she had never imagined it could be worse. Sitting here, she knew that it could. The more she watched her mom with this man, the better that bread tasted.

After they came home from dinner, Genie said she was stuffed and tired and asked if she could be excused to go to bed. She gave her mom a kiss and thanked Gregg for dinner. She got into her pajamas, under the covers, and decided to go away. She dreamed of a time and longed for the day that she would be grown up and happy. She would have a life of *more.*

That life of more had come to someone else in her household. After Gregg left, Jennifer went to the kitchen and got a glass of water. The ice serenaded the quiet house as she walked into Genie's room. She kissed her daughter's forehead and inhaled her skin. For the first time in so long, after such a horrifying depression, Jennifer felt whole again. It turned back a page in her memory's scrapbook, when she was just a few years older than Genie.

At the end of October, when Jennifer was twelve years old, her parents Peg and William called Jennifer and Dotty to say they were on their way home. They owned a retail store and twice a week Peg worked the floor. She told the girls they would be home by six. This night, however, they were late without a phone call and this was unusual.

By seven o'clock, both girls were on the phone calling family and friends. No one had heard from their parents. At seven-fifteen they began pacing. At eight o'clock they started to panic. At eight-thirty they called the police and reported their parents missing. At nine o'clock the doorbell rang.

There was no hesitation, only full hope that her parents would be standing there. Something had gone wrong and they couldn't call. They had been in an accident and had to take a taxi. There had been some terrible disaster but finally now they were home. Jennifer opened the front door. Two policemen and one other man stood on the front porch.

"Are you the daughter of Mr. and Mrs. William Pearson?"

• • •

Twenty years later, as Jennifer stared at her sleeping daughter, hair falling like tattered blankets all around her face, she drew a deep breath in. She had forgotten what happiness felt like. Gregg wasn't just the answer to her emptiness. He would be the answer to Genie's as well. They could be a family again. Jennifer hadn't realized how much she had missed that feeling.

As she turned to leave the room, she glanced toward the window. She let out a gasp as she saw Genie's curtains hanging in strings of fringe. She stood for a moment, unable to move. Her stomach felt weak and sick as she realized that Genie had cut them.

In the window of Jennifer's room, in the house that she had grown up in, yellow curtains with white and orange daisies hung on the rod in shreds. And she remembered the night she destroyed them. It was the night the policemen had come to their door and told them their parents were dead.

Jennifer stared at the curtains. Tears ran down her cheeks. Deep in thought, she looked back at Genie. She stared at her daughter's face, highlighted by a stream of light that the bedroom borrowed from the hallway. She silently verbalized a promise. She made a vow in the form of a prayer. She nodded her head to confirm. She walked over to the curtains, gently slid them off of the rods, and quietly walked out of the room.

CHAPTER 13

The waitress had bright red hair, fake lashes, and fingernails that were red and long. What she wasn't long on was friendliness. Jeff looked up at her and it was clear to Genie, he was about to have fun.

"You two ready?"

Genie spoke first. "I'll have the veggie burger but can you substitute tomatoes for the fries? And whole wheat bread instead of the bun?"

The waitress looked irritated. "And you, Sir?"

Genie watched Jeff as he spoke to the waitress.

"Yeah, I'll have the same thing. But can you substitute a bacon cheeseburger for the veggie burger? And I'll have the fries." Jeff watched the waitress carefully. "And when your tables let up, I want a back scratch." Jeff gestured with his eyes toward her fingernails. The waitress looked at him without cracking a smile.

"You got yourself a deal." She walked away and Jeff laughed heartily.

"Ok, Jeff. I shall change the subject so as not to be a relentless female and drive you away." Jeff smiled and Genie winked. "So, you told me you're a doctor but I didn't ask you if it's a private practice or if you're with a group."

"Bubbles and I have a private practice in town. And we just recently approached a company that rents out private jets. We're trying to make a deal."

"Oh! To commute the rich and famous?"

"Actually, to commute for the poor and famous. Our concept is to cater exclusively to specialists who are urgently needed in remote areas where patients aren't strong enough to survive a trip to the states. We bring the 'hospital' to them."

"What does that have to do with the poor and famous?"

"We piggy-back and coordinate with flights chartered for business people and celebrities. We charge them less than the commercial private jets. They can write off the trip as a charitable donation. And we use the income to fly doctors to these third world areas in need of medical care. We get commissions from the private carriers."

Genie stared at him as if in a trance. He held up the saltshaker. "Here. Smelling salts."

She laughed, slightly embarrassed. After more details and stories about his business, the waitress came back with their lunch.

"One veggie burger and one veggie burger hold the veggie burger. Anything else?"

Jeff flirted. "Yeah, the back scratch when you get a chance."

The waitress giggled and walked away with a smile.

"So what do you do, Genie? Jump out of bottles and make magic?"

Genie laughed. "Well, kind of! I'm a surprise party planner. But yeah, I guess I try to make them a bit magical."

"Genie, no offense, but I hate surprises."

"Why?"

"Well, there's a lot I can't control, but if I can, I like to know what's coming."

"Well, I hate the bad surprises. That's why I make up for it by planning good ones."

Jeff took a bite of his burger. "Did you have some bad surprises in your life?"

"Yeah, I did. My dad died when I was little."

Jeff looked at her with a serious and saddened expression.

"I'm so sorry. That must have been so awful for you. How did he die?"

Genie wondered how he'd react when she said it. "In a plane crash."

Jeff looked at Genie. He didn't say anything and she so appreciated his silence. Then, he looked at her with a gentle smile.

"So are you afraid to fly?"

Genie was blown away by his perception. She nodded.

Jeff looked down at his plate, took another bite and wiped his face with the napkin. He looked up at her for a second as though he was going to say something. But he didn't.

"What?"

Jeff shrugged. "Nothing."

"No, you looked like you were about to say something. What was it?"

Jeff laughed. "You remind me of those little Chihuahuas that bite at your ankles." He looked at his watch. "Oh Genie, I gotta run soon. I have a meeting in thirty minutes."

Genie felt her stomach drop as the Chihuahua inside started jumping. She had said something wrong. He didn't like her. He hated those stupid little dogs...

"But I didn't mean to cut off the conversation." Jeff was hurried but sincere. "How about Starbucks on Hudson in the morning? Eight o'clock, ok?"

The Chihuahua happily picked up her bone.

"You got it."

CHAPTER 14

Genie walked back to the office in a dizzying mix of emotions. As she approached the office, Steven was coming out. "Steven, where are you going?"

"I'm in the mood for a burger. Want to come? You could eat the tomato."

Genie laughed. "No, I just ate. But if you go drive-thru I'll come with."

"How 'bout a walk-thru. I don't have my car."

Genie grabbed his arm playfully. "I'll drive! I'm parked in the back-thru."

As they drove together, Genie's euphoria was transparent.

"For someone who's afraid of flying, you sure are cruising high! Feeling a little queasy?"

"Steven, you won't believe this but of all the jobs he could have... it's gotta involve fricking airplanes!" Genie inched the car up to the order box and spoke. "Can I please get a double cheeseburger, ketchup only, small fries, and a Coke?"

Steven looked at Genie with amazement, shaking his head. "Excuse me, but do you know that you just placed your order with the garbage can?"

Genie looked behind her. No doubt about it, she had ordered from the garbage can but it didn't mean she had to admit it. Without a change in expression, she looked ahead to the actual order box. Casually, she pulled up to it.

"I repeat. Can I please get a double cheeseburger, ketchup only, small fries, and a Coke?"

Steven stared, eyebrows raised, clearly very happy.

When Genie got the food, she innocently handed Steven the bag. He shook his head again.

"Steven, I swear, the second he said the word airplane, I got shivers up my spine."

"Well, Genes, you know what they say. You fall for the ones who bring up your pain."

"Oh, really? Well, those are the perfect ones to stay away from." Genie stole a fry.

"Well, you could. But it'll just come up again with somebody else."

"Not for me. If I date somebody who drives cabs, it won't be a reminder."

"You'd be bored in a cab. And the way life works is that you'll marry the cabbie and he'll win a hot air balloon in a raffle." Steven grabbed a few fries and handed one to Genie. She took the fry and spoke while she chewed.

"Why would anyone choose to be with someone who brings up pain?"

"I don't think they choose it. It happens. And it happens for a reason."

"Yeah, to ruin your life and break up the relationship. Give me one more fry but no more after that." Steven handed her a bunch of fries and she took them.

"No, Genes, to get you stronger. But it's a bit of a turbulent ride. So both people have to be willing to see their own shit. Otherwise somebody's going to get hurt."

"Yep. That would be me. That's why I like it safe."

"Well, you could marry Danny."

"Danny's a friend with sex on the brain." Genie reached over for more fries and Steven slapped her hand.

"He doesn't challenge you either. But he's easy and safe. Just how you like 'em."

"Steven, half the time love doesn't work out even when both people try. And I'm not cut out for another crash."

"You may crash but you won't die. You'll just get shaken up, that's all."

"Oh, yeah? How do you know? And what's my protection?"

"Build your confidence, Gene. It's the best parachute on the market."

CHAPTER 15

Tonight, T.L.C. stood for Television and Lean Cuisine. Genie was cozy in sweats and worn out socks, on the sofa with a soft throw, cell phone close by so she wouldn't have to get up, and her favorite show was on. Suddenly, she heard a knock at the door.

This was one major bummer.

She got up and looked through the peephole, but no one was there. She went to sit down, but heard the knock again. She wasn't afraid, since the building security was tight. She opened the door and there was Casey, the little Genie from Halloween, sub-peephole height.

Genie laughed. "Hi Casey!"

"Hi Genie."

"Come on in!" Surprising to herself, Genie didn't mind the interruption. Casey walked into Genie's living room and looked around. She looked quite different out of costume. She was chubby and rather sloppy. She didn't seem as bright and cheerful without the makeup, chiffon, and sequins. Genie was unsure of how to entertain her new friend.

"You want to see my apartment?"

Casey nodded shyly. "Sure."

"You want to see my Happy Room?"

Casey perked up. "You have a Happy Room?"

"I sure do! I'll show you." Genie led the way for Casey to follow.

The room was not large, but it was any girl's dream of happy. There were basically two colors to the room, white with accents of powdery blue, and a splash of pink in the flowers. The room had large windows that looked out on a balcony full of potted flowers and trees. The furniture was all creamy linen. The pattern on the rug almost looked like a crisp tablecloth; a baby blue background with white lacey looking lines that made diagonal squares. At the foot of the chaise was a small, antique bench that had been distressed-painted in a brighter baby blue. A tall, white, French antique pitcher was filled with peach peonies. Tables and lamps picked up the theme; it was a room that felt like crème fraiche. Casey looked at the room and gasped.

"You like it?"

Casey was glowing. "I love it!"

Genie was so happy she *got* it. "Doesn't it kind of make you feel happy?"

Casey bellowed, "Duh!"

Genie laughed. "I'll tell you what. Every time you come over, this is where we'll hang. And we'll talk silly stupid girl stuff. Deal?" Genie held her hand up in a high five.

Casey slapped it right back. Were awkward pauses normal with kids or did it mean Genie should keep them talking? Casey walked up to the bookshelves and began picking up picture frames. "Who's this?"

"That's my brother, Luke. He lives about a half hour from here."

"Is he married?"

"No."

"Does he have a girlfriend?"

"He did but they broke up."

Casey responded. "I had a boyfriend. He kissed my arm when I was writing on the chalkboard. Then the next day he ripped my new coat on the playground!"

Genie laughed. "Boys are mean when they want you, Case! You just have to wait until they grow up and learn to be nice."

CHAPTER 16

Deciding what to wear for a coffee date before work presents the same dilemma as a "Come as You Are" party planned for New Year's Eve. Do you *really* wear what you'd normally wear, or do you fudge it up a bit? Genie went with the fudge. A chocolate brown satin tank that showed just a bit of skin on the side, a cropped, knit, stark white, button-down sweater, unbuttoned, and brown Theory pants worn low. She didn't quite sport the business look, but she was dressed to close the deal.

Jeff was waiting inside, dressed in a dark suit with a crisp striped shirt. He greeted Genie with a kiss on the cheek, morning fresh cologne, and the sexiest coffee breath. Starbucks never felt so good. He was *so* upbeat in his greeting it seemed fake. The funny thing was, she knew it wasn't fake at all. This was Jeff.

"Jeff, do you always wake up this dapper in the morning?"

Jeff gave a dumb and innocent look. "*Dapper?* You mean the things babies wear just before they're ready for Pull-Ups?"

Genie smiled. "That would be a diaper. Dapper is a happy mood."

"*Oooh.* Yes, I'm always dapper in the morning. Although something tells me you could change any man's dapper! Especially a poopie dapper."

Genie laughed hard. "Yes, I can make a mess on your dapper, that's for sure."

"Maybe I'll take you out for dinner and get in *your* dapper."

Genie wore a frisky smile. "Nobody gets in my dapper on the first date."

"No? How many dates does it take?"

"A lot! Has to be long enough to weed out the dumpers."

This started them up giggling right away. Jeff bumped up against Genie's arm and motioned. "Come on over here, I got us a table."

Jeff pointed to a table where a cup of steamed soy was waiting for her.

"Oh, that's so nice." She picked up the cup and walked toward the sweetener stand. Jeff followed her. She took some packets for her soy and stuffed a few in her purse. Jeff was watching the whole thing, shaking his head and laughing.

"I can't believe you steal those."

Genie was flippant in her defense. "I do not steal!"

Jeff attacked in play. "What do you call that?"

"Well, they don't charge for them. It's there for the taking. It's unlimited and unrestricted for me to sweeten my beverage."

"I think they mean *current* beverage."

"As a matter of fact, that's why they charge so much. They know people..."

"Steal?"

"Use freely."

Jeff loved screwing around with her. That was evident. "Genie, do you ever use those to sweeten things other than drinks from Starbucks?"

"Yeah. I use it for my lemonade and my yogurt. And my..."

"And Starbucks is so generous that they're willing to invest in sweetening all of your unsweetened drinks and foods?"

"Well, actually yes. My friend read an article about it. They want their customers to feel comfortable taking what they need."

"*Really?* Can you stick that chair in your purse?"

Genie looked at Jeff straight in the eye and stuffed a few more packets in her purse. Jeff shook his head and laughed. They walked to the table, sat down, and spent the next thirty minutes talking about Genie's work, more about her dad's death, they gave some basic family history and then they had a stir stick laser beam fight.

"So Gene, how come this is so comfortable?"

"I don't know. It *is* though, isn't it?"

Just then Jeff's phone chimed with a text. He looked at the phone but didn't answer the text. Then he put it in his pocket.

Genie mocked. "I hope that wasn't a sick patient!"

Jeff hesitated with an odd expression. He spoke carefully.

"Actually, I wanted to talk to you about a situation I'm in. Well, *in* but getting *out of*."

Genie didn't say anything.

"I've been in a relationship, but we haven't been getting along, and it's ending."

Genie's stomach dropped. She *knew* this was going to be like the perfect dessert. Two bites in and you find a hair.

"It's *ending?*"

"Well, I've told her that it's not working out. And even if I hadn't met you, I'd be getting out. So you're not responsible for the break up."

"How long have you been together? What's her name?"

"A year. Just under, actually. Her name is Lindsey."

"And you're sure it's over."

"Oh, it's over. We don't even spend time together and even though I haven't technically broken it off yet, I've been backing off a long time."

"Why didn't you just tell her before? I mean instead of backing off?"

"I wanted it to just kind of end on its own."

Genie knew instinctively she couldn't get caught up in this.

"Jeff, why don't you call me when you're out of it?"

Jeff looked genuinely disappointed and spoke slowly. "I can do that. But I was wondering if you'd like to go out to dinner Friday night. Just buddies, if you want." He got coy and sexy again. "Until I break it off for good and try and get in your dapper." Genie smiled.

"Do me a favor, Genie." He pulled out a business card. "Just text me your phone number and address, ok? We will keep it clean, I promise. I just need to do this the right way."

He kissed her cheek and walked out the door.

CHAPTER 17

So maybe her mom's new boyfriend wasn't so bad after all. To Gregg's credit, he hadn't given up on Genie when most men would have run. Gregg saw Genie's anger as nothing more than fear. He set boundaries with her bratty outbursts, but with sensitivity, consistency, and kindness. And then one day, walking home from the park, Gregg popped the question.

"So Genie. How long have we known each other?"

Genie kicked a stone on the sidewalk. "I don't know. Pretty long. Why?"

Gregg spoke gently. "Well, would you say we're pretty good buddies now?"

"Yep." Gregg kicked the stone that Genie was kicking.

"Would you say we're good enough buddies to be family?"

They both stopped. Genie looked up at Gregg. "You and my mom are *getting married?*"

"Well, I haven't asked her yet."

"You're asking *me* first?"

Gregg smiled. "To quote a famous little girl... *yep.*"

"What if I say no?"

"Then I don't ask her. Is that your answer? No?"

Genie settled down, kicked the stone again and started walking. "Nope."

Gregg laughed. He patted Genie on the top of her head. He kicked the stone. "So how should we ask her?"

Genie stopped again. "You're not going to ask her *in private?*"

"To quote a famous little girl... *nope.*"

Genie smiled and kicked the stone while she spoke. "Well, *I* think we should surprise her."

Gregg laughed. "Good idea! With a ring?"

"No way! She'd be expecting a ring." Genie kicked the stone. "But she'd never expect a cat."

Knowing how much Jennifer hated, no, *detested* cats; the idea became hysterical to Gregg.

• • •

Two weeks later, Gregg and Genie put the plan in motion. They went to the shelter, chose a white kitten, wrapped him in a box, and went back to the house. Jennifer was sitting at her desk. She stayed seated but turned to face them. Gregg put the box in her lap.

"What's this?"

Gregg answered her. "Read the card."

Jennifer opened the envelope, took out the small card and read it to herself. *Will you marry me-ow?*

Jennifer's face became blank. She looked at Gregg and Genie who were looking at her and waiting. Suddenly, the box jumped. Jennifer jumped out of her chair screaming, and the box began to fall. Gregg caught it and handed the box to Genie. They both watched Jennifer and her flurry of responses.

"Gregg, what is going on! What is in that box! And what's the 'marry me' part? Is this a *joke?*"

He smiled and took her face in his hands. He looked into her eyes. His own eyes welled up with tears. Now she knew exactly what this was—she just couldn't believe it. It wasn't that they hadn't discussed marriage. It wasn't as if they hadn't broken up several times because of Genie's lack of acceptance. But it was never Gregg who ended it. Each time it was Jennifer, and every time, one of them somehow brought them back together.

"Jenny, I love you so much. I want to be with you always. Will you marry me?" He smiled and wiped his own tear.

Jennifer looked at Genie who was smiling ear to ear, mouth full of gaps from missing teeth, bursting with excitement. Jennifer's eyes filled with tears. She put her arms around Gregg and hugged him. And as she held him, she saw everything that came before him.

She saw her mom and dad, their wedding photos, their home, and the policemen at her door. She saw the first day she met Jimmy, the way he'd proposed, and how handsome he looked at their wedding. She saw Genie's birth, her first years, and an image Jennifer wished she could permanently erase from her brain; the kidnapping of Genie's happy nature after hearing her dad was gone.

The only saving grace on that nightmare day was that Genie had missed watching her mom get the phone call from Dotty. Genie had missed Dotty rushing to the house to stay with Jennifer as she tried to get through to the airlines. Holding hands as they called the crisis number, being put on hold, and having to wait to hear if her husband had actually been on that plane.

Genie had thankfully missed the moment when the woman on the other end of the phone confirmed that Jimmy's name was on the list of deceased. Genie missed Dotty holding her sister's head as she threw up in the kitchen sink because she couldn't make it to the bathroom.

Genie would have her own memory's pictures, no doubt. But as far as Jennifer was concerned, these were close-ups she didn't need. Each day after the crash, Jennifer got sicker and weaker, but far worse than that was the fear. Would she ever feel better, ever survive this, would she be able to be there for Genie? Would she ever have a life that she could actually live?

Three years later, those questions were answered with another crazy question—*Will you marry me-ow?*

Gregg was looking at Jennifer with the innocence of someone who didn't have those kinds of thought interruptions to such a joyous moment. Someone who lived without the tragedies that recycle in moments like these, diluting their perfection. On the other hand, maybe that was what she loved most, the innocence that Gregg brought. She looked at Genie, who had opened the box and was now holding the little white kitten to her face. What a picture for the album. And Genie spoke the perfect caption.

"So Ringo... how do you like your new home?"

Jennifer released her arms and looked at Gregg. Then she looked at Genie. She smiled. *"Ringo?"*

Genie looked up at her mom. "Gregg says we both get Ringos."

Just then, Gregg pulled a small box out of his pocket and handed it to Jennifer. It was all too much. Really, she gets this? This is her life today? The tears came rolling down her face. She wiped them with the back of her hand. She slowly opened the box and gasped. The ring bounced off light and brilliance. Gregg gently took the ring out of the box, placed it on Jennifer's finger, and studied it on her hand. Another photo for the internal album, and Gregg added the perfect caption.

"So Ringo... how do you like your new home?"

CHAPTER 18

Bike rides were something that Genie and Danny had started in college. They would stop for lunch on campus, run errands together or do it for exercise. Today's cars and gym memberships didn't impose on their longstanding tradition. Early Saturday mornings, no matter who was in a relationship or wasn't, weather providing, side by side, helmets on, the conversations always flowed.

"I went out with Kay again last night."

Whenever Danny had a new girlfriend, Genie felt a drop in her stomach. Rationally, she knew that Danny could date whomever he wanted. And she was generous in her desire to see everyone she loved *happy*. There were just certain things she didn't enjoy sharing with others. One was breakfast unless more than one entrée was ordered. She didn't particularly enjoy lending shoes. And she did *not* like sharing Danny.

"Really? I thought you didn't like her."

"I never said I didn't like her." Danny looked behind them. "Watch out, Gene, let this guy pass." Genie went behind and caught up to Danny again.

"So you *do* like her."

"Yeah, but I know she likes me more. I feel bad." They had slowed down as they got to their favorite breakfast spot. "Let's park behind the building." They parked the bikes and got a table outside overlooking the river. Once they were seated, they picked up the conversation.

"Did you have fun together?" Genie tried to look casual as she looked over the menu. "Can we get two things and split?"

"Sure, get whatever you want. Yeah, we had a great time. I just don't..."

Genie interrupted. "How about two omelets and we share an order of banana pancakes?"

"That's fine."

"She just doesn't do it for you, huh? Would you rather have blueberry?"

"I don't know, maybe it's me. Get the banana, you like them better."

"Danny, tell her you can't see her. Why does she keep calling you anyway? Don't you make it obvious that you're not interested?"

"Well, I am interested. She's a great girl. I just don't have that *feeling*, you know? Maybe I will in the future. Anyway, she's still hung up on her old boyfriend. I can tell."

"How?" The busboy dropped off ice water with lemons.

"She talks about him all the time. Why do girls talk about their old boyfriends?"

"If the new boyfriend is understanding he'll listen and help us through it."

"NOT! If the girl is still hung up, we don't *want* to be the new boyfriend!"

"Hmm. Mental note. No discussing old boyfriends with new boyfriends."

Danny laughed. "Yeah, maybe one day you'll be telling someone all about how you can't get over me." Genie took a long sip of water.

"Well, that's why I can't date you. If we broke up, who would help me through it?"

"I would; one stop shopping for women and their emotional needs. I offer dating, love, breakup sympathy, dining and sex. I'm like the mall."

"Yeah, you'll maul me alright. And you have the emotional depth of paper. So, does Kay know about us?"

Danny knew what Genie was referring to. Over the years, each of them had dated people who had a hard time figuring out their relationship and accepting it without feeling threatened.

"Yeah, she knows. As a matter of fact, she thinks we'll probably end up together one day." Danny looked at Genie. She looked back at him.

"What did you say when she said that?"

"I told her there was no way. We're friends." Genie quickly looked away. There was such a mixture of regret and wonder in her feelings. Funny how the truth can hurt even if it's the truth you've chosen.

CHAPTER 19

A bowl of air popped popcorn, caffeine free Diet Cokes in the can, any romantic comedy DVD on the table that would never get watched because they had far too much to talk about, cherry licorice nips in a bowl, and Genie's best friend Lori. It must be a Friday night. Lori stuffed a large handful of air popped popcorn into her mouth and spoke something that would be undecipherable to anyone but a best friend.

"I donth know rhy you don'th justh marry Danny."

Genie laughed. "You donth know rhy? Because we're not in love is why!"

"Why not?"

"What do you mean, why not?" Genie grabbed some popcorn. "Why weren't you in love with Bradley?"

"I don't know why but I'm still sorry I let him go. It was a mistake. You should get Danny before he falls for somebody else."

"Lor, you're just saying that because you're not with Bradley now. When you had the chance you didn't want him, remember?"

"Genie, it's different. Danny is the kind of guy every girl wants to marry. He has it all."

Genie got up to get another soda and brought one back for Lori. “I can’t explain it, Lor, there’s something cold about Danny.”

“I’ll buy you a heating pad.”

Genie laughed. “I never know what he’s thinking. I can’t even imagine kissing him. It seems so…”

“Gene, remember that guy, Craig? I didn’t want to kiss him but when I did it was the best kiss ever.”

“Yeah, I remember. But what about that guy, Shane?”

Lori winced. “You’ve got a point. I just wanted to throw up right on him.”

Genie laughed. “And guys get so sensitive about stuff like that!”

“Yeah. Nobody wants a Regurgi-Date!”

“You know, Lor, it’s not that Danny turns me off. I mean that one time we got together, it was really hot. I felt so close to him.”

“So, what’s the problem? Why can’t you feel it again?”

“I don’t know. Maybe I’m covering up the feelings and I don’t know it. Or maybe it was just a case of two friends sharing a night. But I know the difference between wanting to kiss someone and *wishing* I want to kiss someone.”

“I hear you, Gene. I get that you don’t want to kiss him. But *I* want you to kiss him.”

Genie laughed. “Oh really! Why?”

“I don’t know. I guess I like the story.”

CHAPTER 20

When it comes to dealing with men with on-the-way-out girlfriends, it's always best to consult the panel. It took two days, two girlfriends, Steven, and even a check-in with her mom for Genie to establish her strategy. She typed the agreed-upon text: *Hi Jeff. It's Genie. Would love to hear from you if and when your relationship ends. Not comfortable getting together before then. Hope all goes well for you both. Genie.*

She got a text right back. *I'm officially single. How about dinner tomorrow?*

For her first official date with Jeff, Genie settled on black skinny jeans with black boots up to her knees and a thin navy cashmere sweater that dropped one side off her shoulder. This was a bold move, mixing black and navy. But *In Style* Magazine had reported that this color combination was all over New York. This made Genie a trendsetter in Chicago, and when conservatively handled, she liked that. What she didn't like was the total insecurity of these decisions since being a trendsetter wasn't anything close to who she was.

Jeff texted that he was parked downstairs waiting in the turnaround. She checked herself one more time in the mirror before heading to the elevator. She walked into the hallway and pressed the down button. Suddenly, she felt a panic. Was it too late to change to black and gray? She raced back to the apartment, found the gray sweater in the heap of rejects on her closet floor, changed on the fly, took one more look in the mirror and breathed a sigh of relief.

The elevator was empty. This meant one more swipe of her lipstick wand. When she reached the lobby, she gave a high five to Johnny the doorman, and walked to the circle driveway. *There he was.* Black SUV, black interior, Mahogany trim, and when she got in the car, his cologne smelled so good she wondered if it came out of the vents.

Without so much as hello, Jeff asked... "You like Chinese?"

Genie put her seatbelt on. "Yeah, is that what we're having?"

"Nope."

"Then why did you ask me if I like it?"

"I just had a feeling you wouldn't but wanted to see if you were raised with any manners."

"Oh, I was raised with plenty of manners." Genie gulped and brought up one of her manly burps. They looked at each other and Jeff shook his head and laughed. Genie just smiled daringly, kind of impressed with herself for being herself.

"So, where are we eating then?"

"We're eating at The Pink Carnation. Have you been there?"

"You can't get into that place unless you call weeks in advance!"

"Well, I have a connection. So we're in."

"I'm impressed! I heard it's great but noisy. Hard to talk."

"Well there's a plus!"

Genie looked at him. "Not a big talker, huh?"

"No, I don't mind talking."

Jeff looked at Genie with a serious put on face. "So Genie. Are we done talking?"

Genie smiled. "No. I want to know it all. I have to see if I like you."

"Well, with me there's not much to know."

"You mean you're all muscle? That's all there is to you?"

Jeff laughed. "Why, thank you!"

"You must work out a lot, huh?"

Jeff spoke humbly. "I try to stay in shape. I was trained in Martial Arts for many years. I always enjoyed athletics."

"How high did you get? Black belt?"

"Many, actually. I competed for a long time until my shoulders got too messed up and I had to give it up. But I practice the principles every day."

"What are they?"

Jeff was disciplined, even in his tone. "True strength isn't just a physical thing. It's an intense focus. And when you're fighting someone, it's not just about moves and throws. You can use your mind to tap into your own strength, and at the same time find your opponent's weakness. That's the art."

Genie looked at him coyly. "So what's your weakness? Or don't you have one to find?"

"Oh, everybody has weaknesses. But I'm pretty simple. What you see is what you get."

"Yeah, me too."

Jeff laughed. "Why don't I believe that?"

"I don't know. Why don't you?"

"I've never met a woman who is as she appears."

"Well, every one of my girlfriends is as she appears. But I've never met a man I can read."

Jeff laughed. "Men are *so* easy to read!"

"Only on the front cover!"

Jeff laughed, reached over and put his hand on Genie's leg. "You're gonna be a handful, aren't you?"

Genie put her hand on top of his hand. "I don't know. It depends what comes after page one."

CHAPTER 21

Gregg made sure that the flower girl carried a bouquet of Gerbera Daisies. Genie wore a lavender dress and her mom's suit was winter white wool. Gregg wore a black suit, with a crisp white shirt buttoned to the top, no tie. The guest list was small, but traditions were kept, right down to the white satin runner.

There were two honeymoons. Genie was invited to one. She got to spend three days in Disneyworld with her mom and Gregg, and the next three days home with Aunt Dotty and Ringo. Once the travels were over, Genie nestled in her family of three. Until one year later when someone had the horrible idea of making it a family of four. When Luke was born, the whole house smelled like a diaper.

Luke this, Luke that. Luke is crabby, Luke threw up, oh look how cute he looks now. Everyone came to the house to bring a present for Luke. They all wanted to hold him. Genie was quite sure that she had never seen anything as ugly and stinky as that drooling, noisy excuse for a brother that cried for no reason at all.

Three months after Luke was born, Genie woke up in the middle of the night. The house was dark, and as she made her way to what she thought was the bathroom, she opened the door to the nursery instead. Luke opened his eyes, looked at Genie, and started to gurgle and smile as though he was excited to see her.

Genie walked up to the crib. Luke was lying on his back. The moonlight was sneaking in through the window like a flashlight on his face. He was kicking his legs and flapping his arms. Genie smiled at him and he smiled even bigger. Genie finally felt a thread of connection.

"Hi Lukey!" Suddenly Genie had an overwhelming urge to hug him. She reached in the crib, picked him up, wrapped his blanket around him, and sat on the rocking chair. From that day on, Genie had a sweet little brother. This worked for about two years.

Genie was trying to explain why she had thrown her slipper at Luke. He had taken the stuffed animals off of her bed and gotten blue paint on them. Last week he had ruined her artwork from school. Before that he broke her bracelet. Instead of receiving compassion for her frustration, she got punished and sent to her room. Jennifer came in the room after an hour had passed and sat with Genie on her bed.

"Genie, you can't throw things at people just because you're angry. It's not right."

"Why does Luke get to do everything wrong and nobody talks to him?"

"Genie, Gregg is taking Luke for some ice cream. You can go but you need to behave."

"How come Luke gets to go no matter what and I only get to go if I'm good?"

"Because you're old enough to know the difference."

Genie began to scream. "I was good! Luke was bad! I didn't do anything wrong!"

"Yes you did, Genie. I understand you had feelings. But you don't get to act out on them. If you do, you will be punished."

"Why do I have to be punished from *Gregg?*"

"Well, maybe that's the only way to teach you. You obviously haven't learned the lesson. So I think it's best you stay home."

Jennifer walked out of the room. Genie's body stiffened in pain. The anger was pushing from inside her, racing to find an unguarded outlet. She got on her stool, reached up, and pulled down her photo album. She leafed through the pages until she found a photograph of her mom. She cut it into pieces. Each cutting that fell to the ground was a feeling she couldn't have. A word she couldn't say. The more she cut the picture, the better she felt, and the more her breathing calmed.

When she was finished, she put the small pieces in an envelope. She tucked them away carefully under her biggest bear. She laid her head down in his lap, stroking the fur and bringing it close to her face. Finally, she had spoken.

CHAPTER 22

The Pink Carnation Cafe looked like a cross between Sex and the City and The Easter Bunny. It was sexy sweet. A waterfall and stream meandered through the room. Pink carnations, without their stems, floated in the water like swans. Once they were seated, Genie caught Jeff looking at her with a mocking expression.

"So Genie, do you come with a manual?"

Genie laughed. "What a great idea! 'How to Maintain Your Genie.'"

From there, the conversation got deeper. Jeff's parents had divorced when he was nine. His mother had a drinking problem and Jeff had spent the better part of his childhood in fear of her drunken outbursts and disturbing behavior.

Genie told Jeff about her mom, Gregg, Luke, and moving Luke into college last September. They talked about their own college days and how wild Jeff had been.

"Did you have a girlfriend in college?"

Jeff laughed. "Yeah, I had a few."

"What happened?"

Jeff had a relaxed tone. "Usually they wanted more and I couldn't give it to them."

"Why not?"

"I don't know. I guess I didn't feel that much for them."

Genie felt like a reporter. But she wanted to know it all. "What about the girl you just broke up with?"

"Lindsey? She was great. Just didn't work out."

"So you've never actually been in love?"

"I'm not sure. What about you?" Then came his daring look that Genie knew by now to be trouble. "Have you been in love?"

Genie was matter of fact. "I had a boyfriend in college I was *totally* in love with."

"So why did you break up?"

"He wasn't sure he wanted kids. I couldn't take the chance, so we broke up."

"What happened to him?"

Genie laughed. "He got married and had a kid!"

Jeff laughed. "Well, I love kids. Can't wait to have them."

"Sounds like you've never been much of a relationship person though."

Jeff shrugged. "I always enjoyed the chase and then once I had them, I kind of lost interest."

Genie and Jeff looked at each other and held the gaze. Jeff picked up his water glass, took a sip, and set the glass back down. He smiled. He had a way of looking at her that felt like a cornea trespass.

"So Gene. You think that's what we'll do here? Go for the chase and then get rid of each other like a piece of gum that lost its taste?"

"Well, if history would repeat itself..."

Jeff laughed. "Then we'll both be stuck on the bottom of someone's shoe, right?" Genie smiled. "Gene, do you believe that people like us can find anyone who challenges us enough to stay long term? Or do you think we'll just always need a new chase?"

Genie smiled. "Yes to both. The challenge is in the relationship. And that becomes the chase, over and over again."

Jeff looked at her with a pensive grin. "So you think there's a right one out there?"

"Yeah. But you need to kiss some imposters."

Jeff looked at her and smiled. With his right hand, he lifted his wine glass to toast. Genie followed his lead by lifting her glass as well.

"Here's to *the right one.*" Both of them took a sip from their glass. Immediately, Jeff lifted his water glass in his left hand.

"To the right one with a *chaser.*"

Jeff pulled the valet ticket out of his pocket as they walked away from the table. They walked outside and both commented on the breeze. Jeff hesitated before handing the ticket over for the car.

"You want to walk off dinner a little, Gene?"

Genie felt a chill in the air but didn't want the evening to end.

"Sure."

The wind started to blow and Genie felt the cold air on her bare arms and feet. She felt a shiver but tried to conceal it. Jeff noticed it right away.

"You cold? I'm sorry. You wanna go back?"

Genie's tone was sweet and grateful. "No, let's walk."

Jeff's tone was enticingly warm and sincere.

"Genie, it's so warm out! How could you be cold?"

"I always get cold."

"Well, here, let me warm you up." Jeff took off his worn, brown leather jacket and wrapped it around Genie's shoulders. She could smell his cologne on the collar. The warmth of his body still on the jacket penetrated through to her insides. Then he put one arm behind her and the other arm in front of her as he hugged her from the side.

His wine scented breath was warm on her cheek. She wanted to kiss him so badly but she didn't dare turn her mouth toward his. He cuddled and nuzzled her as they walked.

Jeff spoke softly. "You know, you remind me of my mom before she got so bad."

"Is that a good thing or a bad thing?"

"Oh, she was an incredible mother. Like I told you, she went through really bad stuff later though and… I don't know, everything changed."

"What kind of bad stuff?"

"She got really ugly and violent when she drank. Once, she took me to the grocery store. She had a huge headache and it put her in a horrible mood. She didn't feel like going in the store so she gave me money and a list while she waited in the car."

"How old were you?"

"I was about eleven. I got everything on the list except for one thing. It was this certain kind of cheese she liked. When I came out I told her they didn't have it. She started arguing with me, telling me they always have it and I hadn't looked hard enough. I told her I *had* looked hard. It wasn't there. She got really mad. She stormed out of the car, went inside the store and came out with a paper bag."

Genie could feel her own fear rise as she pictured this small boy in the car, seeing his mom carrying the bag. Jeff continued.

"She got in the car and didn't say anything right away. Then she turned to me, opened the bag, flashed the cheese in my face, and screamed at me for lying. I told her I wasn't lying; I just hadn't seen it. The more I defended myself, the angrier she got. Then she started hitting me in the face with the bag; over and over until the bag started cutting me. When she saw the blood she started crying and apologizing. She tried to hug and hold me but I didn't want to hug her back."

Genie felt such emotion it brought her to tears "Oh Jeff, I'm so sorry. I can't imagine how awful that was."

"You know, I got used to it. The thing is, when she was good she was great. She was really loving and affectionate. She was more fun than anyone I'd ever known. You actually remind me of the good part of who she was. And when you got cold it reminded me of the good times when I was a kid."

Genie was touched. "Really? Why?"

"My brother and I would play softball in the street and my mom would always tell us to put on a jacket. We weren't cold, but *she* was!" Jeff laughed warmly with the memory. "She'd come running out with sweatshirts, we'd put 'em on and we'd just sweat our asses off! Just 'cause it was easier than hearing her complaining about how cold we were."

Genie smiled. "Are you still close with your brother?"

Jeff paused before he spoke. Genie sensed she was about to hear more bad news.

"He died in a car accident. Left behind a wife and two great boys. Anthony and Jonathon."

Genie's heart sank again. She spoke softly. "Oh Jeff. How in the world did you survive all of this so well? And those poor boys."

"The one good thing that came out of it is my relationship with them. I kind of became…"

"A second father." Genie smiled sadly. "You became their Gregg."

Jeff smiled. "I guess I did."

"You saved them, Jeff. Do you know that?"

"Well, it's a way to keep my brother alive. So it works for me too."

"You must miss him so much."

"I think about him every day—like now, when the air is cool but I don't feel it. 'Cause I know he wouldn't feel it either." Jeff looked tenderly at Genie and rubbed his jacket into her shoulders. "Guess you'd be running after me just like my mom, huh?"

Genie smiled. "Yeah, I guess I would. And you'd sweat your ass off for me too, right?"

Jeff laughed. "I think I already do."

The words stunned her. She nuzzled up closer to him.

"Genie, where did you come from? I don't think I've ever felt so comfortable with anyone so quickly. This isn't stuff I typically talk about, you know?"

Jeff held her tight and their walk was now synchronized. Genie felt the same comfort. As they noticed their steps had joined each other's, they adjusted their hips side by side. It was unspoken and yet acknowledged.

As they got to the next block, Jeff pointed toward one of the town homes.

"My buddy lives in that brownstone over there. You want to see if he's home?"

"Sure, if you want to."

"I'm sure he's not home but we can just say a quick 'hi' if he is."

Jeff let Genie walk up the steps ahead of him. When they got to the top, he rang the bell. Just standing next to him was enough to make her heart race. After about twenty seconds without a response, Jeff turned to face Genie.

She looked up at him, assuming he was going to suggest that they leave. Instead, he just rested his eyes on her face and looked intensely into her eyes. She looked at his eyes, and then brought her gaze down to his mouth. Her eyes followed the carved lines of his jaw. She saw him moving closer and she wasn't quite ready for that. She didn't want to give up looking at him. It was almost not worth the kiss.

As if her eyes couldn't let go of watching him, she backed off ever so slightly just so she could watch him longer. Once his mouth was on top of hers she moved back once again. The more she moved back to watch, the closer Jeff moved in to find her.

His mouth was warm in the cool air and he smelled like wine and cologne. He kissed her softly at first and she felt awkward kissing him. It wasn't what she expected. Something seemed to be missing. She felt a slight tinge of disappointment. It just wasn't clicking for her.

All of a sudden, Jeff gently snuck his tongue past her lips. Finally she gave up the fight to watch, and gave into receiving the kiss. He pressed harder with his mouth. It caused her to make a short gasp. She kissed him and she kissed him hard. He matched her vigor with his own. The more they kissed, the more she wanted, and with greater intensity she reached into him. Genie kissed his cheeks, his mouth, his neck and his nose. She kissed every inch of his face.

The force behind her passion could have knocked any man down to the ground. But Jeff synchronized his mouth with her movements and came back with equal force. Genie had no idea how long they were there, or anything that took place around them. Nothing else mattered in that moment. She was buried alive in this man.

CHAPTER 23

The cereal box had mystic powers. No matter how many times Genie put it away, it seemed to come back out again. Yesterday's ordinary bran flakes were today's exotic love affair. Genie's energy was so high her fingers were literally shaking. Eating the cereal felt like a revved up engine racing in the Indy 500. Genie Lamborghini.

When the phone rang, she answered. "Hell-hello?"

"Hey. What's up?"

Genie spoke through the crunch of her cereal. "Hey, Dan! How ya doin'?"

"I'm good. What are you eating?"

Barely audible. "Therial."

"Why is it so loud?"

Smacking. "No milk."

Genie was pushing her hand through the cereal box and the wax paper was crackling.

"Why are you snarfing down like that? Burn up a lot of calories last night?"

"No, nothing like that. But we really had fun."

"Did you keep your clothes on?"

Genie stuffed another handful of cereal in her mouth. "All of them."

Danny laughed. "Don't most girls lose weight when they fall in love? What's with you?"

"I woke up really hungry, that's all. I'm putting it away now." Genie closed the bag and began closing the box. "How was Kay?"

"Well, I just got home, if that's any indication."

Genie felt a pang. She reopened the bag and reached for more cereal. "Well, how was the date other than that?"

"Who cares?"

"Oh, right. I forgot." Genie took smaller handfuls hoping not to be heard. "Sex for a guy is like a milk carton. Don't need to look at the date. As long as it doesn't smell bad you can..."

Danny was humorously defensive. "Oh, come on. It's not like that at all. Sex is more like renting a movie from Netflix. Once I've seen the whole thing it seems pointless to check it out again, you know?"

Genie screamed. "You are so bad!" She closed the bag and box, and put it in the cabinet.

"I'm just playing with you. I like Kay a lot, actually."

"Good. Great! Listen Dan, I know we're supposed to go for lunch but I just ate all this cereal. But I'll still go if..."

"Genie, that's why I called. I wasn't sure if we were on or not and I told Kay I'd take her out for lunch."

Genie paused, trying to decide if she was mad. "Oh."

"You can come along if you want. I'm sure she wouldn't mind."

Decision made. She *was* mad. "No, Danny! I'm not coming along with you and your date. We always go out for Sunday breakfast when we miss the Saturday ride."

"Oh, so you can cancel for Captain Crunch but I can't for Special Kay."

Genie overlooked the pun, difficult as that was.

"I would have still gone!"

"And I'm still inviting you."

"It's so different! You cancelled for a person."

"You cancelled for a box!"

Genie spoke in a pout that even she knew was stupid. "Fine. Whatever. I'll just talk to you later." Genie hung up the phone.

Thoughts of Kay started running through Genie's head. Who the heck was she, and how dare she think she can have my Sundays? *And how could Danny leave me alone without asking if I cared?* Genie grabbed the cereal box again, stuffing handfuls in her mouth as the thoughts did somersaults. She had to fix this feeling; it just felt too bad to hold on to. She called back Danny.

"Yes, Dear."

Somehow, Genie felt calmed just hearing his voice. She still couldn't get any words out.

"Genie?" Danny was affectionate in tone. "Usually when someone calls, they say something."

Genie still didn't speak. Danny was silent. The line was perfectly still.

"Gene? I know you're in there. Come on now. *Boo!*"

Genie laughed. "Sorry, Dan. I called to say I know I was being stupid."

"No, I should have talked to you before I asked Kay. You're right, we usually do spend either Saturdays or Sundays together. My bad."

"Well, girlfriends tend to mess up everything, don't they?"

"So do boyfriends."

"Yeah, you're right. Ok, well... have fun today."

"You too."

After they hung up, Genie walked back into the kitchen and opened the door to the fridge. She closed it and opened cabinets. With knees on the counter and a stretch above, down came the box of Wheat Thins which, when eaten in one sitting, would be more appropriately named Wheat *Fats.*

This was nothing Genie had experienced before. It felt like a switch had been flicked. She couldn't get enough food in her mouth and she felt powerless to stop. Not only was she feeling incredibly full, her stomach was beginning to hurt. It didn't matter. All she could think about was what the next bite would be.

The crackers were good, but how about adding spray butter? What about grabbing peanut butter and jelly and making a cracker sandwich? Hey, screw the crackers! Let's just make a sandwich with bread! The more food she stuffed, the more crazed she felt inside.

Finally, Genie felt an end to the madness. She was winding down now but needed to end on a sweet note. She opened a bag of bittersweet chocolate chips. Somehow it still didn't feel like an ending, so she topped it off with a cup of hot chocolate.

When the eating had run its course, Genie was left with the crash. She felt so sick and cramped that she could barely walk to the bathroom. She wondered if she could throw up. There was no way she could force it, but wished she could. At this point it seemed like the only way to get rid of this poisonous feeling.

Genie looked in the mirror. She had never seen herself look this bad. Her stomach was distended, her face was pale, and her expression almost scared her. She imagined the food going through her system. She counted the calories in her mind. She visualized the inside mechanics of calories turning to fat. The damage was done. She would gain so much weight. There was nothing she could do now.

Genie looked in the mirror and hated whom she saw. She was angry for having done this. She began to brush her teeth but all she could do was cry. In that moment she made the decision to hit the gym. She could wear a big t-shirt to cover her stomach. If she worked out really hard for a couple of hours, maybe she could reverse the damage.

CHAPTER 24

Gregg's 40th birthday was coming up. Jennifer was planning a party to surprise him at Fresco's, an Italian restaurant where they would supposedly be meeting another couple for dinner. On the Tuesday night before the Saturday of the party, the new manager of Fresco's called the house to let them know that because a pipe that had burst in the dining room, the party would need to be cancelled. Even more unfortunate was the fact that Gregg had taken the call.

Jennifer was devastated that the surprise was ruined. Gregg thought it was funny and tried to make her feel better, but Genie knew her mom better than that and went to work on Plan B. Genie asked Aunt Dotty if she would have the party at her house. Next, how to get Gregg there on a Saturday night. This wasn't going to be easy.

First of all, he didn't like the smell of her apartment and basically refused to go there. Secondly, he hated her cooking and that only made the place smell worse. Thirdly, he thought Dotty was a head case and he could only tolerate her in small doses.

Genie knew Gregg would be so distracted by the guests he wouldn't care where they were. But how to get him there? The only way to make this work was to have the surprise take place somewhere else, and then move the guests to Dotty's. Genie went to her mom with the plan.

The Saturday night of the party, at six- thirty, Gregg called Dotty's home and asked to speak to his wife.

"Jen, why aren't you home yet? You've been gone over an hour."

"Oh sorry, Honey, Dotty had some friends here and I just got to talking..."

"Well, where are the damn diapers? I've looked everywhere!"

"Oh Honey... did you check the closet?" Jennifer could hardly keep from laughing.

"Of course I checked the closet. There aren't any."

"Did you check the drawer of the changing table?"

"OF COURSE I CHECKED THERE! I need you to pick some up on your way home. And you need to come home now. Luke's diaper is soaked."

"Oh Sweetie, could you get them?" *Sugar sweet.* "I'm having so much fun here."

"Are you kiddin' me? You want me to take Luke... oh man, hold on, someone's at the door. Get your ass home right now, Jen!"

It was Mrs. Duffy from next door. She was one of those neighbors that always needed to borrow something. And usually that something was Gregg. Could he come over and fix the washing machine? Could he just replace some screens? Does he know anything about hornets' nests? She noticed his outdoor grill is on... could he throw on her Porterhouse?

Gregg opened the door because if he didn't she would just keep knocking.

"Hello Gregg, how are you, Dear? I was wondering if I could borrow some sugar. I'm baking cookies for my grandson tomorrow."

"Oh Mrs. Duffy, could you wait, I've got Jen on the phone and I'm out of diapers..."

Gregg spoke in the receiver again. "Jennifer, are you getting those diapers or not?"

"Oh Sweetie, why don't you ask Mrs. Duffy to watch Lukey, and then you can go get diapers? She loves staying with him. And then you can come over to Dotty's."

"There's no way in hell I'm going to Dotty's. You get the diapers on your way home!"

Jennifer faked her anger. "Well, there's no way in hell I'm coming home now!"

Mrs. Duffy began to speak to Gregg. "Dear, why don't you let me watch Luke and you can run to the store and pick up some sugar for an old lady."

At this point Gregg was beside himself with frustration. He slammed down the phone, took a deep breath so as not to abuse an old lady, and told her he would be happy to go. He threw on a jacket, got in the car, and honked at anyone in his way whether they deserved it or not.

At seven o'clock, Gregg walked into the grocery store. He knew the diapers were in aisle seven. As he turned the corner at the end of the aisle, he saw a huge crowd of people toward the other end. He couldn't imagine what could draw such a crowd in a grocery store on a Saturday night. As he got closer, he began to see familiar faces. Neil and Penny Thatcher, his secretary Kathy, the Greens, the Jensons, the Chambers, Cohns, and Glickmans; so many more... Jennifer, Dotty, Genie...

"SURPRISE!!!!!!"

Gregg stood stunned. Jennifer was crying. Dotty was exploding in laughter. His friends approached one by one, all wanting to exchange their stories of how this had transpired. After many questions and answers, Gregg found out who was responsible.

He broke through the wall of bodies and made his way toward Genie, who was standing next to Aunt Dotty. Gregg looked at Dotty and gave her a heartfelt hug. And then he knelt in front of Genie.

"Sweetheart. In my whole life, no one has ever put so much time, effort, or… creative *brilliance* into something just for me. And there's not an adult I know that could have thought of this or pulled it off."

Genie had no words. She just looked at this man she loved. Gregg smiled at her silence, since it was so out of character for her. And as he spoke, his throat closed up in emotion, causing his voice to crackle.

"I don't think I've ever felt as loved as I feel tonight. You are the best daughter a man could ever hope for. And one day, I'm going to be there when life throws *you* a surprise."

Meanwhile at home, Mrs. Duffy went to Genie's room, opened the third drawer of Genie's chest to find the package of diapers that Genie had hidden. Luke's diaper was soaked and it needed to be changed, just as Genie had planned.

CHAPTER 25

Tuesday morning Genie walked into the office. Steven took one look at her and knew it would be a long day.

"Why the face?"

Genie didn't answer.

"He didn't ask you out again?"

Genie looked through papers on her desk as though she hadn't heard him.

"Genie. You said he left a message on Sunday. Why would he do that if he didn't want to see you again?"

Genie spoke in a monotone. "He's polite. He left the message so he wouldn't look bad."

"Did you call him back?"

"I called him back the next day. He didn't pick up and he didn't call back."

"Did you leave a message?"

"Yes, Steven."

"He called you Sunday. Why did you wait until Monday?"

"I didn't want to look desperate."

"That *is* desperate."

"Whatever. It's obviously done. Where are the files for the Zuckerman party?"

"He'll call today."

"How do you know?"

"He needs to wait a day because you did."

"Why would he wait a day?"

Steven looked at Genie. She stared back at him. She raised her eyebrows, which made him laugh and shake his head. Genie began to go through her call list and Steven walked into the bathroom.

About two hours later, Steven answered the phone, put the call on hold, and looked at Genie without expression.

"It's for you."

Genie didn't look up. "Who is it?"

Steven stared at Genie until she looked at him. He smiled and raised his eyebrows.

Genie whispered. "It's *him?*"

Steven whispered. "It's *him.* And he's on hold so we don't really need to do this."

Genie whispered. "Do what?"

Steven whispered again. "*Whisper.*"

Genie perked up just a bit but did not reach for the phone. Steven watched her shuffling though her papers. "Genie, pick up the phone. He's waiting!"

"He can wait a minute. I'm busy."

"Busy with WHAT? You're not busy! You're making him pay. He didn't do anything wrong. Now pick up the damn phone, Genie!"

Genie took a deep breath, rolled her eyes, and rested her hand on the phone. She brought the receiver close to her ear, but not actually touching it. She pressed line one ever so sprightly. She didn't just speak her name. *She sang it.*

"Genie Buuuurrrrns."

"Yep, you are."

Genie felt alive inside, just hearing the sound of his voice.

"I are what?"

"You are a Genie that burns. Ever since I got home Saturday night, I felt like something got out. Then I realized it was you. Somehow you got out of the bottle and now you're everywhere. And I can't put you back in."

Genie couldn't believe what she was hearing. With a warm and flirtatious spirit, she dove right in.

"Why would you try?"

"Loose Genies can cause a whole lot of trouble. And I don't like trouble."

"Well, Genies bring magic. That's what my dad told me when I was a little girl."

"Well, I guess your dad didn't watch, "I Dream of Jeannie." She caused Major Nelson so much trouble that he died."

"That was the *actor* that died."

"What*ever.*"

Genie laughed.

"So, Genie Burns, I'm watching the Championship tonight. You want to come over? I make a mean salmon."

"Can't."

"Why not?"

"Don't take last minute invitations. And I don't go to men's homes who I don't really know in case I get attacked."

"Well, you *do* know me because I've told you more than I've told other women cumulatively. And I promise I won't attack you. But unfortunately, I can't speak for Stanley."

CHAPTER 26

The first walk into a man's abode is a relationship changing moment. If you really like him, you will undoubtedly find something that you *don't* like. Or, if you aren't sure how you feel about him, and his place is great, he can potentially climb up the chart. Genie's introduction to Jeff's home was... could only be described as... *eventful.*

Stepping in the foyer of this renovated brownstone, Genie looked around. The colors were natural beiges and tans, the walls were covered in bamboo grasscloth, and the floors Genie guessed to be limestone. The artwork was surprisingly traditional. The antique chair and table in the entry were magnificent pieces, and Genie assumed were quite expensive. The windows were large allowing full streams of natural light. As far as Genie was concerned, this man was not only crush material. He lived in crush materialistic.

Suddenly, without warning, barreling down the stairs in thunderous steps, was an animal that could only be described as a one hundred and fifty pound frightening hurricane of knee deep, snow white fluff. The only thing more amazing then his size were the two side by side strings of drool, wagging in sync, almost as fast as his tail.

"STANLEY!!!!!!" The excitement that Jeff had in greeting this abominable psycho monster told a story in itself. These two creatures obviously had a *relationship.* And Genie was quite sure that no man, woman, or beast would ever come between them.

Jeff bent down, eye level, staring Stanley down. Stanley stared back. Jeff waited, daring him without fear. Stanley stood in his spot, staring intently, barking but not moving an inch. One would think this was a moment to gently walk away. Or perhaps offer a treat; something to calm the dog down. *Not so much.*

Jeff took a giant frog leap toward Stanley, landing with a thud. The dog went crazy, barking, seeming ready to pounce. Anyone watching this would know without doubt, that one of them would end up dead. And it wasn't going to be Stanley.

Seconds later, another thunderous sound. This one, however, was not animal. This was a female shriek. It was high pitched and bitchin'. It was strong and not to be reckoned with. It was truly, the only voice you'd ever expect could have survived that dog.

She didn't sound like a girlfriend or wife he had forgotten to mention he lived with. She sounded big. She sounded strong. And she sounded like she ran the show.

"JEFFER-EEEEEEEEEEEEEEEEEEEEE?"

Jeff laughed. He looked at Genie with a subtle, innocent announcement.

"You're about to meet *Helen.*"

Genie whispered. "Who's Helen?"

"She's my housekeeper. She's been around since I was little. She's family," and this part he spoke just an octave higher, "and she hears *everything.*"

From upstairs, the voice could be heard cackling like the Wicked Witch on Adderall, and then screaming down again.

"That's right, Baby! You Goddamn know I do! And don't you be giving me none of your *bull*shit. I'll whip your ass so fast you won't know what be happening to you. You Goddamn *hoe*."

Jeff called out, "Hey, you're scaring my girlfriend!"

"You tell her she be best to find herself a real man. Not a goddamn hoe like you and yo bad self!" Then the cackling laugh again.

Genie looked at Jeff. He looked at her with an innocent, shoulder shrug.

"Welcome to my home!"

They climbed the stairs, which wasn't easy since including Stanley, there was basically four hundred and fifty pounds competing for space on each step. At the top of the stairs, there she was, looking right at Genie. She wasn't tall but she was big. She had dark skin, dark hair, and she was dressed in cuddly sweats.

"Hey, Baby! Come here and give me a hug."

Helen opened her arms to Genie and pulled her in. Genie rested her body against Helen's, which felt like soft, doughy memory foam. It so contorted to fit Genie's body that she couldn't believe this was free. She would have paid top dollar, at least once a week. She would choose it over a mani/pedi and even a hot-stone massage. She would ask Helen for gift certificates to give to her girlfriends and hand out at holidays *annually.*

Helen, Jeff, Stanley. *Thunder Love.*

CHAPTER 27

Jeff had spoken the truth. His salmon was deliciously mean and there was no risk of attack. To the contrary, he was very involved in watching the game and screaming at the refs. Genie would have never accepted this in anyone. Even when Danny tried to watch sports, just the sound of the games made her scream. Jeff pulled her next to him and pretzeled his legs around her.

"Jeff, I used to hate when Gregg watched sports with Luke. I always felt so left out."

Jeff put his arms around her waist. "Tell you what. I'm not *lettin'* you out." Jeff gave up watching the game and spent the rest of the night kissing Genie. It was as if their lips were playing games without any regulations. It was enticing and erotic. It was packed full of fun. It was everything kissing should be.

After the game, rather than the kissing leading to sex, it led to more information. Genie felt like the conversation advanced them to the equivalent of six months of dating, rather than the few dates they had. Talking to Jeff was so easy, comfortable, and relaxing. Each topic they covered connected them more, so the kisses intensified.

From the stories Jeff told, Genie got the sense that he had a strong and grounded sense of himself. He talked about his philosophies relating to stress. He woke up every morning feeling positive and happy. When Genie rolled her eyes, he challenged her to see that living that way is a choice. If situations in his life became difficult, he was determined and focused with the unyielding belief that it would all work out in the end. He wouldn't even allow himself to assume anything less than that.

When it came to family and friendships, he spoke of an iron clad commitment to them. He described friends who lived with him when they ran out of money. One guy, Vince, even stole from him, but Jeff never gave up on him. Today, Vince is married, holding down a great job, and just bought his first home. The more questions Genie asked, the more she found out about Jeff and his life, the more enticing he was.

Jeff asked Genie about her childhood, her relationships with her family, and more of her feelings about her dad. She revealed some of the insecurities she'd had in the past with men, and the fears she had about losing people she was close to. Between her sentences, Jeff would kiss and hug her. She felt like she was talking to the best friend in the world who doubled as a high school crush.

The fact that Jeff hadn't pushed sex that night meant so much to Genie. She wasn't sure at this point if she would have been able to say no if he had. But she knew it was better not to. Feelings wise, this was moving quickly enough. And as happy and excited as she was, the larger part of her felt fear. Genie could already tell at this early stage, she was in way too deep.

CHAPTER 28

One unreturned phone call from Danny could mean he was busy. Two unreturned calls could mean he was busy and then fell asleep. Three could mean only one thing. Danny was dead. There was no other explanation. Well, maybe a hostage situation and at this point, that was still something to hope for. In her denial that Danny was gone forever, Genie dialed him one more time. Danny picked up the phone. *He was alive!*

"Danny? Dan!"

"Genie? What's the matter?"

Genie had started to cry upon hearing his voice. "Dan, are you alright?"

"Of course I'm alright. I just got home."

Genie couldn't stop crying. The relief of hearing Danny's voice was enormous. "Why didn't you call me? Didn't you get my messages?"

"I was going to call you tonight." Danny was alarmed. "What happened? What's the matter with you?"

"We haven't talked since Sunday. That never happens! When I realized it, I got scared."

Danny was soft in his tone. "Genie, it's only Tuesday."

Sniffling. "Well, what have you been so busy with? We usually talk every day."

"I was with Kay on Sunday and then she ended up coming over last night too."

Suddenly, Genie's fear and relief were gone. Anger had crashed the party and chased the others away. "*Kay?* You were with Kay on Sunday *and* Monday? Next she'll be moving in! I thought you didn't even like her!"

"What, I'm supposed to measure each day on the Genometer and report my findings to you?"

"I'm not saying it like that. I just don't understand why you're spending so much time with her so soon. You don't ever do that."

Danny softened his tone. "Look, Gene, I'm sorry you were so worried. Next time I'll make sure to get back to you sooner, ok?"

Genie softened. "Sorry I got so mean. I guess I'm jealous. I don't like someone else taking up your time."

"Ok, Genes. I'll just chase your ass every day."

"Dan, girls like when you chase their hearts."

"Asses are easier, Gene. You can see them."

"Hearts are better, Dan. You can feel them."

"You can feel an ass too."

Genie laughed and blew her nose.

"Danny, I know you're going to have girlfriends. I just feel like I'll get replaced and lose you."

"You'll never lose me. If I gave you up I'd get to order food I like. Bad for my girlish figure."

When they were settled and laughing, they agreed to talk later. Genie hung up and without thought, made a beeline for the kitchen. Since the last eating explosion, she had cleared the cereal box and crackers. As she rummaged through the limited choices,

Genie discovered that creativity goes a long way. She opened her bottom cabinet, aha! A slivered lining! Genie combined slivered almonds with raisins, put them on slices of apples, and voila! *Crunch.* But no reason at all to stop here.

Turkey and cheese rolled with the devil, MAYO! It tasted so good it made her long for a sandwich so she used a half slice of bread. No full sandwiches allowed... way too fattening. She had six of those half suckers until she moved on to frozen yogurt.

When Genie had finished, this time she didn't look in the mirror of hatred. Instead, she put on her gym shoes and headed out for a run. Her stomach felt like a dryer spinning too heavy of a load. But calories needed to be burned and that was all she could focus on.

Genie *Burns.*

CHAPTER 29

It felt dishonest. Not because she was doing anything wrong. But if Genie didn't tell Jeff about her relationship with Danny, and even some of the confusion she felt, she would feel like she was keeping a secret. They were walking with frozen yogurt cones and the words came out between licks.

"Jeff, I have to talk to you about something."

Jeff spoke with affectionate sarcasm. "I'd like the short version."

Genie leaned against him in fun, overlooking the comment. "I have a friend. He's just a friend, but... we're very close."

"Ok." Jeff waited for her to continue.

"He dated my college roommate. I mean there was one *kind of* night that was a mistake a long time ago but since then, we've only been friends."

Jeff waited and listened without speaking.

"He's been dating a girl named Kay. This is the first time, since college I mean, that he's getting involved with someone. And I know I sound like a hypocritical idiot since here I am with you..."

Jeff was quiet and soft in his tone. "And you're jealous of Kay."

Genie felt terribly uncomfortable discussing this with Jeff. She knew she would die if Jeff told her that he had a female friend equal to Danny. She began to feel panicked inside, knowing she might lose *him* too.

Jeff's tone was soft. "Does it make you feel like you want to try having a relationship with him?"

"No. But I never expected to feel this way."

"Gene, it's natural for you to feel jealousy. You're close with him and if he all of a sudden has feelings for someone, you're going to have a reaction. Anyone in your position would."

"Would you?"

"Well, I probably wouldn't be as emotional about it as you, but sure, I'd feel like I was losing part of a friend."

"But I didn't just get emotional. I lost all control. No one else would have done that."

Jeff put his arms around Genie and it made her feel incredibly grateful. "Genie, you had some tough things happen when you were little. You're going to handle things differently than someone else who didn't have those things happen. And my guess is that when you're close to someone, you'll become fearful if you feel like you're losing them in any way at all."

"How do you know that?"

"Because of my brother."

Genie licked the sides of her cone. "You did that when he died?"

"Well, actually, I watched it more in my mom. After he died, if I did anything that she considered dangerous or risky, she went nuts."

"What did you do that was dangerous?"

Jeff laughed. "Anytime I went to the bathroom with the door closed! I had to check in all the time or I'd get these panicked phone calls from her. It was very hard."

"She wasn't like that before?"

"No, not really. I mean she was always concerned about us. But not overly so."

"So how did she get better?"

"She didn't. When she died, I missed her horribly. She was an incredible mom. But honestly, part of me was relieved to be able to do what I needed to do without constantly worrying about her feelings."

"Yeah, well that's why I don't travel. I know I have issues with that too. I just do the best I can to stay out of situations that get me crazy. But sometimes I can't avoid it."

"Well, if you're going to get close to people, you're going to feel that at times. But you can't live your life in fear either. You'll just know that the feelings will come up and you'll learn how to deal with them more rationally."

"I don't think I can. I've tried before. They come up on me and there's nothing I can do."

Jeff was quiet. He smiled. "Well, I know one way I can help you."

• • •

Genie had a pretty good idea as to what Jeff would suggest as a stress buster. He was, after all, a guy. And Genie was, after all, ready. When they got back to her apartment, Jeff grabbed her hand, positioned her standing and facing him, and told her to close her eyes.

He moved to stand close behind her, reached around her and took both of her hands. She could feel his breath near her ear and she felt the warmth of his torso behind her. She waited to be kissed and undressed. This was going to be *great.*

"Ok Genes, I'm going to help you breathe. This is going to relax you anytime you feel like you're losing control. Just stand here and I'm gonna show you how, ok?"

Huh?

He began to speak softly in her ear. "Gene, I want you to draw in air, but you need to concentrate on taking the air in from here." Jeff put his hand on her belly. "Not here." He put his hand on her chest. Having him touch her that way was the most amazing feeling in the world. And yet she knew he meant nothing by it. He took her hand and placed it on top of his hand, pulling his own hand away so that her hand rested on her abdomen.

"Breathe in slowly through your nose, and blow the air out through your mouth." As she breathed, he reminded her to let go of the muscles in her stomach and let it stick out. She felt self-conscious about sticking out her belly like that. Wasn't it doing enough of that these days? As Genie began to breathe, eyes still closed, she could feel him moving closely around her. His voice wasn't a whisper, just low and soft. He took her hands and gently put them to her side. He moved from one side of her to the next, making circles around her, stroking her hand and her arm.

Jeff stayed close in with his steps and spoke quietly. "I want you to imagine your thoughts becoming lighter. It's not that they aren't there. It's more like they're slowly filling up with air and floating above your head." In between his words, Jeff matched the timing of Genie's breaths with his own, leading her to breathe and release the air.

"If you feel them becoming heavy again, release a puff of air and watch them float to the side. Once they're away from the center of your thinking, you'll see a clear opening. That's where I want you to focus and breathe."

Each time Jeff stroked Genie's arm down to her hand, her fingers found his and tried to hold on to them lightly. Jeff allowed the hold just for a moment and then gently released her touch. He continued to give directions to breathe, following each breath she took.

At first Genie had been so taken with Jeff that she couldn't put the thought of him outside of her head. But now, with her eyes still closed, she was beginning to fall into a sense of peace and calm that she had never felt before.

Jeff was talking less now, just sharing her inhales and exhales. At times she became more aware of him, other times she was floating away. Finally, he talked her through letting herself come back and eventually opening her eyes. When she did, she felt like she had left this world and come back to a different one. She had never felt so at peace.

"This is really going to help you. We can practice more, but eventually if you can do this on your own when you're feeling a panic attack, it'll calm you."

Genie stood in disbelief. She felt like Jeff had lifted her up, held her close, wrapped her in a blanket, and rocked her like an infant.

Without thinking, she reached up, held on to him and kissed him in gratitude. By far, more than any physical or sexual moment she had ever spent with a man, this was the most intimate experience of her life. She had never felt more taken care of.

"Jeff, I can't believe how that felt."

"It feels good, doesn't it?"

They looked into each other's eyes.

"Jeff, it felt so… *intimate.*"

Jeff looked in her eyes and smiled. "It did for me too."

And somehow she had known that already.

CHAPTER 30

Steven was stuffing half a turkey sandwich into his mouth. Genie was stuffing the other half into hers. With lettuce coming out of her mouth as she talked, and a desk full of lettuce and crumbs, Genie asked a question that she had been pondering.

"Steven, how does a girl know if a guy she's dating is gay?"

Steven's laugh caught him by such surprise that a big piece of turkey fell right out of his mouth, and then some. He spoke as he was wiping the spritz.

"Well, let's see. If he asks to borrow your clothes for your date; if he thinks you need to buy his brand of mascara rather than the cheap stuff you wear; if you get into bed with him and he asks to bring his boyfriend, or if he asks if you've got a brother for him... I'd say those are tell-tale signs."

Genie finished chewing the bite in her mouth and chugged from her water bottle. "Well, here's the thing. Jeff and I have been dating for over two months now. We've gotten very close. He's introduced me to his friends and his family. He spends tons of time with me; calls and texts me constantly. But he's kissed me and that's all. Something's wrong with him, don't you think?"

"Genes, maybe he just doesn't find you attractive." Steven stared at Genie with an intense smirk on his face, eyebrows raised in jest.

"Steven, I'm beginning to think that must be it. In that case I hope he *is* gay! Oh, my Gosh, I can't introduce him to you. I'll end up your bridesmaid!"

"Genes. Aren't you glad you don't have to fight another one off?"

"No! At least I'd know he wants me."

"He wants you. *Bad.* Trust me. He's holding back for a reason."

"And the reason is he's gay. Or he's getting it someplace else. Or he thinks of me as a friend."

"None of the above. He just wants it to come from you."

"Why?"

"He respects you, Gene. And he might be afraid you'll reject him. I mean, hey, he can probably tell you're a total prude. Did you tell him about your mom and the '*rule*'? No titty without commity?"

"No. Unfortunately it doesn't seem to be a problem."

"Well, I'll tell you what—do something bold and slutty for once. He'll be all over you. If he's not, give him my number and I'll let you wear whatever bridesmaid dress you want. Just stay away from mauve."

• • •

Lover's Arrest was a shop for lovers. Genie had never actually stepped inside, but she had enough friends who had. She looked at the various lingerie and costumes. One option was the policewoman costume. It came with high black patent leather boots, chains, and handcuffs. *No can do.* How about a French Maid? Nah, what would she do, clean the grout? Sex Kitten with ears and a tail? Jeff was allergic to cats. I Dream of Jeannie with below the hip pink balloon pants, and a cropped pink sequin bra? *Bingo.*

Genie bought the costume, made two stops, raced home, took a shower, and put the costume on. It came with a hat; a pointed cone shape that stood on top of her head. There was a pink transparent veil that draped down from the point at the top and tied under her chin like a scarf. She put her hair up in a high ponytail, put on dark eyeliner and pink lipstick. She checked the clock, then the mirror. Seven minutes to go.

She raced into the living room and set the boom box by the front door. She put the CD in place. She lit votive candles all around the room and put the lights on dim. Next to the couch, she took the massage lotion from the bag and set it on the coffee table.

What else? Oh! She got the blindfold and hung it on the outside doorknob of the front door. She wrote the sign in marker and taped it to the outside of the door, just above the blindfold. She looked around the room to see if anything was missing. She couldn't believe she was doing this but nothing would stop her now.

She stood at the door and listened. Finally, after a few minutes, she heard him come up to the door. She put her ear to the door and heard him mutter something to himself and laugh. She heard him take the tape and paper off of the door. When the doorbell rang, she flipped the switch of the boom box. The song "Genie in a Bottle" started to play. She opened the door and there he was, standing with the blindfold on, just as the note had instructed.

"I'm here to see a lady about a bottle?"

Genie didn't say a word. She took his hand and slowly led him into the apartment. She kissed him on the side of his mouth and walked him over to the couch. She sat him down and started taking off his shoes.

He squirmed and giggled but didn't say a word. Genie took off his socks. She leaned over him and kissed him again, this time right on his mouth. He had lost the laughter and replaced it with a quiet intensity, waiting. Taking in the moment, he kissed her. And when he tried to kiss her more, she seductively pulled away.

Genie took the bottle of lotion and began massaging Jeff's feet. At this point, he leaned back into the couch and relaxed. She watched his face in the blindfold. He looked so beautiful and sexy. He reminded her of some masked man in a storybook who steals the princess back from her captor. She had never felt such desire for a man in her life.

When Genie had finished with his feet, she went to the top button of his shirt. She unbuttoned it slowly to reveal soft curls of hair that spread across his chest. She took the shirt completely off. His shoulders were large and strong. His arms were magnificent. She gently pulled him toward her.

She took more lotion from the bottle and spread it between her hands. She began to rub his shoulders and his arms. She pulled him in even closer. As he leaned into her, she reached behind him to rub his back. As she did this, she began kissing him all over his face, everywhere but his mouth. She could feel every response he had and she could see it all on his face. Then she pulled off his mask.

Jeff squinted as his eyes adjusted to the soft light. He looked at Genie sitting on top of him. His eyes scanned her face and her hat. He looked down at her body and the costume. A faint smile came across his face but it wasn't a smile of laughter. It was a smile of desire.

He looked in her eyes, grabbed her face with his hands, and pulled her mouth into his. He kissed her so intensely it made her dizzy. His mouth was warm, his lips were soft, and his eyes were inside of hers. He didn't take them away. She tried to pull back to look at him, but he pulled her back into his kiss.

With every touch, every smell, every glance, and taste; the laughter, the eyes, and the tears, Genie fell deeper in. There were no inhibitions; no holding back. Nothing felt cheap or forced. Genie had always known that sex alone wasn't enough. She saw his emotions, vulnerability, and trust. No matter what happened from this day forward, it was a part of their history now. And in their minds it linked them forever.

CHAPTER 31

"Wake Up Call" was the best breakfast place in the hood. The lines were long but the turnover was fast. After twenty minutes they were seated. Five minutes after that Genie put the menu aside. Jeff folded his and put it to the side of the table.

Genie looked at Jeff. "What are you having?"

With a light and matter of fact tone he replied, "I'm having pancakes."

Genie was playful. "Don't you want banana pancakes?"

Jeff was not. "No. I like plain pancakes."

Still playful. "But banana pancakes are better. Have you ever had them?"

Still not. "Yeah, I've had them and I like plain pancakes better. Why don't you get banana pancakes if you like them so much?"

"'Cause I don't want a whole order. I only want a couple bites of yours."

Jeff smiled. "Well, you are welcome to have a couple bites of my *plain* pancakes.

"Jeeeeeeff?"

"Whhhaaaaaat?"

"Can't you just order banana ones? It's not like you hate them. If I get a whole order I'll eat the whole thing and I don't want to eat the whole thing."

"Then don't eat the whole thing. But why should I have to order what I don't like so that you don't eat the whole thing of what you do like?"

"Well, Danny does. I thought guys don't care about stuff like that."

Jeff's lips drew a smile but it wasn't the happy kind.

"When you say *stuff like that,* you mean we'll eat things we don't like so that you can have some?"

Genie tried to look coy and adorable. But Jeff had major antibodies going and adorable was a germ to attack. She almost felt afraid to speak, but she wasn't sure what she was afraid of.

"Yeah, Jeff, a lot of guys order what their girlfriends like. You know, 'cause they don't care."

"Well, I'm not a lot of guys. I'm me. And I like to order food *I* like."

The waitress came to take their order.

Jeff spoke like the boss. "I'll have *plain* buttermilk pancakes and a small orange juice." Just hearing the words, but especially the tone, took Genie aback. She tried to let it go but it sat there inside of her, heavy like plain pancakes.

Genie placed her order. Aside from the recent, private, unexplainable binges, which were countered with heavy workouts, her meals were still balanced and healthy. "I'll have the veggie egg white omelet with a little mozzarella."

Jeff looked at her with a playful smile. "You can still have a couple bites of my plain pancakes."

Genie looked at him and gave him the most smile she could fake. It wasn't that she thought he was wrong. Rationally she knew that he should be able to have what he wanted. She certainly wouldn't want anyone telling *her* what to order! But even knowing that, there was something that didn't feel right.

"Hey Gene, I gotta get a birthday present to send to my dad. Want to come and help me pick it out?"

There was nothing she would love more than to go with him. But what to do with it? The *feeling.* It was there. And it made her unable to answer the question.

Jeff looked at her. "Don't tell me you're mad about the pancakes?"

Genie didn't say anything. *Busted.*

Jeff laughed as though he had never heard anything so funny in his life. Then he looked at Genie and saw she wasn't laughing.

"Genie?" Jeff looked at her right smack in the eye.

She looked up like a child who didn't want to look up.

"Cut that shit out." His look was so intense. He said it like he meant it. And the way he looked at her made her melt. The anger dissolved along with it.

Later, as they walked out of the clothing store, birthday gift in hand, Jeff put his arm around Genie and pulled her in at his side. He bumped against her and she shyly looked down to the ground. Jeff bumped into her again in fun. She had no idea what it was or why. But she felt something pulling her from deep inside. What had almost seemed like a turnoff before, had drawn her in even deeper.

"Jeff?"

"Gene?"

"I love you."

Jeff looked deeply into her eyes. "I love you too, Sweetheart."

When he kissed her, she detected a faint smell of maple syrup. It reminded her of how upset she had been. She felt so ashamed of herself. How could she be so selfish? She looked at him again, and loved him even more. Then she took him home and showed him.

CHAPTER 32

Genie was at the office, feeling the need for a love break. She called Jeff at the office.

"Hi, Sweet Love!"

His tone was curt and abrasive.

"What's up."

Genie was so unsettled by his cool response that her voice turned to freezer burn.

"Nothing's up. I just called to say hi."

Now Jeff was unsettled by the tone of *her* voice. "Listen, Gene, I've got another call coming in."

"Fine." Genie hung up the phone and slammed it into the holder. Steven, startled by the sound, looked up with a questioning expression.

"Steven, he can be so mean. He talks like a truck driver."

"He asked for your handle?"

"It's the WHAT'S UP. He talks to me like I'm a guy. But this morning he was so sweet."

Steven was full of excitement. This was his favorite part of the job. Taming Genie.

"Wow, Gene. That *is* bad. What could he be thinking? Do you suppose he's got an illness or something? Like a Bipolar disorder possibly?"

Genie looked at him, not amused. Steven kept going in fun.

"I mean, what could *possess* a man to speak warmly with affection in the morning, and then suddenly turn into a tobacco chewing, spit it out on the sidewalk, hack it up kind of guy just a few hours later!"

Genie was silent.

"Genes, do you think that just maybe he was at the office and dare I say... *busy?*"

"Ok, ok, ok. It's just that I got all caught up in feeling close. I was taken aback."

"Genie, you weren't taken aback. You were taken abitch."

"Fine, fine, fine. I'll call him back and be nice."

Genie dialed Jeff's cell. No answer. She waited for the voicemail.

"Hi Honey. I just remembered something I had to tell you. Call me when you can."

An hour went by and Jeff hadn't called back.

"Steven, usually if I call Jeff he calls right back. I think he's mad."

"Genie, the man works."

"Steven, I work too!"

"Yeah? *When?*"

Genie couldn't get her mind off the unreturned phone call. This thing had to be fixed.

"Steven, I'm calling him back. I'll fess up. Tell him I was out of line."

"No, Genie. Leave the poor guy alone. Call the florist instead. They need to know how you want the tables done for Saturday."

"Oh, right. No problem. Right after I call Jeff." Genie picked up the phone.

As though she had lifted her hind leg and was about to pee on the rug, Steven shouted, "Genie Burns! No! Don't you dare call him! He'll call you later."

"Fine, fine, fine."

Genie sat at her desk. She got the florist's number. She noticed Steven was now making a phone call. Slowly, she grabbed her cell phone and quietly walked to the bathroom. She pulled down her pants, sat on the toilet, and began to dial Jeff's number. Suddenly, the bathroom door burst open and crashed against the wall. Steven stood in the doorway, looked at Genie on the toilet, and spoke with authority.

"Genie Burns. Don't you talk shit! Hand the phone over now."

And hand it over she did.

CHAPTER 33

Genie and Jeff were coming up on the day that would mark six months of dating. She had met his family and he had met hers. They had met the majority of each other's friends. They had shopped, cooked, seen movies and plays, gone to quite a few sporting events, seen live music, danced, boated, worked-out, rollerbladed, and cuddled at home together. They were a *couple.*

To celebrate the anniversary night, Genie had spent weeks planning and creating romantic gifts. One was a collage she had worked on all week. She had planted it in his closet the night before as she left his apartment, so he'd find it as a surprise the next morning.

At her office, she received a package. She opened it to find two stuffed bears, each holding a champagne glass. One was a girl bear and one was a boy. They were absolutely adorable. Genie called Jeff right away. He didn't answer so she left him a message, going on about the bears. She told him from now on, Bear would be his pet name.

During the week they had made their anniversary plans. For dinner, Genie had offered to cook at her place, but Jeff preferred she come to his home so he wouldn't have to leave the dog. She parked half a block down from Jeff's front door. This wouldn't have been a problem had it not been for the three-course anniversary meal she had cooked and transported in Rubbermaid, one of which had just popped its lid.

Juggling her heaping bags of food, brightly wrapped gifts, and overcooked expectations, she looked like a cross between Martha Stewart, Santa, and Meals on Wheels. She waited for Jeff to open the door in holy amazement. Instead, he opened the door with the same greeting he'd give the mailman if he had envelopes *and* a package.

"Let me take those from you." Then eight more fighting words. "Do I need to turn on the oven?"

Jeff began searching for a pot. Genie began searching for a way through the letdown. *Connect.* So she went up to Jeff and hugged him from behind. He put his hands on top of hers and danced his hips side to side in exaggerated steps.

"Jeff, did you see it?"

"See what?"

"The collage!"

Jeff looked like he had forgotten all about it. "Oh, yeah! It was very cool. *Thank you.*" He gave Genie a quick kiss. He put food in Stanley's bowl and began talking to the dog. Genie's stomach dropped. She would have expected that response from a *card.* Trying to conceal the hurt, she served the dinner and they sat at the coffee table. When they were finished, Jeff looked at his watch.

"You feel like going to a movie?"

Genie felt destroyed and she couldn't drop the feeling from her tone. "Whatever you want."

Jeff picked up on the change in her mood and added a cold tone of his own. "Well, why don't we see the new Matt Damon movie?"

"That's fine."

As they were driving to the theatre, Genie knew the tension between them was growing. She chose her words carefully, kind of like elevator music.

"Jeff, it's really hard when you put so much work into something and the other person acts like it was no big deal. I did all that with such love and you just acted like..."

Jeff's tone was hard and defensive. "Genie, I did appreciate it and I told you that."

"Yeah, I got a sentence and then the movie listings. I mean, you didn't even call me when you got the collage."

Jeff was heated. "I knew I'd see you tonight and I was very thankful when I saw you. I'm sorry my response wasn't good enough for you!"

"It's just nice to feel appreciated, Jeff! I worked so long and hard on that stuff."

"I couldn't appreciate you more. But just because I don't express it the way you need me to doesn't give you the right to get mad."

"I wasn't mad, I was hurt."

"You were mad and the whole room became an arctic chill. Look Genie, I refuse to get into an argument with you about something so ridiculous. And I refuse to get blamed for something I didn't do. If you're a person who's going to get upset about the way I talk, I'm not going to want to be with you! Nobody would!"

"And if you're going to scream at me when I express myself, I'm not going to want to be with *you* either!"

Jeff parked the car and faced her. "I refuse to discuss this any longer. You've now ruined an entire evening. We can go to the movie but this discussion is over."

They walked into the movie. Neither one said a word the entire rest of the evening. Jeff dropped Genie off at her apartment, and gave her a kiss on the cheek. When Genie got home she felt awful. She wanted to fix this somehow. She called Jeff. He didn't answer the phone. She left a message to please call her back. He didn't and she tried again.

The more that Jeff wouldn't answer his phone, the more messages she left. She tried to explain her feelings. She was sorry if she was stupid. She told him that she loved him. She wasn't even sure what else she said. The crying wouldn't stop. And all she knew was that for Genie and Jeff, it was an anniversary without the happy.

CHAPTER 34

"The person you have called..." Genie knew this automated lady's voice so well she thought she should buy her lunch. She would actually use that opportunity to explain the irrational, crazy messages she had left for Jeff. On the other hand, she figured the voicemail lady probably dated automated men who pulled the same crap on her. Maybe she and Genie would become lesbian lovers and vow to pick up the phone.

It had been two days since their anniversary. The longer Jeff waited to call her, the more of her efforts he didn't respond to, the more panic and pain she felt. She knew he was gone and the relationship was over. She could hardly function.

When the phone rang and Genie saw Jeff's name pop up, her heart raced with relief and fear. She didn't know what kind of news this was, or even what she felt herself.

"Hi." His voice was soft and gentle.

"Hi." She matched it.

"Genes, I'm sorry I haven't gotten back to you but I had to just sit back a bit and think."

Genie didn't respond.

"I don't ever want to fight with you. I understand you get hurt. I understand you have issues. What you need to understand is that I have issues as well."

Genie continued to listen.

"I spent years with anger directed at me when I was a kid. I told you that my mom yelled, screamed, hit us, and blamed us for things that weren't our fault. When she'd come home, I never knew if I'd be hugged or get the shit beat out of me. When it happens today, it literally makes me sick. That's why I've just learned to stay away from it. But with us, it seems I'm always doing something to upset you and I swear, all I try to do is love you every day."

"Jeff, I feel the same way. I love you so much. That's why some of the things you say and do hurt more than they would from somebody else."

"But that doesn't give you the right to blame me just because your feelings get hurt. I order plain pancakes instead of banana and you get mad at me."

"Jeff, that's a bad example. I admitted that was silly."

"Right, but it shouldn't happen at all. And then when I didn't measure up to your standards of a thank you, you got upset with me again."

"Well, sometimes people get hurt over silly things. It's human."

"It's childish, Genie. I shouldn't have to baby-sit you and your feelings."

"It's not baby-sitting, Jeff. I was hurt about something and I expressed it. I know there have been times that you've been hurt or upset by something. I can feel it. You back off and don't give me any information. I think that's even worse."

"There's nothing wrong with somebody backing off a bit if they've been hurt. That *is* a human response. But if you're going to scream at me..."

Genie gave a frustrated laugh. "Jeff, I so didn't scream! I was so careful with my tone."

"You don't have to be yelling for it to feel like a scream."

Genie stopped in thought. She understood what he was saying.

"Jeff, I admit it's my own insecurity and I'm sure I overreact. I'm sorry. I just wanted to be appreciated, that's all."

Jeff's tone softened. "It pushes me away, Honey."

Genie felt like a kid who had been refused by Santa, when all she had asked for was gum. And wait a second. She had confessed her part, *where was his?* "But you wouldn't talk to me for two days because of one comment. That's not right either, ok?"

Jeff's voice was louder now. "You just admitted you were wrong and now you're trying to turn it around on me again. Stop back peddling, Genie!"

Genie's voice rose up to Jeff's. "I'm not back peddling! There are two people here. We both have a side. I'm seeing yours and you're not seeing mine!"

"I disagree. I think it's wrong to get mad at someone for something small. But if you're going to do that, you'll have to accept my response. And my response is to leave."

"Jeff, that's what makes it worse. The way to stay good with each other is to drop it."

"Why do you get to make those rules?"

"They're not rules. They're strategies for getting along!"

"No, they're Genie's strategies for getting along. Jeff's strategy is you don't sweat the small stuff. Look Genie, I called to tell you how I felt and now it's turned into another fight."

"Well, if I tell you how I feel, I get hung up on!"

Now Jeff's voice was louder. "You bring it on yourself! You are relentless and you won't stop. I'm hanging up."

"Don't hang up!"

He did.

Genie couldn't take another two days with the voicemail lady. Without a thought as to what she was doing, she got in her car and drove fast. She burst into Jeff's apartment on a mission to find a monster. What she found instead was a cuddly bear. He was on the sofa, lounging in sweats, ballgame on low volume.

"*Hiiii* Ginomatic." He made it all go away.

Jeff scooped Genie up like a load of firewood. They hugged for a long time. He stared with intensity, directly into her eyes. Genie studied every line of his face. She watched his eyes move up and down as though he recorded each of her features. He pushed strands of hair away from her face and he smiled with warm gentle kisses.

"Genie. I've never felt this way about anyone. Nobody ever got in like you have and nobody will again. This is it for me, you understand?" She nodded. Jeff smiled, kissed her, and spoke softly again. "It's like you're part of my core now. *Don't fuck it up.*"

They held each other and Genie cried. Jeff held her tight and buried his face in her neck. The intimacy that followed was genuine, solid, and bonding. It turned into passion so intense it actually made their lips bleed. Her chin was raw and chafed.

Genie and Jeff were hitting parts of their past that didn't want to be found. When her part found his part in a heated fight, it was razors against cutting knives. But here in each other's arms, eyes, and souls, it was beyond anyone's imagination.

Even theirs.

CHAPTER 35

This year's model of boyfriend was certainly buffed and in mint condition; until you looked under the hood. Between Jeff's migraine headaches, knees without cartilage, multiple shoulder surgeries that didn't quite work, hip, elbow, and back pain, and periodic immobilizing foot cramps, Jeff was like the Tin Man without an oil can. But he still worked out every morning.

Genie had changed her workouts to mornings instead of evenings so they could have the time together. Jeff had just finished doing weights and Genie had run on the treadmill. They met up at the Club Grill, towels around shoulders, eyeing the breakfast menu.

"Gene, there's something we need to talk about."

"*You* want to talk? I knew one day you'd be me!"

"Gino, if I ever turn into you, just shoot me, ok?"

"So what do you want to talk about, Bear? The Dodgers? Miami Dolphins? New York Jets?"

Jeff looked at Genie in amazement. "Man, you really *are* a Genie. The New York Jets and Miami Dolphins are pretty accurate. I need to take a *jet* to *Miami*. And I want you to go with me."

Genie looked at him, knowing already this wasn't her idea of a fun conversation.

"I have a friend from college named Louie. I don't know if I've told you about him. His ten year old son, Pete, was in a car accident a year ago and he's paralyzed."

"Oh, how awful! Do they think it's permanent?"

"They think it might be. But he's a pretty determined little guy. I'll tell you more about him another time when we're not rushing to work. Anyway, I want to use a company jet to take Louie, his wife Anne, and Pete to Disney World. I'm already set up with the ambulatory service. So, all I need is you."

"Jeff, me on a plane now? There's no way. The whole idea makes me shake."

"So, you just move past it. Everyone has fears but you can't let them hold you back."

"They haven't held me back. I'm happy where I am. Traveling has never appealed to me."

"Right. But you're in a relationship now and it's with someone who needs and wants to travel."

"I'm not asking you not to. I'm just saying maybe it's something you do on your own."

Jeff smiled but it wasn't one of those happy smiles. "Then our relationship isn't important to you. If it was, you'd get on an airplane."

"Jeff, maybe you just need to accept that I have that fear. I've had it since I was little. Can't we do something special here for them? In town?"

"Genie, I'm going to be traveling to New York for business pretty frequently now. I want you to be able to come with me sometimes. There's so much you're holding us back from."

"But lots of men travel for business without their wives or girlfriends. And we can take vacations more locally for now and then later when I..."

"Listen, I'm not going to argue with you."

"Jeff, I wasn't arguing. I'm just telling you..."

"It's fine, Genie. Really. Listen, I need to get to the office. I'm gonna skip breakfast today if that's ok." Jeff started to get up from the table.

"Do you have to go? Can't you stay for just some coffee?"

"I really have to go." Jeff kissed Genie on the cheek and walked into the locker room. She left the table, walked to the locker room, showered, changed and went to the office. She tried to reach Jeff all day but he never got back to her. Finally, toward the end of the day, she received a text from him.

Really busy day. Plans with my buddy tonight. Love you. Have a great night!

Genie knew exactly what that was. A candy coated M&M with bullshit that melts in your mouth. She texted him back.

Jeff, why didn't you call me all day? Are you upset with me?

No answer.

Jeff, please just talk to me. If you're upset, let's talk about it.

No answer.

She waited a couple more hours. Her stomach was in knots and she needed to untie them. She dialed his cell again. She sent another text.

You can't do this. I need to talk to you. Please stop with the punishment.

No answer. Two hours later, the pain in her gut was cutting. Genie got a text back.

Genie, there you go again, flying off the handle. I wasn't punishing you. I left my phone in the car. I'm going to bed. Goodnight.

Genie dialed Jeff's phone but he didn't pick it up. The next time she called, the phone had been turned off. When she called him the next day, it would ring once and then go immediately to voicemail. She knew he was pressing decline.

The more that Jeff wouldn't talk to her, the more obsessive and crazed she became. She knew this was all her fault. It was her issue, after all, and he could find a girl who would travel. Which fear was greater, though? Flying or losing Jeff? Genie felt like she was being accused of a crime, not knowing what the verdict would be.

How does the jury find the accused?

Feeling guilty.

Sentence?

Solitary Confinement. No phone calls allowed.

CHAPTER 36

In one of those memorable Psychology classes in college, Genie recalled seeing a movie called *Sybil*. It was the story of a woman who had multiple personalities and at the time, Genie couldn't quite grasp the concept of these vastly different women living inside one body. Until, that is, she found herself leaving messages for Jeff. Genie had not only personified four different women. She brought them all out in one day and each of those lovely ladies sent their own text to Jeff.

The first lady, Gabby Golden, wants to see the good. She hopes he will listen and hear her. Maybe he'll even confide, be open, and trust. So she sends a text.

Hi Jeff. I love you and just want us to take care of each other. Please call me back.

She hears nothing back from him that day.

The second lady, Bitchit Jones, is enraged at his lack of response. How could anyone be so bullheaded not to acknowledge the efforts that Gabby put forward? Bitchitt calls and tells him that she wants this relationship to end. She hears nothing back.

The third lady is Lotta Lovett. She can't stand the idea that these two people who love each other are fighting. The anger sits inside and feels bad. So she sends a rational text that is kind and empathetic. And when he doesn't respond, we meet Harriet Hysteria.

Harriet sobs and cries and pleads for a discussion to heal this. When there is no response, Gabby, Bitchitt, and Lolly come to Harriet's aid. As Jeff hears from the whole gang in panoramic texts, he sends Genie a text and it kind of looks like this:

Genie, you are a lunatic. One minute you love me, the next minute we're breaking up, then you love me again, and then I'm an asshole. I have done nothing at all to bring this on. I refuse to engage in this drama. Goodnight.

Gabby, Bitchitt, Lolly, and Harriet read the text from Ralph Rationalit, Peter Patronizit, Larry Lyitt, Matthew Blamit, and Lyle Lovit. Then they took every picture they had of Jeff, every gift he gave to them, and put it in a hefty bag. They took his name out of their phone and deleted all of his texts. They were clean of him for tonight.

CHAPTER 37

Lori opened the door and greeted her Friday night guest.

"Genes, you look like crap."

"Gee, thanks Lor. Nothing like a good friend to cheer you up." Genie walked into Lori's apartment, sat on the sofa, grabbed some jelly beans from a bowl on Lori's coffee table and began eating them by the handful.

"And I've never seen you eat so much junk. What's going on?"

"Why, do I look fat?"

"Well, I can't tell. But your clothes look like a one year old's bib."

Genie looked down at herself. This was all too true.

"I don't know why I'm eating so much. I think it started when that cupcake store opened on my corner. Every time I walk by it I have to stop in."

"Genie, that cupcake store opened a year ago. And you didn't have a cupcake problem before you and Jeff started dating. I've been watching you over the last month and I'm telling you..."

"What are you saying?"

"I watched this happen to my sister, ok? She was all stressed over this group of kids in high school and she started bingeing like crazy. My mom found a woman for her to talk to and I know she's still seeing people because my mom referred her best friend's daughter there a couple months ago."

"Lori, that's just ridiculous. I have no problems with any of my friends."

Lori rolled her eyes. "Genie. You're eating because your relationship with Jeff is stressful for you."

"It's stressful but that has nothing to do with my eating. I just love these cupcakes! Do you know they insert frosting in the middle? They drill it in. It's the Tunnel of Love. "

"Yeah? And your relationship is the Temple of Doom."

"Well, I know one thing. I'll lose him if I don't change."

"Genes, what you really need to change is your clothes."

Genie laughed. "Next time I'll be sure to dress fancy for my binge. Upscale for my up scale!" Genie walked toward the kitchen and opened a cabinet. "Oh wow, sour cream and onion! How do you keep this stuff around?" She reached in the bag for a handful.

"You know Gene, I hate to say this, but there's another option here."

"I know, I saw the pretzels. Lower in sodium, right?"

"No, not the pretzels."

Genie scooched on her knees down the counter to reach more cabinets. Lori watched her and spoke calmly.

"Genes, maybe you should see other people. You know there are other fish in the..."

"Goldfish! *Good call.* Have you tried the Flavor Blasted?"

"Ok, Gene, be loyal and keep on eating. When Jeff finds out his swan is a swine, you'll be flying solo."

"Jeff doesn't love me for my body." Genie opened a Pop Tart.

"Of course he doesn't. He loves you for your healthy mind!"

"My mind is just fine. All I need to do is get my body back. What's the fat grams on these?" Genie took a bite and began to read the box.

Lori was quiet, and then she spoke. "Her name is Ellen."

"Don't be ridiculous. I don't need to talk to anyone. I'm just in a munch mood today. Probably getting my period." She jumped off the counter and went back to the bag of chips.

"Well, she's really good. She specializes in eating disorders."

Genie got defensive. "Are you kidding me? I eat some chips and all of a sudden I've got a label?" Genie knocked the bag of chips off the counter and they spilled out on the floor.

Lori had humor in her tone. "I'm going to get a broom. And don't you dare eat off the floor."

"Lori, that is so sick."

Genie picked up some chips and put them into the garbage. The thoughts were racing in her head. She couldn't believe that Lori accused her of having an eating disorder. And a therapist? *She's the one who needs therapy, always accusing me of being so crazy.*

Genie heard Lori down the hall in the broom closet. She quickly opened the garbage, grabbed a handful of the chips and stuffed them into her mouth. And out loud she screamed out to Lori, "And I would never eat off the floor!"

• • •

It wasn't the chips from the garbage. It wasn't the sudden run to McDonalds on her way home from work the next day. It wasn't the plow through the cabinets, or the box of Frosted Flakes. What finally pushed Genie to make the call was that it wasn't going away. She was afraid it would never stop. She got Ellen's number from Lori and set up her first appointment.

CHAPTER 38

The sign on the glass door said, "Eating Disorders Clinic." Confidently, not belonging, an alien from Planet Normal, Genie checked in at the reception desk and was given some forms to fill out. She sat in the waiting room and counted about ten people. Among them were two young men, the rest women, varying in age and size.

Genie felt incredibly self-conscious. This wasn't like the hair salon where people looked up and smiled. Genie casually picked up a few magazines and brought them to her lap. She looked up to see a skinny woman, mid forties range, giving her a nasty look. Genie thought to herself, What the *hell* did I do to you? Then a heavier woman looked at Genie and smiled. Genie smiled back and decided to make a friend using just a pinch of eating disorder humor.

"Wouldn't you think, I mean knowing the reason we're here, that if they're gonna make us wait, they'd at least offer up some crudités?"

The friendly woman laughed. "Yeah, how about a bowl of candy!"

Genie laughed. "I guess nobody can afford to put food in this waiting room!" The woman laughed and spoke to Genie.

"Well, you don't look like you'd tap out anyone's budget!"

Genie smiled. "Thanks, but trust me. I'd make you proud." The woman laughed. Genie smiled warmly. "I'm Genie. Nice to share this embarrassing waiting room nightmare with you!"

The woman laughed and said, "I'm Leanne. Glad to meet you, too!"

The skinny woman was now looking at both Genie and the other woman. Her scowl had now doubled in nastiness and it was so noticeable that Genie and her new friend shared a glance. They couldn't help but giggle under their breath, because this woman's expression was actually priceless. Genie couldn't resist.

"Well, they'd bust the budget feeding us. But I think they could afford to feed *you*."

The woman looked at Genie with a hoity toity smile and didn't say a word. At that moment, Genie's name was called. She said goodbye to Leanne, and then turned to face the skinny woman.

"Lovely talking with you. Maybe one day we can meet for lunch! And not to worry, you can throw it up right after."

A woman came up to Genie and led her back to the office. Once they were inside, she introduced herself as Ellen. As far as Genie was concerned, this woman did not look like a therapist. She looked more like someone who would lead a hike and come back to pitch a tent. She had an attractive, athletic, outdoors look. She was too thin to trust as far as Genie was concerned. But whatever she was doing to look like that was worth the waiting room nightmare.

The office was small, but comfortable. Genie sat on a small sofa and Ellen sat at her desk, her chair turned sideways to face Genie. There were pictures of Ellen's kids on the windowsill. Genie saw a crumpled brown paper bag from The Corner Bakery. *Really?*

After taking down some information from Genie, Ellen asked her first question.

"So Genie, tell me why you're here."

Genie spoke slowly. "I think I might have an eating disorder."

"And what makes you think that?"

"I'm bingeing like crazy. I can't stop."

"Have you had this problem before?"

"I've eaten a lot before. But never like this."

Ellen was matter of fact. "Are you purging?"

"No, I just exercise it off, or try not to eat much the other days."

Ellen wrote in her notebook as she spoke. "Is something going on that's significant or that's making you unhappy?"

"No, I have a really great life."

"Were there any traumas or unusual events when you were a child?"

Genie felt somewhat of a jolt. "Well, yes. My dad was killed in a plane crash."

Ellen looked up from her notebook. "How old were you?"

"I was nine."

Ellen nodded. "Genie, it's not uncommon for people who suffered loss or abuse as a child to have food issues as adults."

"Well, I don't think that has anything to do with my eating. I haven't had problems like this before."

"I understand. But it's possible that something in your life today is triggering those old feelings. Because they're too painful, food becomes an unconscious destination to avoid them."

"I don't know. I just don't think that's it."

Ellen looked up again. "When did the bingeing start?"

"It started a few months ago. But it's gotten really bad in the past few weeks."

Ellen nodded. "And what are you hoping for by coming to see me?"

Genie laughed. "I'm hoping to stop stuffing my face. And I want to take off the extra pounds I've put on.

Ellen smiled kindly. "Is that all?"

"Well, yeah. If I could stop the bingeing, I could handle the rest."

Ellen uncrossed her legs, shifted to the other side, and crossed them again. "Well Genie, you've actually got that reversed. If you could handle the rest, you wouldn't be bingeing. But I can help you."

"Oh good. Do you have some special diet plan or something?"

"Well, the bingeing isn't a food problem."

Genie laughed. "Hah! What kind of problem could *too much food* be?"

"It's a feelings problem. There's something going on inside you and until we figure it out, the bingeing will keep on happening."

Genie was politely defensive. "I've had lots of feelings about lots of things but I never bought out Seven Eleven!"

Ellen smiled. "Well, a binge is more like a scream."

Genie looked at her oddly. "I don't understand what that means."

"Here's how I can explain it. If a child was screaming in pain and you were watching a show and ignoring her, what would the child do?"

"Scream louder."

"Right. And when would the child stop screaming?"

"When you listened and took care of her, I guess."

"Exactly. There are feelings inside of you that are screaming to be heard. You're ignoring them by watching a food show." Ellen paused. "We need to turn down the volume on food, and turn it up on the feelings. We need to listen and find out what's causing the pain and then we need to make choices to manage and minimize it. When we do that, your bingeing will ease up."

Genie thought to herself, this was clearly not the diet she had in mind. Where's the low carb one?

"How long will it take?"

"It's different for each person."

"What do I do about the bingeing right now? Is there anything to help it?"

Ellen nodded. "Structure. It's the most important tool you have to fight bingeing. Breakfast, lunch, dinner and designated snacks in between."

"Should I eat all protein? Cut out sugar and carbs?"

"Not at all. *Deprivation leads to bingeing.* Eat foods you like and crave so long as you eat them with structure."

"But how am I supposed to find the feelings? Or those screams you're talking about?"

"Write down everything you eat, the time you eat it, where you are, and who you're with. Don't try and force changes, Genie. Just start to notice your patterns. When you're comfortable, food won't be such a problem. When you're upset, or going against what you really feel, it will be."

"Huh. So food is like a radar detector?"

"Exactly! It's a built in alarm. Beep, beep, beep. And we're going to teach you to listen."

CHAPTER 39

Genie slammed down the phone. Steven jumped and looked up. Genie was on fire. "*Ass*hole!"

Steven perked up, ready for the elect Genie campaign.

"I thought you two made up. Don't tell me. He left hair on the soap. That *animal!*"

"Steven, we have so little time as it is with his traveling, he never confers with me, and he just makes plans with everyone else all the time. It's always this friend, that friend, and now it's some guy, Richie."

"*Guy Richie?* Madonna's ex-*husband?*"

"Steven, shut up. This is how he talks to me." Genie began imitating Jeff, talking in a gruff voice twelve octaves lower than her own.

She pressed her chin against her neck and made a stern face as she mocked him.

"Genie, I am who I am. I'm fiercely independent. I have many friendships that I need to foster and nurture. If that doesn't work for you, go find yourself a boyfriend who has more time. But just remember..."'

Genie lowered her voice even deeper… ***"I never get upset with you or ask you to change anything you're doing. To me, you're perfect. You're the one complaining here and I'm telling you right now, I refuse to live this way. I know I can find women who appreciate all that I bring.'"***

• • •

When Genie had finished her performance, quite ready for Steven's shared opinion that Jeff was a big mean bully, she looked up and watched him walk from his desk to the files. As she was waiting for his response, she noticed a red licorice twist was hanging from his mouth, wagging as he walked. Genie stared at him intently and spoke in an accusatory tone.

"Steven, where did you get that?"

"What?"

"The *Twizzler*."

Steven looked puzzled. He spoke slowly and carefully. "From- the- bag- on- my- desk. Why?"

"No reason." Genie kept staring at him.

Steven became aware that Genie was studying him. He looked back at her in question. He spoke slowly again. "Do- you- *want*- one?"

Genie paused scientifically. "Well, that's what I'm looking at… '*Do I want one.*'"

Steven stared at her, still speaking slowly. "You are *looking* at that. *Why?*"

Genie was almost whispering. "I'm listening for a beep."

Steven looked at Genie. He looked at the licorice. He put it to his ear. He spoke in a whisper.

"This one's not beeping. Want me to try another one?"

Genie didn't smile and matched his whisper. "Not the licorice, Steven. *Us.*"

Steven raised his eyebrows. "We beep?"

"Well, potentially. That's why I'm looking at the licorice. If I need to eat it, that's a beep. It would mean I'm not comfortable with you. Though it could mean I like licorice too—in which case I should eat it and not deprive myself. You want to hear something crazy?"

"You mean what I just heard is normal?"

"Even though I love Twizzlers, I'm not in the mood for one now so I'm not going to have it. That means you and I don't beep! Oh Steven, I love you!" Genie stood up and hugged him. "You're safe! Let me just write this down."

Genie took out her notebook. As she wrote, Steven stared at Genie, Twizzler hanging from his mouth, gnawing at it nervously until it was gone. When he sat down at his desk, he went to take another one from the bag. Genie looked at him with an intelligent concern in her expression, glasses on the bridge of her nose.

"Steven, you're beeping. You might want to take a look at that."

CHAPTER 40

Sam Carr picked up his brother Alex, to meet the wives for dinner. It was Sam's birthday and they were all celebrating together. On the way to the restaurant, Sam got an emergency call from the office. They needed him to come back and sign some papers he had overlooked on his desk.

It all would have slipped by him except for one thing. When he was looking for stamps in his wife's desk drawer two days before, he came across a bill from Surprise Enterprise. It had the party details including the restaurant, the menu, and the prices. He didn't have the heart to ruin it. And truthfully, it was much more fun piecing it all together, watching everyone lie.

He had to hand it to Surprise Enterprise. He would have suspected a restaurant, for sure. But he wouldn't second-guess a call from the office, asking him to come back in. That happened frequently and his boss wouldn't give a rat's ass about his birthday. It could be his funeral and he still wouldn't get a reprieve.

Alex had called Sam to ask if he could catch a ride with him to the restaurant. He said his wife had his car. Hah, what a lame excuse! They were now headed back to the office for the "big surprise." They probably had the conference room filled with balloons, Italian food in tin containers, and a tacky store bought cake. Not that Sam wasn't grateful, it's just so predictable!

Just as Sam was trying to decide how one fakes being surprised, and he looked in the rearview mirror to check his hair, he became aware of the fact that he couldn't see his reflection. The flashing red lights behind him made that rather difficult.

"*Oh* shit."

Alex looked at Sam. He looked behind them. "Oh *shit.* Are you speeding?"

"Maybe a little, but I never get stopped at this speed."

Sam pulled over to the side of the road. When the cop approached the car, Sam rolled down his window.

"Hello, Officer."

"What's your hurry?"

"No hurry, Officer. I didn't realize I was going so fast. What was my speed?"

"May I see your license please?"

"Sure thing." Sam reached into his pocket for his billfold. He opened it and saw that his license wasn't there. He gave a nervous laugh.

"Uh, you're not going to believe this... but I must have left it at home. Let me call my wife, I'm sure she can bring it." He reached on the console for his cell phone but that wasn't there either. He looked on the floor and asked Alex if he was sitting on it. Alex sat up and felt around the seat.

The officer's tone was curt, bordering on nasty. "Registration and insurance?"

Sam reached into the glove compartment. He rummaged through the contents and felt himself starting to sweat. "Oh man. It's not here. I honestly don't know why... I always..."

"Sir, will you please step out of the car?"

Sam looked at Alex, who couldn't believe what was happening.

He whispered as the cop stepped back to let Sam out of the car, "What's the matter with you? How could you drive without your paperwork? He could take you in!"

"My license is always in my billfold! I haven't used it for anything in at least a week. Maybe it dropped out or something."

Sam stepped out of the car. He was gone for several minutes. As Alex sat anxiously waiting, the cop came up to his window and tapped on it. Alex lowered it.

"Sir, we're going to have to take your brother in. You can't drive this car without proof of insurance so it's best if you come with us."

Alex stared at the cop for a second, turned off the ignition, opened his door, locked the car, and walked back toward the squad car. There was his brother sitting in the back seat looking like some white collared thief.

Sam spoke to the cop from the back. "Officer, we're supposed to be meeting my family. And I believe there's a surprise party waiting for me. My wife..." He looked sheepishly at Alex as he said it. "Is there any way we can do this tomorrow?"

The officer looked at him in the rearview mirror. He looked at his partner next to him—a policewoman who was far too pretty to be a cop unless she was an actress playing one.

"Hey Lani, I say we one up the surprise the wife's got goin', ya think?"

Lani laughed. "Yeah, Johnny, lock up is *quite* the surprise."

• • •

As they pulled into the station, the two cops escorted Sam and Alex inside. They told them to sit on the bench. Ten minutes later, Lani approached them and asked them to follow her. By now, Sam was more than concerned. Alex wouldn't speak to him. Sam had seen him sending text messages, probably letting everyone know that the party was going to have to be cancelled. This was so embarrassing!

Down a poorly lit corridor, passing all sorts of people who looked like they hadn't laughed since the eighties, the two brothers followed Lani up to a closed door when suddenly Johnny's radio paged him. He stood back and told the men to go inside.

Sam opened the door. The lights were off. He was about to go back out and summon Lani when suddenly, bright lights filled the room. Out of the corner of his eye he saw dozens of people. Everyone he knew. In unison, they screamed. *Surprise!* He turned to Alex who was laughing hysterically.

The coach bus was in the parking lot. They would indeed be going to dinner at the restaurant that was stated on the proposal. The one he'd found next to the stamps. The stamps that Sam's wife had asked him to grab. The wife who had followed Genie's instructions.

And who says there's never a cop when you need one?

CHAPTER 41

The after therapy glow. Genie walked into the office looking like someone who had played a round of tennis in ninety degrees, and dried off walking home. Steven looked up from his desk and smiled. Something about seeing Genie after therapy made him feel happy inside.

"Hey Genes. What's the matter? Starbucks wants their Sweet-n-low back?"

"No."

"Egg whites didn't laugh at your yolks?"

"No!"

"Too many Doritos last night?"

Genie was dull and matter of fact. "I'm trying not to eat when I feel upset."

"What? Who is giving you this awful advice?"

"My therapist, Ellen."

"Tell her to mind her own business."

"She says I have to feel my feelings."

"Bull. You don't have to feel anything. Get some Ho Hos and we'll feel the fillings instead."

"She says we all have wounds from our past that we don't think about on a conscious level. When something triggers that old feeling, it's too painful so we instantly run to food to feel better."

"Wow, Gene. She ought to win the Nobel Pizza Prize for that one!"

"Hey, tease all you want. She's not saying people don't realize that they eat for comfort. She's saying they don't realize it in the moment. And they don't know how to stop it."

"Ok, and how should they stop it? I mean according to her."

"They need to feel their feelings even if they're painful. Face and confront issues honestly. We all need to..."

"Oh, and let me guess. You get to bleed out the pain every week in your shrink's office. You'll become a total wreck, won't be able to work, she takes all of our hard earned money, money that *I* have to make because *you* are too screwed up to work. And you know where she probably spends that money? Buying food to make *herself* feel better. She's probably on the phone right now, ordering Chinese."

"She told me today I don't have Object Permanence."

"That's because your dermatologist removed it."

"Not that thing! It's the thing where if something isn't right in front of you, you think it's gone forever—like a toy in front of a baby. If you cover the toy with a blanket, the baby won't know it's still there. But at about eight months old, the baby begins to understand that the toy is there, even though she can't see it."

"Oh, and you ditched class that day, huh? Breast milk hangover?"

Genie laughed. "Well, it's one of the reasons why I have such a hard time when Jeff walks out after a fight or when he leaves town. I think he's not coming back. My dad's death and all."

"So, if all this is true why is it just happening now? Why not before?"

"Well, I'm not sure. I mean I guess I have binged before, I just didn't think it was anything more than loving food and then having to diet it off. She thinks Jeff hits deeper places in me and that's why it's so out of hand. You know, more than in the past."

"What other syndromes do you suffer from? Just so I know."

"I have Separation Anxiety."

"Oh God. Is it contagious?"

Genie rolled her eyes.

"So if you're not allowed to binge, is she giving you some anti-anxiety medication or something?"

"No, I told you. I have to feel my feelings! That's how I'll get stronger. It'll grow me up and make me feel safe inside."

"Genie, there is no such thing as safe. We're all at risk for something. So you just live life as joyfully and responsibly as you can. The more you worry about duckies under blankies the less work we'll get done, and that's making me feel very unsafe."

"Easy for you to say, Steven. You don't have the issues I have. I can't help it that I'm this way. You think I asked for it? You don't think I want to be normal? I missed out on something that *you* had, which was a nurturing mother."

"Oh, you mean the one who disowned me when I came out?"

"Well, she was nurturing before that!"

"I know, Gene. Your pain is worse because you don't have..."

"Steven, you know what I don't have? Brake pads! Most people don't feel what I feel because they have thicker padding."

"Oh, you ditched the day they handed out the pads too, huh? Ok, Genie. Let's have a make-up class. Object Permanence 101."

Steven walked over and grabbed a dishtowel from the kitchenette. He walked back to Genie's desk. He placed it over some files on her desk.

"Ok, Genes. What's under the blankie?"

"My files."

"Which ones?"

"Um, the Handmans and the Millers."

"Good girl. You're cured. Now can we get some work done?"

CHAPTER 42

Genie and Lori were looking through the sale rack of their favorite boutique.

"So Gene, how's the therapy going? I know we walked by a garbage can and you refrained. Things are looking up, huh?"

"I actually think I'm just too much for one man. Maybe I should buy a baseball team and spread my feelings out over all of them..."

Lori laughed. "Yeah. 'Next battered up!'"

"The other day, I got so hurt but I couldn't help it. Jeff kept commenting about how beautiful these women were that he works with."

"Gene, the only time men do that is when they're insecure and want to make a woman jealous. He *wants* you to worry."

"I don't think so. He's not a game player."

Lori laughed. "Oh no? How about the game, 'Telephone'? We can choose not to answer it, hang it up, or read texts and not answer them. How about the game, 'Spin the Bottle?' He makes you bottle up your feelings, hits your insecurities, and then he watches you *spin*."

"Lor, I don't think he realizes he's being insensitive."

"If that's the case, he can still apologize. Wouldn't you?"

"The more I get to know him, the more I see he lives to certain principles of behavior and he demands it from the people around him. He just believes you don't make decisions that are based on fear, and you don't sweat the small stuff. He challenges me to be better and stronger."

"Oh, please. He's the one who sweats the small stuff, Genie. You don't ask him to buy you things. You jump at every opportunity to take care of him. You entertain his friends, run errands for him; you do everything a wife does, ok? Your only fault is that you get hurt when he's hurtful, and he gets mad and walks out on that. So, you tell me, in the grand scheme of what you two have and what you've given him, who's sweating the small stuff?"

"Well, he says I act out. I get cold or mad and it's wrong."

"Oh, you mean you have a FLAW? So what are you supposed to do when you get hurt? Bake cookies?"

"He just says the same thing every time we argue: 'It shouldn't have happened.'"

Lori laughed. "Tell him the hurtful comment *shouldn't* have happened!"

"He says a relationship should be the place you go to get away from stress."

"Then he should have a relationship with a fucking spa."

"Lor, I see both ways of thinking."

"Ok, Gene. Let's say he's right. Your relationship should be that beautiful oasis where you treat each other like a vacation. It sounds to me like it's his vacation."

"I'm not easy going, Lor. So many people are. This is my issue and we both know it."

"Genie, there's a thing called forgiveness. And empathy. You have it for him; he doesn't have it for you. Look how you argue his side. Does he ever argue yours?"

"He doesn't say I'm wrong, just wrong for him. I know there are girls who could do a better job of this. So I better toughen up."

CHAPTER 43

When Cavemen drew pictures on walls, some scientists believe it was because there was no written language and this was the way they communicated the stories of their hunts and days. Genie was relatively certain, however, that it was because they were shutting their women out of their lives, talking to the walls instead.

• • •

This would be their sixth session together. Genie had just finished telling Ellen about the argument with Jeff and how he handled it afterwards.

"Genie, when you were little, what happened when you got angry?"

"I was punished."

"How?"

"Sent to my room."

"Do you remember how it felt?"

Genie pictured herself on her bed, watching her mom leave the room. She could feel the ache in her stomach of not being able to say what she felt in fear of being punished for longer. Suddenly, she felt horrible anger.

"I was so *angry.*"

"Why?"

"Because I wasn't ever allowed to complain. I had to walk through my house being perfect because my mom could blow and go away anytime."

"What do you mean blow and go away?"

"If Aunt Dotty said anything negative at all, or made any small suggestion, my mom would get horribly defensive. Then she'd disappear in her room for days. If I was in a play at school, I was afraid to ask her to come. I was afraid to have friends come over. I never knew what would make her feel pressured."

"And when she was feeling pressured, how did that play out? Did she scream at you?"

"No. I would have welcomed that! She just went away. She wouldn't talk to anyone."

"So who did you go to for your daily needs?"

"My aunt. Or nobody. Then when Gregg came around, that was when she changed. But that made me angrier."

"Tell me why."

Genie felt her throat close. She couldn't believe that talking about this brought up such emotion. "Because I wasn't enough to make her happy. It took Gregg to bring her back to life. Her own daughter couldn't do it."

"So how do you think you interpreted that?"

Genie felt her eyes well up. Her nose began to run. Ellen handed her a box of tissues and Genie put it on her lap.

"That I didn't mean all that much to her. That spending time with me wasn't important. All the moms took their kids on outings. I barely got a trip to buy gym shoes. I did everything with my aunt or on my own."

Ellen nodded. "So you were hurting. And when you wanted to express that you were punished. You lost even more of her, right?"

Genie couldn't answer. The tears turned into sobs.

"Genie. I know it hurts to talk about this. But it's the kind of purging that's healthy. If you can, tell me more."

Genie blew her nose and wiped her eyes. "Ok. Nothing I felt was ever acknowledged. Whether it was being homesick and not being allowed to come home, or not wanting my aunt to take me someplace, you know, wanting to be with my mom instead. Even after the accident. I don't ever remember anyone asking me how I felt or if I was okay."

Ellen nodded gently. "And what did that feel like?"

Genie began to feel woozy. Her eyelids felt heavy and her stomach started churning.

"It felt like," tears began to well up again, "it felt like I wasn't taken care of. Like I wasn't important to anyone."

"Did you feel loved?"

Genie shook her head. "No. I really didn't. I just felt alone."

Ellen looked softly at Genie.

"Genie, your relationship with Jeff carries a very similar dynamic to the one of your childhood. Not being allowed to express a feeling without being punished. Having that person you want more of, leave you behind with your feelings. Can you see that?"

Genie nodded as the tears kept coming.

"And when Jeff shuts you out for having feelings, it's going to bring all of that back up to the surface. It's been sitting there a long, long time."

Genie nodded and blew her nose. She let the tears continue and it felt good to get them out. As she began putting thoughts together in her head, the tears began to subside.

"Ellen, how does someone with my history have a relationship with someone who can't tolerate negative feelings?"

"She makes a choice," Ellen said. "She either finds a man who doesn't feed into those issues with such extreme independence, so little time to spend with her, and who doesn't take off in bad moments… or she commits to this relationship and works very hard. But I want you to think about something."

"What?"

"You bring out bad things in each other. Jeff *would* be better off with someone who doesn't mind his extreme independence. There are women who would see it as a positive. And you *would* be better off with someone who shares decisions with you and appreciates how expressive and communicative you are. A man who sees it as part of your honesty and warmth."

"But he keeps telling me that no two people have what we have. He won't give up on us and he'll hate me forever if I ruin it."

Ellen smiled and shook her head. "Genie, Jeff's told you how he wants to live. It leaves no room for the way you want to live. I have no doubt that this man is madly in love with you. But I'm not convinced, though he'd never admit it, that some of this distance comes from feeling threatened by you. He's got a lot of deeper issues that you've tapped into and it's actually too painful for him to see them. It's much easier to blame you, especially since you're the one willing to go there."

"You're saying he'll never go there?"

"From what I hear, no. I don't think he's capable of it. Genie, Jeff suffered a lot of trauma as a child. He was mentally and physically abused. A negative feeling of any kind will be intolerable for him. He wants to live in a happy place, away from the feelings of his past. Because he's so in love with you, if he perceives you as being unhappy with him, he'll shut down and go away. It's just too painful for him."

"I understand that. I guess I just don't see why he gets so mean."

"Well, that's pretty common. Part of him is that little boy who you have empathy for. Part of him takes on the role of the abusive parent. He's probably, in moments, very much like his mother but he's not going to want to see himself that way. If you accuse him of that he'll rebel. He'll strongly resent you for the mere suggestion."

Genie nodded. "And because my past didn't allow me to express myself, I'll resent him for not allowing it today. We need opposite things to be comfortable and happy."

"That's right. At least with each other."

These were not words Genie wanted to hear. The notion that they would be better off with other people was not a place she could go. Her eyes welled up with tears again, and she almost felt like begging Ellen to find a way past that opinion.

Genie's voice was shaking. She spoke quietly and carefully.

"But I love Jeff. And I know he's right about so much of what he says. I mean separate from his issues."

Ellen was quiet and soft in her tone. "Jeff can't work with who you are, Genie. I think he's been clear about that. You need to be with someone who sees your flaws with endearment and humor, not rage."

"I don't want to give up unless I know I've done all the work I can to get past my own stuff. If we're not right at that point, I'll be able to walk away."

Ellen looked at Genie for a moment. Their eyes met and held the glance. With a supportive demeanor, as though she were sending her off on an expedition, she packed her bag with tactics. “Okay, Genie. Therapeutically, I’m not sure I would support you being in this relationship. But, I also see it as a wonderful opportunity for you to challenge your issues and grow stronger. You’re going to need to work exceptionally hard. Is that what you want to do?”

Genie’s eyes lit up like a child who was told she could keep the stray puppy she found.

Ellen smiled. “Ok. The next time you get a hurt feeling, your job is to fight those feelings with questions. ‘Did he really mean to hurt me? Is this something that would seem really unimportant in a week?’ And you’re not going to say a word until you’ve had some time to bat it around in your head.”

Genie pictured the moment. She had learned to see her own patterns. “If I’m hurt and can’t bring it to him, I’ll end up stuffing my face.”

Ellen nodded. “Genie, that’s a self-esteem issue. If we can get you to feel ‘full’ in your life, secure in your ability to take care of yourself, and not so needy of Jeff’s affections, you’re going to be able to feel a feeling without diving into that hole. Instead, we’re going to get you to *see* the hole, but walk around it.”

“That’s impossible. I am a hole diver.”

Ellen laughed. She sat up tall and slapped her hands to her knees like a coach explaining a play. “Ok, Genie. Here’s the plan. You’re going to structure your food in meals and snacks, just like we talked about. Give yourself what you need in terms of cravings, but you don’t get to have all you want. There are limits regarding your health. Right?”

“Right. So how much? What kinds of foods?”

"All kinds of foods. Be health conscious and keep portions reasonable. Have a treat every day if that's what you crave but commit yourself to structure."

"Ok, so that works on a normal day, but what about a bad one?"

"Have a mantra in your head: *Food only adds weight gain to the feeling which already feels like crap.*"

Genie nodded and added, *"And bringing it to Jeff only starts a fight, which makes me feel like triple crap?"*

Ellen nodded. "Now, if you really need to eat, *eat.* I don't want you to get hysterical or panic when you feel yourself reaching for food in those moments. Although it doesn't seem like it, allowing the food will take down the quantity."

"Ok, so what you're saying is that when I feel like I'm going to binge, I should just allow it?"

"*Negotiate it.* Allow food, but try to remain calm so you can harness the binge."

Genie was eager to learn. "And how do I hide the feelings from Jeff?"

Ellen smiled. "By becoming a brilliant actress. If you have to leave a room, leave a room. But under no circumstances are you to bring those feelings to Jeff. Journal them and we'll discuss them here. Call a friend; that's what they're for. If we can get you to the point where you're not reacting in the moment, we'll be able to decide if the feeling is one to bring to him, or one to deal with on your own."

Genie nodded.

"And don't forget, Genie. Anything you say, can and will be used against you. He will misinterpret and spin just about anything if it's in a negative tone or about him. He'll get bullish and irrational. The way to get what you want is in a positive way, ok?"

Genie felt pain in her stomach. "Ellen, I don't think I can live that way. It doesn't sound real or honest."

"You don't have to live that way."

"But I can't give him up either." Genie stared at Ellen. "My stomach is in knots."

"Genie, you two are in love with each other. You each have a lot of pain from your pasts. What I want you to visualize is a fifty story high-rise building. The view from the top is amazing but it's a long way down to the basement. We want you to live somewhere in the middle without those damaging drops."

"So I need a relationship on the twenty-fifth floor?"

Ellen smiled and nodded. Genie seemed to speak from a haze. "It's so strange. I feel so afraid. I can't even tell you what it's about."

"Well, there's a little girl inside that is absolutely terrified. But the adult in you is going to take her hand and let her know that you'll be listening to her feelings and making decisions in her interest. Jeff isn't the one to take care of her. *You are.*"

Genie looked at Ellen. She looked at the picture of Ellen's kids, lined up on the desk.

"Ellen, I bet you're the greatest mom."

Ellen smiled. "And one day you will be too."

Genie looked at Ellen. The tears ran down her face.

"You think I'll really be that lucky? To have all this in the past and have kids?"

"Genie, if you can beat this now, and become healthy in your own life, you will end up in a relationship that brings out all of your wonderful traits. Whether it's with Jeff or someone else. And you'll be an amazing mother. Always remember. Possibility begins with a choice."

CHAPTER 44

"Steven, I have another assignment from my therapy."

Steven was looking at a file. "What Mission Impossible is it this time?"

"I can't bring any of my hurt feelings to Jeff. I have to take them someplace else."

Steven looked up at her with an intense and suspicious look. "Oh no, Genie."

"Steven, come on. That's what friends are for! *Ellen said.*"

"No way. I don't want your feelings! They'll crowd the office, clog the vents, and we might lose our Internet connection. Look in the Yellow Pages and see if there's a feelings depository for the needy."

Genie pouted in fun and then she remembered. "Oh Steven, I forgot to tell you. Your mom called. She's coming in town for some sort of opening and she wants to have dinner with you."

Steven stood in shock. Genie looked at him.

"Don't you want to see her?"

"Hell, no."

"She's your mother, Steven."

"She gave birth to me."

"I think they define that as mother."

"I define it as birther."

"Well, your birther wants to have dinner. You better call her back."

"*Bertha.* That is the perfect name for her. I shall call Bertha when I'm good and ready."

• • •

Later that evening, after dinner, Casey was in the Happy Room, beading a bracelet for Genie.

"My grandma's putting me on diet food and no treats allowed. I think she thinks I'm fat."

Genie was disgusted. "You are not fat. And hey, I've had some problems with food lately too. I think most people do."

"*You* do? But you're not fat." Casey reached in her box, looking for more blue beads.

"Lots of people have problems with food and many of them are not overweight."

"What kind of problems?"

"Well, I didn't realize it before, but sometimes I eat when I'm upset. So I'm learning that instead of eating, I need to feel my feelings."

"What kinds of feelings?"

Genie found a blue bead and handed it to Casey. "Sad ones. Hurt ones. Angry ones. Bored ones. Yellow ones. Pink ones."

Casey laughed. "Mine are striped."

Genie looked at Casey. "You know, Case, as you get older, you're going to see all sorts of people doing all sorts of unhealthy things with food. Some will eat too much. Some will not eat enough. We want you right in the middle."

"Like Goldilocks in Baby Bear's bed. Not too small, not too big?"

"Yep! We want you to be juuuuusst right!"

"Genie, I heard about a kid at school who throws up every time she eats."

"Oh my Gosh, already?"

Casey looked up from her painting. "People do that a lot?"

"Yep. Some people do. But you can throw up feelings instead."

"Gross!"

Genie laughed. "It's called talking."

"Talking is throwing up?"

"Yeah, in a way. I mean, we throw up because there's something inside of us that's making us feel sick, right? And when it comes out, don't we feel better? Well, sometimes feelings can make us feel kind of sick too. If we talk, we get some of that sickness out of our insides and we end up feeling better."

Casey looked back down at her mug. "Talking doesn't make my mom come back."

Genie stared at Casey for a moment. "No, Honey it doesn't. But even if the thing can't change, it still feels better to share."

"Does everybody need to talk?"

"No. Some people feel better not talking. So you have to be careful who you bring your feelings to. I'm kind of learning that too. But most girls, I find, do need to talk. Especially girls like the one you know who throws up. She needs a friend."

"Maybe I should see if she wants to come over one day. Try and be friends with her."

"That would be great! And you can always talk to me."

Casey was quiet. She dipped her brush in the water and started with another blue tone.

"Well, I get really sad when I'm at my friend's houses and they have moms and I don't."

Genie felt a dull ache. "I know that feeling, Case."

"'Cause of your dad?"

"Yes. And when my mom would go in her room and leave me by myself, I remember going in the kitchen and eating. Do you think you ever do that?"

Casey thought about it. "I eat when I come home from school."

"Well, that's normal. You're probably hungry for a snack. So you should eat. That's the other thing I'm learning. I have to eat when I'm hungry."

"But Genie, I eat more than a snack. That's why my grandma's getting mad at me."

"Well, let's have a treasure hunt for feelings, ok? And we'll use the food as a clue. So Case, when you come home from school, what do you think the feeling is?"

Casey whined. "Bored."

"Good girl! That's one feeling. So we'll work on finding things that interest you. What else? Anything going on at school that's stressful?"

"Well, the kids tease me. They call me Spacey Casey. Some of them call me 'Case of the Runs' or 'Case of Dough.'"

Genie felt so sick for her little friend. She wanted to punch out every one of those brats.

"Honey, we need to deal with these kids."

"How do we do that? They won't stop."

"Ok, Miss Casey. We're going to finish up painting. We're going to talk to Grandma first, and later we'll figure out what to do with those nasty, mean girls."

CHAPTER 45

Genie and Lori were in their sweats in the Happy Room, reading the Sunday paper.

"Lor, I'm reading about Barack and Michelle Obama."

"What about them?"

"The strain of a presidency on a marriage. Can you even imagine what it's like for her? I mean, like part of me is so jealous. But wouldn't it be the *worst?*"

"Are you kidding, Gene? It'd be fantastic! Look at the life she has! The possibilities, the power, the influence. She's going to make such a difference!"

"Oh Lor, I'd make a horrible First Lady. I can just see it now. I'd be so mad at my husband for putting THE WHOLE COUNTRY before me!"

Lori laughed. "Yeah, Genes. You'd be like, 'What do you MEAN you're too busy to talk. What could be more important to our country than *my* feelings!'"

"And just think. When I got lonely, I'd be eating out of the Presidential *Cabinet!*"

"Ooooh. The ultimate "Peace *Treaty!* But how do you binge with the staffers around?"

Genie pointed her finger up in the air. "You have a stuffing staffing. And you make them sign confidentiality agreements that they can't binge and..."

"Purge the information!"

The girls laughed until Lori got more serious and spoke in a protective tone.

"You know, Genie, Jeff is so in love with you. I saw the way he looked at you when we were all at your place."

Genie took a double take. "Yeah? He was looking at me?"

"He's *spellbound.*"

Genie laughed.

"No, really. I was thinking about how hard he is on you but, at the same time, he sets you up. I think he needs you insecure so that he can feel in control. If you get too healthy or confident, your relationship with him will suffer."

"How can you say that? It's all he would want for us."

"That's what he says. But I think he knows he could lose you. And I think he's more afraid of that than you are."

"I think you've been watching too much Dr. Phil."

"No, my extensive knowledge of the damaged male psyche comes directly from my studies performed on that guy, Barry, I dated in Miami. I became an expert on confident men who are scared little boys inside."

Genie shook her head. "Well, thanks for the free analysis, but Jeff is not Barry. *Nobody* understood what you saw in him. We couldn't even talk to you back then. I wasn't sure if we'd be friends again."

"I know. It's embarrassing. But man, I was so *into* to him. He was totally fun and sexy. He was always telling me how beautiful and great I was. He was with me every day and he would brag to everyone about me. He made me feel like I was Heidi Klum. The sex was *awesome*. I felt really lucky."

Genie shook her head. "Yeah, he did a real number on you. Man, did he turn out to be a scumbag, all the lying, my Gosh! I remember he kept coming back to you and you'd still go back to him. How did you finally let go?"

"Well for one thing, I read the break up books. They said the only way to really get over someone is zero contact. And Gene, he went to other women so fast his dick left skid marks."

Genie laughed. "Lor, what a beautiful image. *Really.*"

"Well, all I know is that when I got healthy and became aware of his 'other side', that's when things got worse. And eventually they got creepy."

"What do you mean by creepy?"

"Ok, so he was a businessman, right? He had a million friends and he gave to charities… I mean he was an upstanding guy."

Genie shook her head. "There were a lot of people who didn't like him, Lor."

Lori was defensive. "You think I didn't know that? But nobody would have thought he was capable of what he did."

Genie's curiosity was piqued. "What did he do?"

Lori paused before she spoke.

"Before we broke up, unbeknownst to me, he had downloaded spyware on my phone and on my computer. That meant that after we broke up, he was listening to my phone calls, reading my texts, going through my emails, had my contact list, had access to basically everything on my computer, and he even had a GPS on me."

Genie was stunned. "What are you talking about?"

"Oh Genie, it was a nightmare. I had to go to AT&T five times. I was on a first name basis with at least ten Apple Care guys. I even dated one of them."

"Holy shit, Lor! So how did you figure it out?"

"I didn't. His old girlfriend called me and told me he did it to her. She was worried for my privacy. Every single thing that had happened to her had happened to me."

"Did you prove it?"

"That was the worst part. I hired a computer guy but a lot of spyware isn't traceable, neither is spoofing. And he did that too."

"Spoofing?"

"When someone sends something that looks like it came from someone else. I could send you an email from Hannah's exact email address so it looks like it's coming from her. I can also text you so it looks like it's coming from her exact phone number. It would appear as an addition to the text screen you guys already have going!"

"Are you *kidding?*" Did you confront him? Report him?"

"Both. You know what he said? That he's a computer idiot and it couldn't be him. Then he turned it on me and accused me of trying to make him look bad. Like he has no idea what I'm talking about or why his old girlfriend would make up such lies."

"Oy."

"Oy is right."

Lori looked at Genie directly. "I know you're not going to like hearing this, but Jeff shows some signs of being a Barry. I mean, I'm just saying."

Genie's tone was defensive. "Lori, that's not true. Jeff is difficult. But I see that a lot of it is stuff I bring on."

"That's because you're in it. If you were outside looking in, you wouldn't want this for yourself."

"Well, I'd want the good parts and I'd hope the bad parts would get better. They have already."

"Maybe, Gene. I hope so."

"You know, Lor, when I was a kid, during the unhappy times, I'd lay awake in bed and write scripts in my head. I would kind of design who I wanted to be. I felt so mousy and lonely, and all I wanted was to grow up and fall in love. I did this every single night and you know, even with all the bad stuff... Jeff is everything I dreamed of."

Lori looked at Genie, raised her eyebrows and smiled a bit sarcastically. "Your own little fairy tale? How nauseating."

Genie laughed. "No! It wasn't like that. There would be problems and things to conquer. My creations were imperfect, but all with happy endings."

"That's really pathetic, Gene."

"Well, it's better than falling for assholes."

"Which you've clearly done!"

Genie smiled and surrendered. "Why do we like the assholes?"

Lori shook her head. "I have no clue. I guess they're fun and enticing. They have a way of making you high."

Genie laughed. "So does cocaine. Maybe women need to learn the virtues of homeopathic relationships."

"Now you're talking, Genes! Why don't you write the manual on that? Do something useful for once in your life. You majored in journalism!"

Genie laughed. "But I'm a binger. I'd hate to end up eating my words!"

Lori laughed. Then she looked at Genie with a calm and confident smile.

"Just write the truth, Honey. Those are words you never have to eat."

Genie smiled. "My grandfather used to say, 'When you tell the truth, you don't have to have a good memory.'"

"So do it! Write a novel!"

"Maybe one day. Right now I've got to go meet Jeff for lunch. And the title of this book would be, 'Three Men and a Baby *Reversed!*'"

CHAPTER 46

The triplets were in their bouncy seats on top of the kitchen table. Jeff was holding one bottle up to one, and a second one up to the other. Genie was in the nursery, changing the third one's diaper. Jeff called out to her.

"How do Sue and David get through one day with these things? We've been here an hour and I'm exhausted! I think my wrists are detaching!"

Genie laughed. When she finished changing Nikki's diaper, she picked her up and carried her back to the kitchen.

"Bear, I so appreciate you doing this with me. It means so much to Sue. They would've missed her parents' entire surprise party. I owe you big time."

"No problem, Gino. I think it's nice that you offered to help them. But I see why their baby-sitter cancelled!"

Genie laughed. "I know!" Genie looked at the babies sucking from the bottles. The milk making bubbles around their mouths, and the wide-eyed, curious expressions in their eyes. She smiled with total adoration. "These guys are work but man, they are *really* cute."

Jeff began making silly faces at the babies. He buried his nose in their tummies, tickling them and smiling bigger. They cooed and giggled, and she found Jeff so adorable she enjoyed his show more than they did.

Later that night, when they got back to Jeff's house, they got into bed. Jeff turned on old comedy reruns and they cuddled. They talked about the babies during commercials, laughed together at the show, and when they couldn't keep their eyes open, they turned off the TV and the lights. Jeff nuzzled his face in Genie's neck. He kissed her all over her face and then he rested his head on her chest.

"Jeff?"

"What, Honey?"

"Tonight felt like a flash forward, you know? Did you almost feel like those babies were ours?"

Jeff smiled. "I did. And it felt great. You'd be an incredible mother. I would love to have a baby with you. I know we're almost there, Honey. We're doing so much better."

"I know. We've been getting along pretty damn well lately, huh?"

"Yep. I think we're past the worst of it. I told you before. I want this relationship to work and I'll stretch myself, ok? I put up with more from you than I would anyone else. That should tell you a lot."

Genie kissed Jeff on the cheek and held on to him. "Oh come on, I'm not that bad! And I don't want to be with anyone but you, not ever. You'd be the best dad in the world. You got such pleasure from them. You didn't even begrudge it."

"Are you kidding? They were awesome. I'd go back again, and I mean it. Let Sue know, we can help them out anytime."

* * *

The next morning, they both went to work. Genie was full of love, full of Jeff's encouragement, knowing they had come so far. She called him up at the office to see about getting together that night. Jeff said he had already made plans. He informed her that he was pretty booked up this upcoming week, but she was welcome to join him some of the nights. Somehow, though, Genie thought she didn't always want to be the third one invited. And did it always have to be *his* friends?

That night, she came home and made herself a salad. She went online, answered some emails, and thought about their time with the babies. She flash-forwarded to what life might look like if they were together in the future. She imagined herself home with the kids. Would Jeff be home with her? Would he discuss plans and schedules with her? Or did being Jeff's wife just mean she'd earn the title of being welcome to join.

Genie sat in front of the TV. She couldn't concentrate on the program. The more she thought about a future with Jeff, the more thoughts that ran around in her head, the more focused she was on the kitchen, and what she felt like eating. Genie could feel the binge about to happen. The switch was flicked, the binge was in pre-launch, and there was nothing she could do to escape it.

CHAPTER 47

"Ellen, this therapy isn't working. I'm getting worse. I'm seriously considering quitting. No offense, but it's a lot of money and nothing is changing."

"Ok. Well, first of all, the decision to quit therapy isn't anything I'm going to argue you out of. But remember what we said at the beginning? When you open the door to feelings, you don't always like what you see."

"That's what I mean! If I hadn't opened them I'd be so much better off! Seeing them makes me eat more!"

"Well, if you hadn't come in you would still have the food problems without any awareness of the feelings behind them. You've made the connection between the feelings and the episodes of eating. That's huge!"

"But I'm still eating!"

"Well, it takes time. In some form, you've been emotionally eating for years. It's not going to end in a month. It's like you're cleaning house, Genie. You're getting rid of old stuff and replacing it with new behaviors. It's not a one-day project. But you're doing a great job."

"How am I doing a great job? I'm falling apart."

"Well, you're falling apart in moments. You're also functioning beautifully at work. You're maintaining a relationship that happens to hit every sore spot you own. And you're working through feelings and choices."

Genie shrugged. "Yeah, but I'm so tired of the bingeing."

"Genie, most people who have food issues are, certainly in moments, living a false self. They're in uncomfortable situations or relationships. What we want is to get you operating from your true self."

"What does that mean?"

"Your true self is who you are and what you feel. When you're living true, you'll feel healthy and whole. It doesn't mean you won't have pain and discomfort or that relationships won't be difficult at times. Those are all part of living true. But when someone is living from a false self, they are either operating in avoidance or living a lie. Their choices can become obsessive. Their behavior can get reactive and destructive, even if they can't see it."

"Do you think I'm living from a false self?"

"Let's try looking at it this way. Who are you with when your eating gets out of control? Let's go through the people in your life. Starting with your mom."

"Oh Man, the second I walk in her house I head for the food."

"Well, we know there are a lot of feelings going on inside you."

"Great. Now what?"

Ellen smiled. "You address them."

"I did."

"You did *here*."

"Oh shit. You mean tell *her?*"

"What do you think about that idea?"

"It's terrifying."

"Why?"

Genie laughed. "I'll get sent to my room."

Ellen didn't laugh. "Meaning what?"

"Meaning I'll lose her. She'll back off. She won't talk to me."

"If she doesn't talk to you does that mean you've really lost her?"

Genie smiled. "No."

"What does it mean?"

"She's upset."

"Right. And that's ok. She can get upset and you can still have a relationship. She's never actually left you, Genie."

Genie smiled as her eyes watered. "So you're suggesting I tell her what's inside me?"

"I'm suggesting you make that decision but don't base it on the fear that she'll punish you or leave. That's a child's view. Base it on who you are and how you need to handle these feelings that have built up inside you." Ellen paused. "What about your brother?"

"Luke? I never overeat around him."

"Gregg?"

"No. As a matter of fact, if Gregg is around I eat normally even if my mom is there. It's being alone with her that gets hard."

"Your girlfriends? Steven? Danny?"

"Lori and I eat for sport but I don't binge. With Steven and at work, it's never a problem. Danny..."

"You notice yourself eating more when you're with Danny?"

"Historically, no. But I just realized that lately I will hang up the phone with him and grab the cereal box."

"What about when you're with him?"

"No. I eat comfortably around him. I love going out to lunch with him. We split stuff and..."

"Can you recall what's going on in these phone conversations lately?"

Genie thought back to the last talk. She laughed and nodded. "We were talking about his girlfriend. And Jeff I guess."

"Interesting. How do you feel about Danny having a girlfriend?"

"I don't like it."

"Why?"

"I start to feel replaced. I feel like Kay is taking over my favorite girl spot."

"And as a little girl, do you remember having that feeling in your life?"

Genie thought about the feeling. Her response was immediate.

"Yes. I felt it when Luke was born. My time got split. And I felt like he was favored."

"So is that your fear with Danny? That Kay will be favored?"

Genie smiled ironically at the connection. She nodded. "That's part of it."

"What else?"

"I feel jealous. And it makes me wonder if I'm losing someone I'm supposed to be with."

"Do you have romantic feelings for Danny?"

"No. But I love him. And he's the kind of person I'd do well with. He's so different than Jeff. Danny's really good for me and I know it. Sometimes I think something must be wrong with me that I don't feel more; that I would invest so much with Jeff who is clearly not good for me, but I'm in love with *him.*"

Ellen looked at Genie. She didn't say anything. Genie spoke again.

"Do you think that's what the food is telling me? That I'm making a mistake?"

"I think it's telling you that you have confusion and doubt. Jeff offers the feelings you want to have, and Danny offers the type of relationship that works for you."

"Right. That's exactly what it feels like."

"Genie, I want to get back to the concept of true self versus false self. Let's look at your relationship with Jeff."

"I know what I feel for him is true."

"Genie, I believe what you both feel is true. What I don't know is if you're able to be who you are with him or be the kind of couple you want to be. And if you can't, you *wouldn't* be living true. And that would cause you to overreact emotionally and with food."

Genie looked at Ellen with the eyes of a frightened doe. "So what am I supposed to do?"

"Ok, here's what I suggest we set as a goal. We grow you up inside. We talk through these issues from your past and how they show up in your relationships. And when you're operating out of a healthier place, we're going to meet a woman with a decision."

"What kind of decision?"

"Either she's so secure and comfortable with who she is that she won't get hurt by these things that come up with Jeff. Or, she'll see that this relationship isn't the right one and that's why she's been so reactive."

Genie looked at Ellen as though they were about to climb Mount Everest.

"I better get my hiking boots on, huh? Sounds like a tough climb."

Ellen smiled and nodded. "Tough but *extremely* rewarding. And don't worry. We'll take it one step at a time."

CHAPTER 48

Casey was very quiet as she walked down the street with Genie. The sounds of the playground went from faint to loud the closer they got to the school.

Genie looked down at Casey, knowing what she felt inside.

"You know the plan, right?" Casey nodded.

"You're going to be fine, Case. You can do this."

"I'm scared, Genie."

"I'm going to wait right here. And by the way, it's ok to be scared. You're still going to go through with it. You remember why?"

"I remember. Casey standing up for Casey."

Genie gave her a thumbs-up. Casey took a deep breath. Genie watched through the fence as Casey walked over to a group of kids in the playground and walked up to three girls huddled in conversation. When they saw Casey, they all wore mocking faces.

"Oh, it's Pillsbury Dough Girl!"

Casey's face stiffened. She gritted her teeth. She looked down to the ground.

"What's the matter, Casey? Forget your lunch?"

Casey looked up. "No, Taylor, I didn't forget my lunch. Did you forget that people have feelings?"

Taylor looked surprised. She looked at the other girls. She made a fake expression as though she was about to cry.

"Awwww. Boo hoo! Did I hurt your wittle feelings? I'm *sawry.*"

The other girls laughed, but Casey was stoic. "You used to hurt my feelings. You can't hurt them anymore. So you might as well stop trying."

"Aww, do I *have* to? It's my favorite part of recess!"

For the first time since the beginning of school, Casey didn't feel hurt. She just thought the girls looked stupid.

"Taylor, I don't know why you feel like you have to make people feel bad. You may be pretty but being mean makes you ugly to me. And ugly is way worse than fat." Casey looked over the girls who, at this point, were without words. She smiled confidently. "See you guys later."

The girls kept their silence as Casey walked away. They began to talk as Casey got further, but Casey didn't care. She looked over to Genie, standing outside the fence. She stood still for a moment. Genie didn't know how to interpret what she saw because of the distance between them.

Suddenly, Casey sent her a thumbs-up. Genie felt a shiver of relief and euphoria. She cheered and held up both hands to send the thumbs-up back. In that moment, Genie knew what it must feel like to be a mother; to experience the thrill of another person's happiness and the pride in their success. She watched Casey walk toward the building and didn't take her eyes off of her until she disappeared inside.

CHAPTER 49

Genie walked down the corridor. She looked at the numbers on the doors. It was hard to believe that her baby brother had an apartment of his own. She almost wished she would open the door to find him in feetie pajamas, sucking his thumb, standing in his...

"Welcome to my new crib!" Luke's apartment was in typical first week order. Boxes everywhere, no food, not a picture on the wall, but the stereo, flat screen, iPod and computer were wired, hooked up, and running.

"Oh Lukey, it's great!" Genie looked around. After the tour, they sat down to eat Chinese on the floor, while they dove into their old sibling rituals.

"Lukey. Knock knock."

"Who's there?"

"Ketchup."

"Ketchup who?"

They broke up laughing and chanting. "Ha ha catch a poo!"

"Genes, knock knock."

"Who's there?"

"I love mop."

"I love mop who?" They slapped each other a high five. " Ha ha, I love my poo!"

Later, after reading their fortune cookies, Genie found herself gazing at Luke.

"Luke, I'll never forget the day Mom and Gregg brought you home."

Luke, in typical disinterested male fashion, asked Genie to pass the egg rolls.

"You were all bundled up. You were so cute. But I wasn't sure I was going to like you."

Luke took a bite. "Why, what did *I* do?"

"You took my only child spot."

"Oh. Can you pass the sweet n' sour sauce?" Genie handed it to him. "I ended up really loving you. But a part of me resented you too."

"I know. You've told me."

"When?"

Luke laughed. "All my life. You always complained that I got more. You'd even complain if you thought Mom gave me more noodles. You always had to have the bigger bowl."

Genie laughed. "Really?"

"Hell, yeah. I remember one year you even counted how many kids I had at my birthday party so you could make sure to have more at yours."

"Luke, all I did was take care of you and love you all the time."

"Ya, but you bitched about it *all the time.*"

"I didn't bitch about it. I probably just talked about it. They're just feelings."

Luke laughed. "It gets really old."

Genie spoke quietly. "Nobody's ever complained."

"Wrong."

"Well I wouldn't mind hearing your feelings."

"We wouldn't mind *not* hearing yours."

"I'm just expressing myself."

"Genie, you don't express your emotions. You vomit them."

Genie looked at Luke. Luke looked back at Genie. "Hey, Luke. Knock knock."

"Who's there?"

"Europe."

Luke looked at Genie. She smiled back at him. And they spent the rest of the day unpacking.

CHAPTER 50

Pantry, freezer, or fridge? Triscuits, rice cakes, or turtles? The food selection in her mom's house was all that Genie could think of. She knew that the second she walked in the door, she would head straight for the crackers, and then some.

What would Ellen say? Genie sat on the jumping feeling inside her as she walked into the house. Minutes later, she and her mom were sitting in the kitchen together, talking about life's minutia. Suddenly, without a plan, the words came out. Like they had been standing in line for years, and finally heard their names called.

"Mom, I didn't tell you this, but I've gone into therapy."

Jennifer looked at Genie with surprise. "Really? Why? Is everything alright?"

"Yeah. I actually started going because of my eating."

Jennifer looked concerned. "What about your eating?"

"I couldn't control it. And I didn't understand why. Do you want to hear about it?"

Jennifer seemed hesitant. "If you want to tell me, sure." Jennifer took a deep breath. Genie was so nervous to start and she had no idea where to begin. Jennifer seemed to sense that.

"It's ok, Genie. I can take it."

Genie was matter of fact. "The feelings are about you."

Jennifer looked jolted. But she nodded as though this was expected.

"I'm listening."

"Well, after Dad died, everything changed for us. And I was kind of..."

Genie looked at her mom with hesitation.

"It's ok, Genie. Go ahead."

"I was kind of left on my own." Genie's throat closed up as though the sentence did damage to her vocal chords. Her eyes welled up. She choked on the words as they came out.

"And it hurt."

Jennifer looked at her daughter. She didn't say anything and she didn't move. Genie cried, but it was controlled. After what seemed like a long time, Jennifer finally spoke.

"Genie, I'm so sorry I hurt you. I never meant to."

Genie sucked air in hard. She had never expected an apology.

"I know you didn't, Mom. And I don't think I had any idea what you had gone through until recently. What it must have felt like for you to lose someone you loved so much. Especially after losing your own parents so young."

Jennifer nodded. Tears welled up in her eyes.

"Genie," Jennifer wiped her face with the back of her hand as she spoke. She stood up and grabbed a tissue from a box on the counter, "there are many things I would do differently if I had the chance or if I knew what I know today. But what I do need you to know is that..." she wiped her eyes again, "...you have always been my rock."

"But Mom, I needed you to be *my* rock. I was just a little girl. And I had lost my *dad*."

Jennifer's whole face dropped. Genie had never been so sorry to have uttered words in her life. Not because she felt fear, but she couldn't stand seeing the pain in her mom's face.

Jennifer spoke quietly. "Genie, I broke down. I can't explain it. I just did. I could barely get through the days. But if you hadn't been in my life, I'm not sure I would have made it. Even though you didn't know it, you were the reason I held on."

The two women looked at each other. Genie was frozen. Jennifer looked defeated. As if she needed an interruption. Jennifer opened the cabinet and reached for a glass.

"Do you want some fresh juice, Honey?"

The question, as though it had gone inside of her and turned a reaction valve hard, was unexpectedly jolting. It brought up the memory of the days after the accident. Tiptoeing toward her mom's bedroom door before leaving for school. Wanting to make sure she had fresh juice since Genie knew she probably wouldn't get it herself. Genie could still hear the sound of the creaking door to Jennifer's bedroom, and how afraid she was to wake her. After a few failed missions, Genie had found the formula. It had to be a slow turn of the knob, with a push so fast it made wind.

Every day that Genie walked into that dark room, with its shades drawn, stale air pushing against her, she placed the glass in a different spot on the nightstand. The condensation rings dried like the inside of an oak tree, as though to keep track of the number of days their small family was in mourning.

Standing in the kitchen today, the collision of feelings was overwhelming. Genie burst into tears. Jennifer looked at her and felt overwhelming guilt and pain. Genie started crying so hard, and with such ridiculous noises, that it made her laugh. Jennifer walked over to her.

With confidence, Jennifer opened her arms. With trepidation, Genie walked toward the embrace. They hugged, but Genie could feel herself holding back. She could smell her mom's perfume. She could feel her chest move in and out. They continued to hold each other; neither of them speaking a word. But Genie couldn't feel anything.

It didn't happen overnight. But from that day forward, Genie and Jennifer began a new relationship. They started checking in with each other every day. They shared more in the days that followed than they had shared in all the years leading up.

With each conversation, Genie learned more. The more she opened up, divulged, and vented, the more support she received. The more her mom allowed her to speak, the more Genie grew to love her. The more she grew to trust her. The more she felt when she hugged her. And that kept the pantry door closed.

CHAPTER 51

It was one of those negotiable yellow lights. Genie could either slam on the breaks or go through. Seconds later, she wished she had slammed on the breaks. Genie had no idea where this woman's car came from. All she knew was that the car was crying pink tears from someplace near the engine.

Genie never made a big deal about car accidents if no one was hurt. The one place she underreacted and everyone else freaked out. Glass was shattered everywhere. Genie got out of the car and walked up to the other car. She talked to the woman through the passenger window. This was a no-brainer since the window was no longer there.

"Are you ok?"

The woman was crying and shaken but responded angrily. "I had a green!"

Genie was firm. "No, you couldn't have had a green, because I had a yellow."

Within minutes there was an ambulance, fire truck, and police car. And as the hefty policewoman approached her, Genie could tell she was not about to make a new friend.

"What happened here?" she said gruffly.

Genie was matter of fact. "I had a yellow and she appeared in the intersection out of nowhere. I slammed on the breaks but I couldn't avoid her."

The policewoman walked to the back of Genie's car. "Your plates are expired. November thirtieth."

"That was two days ago."

"That makes them two days expired." The officer walked to the other driver and questioned her. After some time, she walked back to the squad car. She was writing for a long time. Finally Genie approached the squad car and spoke to the policewoman through the passenger window.

Genie spoke politely. "Excuse me, were there any witnesses?" The officer looked at Genie with annoyance.

"No witnesses. You admitted running a yellow, so the accident is your fault."

Genie was defensive. "I said the light was yellow as I passed through it. There is no way she could have a green because I didn't have a red."

The other driver was now standing next to Genie. "Of course you're going to say that," she said. "You're lying."

Genie looked at her. "No, *one* of us is telling the truth here."

The policewoman forbid Genie from talking more, but didn't say anything to the other driver who had no driver's license, no insurance card, but for some reason wasn't hated.

When Genie got her ticket, it said, "Disobey solid red signal."

Later that night, minus a car, Genie got the lecture from Danny.

"Genes, you don't say you went through a yellow. You say the light was green."

"But I was just trying to be honest! I mean, I didn't go through a red. She did!"

"It doesn't matter. She's not going to admit it and you'll end up getting blamed anyway. And your insurance is going to go up if that happens."

"Well, I'm going to fight it. I don't think I was wrong, but even if I was, I wasn't the only one at fault. I was just big enough to tell the truth!"

Five weeks later, Genie stood before the judge. She had long blond hair and a soft-spoken demeanor. She asked for both women's accounts of what happened. Then she questioned the officer. The judge nodded and looked over the documents in front of her. Genie timidly spoke.

"Excuse me, Your Honor, may I speak?"

The judge looked up. "Yes, go ahead."

"I told the officer that the light was yellow when I went through it. My honesty caused me to get the ticket. And frankly, this reminds me just a bit too much of my boyfriend."

The judge looked up over her glasses. "Excuse me?"

"Every time my boyfriend and I have an argument, he's just as much at fault as I am but he won't admit it. So I get the ticket. I'm just tired of being honest about what my issues are and getting all the blame. I mean, isn't every fight or upset a two person accident?"

The judge looked at Genie. She spoke to the policewoman.

"Did Ms. Burns tell you that she ran a red light?"

"No, she indicated that she ran a yellow light. I told her that was against the law."

"And there were no witnesses?"

"No, Your Honor."

"Ms. Burns was honest in admitting her responsibility. I don't think she should be penalized for that."

The judge spoke directly to Genie.

"My boyfriend does the same thing. My judgment is fifty percent for each party."

Lawsome!

CHAPTER 52

The doctors are running tests. Within twenty minutes of receiving the call, Genie was on autopilot, packing her bags and heading home. As she drove from college, two days before finals, she longed for *those* tests instead.

Five hours later, she walked into the hospital. Jennifer was in the waiting room, in a trance, with Aunt Dottie by her side. They explained the sequence of events. Gregg had woken up with chest pains. At several points, Genie and Dotty caught each other's glance in acknowledgment of history's replay.

Finally, the doctor came out to the waiting room. Each of their faces turned to him as though the Almighty himself had put on some scrubs and entered into their sphere. They tried to read his expression. Would he bring hope or would he bring death? Genie wondered what it would feel like to deliver messages carrying that kind of weight.

Gregg was stable. The next twenty-four hours would tell more. No matter what question they asked, there didn't seem to be much of an answer. They could see him, one at a time, a bit later. For now, the doctor advised them to go home and get some rest.

When they got back to the house, Jennifer told Genie how much it meant to her that she was home. And then she asked if

Genie minded if she rested for a while since she hadn't slept all night. Genie told her mother she would put some dinner together so it would be there when she woke up.

Genie grabbed her duffle and walked into her bedroom. So many of her belongings were at school and her room didn't look lived in anymore. She opened the closet door and began to hang her clothes. They looked like guests hanging between empty hangers.

Above the hangers, on the shelf, Genie noticed all of her old scrapbooks. She reached to pull a couple of them down. As if history had been tapped on the shoulder, she watched a puff of dust disburse. Memories protected with a "Do not disturb" had just been allowed a trespass. Respectful of the all years they had sat there, she handled them with delicate care.

Genie leafed through the pages of her past. Poems she had written, pictures she had drawn, and photographs she had taken. She picked up the second book and opened it to the first page. What she saw hoisted emotion from deep inside. Her tears made the page look blurry. They rolled down her cheeks, down the side of her nose, and one of them fell directly on top of one of the daisies he gave her.

It was in that very instant that something clicked inside. She remembered the night in the restaurant when Gregg had taken the family to dinner. He had announced he would be traveling and though she hadn't realized it then, Genie had pulled back from their closeness. Sitting in her room, knowing Gregg was in a hospital bed, she prayed that he had never noticed that anything had changed between them. And suddenly, she needed to change it back.

She left the house quickly and drove straight to the hospital. She snuck into Gregg's room before anyone would see her because she didn't know if she'd be allowed in. The room was quiet. Gregg was surrounded by things that didn't belong in Genie's picture of him. She felt a disdain for what she saw and decided *not* to see it. Instead, she focused on the man. The man who had brought her a father; the man who had brought life to her home; the man who had given her a brother, and had looked out for her from day one.

With tears of love and attachment, history and commitment, Genie approached the side of his bed. It felt so good to feel him again. In that moment she made a promise to him and she made one to herself. No matter how much it hurt to love, she would never again let it go.

Genie carefully took Gregg's hand so as not to disturb the I.V. and she gently kissed his forehead. Her face was just inches from his, and all she felt was healed. Being close to him was all she needed and it made her feel strength, not fear. Somehow she knew in that very moment that Gregg would be ok.

As if the cue was planted in spirit, he opened his eyes to see her. His mouth was dry and she watched him struggle to find his voice. He smiled ever so slightly and closed his eyes again. Crackly, whispery, and mixed with air, his words escaped their cell. "That's my Genie. Always on my side."

Suddenly, she was overwhelmed with emotion. It wasn't that she hadn't been with him the last few years. She just hadn't been with him in full. As if those surplus feelings all decided to come through the door at once, Genie felt the most overwhelming love for him. Her tears weren't so quiet and once again, Gregg opened his eyes for just a speck of a second. His lips stretched for a smile.

"Don't worry, Sweetheart. I always come back."

And true to his promise, Gregg was home in a week.

CHAPTER 53

Casey was holding Genie's hand as they walked around the farmer's market.

"Is Jeff coming over today?"

"I don't know. I hope so."

"You really love him, don't you?"

"Yes Case, I really love him. You want to get some grapes?"

"Yeah, I like the purple ones. Do you think you'll get married?"

"We still have some things to work out. But we're doing so much better. I wouldn't be surprised if it happened."

Genie put some grapes in a bag and paid for them.

"But you love each other. So I don't get it. Why wouldn't it happen?"

"Well, relationships get a bit complicated. And even though people love each other, they don't always agree on how to live and get along. You want some mangos?"

"So what? They love each other. Why can't they just figure it out?"

"Sometimes they do."

"I hope you guys do. You have to."

Genie looked at Casey. "Why is it so important to you, Case?"

Casey shrugged. "I feel like we'd kind of be like a family."

Genie was stunned. She had never realized that Casey regarded them that way. She felt an instant commitment to the sentiment.

"Case, even if Jeff and I didn't get married, you and me... we're..."

"I know. We're friends."

Genie smiled. "Is that what you'd like us to be?"

"No. I want a mom and a dad."

Genie felt such an ache for Casey, and in some ways an ache for herself.

"Well, I know you had a mom who loved you very much. And even though she's in heaven, I have to believe she would want you to have someone to help her out down here while she's away. And I imagine your grandma could use some help too. So maybe they wouldn't mind if I looked out for you here on earth."

Casey's eyes opened wide with excitement. "You mean like an Earth Mom?"

Genie laughed. "Yes. I'd love to be your Earth Mom."

"Like forever?"

"Moms are forever, right?"

Casey hugged Genie's waist so hard she nearly fell. Genie laughed at first, but as she held Casey, her eyes welled up. She could feel her stomach tighten with emotion. And yet, she didn't want Casey to see that. She preferred her to believe that to Genie, the question was normal and what she expected.

"So my little earthling...you want mangos?"

"Do you think Jeff wants to get married?" Genie shrugged and laughed. Casey began to scold. "Oh, I get it. You guys are like all the other grown-ups. If you'd act like kids and not make such a big deal about everything..."

Genie laughed. "You know something Casey? You are one of the smartest people I know. *Do you want a mango!*"

"Yes, I want a mango! If Jeff asked you to marry him would you say yes?"

"If Batman asked you to marry him would you say yes?"

"Yeah. If he promised to wear his mask to the wedding."

Genie laughed. "Well, I'd marry Jeff if he took *off* his mask once and a while and let me wear *all* of mine. Like *this* one!" Suddenly, Genie opened her eyes wide like a wild creature, waved her arms around like a hovering monster, and howled like a wounded animal. She laughed an evil laugh and Casey screamed in laughing terror.

Later as they walked into the lobby of their building, Genie stopped to get her mail. She went through to see what was in the pile, not noticing Casey's stare until she turned and looked at her.

Genie smiled. "What, Honey?"

"I love you, Genie."

Genie looked at Casey. She pulled her close kissing the top of her head.

"I love you too, Beautiful Girl. More than you'll ever know."

• • •

Casey's day with Batman. Jeff took her to a movie and shopping for some new sweats and a new backpack. Bags in hand, sucker in mouth, they strolled down the street toward the car.

"Jeff, are you and Genie going to get married?"

"WHOA! Where did that come from?"

Casey pointed to her mouth. "It came from there."

Jeff laughed. "I don't know, Case. I've certainly thought about it."

"Well, why don't you ask her?"

"We're not anywhere near ready for that. We have some things that get in the way. Maybe one day though." Jeff stopped at an art gallery window and looked inside. "You like that painting over there?"

Casey looked. "No. I think it's ugly. What gets in the way of love?"

"Life." They started walking again.

"Why does life get in the way?"

Jeff looked at Casey's face. He had no idea where to go with this one.

"Case, I love Genie very much. And I believe she loves me. I'd love to think that we will get married one day. Ok?"

"What are you waiting for?"

Jeff laughed. "We have some problems that need to be worked out." He patted her head. "Is that ok with you?"

"No, it's not ok. You guys love each other and that's all that should matter. We could all be together."

Jeff stared at Casey. He understood what she needed.

"Casey, do you remember a time when your mom and dad were together?"

"Not really. My dad left when I was little so all I remember is my mom. But I know how it's supposed to be. Kids are the smart ones, don't you know? It's just that nobody ever listens. And by the time we grow up, we turn into dumb adults just like you. And we listen to dumb adults just like you."

Jeff looked at Casey and put his arms around her. He kissed the top of her head.

"Hey, Case. Got any good stock tips?"

CHAPTER 54

Lying on the sofa together at Jeff's house, cuddling and reading magazines, Jeff pulled out a page from *Travel + Leisure* and handed it to Genie.

"Nevis is supposed to be beautiful, and if you would fly, we could go there. Gorgeous beaches, mountains, and I heard in some of the remote areas there are monkeys that just walk around. If you leave your door open, they'll come inside your house."

Genie looked at Jeff laughing. "How would you know that?"

"I had a patient who was from there. He said the monkeys take things from your house and throw them at you!"

Genie laughed and groaned. "Ohhh, I want to go! I want to play with them!"

"Oh, they hate the monkeys. They ruin all their crops. Especially the bananas."

"Well, Bear, do you know what I heard about monkeys?"

"That they see and do?"

"When a big monkey and a small monkey are on the verge of a fight, the small monkey knows it's going to lose. So to avoid getting hurt, it turns to face the big monkey and lets him know he wants to have sex. That's how they avoid fighting."

"Oooh. I like that. Make up sex *before* the fight!"

"Yeah. And then there're these Bonobo monkeys. There's no aggression, they're really kind and gentle and there's never any fighting. But they have sex *all* day long."

"I'm all in. Let's start right now." Jeff began to tickle Genie and she laughed.

"Wait, Jeff! Do you want to be the big monkey or the small monkey?"

"The big monkey."

"I want to be the big monkey."

"Nope. I'm the bigger human so I get to be the bigger monkey."

"It was my discovery. I should get first pick."

"If you weren't going to give me the choice, then why ask?"

"Rhetorical question, Jeff. And we can't both be big monkey."

"Genie. You know why I get to be the big monkey?"

"Why."

"I have the banana."

Genie hit Jeff playfully. She laughed and kissed him on the cheek. Jeff moved in about three inches from her face. He fixed his eyes on hers. He looked so deeply into them. This *Jeff look* was somewhere between a reassuring father, a sexy boyfriend, and one scary motherfucker. It was a look not to argue with.

"Gino. I am never going to want to be with anyone else. I just don't want us fighting, you understand?"

Genie nodded like a little girl being told the rules of conduct.

"You need to stop getting hurt over small things. You need to give me the benefit of the doubt. There's no reason on earth why we can't be together, you understand?"

"Jeff, I'm going to get hurt about things. I'm going to get upset sometimes. It's normal. You know, some of this is about your own childhood and the way your..."

Jeff's voice rose over Genie's. "Genie, this has nothing to do with my childhood. I'm well aware of what I experienced as a kid. Regardless of that, I don't agree that people need to fight or that it's normal. There are couples who never fight."

"Jeff, that's like me saying there are couples who never go on airplanes. And it has nothing to do with my childhood. There are people who don't travel too."

"Genie, stop turning this on me. These are your issues and you know it."

"Oh and you have none?"

Jeff's voice rose higher. "I've never implied I have none. I'm not a perfect person. Nobody is."

"Oh, so what exactly are your issues?"

"I am well aware of what they are. But that's not what we're discussing right now. If you can't tell me that you're not going to be able to hold back from being upset so often and about such small things, it will ruin us. I won't be able to live that way. No matter how much I love you. I know *me*."

"Well, I know *me*. I'm in love with you, I'm sensitive around you, and sometimes you are hurtful. All my friends' boyfriends and husbands are. They don't tell their wives they can't get hurt."

"I'm not going to compare us to any other couple. I'm telling you how I need to live. I'm also telling you that it's a healthy way to live."

"I think it's healthy to be able to share hurt feelings, to discuss them."

"No, Genie. You just accept people for who they are. Life is short. What we have is something that people just don't get. I'll never have it again and neither will you. But fighting takes years off of people's lives. It's unnecessary."

"Jeff, if I express any feeling at all, you get so mad, shut me out, and we fight. Can't you just listen without fighting?"

"No! Because if I don't agree with you, you become relentless!"

"All I'm asking for is the understanding."

Jeff paused. "Genie, we need to be adults. If we do that, we'll be together forever. I'm in. You in too?"

Genie was afraid not to be in. She nodded in fear but had no idea if what she agreed to was something she could do, or even believed in.

In the morning, Jeff got up, got dressed, and stood beside the bed. He stroked Genie's hair back and away from her face. He kissed her on the forehead. She woke up and looked at him. He reached into his pocket and pulled out his folded bills. He thumbed two twenties and placed them on her nightstand.

"Genes, I owe you this for picking up my dry cleaning the other day."

"You don't have to pay me back."

"I don't want you paying for that. But thanks for picking it up."

She kissed him goodbye. She stretched and yawned. And as she looked over to the clock to see how much more time she had before she needed to be up, she saw the folded bills standing in their tented position. She heard the front door close. She looked at the money again, and she sobbed.

CHAPTER 55

The Superman ride was the main attraction of the theme park. The whoosh of the rides and the distant screams made Genie wonder why anyone would self-induce fear.

"Jeff, I can't do rides like this. I get so sick on them. I can only do the ones that don't go upside down."

"Gene, I told you, this ride is so smooth. It's the best one, you're going to love it."

Genie watched the loops and knew that there was no way.

"You don't understand. I get sick talking to someone who has Venetian blinds behind them!"

Jeff put his arms around Genie and gave her a big slurpy kiss on her neck. He tickled her.

"Trust me. You're going to be fine."

As they got up to the car and sat down, a bar came down over her lap. Her head was in some sort of contraption, which didn't allow her to turn and see Jeff next to her. Already she was beginning to panic.

The ride began slowly. It bumped from side to side. She was ok until it began to whip into high speed and drop forward so that she actually faced the ground. Genie tried to scream but she couldn't. She was paralyzed with fear.

As the car soared higher, turning around in a circle, Genie closed her eyes, but it made her sick not to see where she was. She tried opening her eyes but the moving sights made her dizzy. The speed was tremendous. The sickness enveloped her. The ride wasn't ending. She braced herself in a stiff position, trying to hold on.

When it finally came to an end, she felt like she was in a sick trance. She walked with Jeff, who was laughing. She couldn't get rid of the dizziness. She stopped walking and Jeff stopped in front of her, turning around to see where she was.

"Oh, please. It wasn't so bad. Stop being so dramatic!"

"Jeff, I think I'm going to be sick."

"Do you need to go to the bathroom?"

"Yeah."

Jeff pointed to one and told her he'd walk around.

Genie walked into the bathroom and headed toward a handicapped stall. She knew she'd need some room. She sat on the floor near the toilet. She tried to throw up but couldn't.

She didn't know why, but she couldn't imagine going out to that park and facing Jeff again. Not knowing what else to do, she picked up her cell phone, dialed Ellen, and told her where she was.

"Genie, just take some deep breaths. It's not uncommon to feel disoriented emotionally when your equilibrium is off. One is absolutely affected by the other. That's why you're feeling this way."

Genie cried. "No, Jeff is a roller coaster. He's scary. He pushes me to do things I can't do. I don't feel safe with him! He's not for me!"

"Genie, Jeff isn't a ride, he's a man. The relationship has tapped into a lot of trauma from your childhood. You're having a panic attack and we just need to get you to breathe. Put some cold water on your face and let yourself relax. I'll call you in a while."

Outside the stall, there was a line of people waiting for the bathroom. A woman looked under the door and saw part of Genie's body on the floor and had heard she was on the phone. She yelled at Genie.

"Hey you in there! There's a line of people out here! Can't you sit on a bench?"

Genie sat up in total shock. "I was talking to my therapist! Could you not?"

The woman outside yelled back. "What's the problem?"

The women behind in line started chatting among themselves. Another one bellowed out.

"Yeah, open the door! Maybe we can help you. Just let us use the can."

Genie reached up and disengaged the lock, sat back on the floor but didn't look up or over to the woman as she came in, dropped her pants, and sat down on the toilet.

"Man trouble?" said the woman in a firm tone.

Genie nodded.

"Dump him."

Genie whined through tears. "How can you say that? You don't even know him!"

"Honey, if you're on the bathroom floor talking to your shrink, he's the wrong guy for you."

"Well, maybe he'll become the right guy. Or maybe I need to change."

"Dump him. And don't take him back until he says whatever he needs to say to get you off the damn floor."

From outside the door, one of the women called out.

"I'm with her! Dump him!"

"You don't understand. He's everything I want. He's an unbelievable person. He's any woman's dream."

"No Baby. No woman's dream is to cry."

CHAPTER 56

Thirty days had passed. In that month, Genie was down to four hurt feelings, which resulted in four days of shutouts for each one, bringing the grand total of talking days to fourteen. Jeff traveled for three of those days and had plans with friends another seven. That left four days spent together.

Genie was home, walking out of her kitchen, dragging her feet in defeat. She spoke out loud with the voice of a professional newscaster, holding an invisible microphone up to her face.

"Late tonight, an unidentified woman was gang banged by Ben and Jerry, Mike and Ike, Mr. Salty, Chester Cheeto, and even Dr. Pepper. The offenders, not yet apprehended, are still at large." She looked down at her stomach, "*Very large.*"

The next morning she stood at her closet. She grabbed a pair of flannel pants, a big sweatshirt, and headed into the office. Steven took a look at her and spoke with sarcastic cheer. "I forgot! It's theme week at Surprise Enterprise! Pajama day today... and what's tomorrow again?"

Genie shot him a nasty look. "Supportive partner day! I guess that means you get a day off!"

"*Cute Genes*. Speaking of *cute jeans,* too fat to wear your Sevens?"

"Yeah. I have to cancel my appointments today and tomorrow. But I'll be back in my medium fat clothes on Thursday with a goal of thin by Monday."

"What do you think you are? A cop off his beat and now you're demoted to desk job? You can't *cancel* appointments!"

"Oh, no? Watch me."

"Why would you do that?"

"Too fat to go."

"Oh, stop it. You're not fat." Steven shielded his face. "You're just not thin anymore."

"Oh, Steven! Would you look at me on the street and think I was fat?"

"No. I just wouldn't look at all."

Genie squealed. "I'm not attractive *at all?* Like, how would you describe me?"

"Great personality." The phone rang. Steven answered.

"Surplus-thighs Enterprise. I mean, Surprise Enterprise can I help you? Oh, hi Grace. I will be there at eleven, but Genie won't be joining. She's feeling overw—"

Genie bellowed, "STEVEN!"

"...whelmed with work. Too many chips, brownies, and cookies..."

"STEVEN!"

"...to deliver to a ten year old's surprise party."

Genie put her face in her hands and brought them down to her desk.

"See you then, Grace." Steven walked to Genie's desk.

"Genes, what has gotten *into* you? You're a *wreck*."

Genie looked up with mascara bags under her eyes. Her hair was all over the place.

"Steven, remember who I was before? Remember my cute clothes? I used to be such…"

"A pain in the ass. Don't worry, you haven't lost your touch."

"I'm in love, Steven. It should feel good, right?"

Steven sat on the desk next to Genie.

"Hey, maybe this is how you act when you're happy!"

"I think we bring out each other's dark side. We're really nice people when we're not together." Genie got a look like she was going to sneeze. Steven put his hand up as he spoke.

"Oh, God *no*. Cover your mouth, Genie. Last time you sneezed I had to vacuum."

Genie laughed hard and sure enough, something flew out of her mouth and onto her desk. Steven put his face in his hands and shook his head.

"We got into another fight two days ago 'cause I got hurt. He won't talk to me again."

"What this time? He complemented your cooking on the second bite instead of the first?"

"No, I got over that. Steven, he chose *Hitler* over me."

"Excuse me?"

"We hadn't seen each other in so long because of his traveling and our fighting, and he got all loving and sexy and all he talked about on the phone was how he couldn't wait to do this and that to me…"

Steven raised his eyebrow. "Ok, so…"

"So wait. It was ALL he talked about! In text, in email, on the phone. The man was so hot on me he even asked me…"

"Genie, I'd really rather not go the scenic route here. Take the shortcut, please?"

"Ok. So on our first day back together, we go out with friends and the first opportunity we had to be alone, he turns on the TV to watch a special on Hitler."

Steven smiled. "So next time you put on the Jeannie costume, try adding a mustache."

"Steven! Come on! I got hurt. I know I'm not supposed to, but I did. Who wouldn't? It's not like we've been married for years or anything."

"Gene, he just needed some down time before the *get down* time."

Genie laughed. "How do *you* know?"

"I've dated guys like him."

Genie smiled and shook her head. "Steven, you and I have way too much in common."

"Genie, don't get upset. He loves you and he's attracted to you and just because he wants to watch an interesting program, doesn't mean he's not totally into you. Stop getting so hurt."

Genie slammed her palms down on the desk. "I'm so tired of everyone telling me I'm not supposed to get hurt. *Why not!* We were apart a long time! And I'm sorry, but people get pissed and annoyed and hurt at little, stupid shit! It's the way of the world! Like nail clippings on the bathroom floor! Not replacing the toilet paper! Forgetting to buy everything on the list!"

"Uh Genes, you've got..."

"Overspending! Underspending! Not wiping up the counter! Not saying I love you enough! Not being available enough! Asking too much! Giving too little! The stupid, idiotic, meaningless things that people get upset about and you know what? It's accepted as the norm in an intimate relationship. That's why there are BESTSELLER books telling people not to sweat the small stuff..."

"Right Genes, just so you know you..."

"I always hear women talk about the stupid stuff they get pissed about! The stupid stuff their husbands or boyfriends get pissed about! Stupid, stupid, stupid. Nobody thinks anything of it! But with Jeff? Shut out for days, it's forever logged in his memory, I'll hear about it for the next year, and I'm the one with the problem!"

"Uh Genes, can I say something now?"

"*What* Steven!"

"You've got a big piece of something green in your..." Steven pointed to her teeth. "*Really* big."

With a complete change of focus, Genie ran her tongue over her teeth. She took her finger and picked between them. "Here?"

"Next one over."

Steven was smiling, enjoying it all too much. He couldn't resist adding a minute or more to the show. "Genes, you know, you do have quite the little temper there."

"I DO NOT have a temper! I have a temper when I'm not allowed to be normal! You know what it's like not being able to react like the rest of the world? Being accused of being screwed up ALL THE TIME?"

"Ok Genes, let's say it's Jeff's issue. He's too hard on you but accept it and let him come to you when he's ready."

"Well, not to at least answer your phone for days is so immature and punishing. What if he was dead? I'd never know the difference!"

"Oh shit, you're right. We might have to sign for the FedEx boyfriend box!"

Genie smiled. It just felt good to be heard. "Ellen tells me that underneath all of this food is a truth. I just don't see it yet."

"Well, in the meantime, I'm locking up my lunch."

"You know what, Steven? I was supposed to grow up, meet a guy, fall in love, and get married. What a fricking surprise my life turned out to be, huh?"

"Well, you never know, Genes. The surprises are far from over. Now go call Romone. Tell him he's got to be at the location, with everyone set, no later than five. And please don't ever dress like that again. It's killing our chance for romance."

CHAPTER 57

How do you say no to a friend? Jessica, Genie's friend from the health club, had spent the past seven years learning Kabbalah; the ancient and mystical teachings that reveal how the universe works with a set of tools and methods to understand why things happen, and how to receive the "light."

The only light Genie was interested in was Cool Whip Lite. There were no mystical wisdoms when it came to her weight. Those ancient rabbis knew nothing of Kraft Macaroni and Cheese or the stress on girls to be thin. Sure, easy for them to find inner peace. The zipper hadn't yet been invented!

Jessica and Genie were at the club, side by side on the elliptical machines.

"All I'm asking is that you come to the class I'm teaching." Jessica wiped her forehead with the small white towel that hung over her elliptical screen. "It changed my life, Genie."

Genie didn't say anything. Jessica went on. "Every relationship in my life is better. And I think it would really help you with so much of what you're going through now."

Genie spoke through her panting and sweating. "Jessica, I just don't buy into that stuff. I wish I did. And Ellen is helping me with all my problems right now. She's all I need. Kabbalah... it's just not me."

"Genie, it's a ten week course. The people who come are not weirdos, I promise. They're people just like us looking for ways to manage stress and various situations in their lives. It's so powerful, Genie. *Come.*"

• • •

Jessica stood at her podium and greeted people as they came in. There were five tables in the room and the students were told to sit anywhere. On each table was a pitcher of water, plastic cups, and two plastic bowls, one filled with miniature Hershey bars and the other with animal crackers. In front of each chair was a small yellow notebook pad with pens scattered on the table.

Genie was relieved to see Jessica had been right and this was not a group of weirdos. As a matter of fact, there were enough Diet Cokes and water bottles to reassure Genie right away that she was among her people. She looked around to see a mix of moms, daughters, professionals, husbands, wives, teens, and singles; a community potpourri.

"Chances are, if you came here tonight, you would like to gain more control and break negative patterns. You want to remove the chaos and live a more fulfilling life. Kabbalah is ancient wisdom that gives us tools to transform. You're going to discover that behind every difficult, annoying, painful event is another event that brings light." And then Genie learned her first Kabbalah term.

"*Bread of Shame* is getting something without earning it. Nothing that's handed to us can make us happy unless we've worked hard, overcoming obstacles to get it." Jessica began talking as if she was an angry parent teaching a vital lesson. It was fun as hell listening to her.

"Is it fun to win a game if there's no opponent? Is it fun to be given everything we want without ever having to earn it? No! *It's boring!* You *asked* for these conflicts in your life so that you could overcome them. So you wouldn't have Bread of Shame.

"Each of us has a history, a make-up of past experiences that leaves us with a need to be healed. Some are small, and some are monumental. If your issue, or the place you need correcting, which is called a Tikkun, is traffic, you will hit traffic every day. If your Tikkun is abandonment, you will be abandoned. If your Tikkun is loud voices, your boss will be a screamer.

"Each of us is given the *exact* obstacle in the form of a person or a situation that hits us deeply, because one day, when the obstacle has been overcome, it will be the result of our own strength and perseverance. We will have earned that peace and contentment. We will have healed that Tikkun. And will the opponent let us stay there?" Jessica paused and looked at her students. "NO! Something new will come our way every single day and challenge us again! Because that is what keeps us alive!"

A woman raised her hand and Jessica pointed to her to speak.

"So is this opponent like the enemy?"

"Great question! No! This opponent is the good guy with the hardest job in the world and that is to work against us; to mess us up; to throw us off our game. Not like the bad guy, but like a coach or a trainer. He will try to pull us to chaos, to reactivity, to bad health, to laziness, to dysfunction, and even to failure. He'll try to ruin our relationships and he'll fool us every day. *Our job is to beat him.* But here's the thing. The obstacle is never the bad guy. The obstacle IS the light."

CHAPTER 58

By the fourth Kabbalah class, Genie was feeling a friendship and connection with the people in the room. Each week there was a lesson followed by a weekly assignment. Jessica's voice was in one side of Genie's brain. Ellen's was on the other. Today's lesson put Genie in the middle, as her very own referee. This happened when Jessica made the following statement: *"Feelings don't mean a thing."*

Genie was destroyed. *What's that? I just spent how many dollars in therapy to learn all about my feelings!* Jessica went on to make her point.

"Most of us live within one percent of our potential, and that is listening and reacting to our five senses. The spiritual world is ninety-nine percent." Jessica wrote it on the board with a marker. "We actually have the characteristic of giving and sharing because we want to be like our creator. We each have a *huge* purpose here. The opponent tries to slow us down."

Genie raised her hand. "I'm not sure I understand. I've learned in therapy to address my feelings and make decisions from there, and that if I don't feel my feelings, I'll go to unhealthy places of distraction. So I don't get it. How can my feelings be unimportant?"

"Great question! It's not that your feelings aren't important. It's how you respond to them. Feelings and thoughts are not real. They are a decision. You can change them and here's what I want you to remember. Your five senses fool you *all the time*."

Jessica looked around the room. This was her sunlight before the downpour lesson.

"How many times have you made up your mind or formed an opinion, based on something you saw, heard, or felt, that you later found out to be false?" The room was quiet. "Come on! Anyone? I know you all have a story." One woman raised her hand.

"My boyfriend and I had been dating only eight months, but we were so in love with each other and everything felt so right. Then suddenly he became really quiet around me. He seemed busy a lot. I was devastated because I figured he was backing off. I had myself convinced we were over. Two weeks later, he asked me to marry him!"

Jessica's face lit up. "So why had he backed off?"

"He was stressed about the ring, the proposal, he wanted everything perfect."

"And you got married?"

"Five years ago."

"Excellent story!" Jessica bellowed. "Your five senses fooled you! Your feelings, which would be very important to you, were based on something that never happened! So, class. Guess who sends those feelings?" Jessica looked at the empty expressions. Finally, a man spoke out.

"The opponent."

"Right! The opponent, who wants you to *earn* your happiness, sends feelings to slow you down, and block you from the light.

Your job is to stop yourself from jumping to words, assumptions, or actions that might be incorrect."

Jessica looked at the woman.

"What did you do when you felt him backing off?"

The woman laughed. "I backed off. I got bitchy."

"Right! Which added to his stress, correct? And it wasn't even stress that came from a truth."

The woman raised her eyebrows and nodded.

"So, what you could have done was to identify the feeling or suspicion and *resist* by doing the very *opposite* of what you would normally do. That's what we're going to talk about today and it's going to change your life." Jessica paused again as she looked at the faces in the class. "Today, I'm going to teach you The Proactive Formula. This is the key to Kabbalah." Jessica wrote it on the board as she spoke.

1. When a difficult situation arises, acknowledge that it came from the light.
2. Identify your reaction.
3. Restrict. Do the opposite of what you would normally do. Go against your nature.
4. When you come to the place where you're not reacting, do something different than you would have in the past, even if it's uncomfortable. *Be proactive.* Jessica faced the class.

"Homework assignment is, find a situation that normally makes you nuts, where you can begin to resist and become calm. Every day, do something different. It doesn't need to make sense. If it's positive and involves giving and sharing, it is the correct response. And one more thing before you go..."

Jessica clearly loved this part. Her eyes held the expectation that she was about to drive the point home. "WHO INVENTED THE

SNOOZE BUTTON?" She looked around the room. "Really! You wake up; push the snooze button over and over. You become lazy and unproductive. So who invented it?"

Several people called out, "The opponent."

"Right! The opponent knows that something from the light is coming your way, *that* day! The opponent wants you to miss the workout that gives you energy and health. Maybe you'll miss the stop to Starbucks where you'll make a business connection. Maybe you'll skip a party and miss meeting your soul mate! Be proactive! Do it differently! Step outside your comfort zone." Jessica banged the last one out big. *"Shake up your life by taking the high road so the light can find its way in!"*

CHAPTER 59

Monday morning. Genie got out of bed, took a shower, and headed into the office. Steven was all excited. He started to tell her about a new client who had called from L.A. and had read an article about them in the newspaper.

Steven explained that this was a strange call but an interesting one. Apparently a man phoned to say that he was planning a wedding for himself and his soon-to-be bride. He wanted to surprise her with the location and the festivities. He wanted it to be terribly romantic and insisted that all of the details remain a secret.

"Steven, I don't know if we should take this on. The risk factor is so high. If she's disappointed in any way he'll be crushed. I mean, it's really sweet and romantic and all, but he might be making a huge mistake. Maybe I better call him and talk it over."

Steven got an uncomfortable look on his face. He almost looked nervous.

"Genes, I don't know how to tell you this without pissing you off, but he kind of doesn't want you involved."

Genie thought, Resist. Restrict. Do it the Kabbalah way. That lasted about thirty seconds. Fuck resist!

"Steven, what do you mean he doesn't want me involved? Who does he want involved?"

Steven started fidgeting with his pencil. "He wants... *me*."

"He wants *you?* You're the food guy. I'm the surprise guy. Who does he think he is? Tell him, no way. You couldn't possibly know what a girl wants at her wedding."

"Genes, just get a grip. Don't take this so personally. The reason he doesn't want a woman's opinion is he knows she'll try to influence him. He wants to do it himself."

"Then tell him to do it himself! Why would he even need us?" Genie took a bag of animal crackers out of her drawer and started stuffing them into her mouth.

"He needs us the way anyone needs a consultant. He needs us to do the footwork on his ideas. He needs our connections. Genie, he has basically no limit on his budget."

"But he's kicking me out of my own business!"

Steven shook his head and rolled his eyes. "Genie, many people calling into companies give their requests as to who they'd like to work with. If it's an attorney, a hair stylist, a doctor... why are you making such a big deal out of this? Put your hurt ego aside and make a business decision for our company."

"Hurt ego? How about *your* ego? How inflated is it now that some big client wants me out, and you in?"

"You are so out of line! A client called and wanted us to do an event. He requested me, the man, as opposed to you, the woman. As a client, he has that right. This isn't Girl Scouts, Genie. This is business."

"It may be business to you, but I put our friendship first. If *anyone* tried to cut you out of any event, I would tell them that's not the way we do business around here. Sorry, Steven, but I would never hurt you that way."

"Genie, it wouldn't hurt me if someone preferred you over me. I would never take that personally. I could give a rat's ass who they want. I just want their business. Our friendship is totally outside of that."

"Ok, fine, Steven. But it does hurt *me*."

"And it's ok if we lose a huge client? Not to mention all of the other potential clients who might hear that we gave up a client because we did pinky swears that we would never betray our oath? C'mon Genes, grow up!"

Some sense was emerging from the rubble of hurt and Genie began to see it. Her opponent won big time today and was high-fiving the devil. She felt like she wanted to cry, so she did. Steven came over, sat down next to her, and wrapped his arm around her neck, leading her into his chest. Genie cried harder and harder. He would have gotten frustrated with her except that she was already so frustrated with herself.

"Oh, I know I'm being such a baby! I thought the therapy and Kabbalah would help."

"Genes, one day they're going to have to open you up and see what happened in there."

Genie spoke through sniffles. "If they did that they'd find out I'm really... *not one of you*."

Steven smiled with an expression of playful suspicion. "You're an alien, aren't you?"

"Yep. E.T in drag." Genie made a deep raspy voice. "Genie, phone home. *Phone home*."

Steven smiled and squeezed her. "Don't worry, Honey. You're going to find your home."

"You think?"

"I know."

CHAPTER 60

Two weeks without fighting might not strike anyone else as a huge accomplishment. For Genie, however, it was like a mid-semester 4.0. Between studying Kabbalah and her therapy, she finally had a chance of acing this relationship. One day she and Jeff would walk up to the podium, wearing their wedding day tassels. The orchestra would play the Pomp and Circumstance Marches. They would be the Couple *Cum Laude.*

Genie and Jeff were on the floor, watching TV, when Genie's cell phone rang. When she saw it was Lori, she decided to answer and quickly get off.

"Hello, Baetch!"

"Genie, we need to talk. Are you with Jeff now?"

"Yeah, we're eating pizza. Why?"

"Call me when you finish if you can get away from him for a few minutes. Don't act like anything's wrong. Or just say I have boyfriend problems."

Genie laughed. "Well, that's always a true statement!"

"Yeah well, so do you, Honey. Call me back."

Genie's stomach dropped. Was Lori purposely messing up this relationship? Did she love Genie, but secretly want her alone?

Was Lori really the opponent, disguised as her trusted teammate? Were Genie's five senses fooling her? When she and Jeff finished eating, she left him to his game, went into the other room, and dialed up disaster.

"Hi, Lor. Before you tell me whatever it is, I want to know why you are always so hard on Jeff. I mean, I love this man, and all you do is look to hate him."

"Genie, I don't look to hate him. I know things have been better and I could choose not to tell you what I just heard but I don't want to see you get hurt, ok? Really. Please trust that I'm your friend and I want you happy."

Genie paused. "Ok, Lor. I do trust that. Go ahead."

"I got a call from Hannah. She was out to dinner with her friend Brittany last night. Somehow your name came up and when Hannah said you were dating Jeff, she said Brittany's eyes bugged out of her head."

"Why? She dated him?"

"Yep. And then some."

"So what, Lor. That's not my business. I never pay attention to that kind of gossip."

"Don't you think I know that? But I think this is stuff you should know."

"Why?"

"Would you want to know if someone had a criminal record?"

Genie felt sick. "Jeff has a criminal record?"

"Crimes of the heart."

"Oh, please. Everyone gets hurt."

"I think you should hear this, Gene. Knowledge is power."

Genie paused. "Ok, what?"

"Ok. So, Brittany and Jeff were neighbors. And he had apparently… *borrowed a few cups of sugar.*"

"So…"

"So, he must've been baking some *big-ass cake* 'cause her sugar wasn't enough. She found out he was also borrowing sugar from…"

Genie was abrupt. "I don't care!"

"Genie, just hear me out. Lindsey was this beautiful girl, a dancer actually, who he chased, treated great, and won over. Once he had her, she found out he was…"

"Lori! What part of *I don't want to hear this* do you not understand?"

"Uh, I guess no part, Genes. Anyway, he then meets this girl out of town and…"

"Lori, stop! I really resent you telling me this. Maybe he was like that with others because he wasn't into them. Nobody can fake that kind of love and loyalty. I can *feel* it."

"All the girls *feel* it. He treats them like queens but behind their backs he's fucking around. He's never been loyal to anyone. The girls he cheats with all believe there's a chance for them to be together one day. And if a girlfriend questions him, he just denies it or claims innocence. I heard he even showed one girl all of his calls and texts so she'd believe him. But he had another phone! He's a total con man and every woman falls for it. They're too afraid not to believe him because then they'd have to give him up."

"Lor, that's not the Jeff I know. People learn from their mistakes or they pull that shit because they haven't met *the one.* I have to judge him right here, with me, today. And he's very real."

"That's how he ropes women in. He knows exactly what to say and do to make them attach to him. He's fun, genuine, humbled, and he comes off principled and honest so they trust him. And since he's good looking, they all think they won the jackpot."

"Lor, I don't want to listen to gossip. And I want you to support me in this decision."

"Ok, Gene. Good luck. I'll support you. But there's one more thing."

"Let me guess. He's a transsexual too."

"He had drinks with Brittany Wednesday night. And he didn't mention he was dating you."

CHAPTER 61

Just as they were about to get ready for bed, a text came in on Jeff's phone. He glanced at it quickly, didn't read it, and shoved it back in his pocket. Genie was hit with a feeling faster than a deployed airbag. But no way was she giving in to it. No tears, no fears, no rage. But no chump either. So she made sure she sounded casual with her question. As innocent as... Would you like ketchup on your steak or A-1?

"Jeff, why didn't you read the text?"

"I'm with you. I'll answer it later."

"But you always answer texts when we're together. We both do. Why not this one?"

"Why are you questioning me like that?"

"We've never hidden phones before. And you *always* respond to texts."

"I don't like what you're suggesting. You think I'm gonna screw around on you?"

"I don't think you would do that. It's just that in the past, you never hid your phone before. So it makes me uncomfortable because it's a change."

"And it makes me uncomfortable that you would think I'm the sort of person who would be this close to you, and be with someone else at the same time."

Genie was careful and slow with her words. "Well, if I got a text, I'd tell you who it was. I'd never need to keep that from you."

"And I'd never ask you to show me a text. I trust you unconditionally. I'll always give you the benefit of the doubt."

"You trust because I offer full disclosure. Anyway, we don't need to fight about it. Honey, I forgot to tell you. I was talking to Lori and guess who she's kind of friends with? Someone you know. A girl named Brittany?"

"Brittany Hager? Yeah, she's my neighbor."

With generic interest Genie asked: "Did you ever date her?"

"We went out once. Never turned into anything."

"I heard you were out with her the other night."

"She called to get my opinion of a business she's thinking of getting involved in."

Genie felt immediate relief: A legitimate explanation.

"Jeff, you want something from the kitchen? I'm gonna get some water."

"Sure. I'll have some."

She went to the kitchen and texted Lori. She wanted to clear Jeff with this proof. *Lor, they had a business meeting Wednesday night. That's legit.*

Lori texted back. *Hmmm. Well he is a doctor. Maybe he gave her an erection. I mean injection.*

Genie texted back. *Very funny.*

Lori texted back. *Ask him about it. See what he says.*

Genie walked back to Jeff with a glass of water. He was now in bed. As she went in the bathroom to wash her face, she called out to continue the conversation. And her tone was as casual as flannel pajamas.

"It's funny, Jeff, 'cause I guess Brittany didn't know we were going out."

"I don't talk about my personal life."

"But you're friends."

"Not close friends."

"Jeff, Lori said that Brittany was at your house many times. It's not wrong. You didn't even know me. But why wouldn't you tell me that?"

"Maybe she was at my house. I really don't remember."

Genie came back in the room and got into bed. She turned to face Jeff.

"You don't remember if she was at your house?"

"Genie, she's a neighbor. I'm sure she was over. What's the big deal?"

"The big deal is that I'm not sure why you'd lie. It's so obvious you guys had sex. She talked to her friends while it was going on."

Suddenly, Genie knew she was in trouble. Big trouble. Not because he screamed. This was more like a bomb in a pillow. Genie swore she could hear his temper ticking as he took is glasses off.

"Look, Genie. You have total control of our future here. And be honest. Don't say what you think I want to hear. Tell me the truth so we can both move on if need be. Do you trust me?"

CHAPTER 62

Lori stuck the sushi in her mouth before she spoke.

"Those are the words of a very clever cheater. No doubt in my mind, Genes. The guy is a brilliant snake."

"Ok Lor, I know he's lying about Brittany but you'd really have to know him. He's afraid I'll judge him. He didn't care about her. He'd think I'd get upset or think it meant more to him. He doesn't want me insecure."

Lori was sarcastic. "Oh, you know you've made an excellent point. This is arrived at I'm sure, by the infinite ways he's shown us that he's ever so concerned with your feelings. And you feeling secure, bless his soul."

"Ok, ok. But then what possible reason would he have to lie?"

"It's still going on, Gene. Or it will be. And he doesn't want you on his case."

"He's totally right. Nobody wants to have someone checking in on their stuff. It's intrusive."

"Or they're actually hiding something. It's relationship blackmail. They threaten you with a break-up if you so much as suspect them. Meanwhile, they get to keep you and the other bitch, or bitches in plural, at the same time. I gotta hand it to the guy, Gene. He's *smooth.* What was his ACT score?"

"What?"

"College entry exams. Did he score high?"

Genie had to laugh. "I can't believe you're asking me that!"

"Good cheaters always score high."

"Lor, based on *my* experience with him, there's no reason for me not to trust him. Unless I've caught him in the act."

"Genie. You weren't suspicious until he hid his phone. And lied about Brittany. Why are you doubting your instincts?"

"Well, I wouldn't want him to see certain texts with my girlfriends. That's a privacy issue."

"What if he thought it was a guy. What if he thought you were cheating?"

"I'd show him to reassure him."

"That's right. You'd have nothing to hide and you'd want him to feel reassured."

"Maybe Jeff is just angry that I don't trust him. I don't think he's a cheater. Not with me. He's really an upstanding person."

"So is Bill Clinton, and Tiger Woods. Cheaters are good people who cheat."

CHAPTER 63

Genie's eyelids felt so heavy she barely had enough energy to wash up. Lori's words wouldn't go away. It wasn't even eight o'clock, but she knew she had to get into bed. She closed her eyes and was almost asleep when the phone rang and startled her. She looked to see who it was. *Danny.*

She hadn't talked to him much at all in the past few weeks. He had been traveling for work, busy with Kay, and Genie had been preoccupied. And on some level, maybe they had backed off from each other a bit. Seeing his name on her phone felt like a big bowl of chicken soup.

"Hello?"

"Hey, Genes. How's my girl?"

"Oh, Dan. It's so good to hear your voice."

"What's the matter? You sound awful."

"No, I'm fine."

"You don't sound fine to me. You want me to come over?"

"Oh, could you?"

"I'll be there in a half hour."

Genie felt revived. She showered quickly because she knew she smelled as bad as she felt. When Danny knocked at the door, Genie ran up and held on to him longer than usual. He felt so warm and cozy. His sweatshirt was thick and soft, and he smelled like a good game of softball.

They sat down on the sofa. His sweater was light blue, his jeans were faded but clean. His face had a Sunday shadow and Genie felt such a lift sitting next to him it took her by surprise. In the most magical way, it reminded her of her dad. He would come home from a trip, sit on her bed, and ask her about her week. She used to study his clothes in the same way. And on Sundays he never shaved.

"So, what's wrong?"

Genie suddenly felt homesick, right there on her own sofa. "Danny, I don't know. I feel so confused about everything." Tears began to roll down her cheek. "I've been seeing Ellen and that's made me so emotional. Work is stressful. Things with Jeff are... I don't even know. I can't tell if we're a great couple or a horrible one. I've never been so conflicted."

Danny opened his arms and Genie rested her head on his shoulder. He smoothed her hair back. She wiped her nose on the back of her hand, sniffing, coughing, and choking.

"Genes. Remember that white sweatshirt I left here?"

Genie wiped her eyes again. "Yeah. What about it?"

"I might need to wear it home."

Genie laughed through her stuffed nose.

"Did something happen with Jeff?"

"I'm not sure."

"You're not sure?"

"No. I'm not sure of anything."

"Do you love him?"

"Yes."

"Does he love you?"

"Yes."

"Well, then you're sure of *something*."

Genie squeezed Danny harder. "Danny?"

"Yeeees."

"The way I feel around you. In your arms. On our bike rides. Every time we're together..."

Danny kept silent.

"I feel so *safe*. It's really the most wonderful feeling in the world."

Danny continued to hold Genie. He kept stroking her hair. She felt like she could hold him forever. A part of her wanted to kiss him but she didn't dare. She leaned back, kissed him on the cheek, got up from the sofa and walked into the bathroom to wash her face. Danny went to the kitchen and pulled a water bottle out of the fridge.

Danny sat down to watch TV. When Genie came back to the room she asked if he wanted a sandwich and Danny said yes. As she was making it, she felt happy, calm, and content. She set the plate in front of him. She sat down next to him, but after a few minutes she sensed something off in his expression. He almost seemed resentful. She couldn't put her finger on it but she got a terrible feeling in her stomach.

"Dan, is something wrong? You seem funny."

"No, there's nothing wrong." Genie was convinced now that something definitely was. His tone was different.

"Why are you acting so cold?"

"I'm not cold."

"You're different. Really, what is it?"

Danny looked at Genie. "Will you stop? You want me to make something up so you can feel satisfied?"

"Dan, please. You're the one person I can count on to be real. What just happened?"

Danny shook his head and smiled. "I can't say."

"Why not?"

"It wouldn't be right."

"What wouldn't be right?"

"Look. You are involved with someone. So am I."

"But if you're having a feeling about something, can't you share it with me? We're best friends."

"That's right. We are." Danny picked up the plate. "Listen, I really appreciate the sandwich but I'm not that hungry. Do you feel like you can get some sleep now?"

Genie started to cry. "Danny, please don't leave right now. Not like this. I can't stand that something's wrong and you won't tell me. Please don't go."

"Nothing is wrong. We are fine, I promise."

Genie looked up at him like a child. As he stood up to leave, Genie grabbed him toward her. She put her arms around his neck. She kissed him on his cheek. She kissed him on his neck. "You promise, really? You promise that we're fine?"

"I do."

He walked toward the door, opened it, and without looking back, he left. Genie sat on her sofa and stared into space. After an hour, she went straight to bed, closed her eyes, and cried herself to sleep.

CHAPTER 64

"*Steven, are you out of your mind?*"

Steven's feet were on the desk and he was leaning back in his chair. "It wasn't my idea, Genes. I'm just telling you what Bill's wishes are."

Genie was beyond frustrated. "Aren't we supposed to surprise *one person* at the surprise party? Not a *hundred?*"

"What can I tell you, Gene?" Steven brought his feet down and sat upright in his chair. "He wants the guests surprised too."

"Why on earth would he want that? Who cares if the guests know?"

"He doesn't trust that someone won't leak it to the media."

Genie tapped a pen on her desk and then put the pen in her mouth. How to get a whole group someplace…

"Ok Steven, tell the guests that Bill is in a movie. And the director is looking for extras."

"I don't like it, Gene. They're not going to fly all the way to some island to be an extra."

Genie had a hopeful tone. "Tell them Brad Pitt plays the lead. Name some other stars too. And say that some of the guests will be picked for a small part."

Steven was sarcastic. "Not bad, Genes. Just hand over Brad's number and I'll give him a call."

"Cute, Steven."

"Genie, come on! You're not thinking. What are we supposed to do when they get there and there's no Brad? Don't you think they might start asking questions?"

"They'll know the stars are going to keep to themselves until they need to report to the set. And the set will be... *the wedding.*"

Steven's face perked up with interest. He was quiet, running it through his head.

"Ok Gene, I've got it. We tell them the story is a romantic comedy and the ending is a wedding on a beach. When the bride gets there and sees the scene, that's when he can tell her. And then we run from the pissed off guests who thought they'd meet Brad Pitt!"

Genie laughed. "No, Steven. We get her to walk down the aisle *without* knowing it's her wedding. It's much more fun."

Steven looked at Genie with a blank face. "What reason would she possibly have to walk down that aisle without suspecting it's her own wedding?"

"Steven, never underestimate the value of over twenty years of my fantasies. I, my friend, have a plan."

CHAPTER 65

Thursdays are spent with Bobby the trainer. He was close to Genie in age, really cute, with a tough edge. While Genie pumped iron, she pumped him for his perspective. Their workout sessions always included recaps of things he did with his wife, and funny stories about their weekends.

Genie was on her second set of squats. "Is Chelsea allowed to get mad at you about stupid things?"

"Are you kidding me? She always gets mad at me for stupid things."

"And you're ok with that?"

"I don't see that I have much choice in the matter."

Genie winced and blew out a puff of air. "Does she ever tell you you're an asshole?"

"Genie, I'm a guy. Guys are assholes."

Genie laughed. "Wow. If I ever called Jeff an asshole I'd lose him for two weeks."

Bobby laughed. "I think that constitutes asshole!"

• • •

Later that afternoon, Jeff and Genie met at the mall for lunch. Afterwards, they decided to walk around, maybe browse in some of the stores. They talked about their days, things going on at work, and Genie began looking at Jeff's face in a subdued stare.

"What?"

Genie smiled.

"What's that look, Gino? What's on your alleged mind?"

"Jeff, you know why I got quiet last night at the game?"

"Why?"

"When the text came in and you didn't answer it, I knew I couldn't say anything. I know you're right, that I just need to trust you. But it's hard. I get insecure."

"Genie, you create scenarios that get us into trouble. You let your imagination run off to all sorts of places. If you can't trust me, it will ruin us because I can't be constantly doubted. Remember… benefit of the doubt."

They walked by a jewelry store.

"Genie, let's walk in here and take a look."

"I don't care about jewelry, Jeff. You know that."

"I know. But I want to give you something so you feel secure. What would you like?"

Genie looked at Jeff. "Nothing now. But one day if we're there… a ring I guess."

"Let's go look."

Genie was shocked. "Not today! I meant in the future."

Jeff smiled. "Let's just go take a look."

Jeff took Genie's hand. They went inside the store. Jeff told the woman they'd like to look at rings. Genie specified something simple. The woman led them to a grouping of rings that were high end, almost antique looking, very classic, and brilliant. Genie tried on a few of them, and Jeff was very involved in the process.

"Genes, which one do you like?"

"I like the first one. Which one do you like?"

"I like that one too. Would you like me to buy it for you today?"

Genie didn't know what to say. Was he proposing to her?

"Jeff, I don't exactly know what you..."

Jeff looked at the woman behind the counter. "Would you excuse us for just a moment?"

The woman backed off quickly. "Of course! Take all the time you need."

Jeff took Genie's hand. He turned to face her. "Gino, I want to spend the rest of my life with you. I know we have issues but we just need to get through them. Ok?"

Genie looked at Jeff. His face was gently smiling and his eyes were so reassuring. She nodded and kissed him. He kissed her back and hugged her.

"I'd like to buy this ring for you today knowing that the next one we buy seals the deal. By then, I know you'll be traveling so we can have an awesome honeymoon. How does that sound to you?"

Genie looked at Jeff. She knew without a doubt that they would be together forever. She reached up and hugged him again. She began to cry. He squeezed her harder. And within thirty minutes, ring on finger, they were out the door.

CHAPTER 66

Genie was in her pajamas, on her way to get a glass of water, and as she approached the kitchen, she heard her mom and Aunt Dottie talking softly. Genie knew this was one of those talks that she wasn't supposed to hear. So she made sure to listen closely.

"I wish I hadn't found it, Dottie. What am I supposed to do with this information?"

"Are you sure it was after you were married? Maybe it was an old love letter and he saved it. Or even forgot he had it?"

"It referred to us. To me."

"Oh, God. I can't believe it. I'm so sorry, Jenny. Do you think it was serious?"

"I can't tell. It seemed affairish, you know? Like over the top but shallow. Not the way he talked to me. Not the kind of closeness we had. It was love gibberish."

"Jenny, I'm sure it didn't mean anything to him. He probably met her on one of his trips away. Men do that, you know? It was just a stupid indiscretion. Don't let it taint what you had. He made a mistake. That's what he would tell you if he was alive today."

"Do you think he would deny it, Dottie?"

"Maybe. If he thought it would hurt you more to know. But I know what I would do. I'd confess it right away. I wouldn't be able to live with the lie."

"Me either. The lie would feel dirtier than the cheat."

Genie sensed that her mom and her aunt might soon be leaving the kitchen. She took her steps carefully as she headed back to her bedroom. She got under the covers and reached for her bear. She had a strange sensation in her stomach. All she could think about was how hungry she was and how she wished she could get something to eat. Outside her bedroom door, Genie heard their voices again as they left the kitchen and headed toward the front door.

"Jen, if I were you I'd just put it away. There's nothing you can do with this information."

"I know. But how do you do that? Put something *away*. How do I stop picturing him with someone else?"

"I guess you let it run around up there until it gets tired. And I think you have to replace the bad part of what you heard with the good part of what you had." Jennifer teared up.

"Jimmy really loved you, Jen. Whatever he did was just him fucking up. You know?" Jennifer nodded, the tears running down her cheeks.

Dotty paused. She spoke quietly and carefully. "Jen. When Jimmy was on that plane, and he knew it was going down… who do you think *he* pictured?"

Jennifer was jarred by the question. She had pictured his last moments too many times to count. She had thought about what ran through his mind as he realized what was happening. The fear, the terror, the thought of his life about to come to an end. She had *obsessed* about it over and over. She had felt so horrible for him, knowing he was thinking about his wife and his daughter, knowing he would never see them again. Now, with this new information, she wasn't so sure that she and Genie were the images he held onto.

After hugging and kissing her sister goodbye, she went back into the kitchen. She poured herself a glass of wine. She sat at the table for another hour. Finally, she walked to her bedroom, took off her clothes and got into bed without turning off the lights. She stared at the ceiling in a trance.

Outside Jennifer's room, her daughter was sitting on the floor. Genie could see the light from under the door. She waited forty minutes until she heard the click of the lamp and saw the room was dark. When she believed her mom was sleeping soundly, she went to the kitchen and got herself a handful of cookies. She returned to her room and within five minutes she was sound asleep.

CHAPTER 67

Looking at Ellen, one would have to wonder. Did *she* ever have sore knees from climbing on countertops?

"Ellen, my eating is over the top."

"Genie, structuring food is the best way to control the bingeing. And if you don't binge, you *will* lose weight since the extra calories come from there. Picking and grazing is begging a binge to happen. A satisfying meal with a beginning and an end is the way to keep your weight in check."

"You know, I don't remember my mom overeating *ever.* Even when my dad died, my mom never overate. Why couldn't *that* have been genetically passed on?"

Ellen laughed. "Genie, when people are in upheaval, it's not unusual to take that to food and obsessing. When we're in deep pain and loss though, like your mom, typically that's when we lose our appetites."

"But I remember her obsessing."

"About food?"

"No, about the crash. She couldn't stop talking about all the things that could have prevented him from being on the plane."

"Yes, but that's not obsessing about a created drama like food. It's obsessing about what really happened. It's like the mind saying, I can't believe it. Your brain keeps replaying the events over and over again. That kind of obsessing, though it doesn't feel healthy, actually is based on a truth or finding the truth. When you plow through the grief, or find the truth, the obsessing begins to fade out."

"So my mom kind of did it right."

"Yes, but what she didn't do following the crash was to *manage* the grief."

"How do you manage grief?"

"In increments. Time for grief, back to life, cry and obsess, run an errand, feel horrible like you'll never survive, then laugh with a friend. That's healthy grieving."

"Oh, there was no leaving it with my mom. It was constant until she met Gregg."

"Right. Had she gotten a job sooner, or forced herself out, or spent time with her daughter, she probably wouldn't have fallen as deeply into the depression. And that's how she left you, in a sense. You're still grieving that today in your relationship with Jeff, every time he leaves."

"I'm not eating when he's leaving."

"Good. That means you're feeling the feelings."

"I'm eating now *before* I'm going to see him. I've noticed now that every time before I have plans to go over to his place, I take longer to get ready. I end up in the kitchen."

"So what do you think you're feeling?"

"Confusion. He's so loving. But I always have to go to him. His place, his friends, his family, his schedule, his rules of how a couple should be and if I have any complaints, I'm just not let into all those places until he decides my time out is over. My punishment for complaining."

Ellen nodded. "That's what we talked about. If you choose to stay in this relationship, it's going to require that you…"

"…Need to be a Barbie doll. Seen but not heard unless it's to agree and support him."

"Genie, deprivation of voice is exactly like deprivation of food. And being a Barbie Doll is classic with eating disorders. So, my question is, what exactly are you getting from this relationship?"

"Being with someone I love, I guess. And who is so in love with me. We make each other laugh. We are intensely in sync and connected. So when things get bad, I just want to get us back there."

"Genie, what do you remember about your father?"

Genie was somewhat taken by surprise. "Not a whole lot. I remember him in flashes."

"What do you remember feeling around him?"

"Happy. I felt really happy. He was so… energetic and full of life. He was very handsome. Women used to flirt with him wherever we went, I remember that."

"How did that feel to you?"

"I liked it. I felt lucky to be the girl he was with. He was wonderful to me. Very attentive."

"What else? What other memories do you have?"

"He was the opposite of my mom. She was afraid of everything. He was fearless. She was rigid and he was a free spirit. I remember when he taught me to ride a bike. She was a wreck and kept yelling for me to slow down. He wanted me to pedal faster until my hair blew back in the wind. He told me that. He wanted me to ride fast enough to feel the breezes."

Ellen smiled. "Did they fight?"

"Yes."

"How did you handle that?"

"I don't remember being concerned. It was normal to fight in my house. Well, normal for *them* to fight."

"And if you had a feeling or complained to your dad?"

Genie thought back. "I don't remember having those kinds of feelings before he died. I think I was really happy. There was balance when he was alive."

"So, when your father died, is that when you became more like your mom? More fearful?"

"That's funny, I never thought about that but you're right. When I lost my dad I lost my own free spiritedness. You know, Ellen, I stopped riding my bike after he died. I didn't ride again until Danny insisted I ride with him."

"And were you afraid?"

Genie nodded. "No, I wasn't. I felt totally safe with him."

They looked at each other intently.

"Ellen, what do I do about the food now?"

"Genie."

"Yes?"

"Do you see what you just did?"

"What?"

"You talked about feeling safe with Danny and you immediately brought up the food."

"Hah. I guess I did."

"Sometimes, feeling safe and comfortable is uncomfortable."

"Huh?"

Ellen smiled. "You are so used to feeling not safe and not loved that it's familiar to you. Feeling loved, taken care of, and safe is... *foreign*. Something to think about."

"Ok, I'll do that. But can you tell me in the meantime what I do about food?"

Ellen laughed. "Know that right now, you're having a tough time emotionally. So you need to take care of yourself. Don't let yourself get too hungry. Remember the rules not to deprive your cravings. Stick to structured meals and snacks. Write it down if you have to. Anything to keep it not chaotic."

"I feel like I'll binge or overeat if I *don't* deprive the cravings. Like I won't stop."

"You haven't been able to stop in the past. But I think that's because the food wasn't allowed. Eat food, leave food. Feel feelings, leave them. Don't look to Jeff to validate them. And in all places Genie, when it comes to food and your life... *Listen to your gut.*"

CHAPTER 68

Steven was up to something. The reason Genie knew this was that he seemed way too keen on getting Genie out of the office for lunch. When Steven went to the freezer and pulled out the white box, Genie finally understood.

Genie was incredulous. "Lean Cuisine? *Really?*"

Steven looked busted and nonchalant. "Oh, is it Lean Cuisine? I didn't notice the brand. I just like Macaroni and Cheese."

Genie laughed. "You lie! Steven, a diet is not the way to lose weight."

"Yeah, well I tried overeating but it didn't take the weight off."

"Steven, a diet is not where you gain control."

"Genes, I don't mean to insult, but you're kind of the last person I'd take diet advice from. Why not stick to something you know like, I don't know… laundry detergent. With all the bingeing I know your clothes must take a beating. So you tell me, Tide or All Temperature Cheer?"

Genie paused as something clicked inside. "Isn't tonight when your mother's coming?"

"Yep. Dinner at six."

"Steven, don't you see? You're eating like crazy because you're so uncomfortable around her and it's making you run to food. Instead of making the connection Ellen's talking about, you go on a diet, distracting yourself from what's really going on!"

The timer to the microwave dinged. Steven pulled out the steaming entree and put it on the counter.

"Genie, don't be ridiculous. Sometimes I just overeat. Everyone does. I diet and it comes off. And I have no problem with Bertha coming. I'll deal with it like I deal with everything else."

"Oh really? And how long have you been *overeating?* Would you say it's been about the last week or so? I mean, coincidentally?"

Steven thought. He flinched a bit. "Yeah. I'd say about a week."

"Uh huh. Hypothesis confirmed. You got anxious as it got closer and began stuffing yourself with food."

Steven imitated a stage actor. "By Golly, I *have* been eating my Frosted Cheeri-woes."

"Don't make fun, Steven. There really is a reason you're eating."

"It's called hunger."

"It's called discomfort. And I think it's because you haven't made a choice."

"I chose Mac and Cheese over Linguini."

"Steven, either A, cancel the dinner with your mom because you don't feel right meeting her, or B, choose to meet her but be aware of the feelings."

"I choose C."

Genie laughed. "Why don't you cancel with her?"

"I can't."

"Well, maybe you need to tell her how you feel. I mean, she *is* making the effort to see you. Maybe she's trying to apologize. But either way Steven, I really do get it now. I mean, I can't always do it but I'm getting better. The control over food comes from taking control of your life and decisions."

Steven walked over to the Lean Cuisine and slowly took off the cellophane. He burned his hand on the steam. He let out a squeal, shook his hand for relief, and as he was about to grab a fork, he suddenly changed his stance. Steven looked over at the coat rack and grabbed a black trench coat. He put it around the back of his neck like a cape. He stood over the macaroni and cheese container and drew himself up like a superhero. He pointed to the food and spoke with a stern comic strip voice. "You! Stop that steaming!"

Genie looked at him, rolling her eyes. Steven continued.

"I've had enough of you and your cheesy ways! Your saucy comments! Your plastic values! YOU LISTEN TO ME!!!!!!"

Genie began to laugh, watching the performance.

"I WILL TAKE NO MORE OF YOUR SERVING SUGGESTIONS! I DON'T APPROVE OF YOUR DAILY VALUES! YOUR DIETARY FIBERS CAUSE MY BOWELS TO MOVE, AND YOUR NUTRITIONAL FACTS AREN'T... *FUN!* I WILL FACE MY FEELINGS. I WILL LOSE POUNDS. AND I WILL CONQUER BERTHA!"

* * *

Later that night, Steven sat in the lounge of the restaurant. As he waited, he reached for some nuts that were sitting in a bowl by his drink. As he brought the nuts to his mouth, he looked around in paranoia and put the nuts back in the bowl.

"Hello, Steven. Sorry I'm late, Dear."

Steven's mother was a tall, thin, attractive woman in her mid sixties. From her Gucci pumps to her Hermes scarf, she was stylish and elegant. Steven stood up and kissed Bertha on her cheek.

"No problem. I just got here myself. Our table is ready though, if you want to sit down."

"Wonderful."

When they had settled in the booth, Bertha began her routine.

"I haven't been in the city for so long I'd forgotten what it looked like."

"I know. You've never even seen my place."

"No, I must get over there sometime. How's the fish here?"

"I don't know, Mother. Last time I was here I had steak. And I think Michael had..."

"Oh, well I'm sure the fish is just fine. Oh by the way, before I forget, do you remember Mary Fine?" Bertha took off her scarf and gloves, folded them neatly and placed them on the seat beside her. "She's getting married next weekend."

Steven didn't respond. The waiter came to introduce himself.

"How are you folks doing tonight? My name is Paul and I'll be your server. Can I bring either of you anything to drink?"

Bertha spoke first. "I'll have a Chardonnay, please."

Steven pointed to his drink. I'll have another Absolute with a splash of cranberry." Paul walked away.

"And your friend Ben just had his first baby. I think they named him..."

"Mother, why don't you look at the menu."

With a subtle surrender she opened the menu and read through the options. A minute later, Paul returned with the drinks.

Bertha spoke. "How's the sea bass?"

In a flagrant and upbeat tone, Paul responded. "I absolutely adore the sea bass. It's a very rich fish as you know but the sauce is actually very delicate. It's a divine blend of natural juices, a hint of fennel, reduced in wine, and..."

Bertha had a pained and irritated expression. "Thank you. I'll have the Caesar salad and the Amish roasted chicken."

"Delicious as well. And you, Sir?"

"I'll trust your recommendation and try the sea bass. I'll have the spinach and beet salad to start off."

"Terrific."

When Paul left, Bertha opened her napkin with obvious irritation. When she spoke it was almost as though Steven wasn't there.

"I don't understand why they have to force it down your throat."

Steven knew exactly what she meant. "Force what?"

"Their..."

"Their what?"

She spoke in a whisper. "They don't have to make it so obvious."

"You mean they don't have to act like '*fags*'?"

"I never said that!"

"You didn't have to."

"I have nothing against anyone making choices for themselves. I just don't see why it has to be advertised in that... style, that's all."

"And what style is that?"

"They don't have to talk and dress that way... as though they're wearing a big sign that says 'I'm a homosexual'. Why do they have to flaunt it?"

Steven was angered beyond control.

"I don't know, Mother. Why do you wear five-carat diamond rings and clothes with price tags that could feed a family of twelve? I understand you have money and all, but why do you have to flaunt it?"

Flabbergasted. "That's entirely different and you know it."

"How?" said Steven arrogantly.

"I don't wear jewelry to flaunt wealth. I wear it because it..."

"It lets everyone know who you are. That you're just a bit better than everyone else. But I see your point. The nerve of somebody to talk or dress in a manner that reflects who he is. It would be a whole lot more respectful if he let us know his financial status instead."

"Steven, you are twisting this to support your own lifestyle."

"No, I'm just calling you on yours."

There was a silence as she caught her reaction. "One is simply a style of dress. The other is a sexual preference that needs to stay private."

"Did Paul describe his sexual encounters? I thought he was just talking about the fish sauce. Oh wait! How did I miss it! *The natural juices!* Mom, I gottta hand it to you, you really know your stuff!"

She slammed her palm on the table. "I've heard enough!"

"No, you haven't. I want to know why you can't accept people, or your own son for that matter, for who they are. Who are you to judge?"

"I don't judge. I just..."

"What, Mom? You don't like me?"

With her voice cracking, on the verge of tears, she said: "Of course I like you. I love you."

"Then why did you cut me off?"

"I didn't cut you off. *You* backed off from *us*."

"I backed off from you because you made it clear you didn't approve."

"We didn't disapprove. We just felt uncomfortable, that's all. It's not what we ever expected."

"Yeah, well I guess we both got surprised then. 'Cause I never expected that I'd be rejected by my own family."

Paul approached the table with the salads. "Here you go. Fresh pepper?"

Bertha looked up at Paul. Her eyes welled up with tears. Her face softened.

"Yes, thank you so much."

Paul smiled warmly. "My pleasure. Enjoy your salads."

Bertha spoke abruptly as Paul turned from the table.

"Paul!" The waiter turned around and took a step back to the table.

"Yes, Ma'am."

"Is it too late to change my order? I'd like to try the sea bass."

Paul smiled. "It's never too late to change."

CHAPTER 69

It was the last Kabbalah class of session one. Jessica reviewed what they'd learned so far. She asked the students to tell stories of situations they had handled differently since starting class. And then she got a look that said, I'm about to teach you something *big.*

"I want you to take a piece of paper and fill it up with your doubts. Whatever you want in your life, but doubt you can make happen, write it down— and be sure to fill the whole page."

All of the students began to write. Half of Genie's page was filled with her fears and whether she could overcome them. The other half was filled with doubt about Jeff, about trusting him, about whether he could be a good partner, and whether they could ever really get along.

Jessica spoke again. "So here are some facts. Thoughts come into our brain. Chemicals are released and then they turn into feelings. What we do with those feelings is a choice. It's a decision. Remember, feelings don't mean a thing. Doubt is the work of the opponent. Sometime soon, when you are ready, you're going to take that sheet of doubt and you're going to burn it. Doubt no longer has a place in your life. Instead, you're going to replace it with a new word that comes straight from the light. That word is *certainty.*"

Jessica stood at her podium, looked around the room, and smiled. Her voice was loud and spirited. Her energy was undiluted.

"The light loves you. The light wants everything good for you. If there's something you want, it's there. Anything at all, it's actually waiting for you. That is a spiritual, universal fact. Certainty is a decision. So whatever it is that you want, but doubt, throw away the doubt and proceed as though you know for certain it will happen."

Genie raised her hand. "So what if your doubt was right? Like it came from your gut as a warning, you throw away that doubt and you end up getting burned."

"Great question! The thing is, you can never get burned from the light. Because even if it turns out that the doubt came from an intuition that was correct, you will have new information, and you'll be in a different place where you can make another decision with certainty. When you live the truth only, and when you follow The Proactive Formula, giving, sharing, resisting, and receiving light, you are protected. Step outside of your comfort. Do the opposite of what you normally do. The light will take care of you always."

Genie drove home after class with a plan of *no doubt.* She would fly in that plane. Her relationship with Jeff would be great and they'd live a long life together. The happiness she felt from those decisions, and the certainty she felt, was enough to make her fly home. What she learned, however, was that The Proactive Formula should never be decided upon while operating a vehicle. The only light that comes from that is the flashing one that pulls you over and costs you a day in court!

CHAPTER 70

The snooze button lost again. The next morning, Genie woke up with an energy that was unyielding. Jeff would be leaving the following week for New York. Genie went online, bought an airplane ticket to accompany him, walked into the office and jumped on Steven piggyback style.

Steven yelled at her. “What are you doing?”

“Going on a fairy ride!” Steven backed up toward the desk and unloaded Genie on top of it. “Steven, I want you to be the first to know. I made a reservation.”

“Wonderful. But don’t forget, I don’t like French or Thai.”

“It’s American.”

“Make it a steak house.”

“Steven, American *Airlines*.”

“Genie, the airlines don’t serve food anymore. Can’t you pick a better place?”

Genie laughed. “I’m going to meet Jeff in New York next Thursday.”

Steven turned around and faced Genie. “What kind of drugs have you got?”

“Airborne.”

"Oh boy. And I've decided that the week leading up to that, I will be out of the country. Not available by text or by phone. I'm putting a freeze on all our credit cards because I'm afraid you'll eat us to debt."

"Hey, thanks for the support, Steven! I'm so easy going I'm traveling carry-on."

"Yeah, you'll *carry on*, I'm sure. And I've got news for you, Sister. When American Airlines finds missing baggage, they return it. So don't leave a return address on your issues."

• • •

Genie showed up at Jeff's unannounced. She pushed him back from the front door into his foyer, and told him to stand against the wall.

"Genie, what are you doing?"

"Just watch."

She stood on the opposite end of the room, held her nose, took both of her feet together and made a huge jump to the center of the room.

Jeff laughed. "What was that?"

"I just jumped in the pool with you. I'm two feet in! *No more fear.*"

Jeff smiled. "Oh yeah? How so?"

"I decided to make reservations to fly to New York and I'll meet you there next week!"

"You're really doing it?"

"Yep. Are you happy?"

Jeff smiled. "That's awesome, Gino." He wrapped his arms around her. She was so full of excitement and energy it moved her to the next topic.

"Jeff, I really just stopped to give you the news. I kinda gotta go."

"Go where?"

"I want to take a look at that car I'm thinking of buying. I'd like to get it this week if I can. Want me to call you later?"

"You want me to come with you? I might be able to talk him down more."

"Are you kidding, I'd love it!"

• • •

Joe was the salesman who offered Genie the best price and payment plan. They all stepped into his office while he ran the numbers.

"As I told Genie, I can give it to you for $40,000 and that's down from the sticker at $42,000. If you put down $6000 with a finance charge of 6%... it's about $550 a month."

Jeff spoke to Joe. "So if she buys the car today, what's your best offer?"

"Well, that's a really good offer."

Jeff was gentle but confident. "I understand. But I'm looking for an even better one."

Joe moved about in his chair. "Well, I could maybe shave $20 off the monthly. But other than that, I really can't do anything more. See, we're not like other dealerships. We price our cars to sell so we have less room for negotiation."

"And what about the down payment? $6000 is more than she wanted to pay. Can you bring that down?"

"Not really. That I can't move on."

Jeff looked at Genie. "Joe, will you excuse us?"

Genie walked out with Jeff. "I think there's room. The economy sucks right now and he's gonna want to sell that car. Let me see if I can get him down."

"Jeff, he said that's his lowest."

"Just go along with me, ok?"

They walked back into the office. Jeff held his hand out to Joe.

"Joe, thanks so much. I think we're going to shop it a bit more. Here's my card."

"Thanks, Jeff. So what if I could get that monthly down $40 instead of $20?"

Jeff shrugged. "That's better. But I'm looking to bring down the down payment. We'll call you." Jeff led Genie out the door.

As they walked toward the parking lot, Genie was crazed. "Jeff, what are you doing?"

"We haven't gotten the walk away deal yet. Just wait."

Sure enough, Joe came out to the parking lot as they were about to get in their car.

"Jeff, I can bring that $6000 down to $5500."

Jeff shrugged. "That's better. I've just got one more guy I want to talk to. I'll let you know on Monday." Jeff motioned for Genie to get in the car, and then he drove away.

"Jeff, you're blowing it! There's only so far he can go!"

"And only so far you can go. Somewhere in the middle is the price where everybody stretches but still gets what they want. If we can't find that place, the deal doesn't happen, right?"

"I guess. But I really want it."

"So does he. If he can budge, we'll hear from him soon. In the meantime, you hungry?"

Thirty minutes later as they sat at lunch, Jeff's cell phone rang. Jeff looked to see who it was. He smiled at Genie and took the call.

He talked a few moments but the restaurant was loud and Genie couldn't hear what he was saying. Finally he hung up. In an almost arrogant way, he took a bite of his sandwich.

"Jeff!" He looked up with innocence, chewing and smacking his lips.

"Stop that!" Genie was laughing. "What happened?"

"Sixty bucks off the monthly and $1000 off the down payment."

"No way! How in the world did you do that!"

"Genie, always remember. It's not in the conversation. You've got your best shot when you walk."

CHAPTER 71

Genie woke up startled but she didn't know what had woken her. Her vision was blurry and she couldn't move. As she tried to focus, her eyes were drawn to the chair in the corner of her bedroom. She saw a figure there.

"Dad?"

"I'm here, Blue Genes. Right here."

"It's really you?

"Not exactly in the flesh. But it's me, Sweetheart."

Genie sat up in her bed. "After all this time?"

"Honey, I wish I could see you more often. They're a bit stingy with the passes up there."

Holy shit. That was exactly something he'd say. She was frozen, not knowing what to do. Suddenly she felt like a five-year old girl. "Daddy, can I just have a hug?"

"We hug every day. You just don't know it."

Genie looked around the room recording the details to make sure she was really awake.

"Genie. You need to know that flying isn't what killed me."

Genie looked at him again, in shock. "What are you saying? Of course it did."

"No, the crash did. You can fly and *not* get killed. I need you to understand and believe that."

Genie stared at him.

"And Honey, you can love without being in pain. When you fall in love and it's right, you don't crash."

Genie cried, "But Dad. What if he says I'm the one causing the crash?"

"You give him a kick on the way out the door. If someone really loves you, unselfishly, they won't let you crash. You deserve better than that. You hear me? You do."

Genie looked at his face and studied it. He was exactly as she remembered. And then a thought came into her head. She wanted it to go away, but it was bigger than her power to thwart it. She had to ask.

"Dad. Please forgive me for asking. I have to know. *Did you cheat on Mom?* Was what she found out true?"

He looked her straight in the eye.

"Yes. I was unfaithful."

Genie was stunned. *"Dad."*

"Genes, I'm only sorry I couldn't have been there to make it up to her. I loved her very much. It was my problem. It had nothing to do with her. You tell her I'm sorry. You hear me, Honey? I'm so happy that she's happy. And I know you will be too. That's why I'm here. To let you know that you're going to be ok." He gestured up toward the ceiling with a nod of his head. "I've made some good connections."

Genie began to sit up. She wanted to go hug her dad. She felt more for him now than she ever had. As she stood up and began to head toward him, he slowly faded away. But Genie wasn't upset. She had never been so sure of anything in her life.

He was *with her.*

CHAPTER 72

An average flight to New York, booked in advance, wasn't outrageous in price. But when you tack on the self-help books, motivational tapes, and panic attack phone calls to Ellen, this was one costly overcome fear. The motivation was high. Like Dorothy delivering the witch's broom to the Wizard, it was the deed to a life with Jeff. Three clicks of her heels to go home.

For two days before the trip, Genie sobbed on and off in fear. The light had disappeared and she was under a dark cloud of panic. She unfolded in tears with Jeff as he told her she didn't have to do it. But he talked her through it on the phone, and explained exactly what she should expect. He would pick her up at the airport as soon as she landed, and they would be together.

The morning of the flight, she kept her deal with karma. She gave herself plenty of time and made her bed perfectly. She even wore new underwear; a ritual that always brought a good day. Her hair was good, her outfit was cute, and she still had time for Starbucks. The flight was delayed a few hours, which she was actually grateful for. Around five-thirty, there she was, seated on an airplane.

In all the years she had imagined this moment, wondering if it would ever be, she pictured herself a nervous, crying wreck. Paging the flight attendant in a panic. Having them stop on the runway. Running off the plane and back to the terminal. Instead, she picked up one of her seven magazines, popped an Altoid, and waited for the flight to take off.

In the oddest way imaginable, it felt ok. She breathed, just like Jeff had taught her to do. She pictured her Happy Room. She thought about the people she loved. She imagined a light like a laser beam making a circle of protection around her. The airplane began its race down the runway, and lifted up off the ground.

It was sundown. The colors of the sky were magnificent and the ground appeared to be on a slant as the plane pointed up toward the sky. Gazing at the scene below and the colors surrounding the wings, Genie rested her head back. She surrendered her posture to the flight's position, as if to allow it to carry her.

She thought about her dad, her family, and her friends. She thought about her job, Steven, and her life. She felt insurmountable gratitude for everything that brought her to this day. She surrendered even to *that.* This moment, this flight past her fear, was the thrill of her life so far.

Jeff had told Genie he would pick her up in baggage. What he hadn't told her was that once she got there, she would be greeted by a limo driver holding up a sign that said "Gino". He had failed to mention that the driver would also be holding a giant stuffed bear wearing a pilot's uniform. And he somehow missed the part about the champagne and still warm banana pancakes that would be waiting in the car, along with one very affectionate boyfriend.

They spent the weekend together. Jeff was happy, loving, and grateful. Suspicious things didn't seem so suspicious anymore.

She was with this man she loved and adored. Genie felt *confident.* So why does that thing have to come along and blow such a winning streak?

Didn't opponents *ever* call in sick?

CHAPTER 73

Their first day back home, Jeff had a dinner meeting downtown at six-thirty. Genie, the never questioning, trusting soul she was now, simply made suggestions around it. Knowing on weekdays he was always in bed by nine-thirty at the latest, she figured she'd treat her man right. Jeff was always disappointed when she preferred to sleep at home. She knew he would love this effort.

"Jeff, why don't you call me on your way home? I'll come spend the night."

"Sounds like a plan. I'll call you."

When nine-thirty rolled around, and she hadn't heard from him, she laid on her bed with a book. She wasn't feeling great anyway. She thought to call him but didn't want to bother him if the meeting was running long. She fell asleep. At midnight, a text came in.

On my way home now. Long night. Didn't want to wake you. Love you so much. Talk to you in the morning, Sweetheart.

Something didn't sit right. But she held down the fort of trust with a text back to him.

Sorry you had such a long night. I wasn't feeling so hot myself. Love you too.

Jeff texted back.

What a crazy coincidence! I got so sick I had to lie down! Are you ok now? Hope you're feeling better!

You had to lie down? Where? Weren't you at a restaurant?

At a hotel. They gave me a room so I could rest.

Genie could feel the sensation. It was like walking down the hallways at school, passing the fire alarm that sits behind a sheet of glass. That comment was the hammer. Was there enough smoke to grab the hammer, break the glass, and pull the cheating lever?

Why didn't you call me?

Too sick.

Why didn't you stay the night?

Wanted to get home to the dog.

You always call me when you're sick. And you never worry about waking me up. We had plans to see each other. I don't understand why you didn't call me.

You didn't call me either.

You were in a meeting, Jeff! You said you'd call on the way home.

I did.

Genie had been with Jeff many times when he felt a headache coming on. They weren't infrequent. They also weren't sudden. Usually, he didn't even mention it; she would just notice him being quiet. If she offered to get them out of wherever they were, he was fine to stay. Or he'd leave and want to get home. Never did he have a headache and leave to go lie down somewhere *else.* It wasn't even in his nature.

Genie didn't text back right away. She didn't want to jump. She played it out in her mind. Jeff at a business dinner, feeling sick, getting a room or asking someone to get him a room. Laying down by himself on a hotel bed for a couple hours, too sick to call, afraid to wake her, and then getting up to leave. She knew one hundred percent this story wasn't true. She took the hammer and busted the glass.

Jeff. I'm sorry but I'm not comfortable with this. I've never heard of someone at a business meeting getting sick and taking a room for a few hours. And if it did happen, he'd call his wife or girlfriend to tell her what was going on, especially if they had plans to be together. If you were well enough to get a room, you were well enough to call. And if you weren't, you'd be sick enough that you'd want me to know. Or come down and be with you, just like you have in the past. You've never worried about waking me up. You send me texts in the middle of the night with a joke! This story doesn't add up.

And the text came back.

I do not like what you're suggesting! I was so sick and all you can do is accuse me of something horrible. You haven't even asked what happened. All you're concerned about is yourself. You are the most selfish person I've ever met. And I actually asked how you were! If you don't apologize for this, I don't want to see you ever again. And I mean it Genie. I'm tired of not being trusted."

She texted back.

I'm not going to apologize. That is the most ridiculous story I've ever heard. And if you can't see how bizarre it sounds, or even how unfair the delivery was, then you're right. We don't have anything to talk about and we should just break up.

CHAPTER 74

Two Face. What is it about little girls and their fascination with Batman and his rivals? When Genie was little she fantasized that he would come to take her away. Marry her in Gotham City. Be the father of her little Bat-babies.

Genie, Casey, and Lori were sitting in the Happy Room. Lori was holding Casey's Two Face action figure. She spoke with sarcasm.

"You know Gene, this guy reminds me of someone. I'm trying to think who..."

Casey jumped in.

"Lori, do you know how he got to be Two Face?"

"Well, the Two Face I know that dates a friend of mine starts out as a great guy, has everyone fooled, and then his alter ego comes out."

Casey responded with innocent excitement.

"That's this Two Face too! He's like a lawyer or something named Harvey Dent. But he gets this mob guy Maroni in trouble. Maroni throws acid on his face. So half of him is *really* gross and half of him is like normal."

Lori looked at Casey in amazement.

"Case, I think you're a Two Face. Half kid, half genius."

Casey laughed. "So wait, this is *really* awesome. I learned about it in English. The guys who wrote Batman used examples like… I don't remember their names but they were really creepy. One guy with a mean side *and* a good side."

Genie nodded. "Jekyll and Hyde."

Casey perked up. "Right! Those guys. They made Two Face just like them. My teacher says kids who get abused by their parents can grow up to be like Jek…um…"

Lori interrupted. "I remember that from psych class. I think it's called Jekyll and Hyde Syndrome. Dual personalities."

Casey nodded. "Yeah. Two personalities. They have a good side but they use it to cover up really bad things they do."

Lori loved this. "You know, Case? The guy I know that dates my friend was abused as a boy. He has two sides too and he covers his bad side up with lies. Isn't that *amazing?*"

Genie shot Lori a look. Casey continued without notice.

"Do you guys know about the coin?"

Both women shook their heads.

"Maroni had this lucky double headed coin. The day he threw acid on Harvey Dent's face, this coin fell out of his pocket. Harvey Dent picks it up and keeps it. He takes a knife and scratches one side of the coin, so it's like his face. All messed up. And he like goes crazy about the coin. Like the whole idea that one side's good and one is bad. So whenever he had to decide whether to off a guy, he flipped this coin. When it flipped to the scratched side, it made him think about his own face. He'd get all mad and then he'd kill his victim."

Genie was pensive. Lori picked up her Diet Coke, took a sip, gave a small belch, put the can back on the table and jumped right out with a comment.

"Hey, Gene. If I were you Honey, I'd check Jeff's pockets for double headed change."

CHAPTER 75

Genie and Lori's mouths were wide open in shock. Lori's was full of oatmeal. Sitting at the table of their favorite breakfast place, Steven had just given too many details about his hot night with his boyfriend.

"Oh Girls, don't be such prudes."

Genie defended. "I am not a prude. I can be downright raunchy."

"Oh, please. What's really raunchy for you? Sex in a low thread count?"

Lori laughed. Genie spoke. "I would never tell."

Steven answered. "Then you're a prude, Dude."

Lori put another bite in her mouth before she spoke.

"I'm not a prude, Dude! I'll tell!"

Steven started to get up from the table. "We're going to be late for the movie. Let's pay the check and talk smut while we strut."

Genie giggled. "Yeah, the movie's rated PG and the walk's rated NR17."

Steven paid the check. They walked out the door and headed down the street toward the theatre. Lori started right in.

"Ok, so last night Todd got a new video camera. He wanted me to..."

Genie interrupted. "You didn't."

Lori was defensive. "I had to."

"You *had* to?" Genie reprimanded. "Lori, you could end up on YouTube!"

"That's what I said! But he said it's a way for us to be close. When I said I wasn't comfortable, he kind of backed off. He was hurt I didn't trust him. So I did it. I took one for the team."

Genie was incredulous. "Oh my God! Why is it that you slam my boyfriend but yours pulls that shit and it's okay?"

"It's totally different, Genie. He's not..."

Steven interrupted. "Lori, he knew you were uncomfortable and he manipulated you into it."

"But Steven..."

"Ladies, I'd like to introduce you to my Sour Patch Theory."

Genie and Lori laughed. Genie spoke first. "Like Sour Patch candies? I *love* those!"

Steven the professor made his point. "You may love them. But they are a passive aggressive candy. Genie. What is the first taste of a Sour Patch candy?"

"Sweet."

"That's right." Genie nodded her head, proud that she knew the answer. Steven directed the next question to Lori.

"Lori, once you get past the sugar, what is the second taste?"

"Sour."

"And what is the final taste?"

"Sour."

"Excellent. And rather than end on the sour, you pop another candy to experience the sweet. Would you say that describes the Sour Patch experience correctly?"

Genie was excited. That's what I do with Jeff! The sour is so bad, I have to always run back to him to return to the sweet."

Steven took his proverbial teacher's stick and whacked Genie's proverbial desk.

"Genie, please. Everything's not about you and your little boyfriend. May I continue?" Genie nodded like a scolded student. "As I was saying. Would you buy the candy without the sweet beginning?"

Lori answered. "No. Too much sour."

The girls were silent. As they walked up to the ticket counter of the theater, got their tickets and paid, the professor went to close the lesson.

"Ladies. I am not for a moment suggesting that you break up with these men. What I'm suggesting is that you understand what you're dealing with. Don't let them control you or take advantage of your loving natures."

Genie spoke. "Jeff says I'm the one who's controlling. Trying to get what I want based on my feelings and getting mad when I don't get what I want."

"He's right. The difference is it's upfront. It's honest. And it's negotiable. What these guys do is underhanded and it's damaging to the relationship. The point is, be aware."

Genie was hesitant. "Steven, there have been things lately with Jeff that are suspicious. Between some stories from his past, situations, mean things he says that really, nobody nice would say… there's just so much that doesn't add up to honest or even kind."

"Genie. You always sucked in math. But think of Jeff as a story problem. If everything he says and does doesn't add up, switch around the properties. Always try and find something that makes sense, other than him being a bad guy. You're looking for the square root of Jeff. And at some point, your equation will result in the correct answer and then you'll know who he is."

"And if he turns out to be..."

"Then you'll know it. And you won't go back to him for the sweet. That's when you'll know the relationship is over."

"I can't imagine living without Jeff's sweet."

"Maybe you won't have to. You guys will work through the bitter parts and end up M&M's."

Lori broke in. "Yeah, the ones with nuts!"

Genie stood behind a man at the candy counter. He had just bought a bag of Sour Patch candy. He turned to face Genie as he was walking away. Without a thought, she spoke to him.

"You really need to be more honest about who you are and not be so passive aggressive!"

The woman beside him looked at Genie, then faced him, and slapped him in the face.

"I knew you were cheating on me!"

The man was in total shock. "I've never seen this woman before in my life!"

The woman yelled. "Liar! Then how did she know you're passive aggressive! I am so tired of your shit!" She looked at Genie.

"You can have him, Sister."

Genie looked at the woman. "No thanks. I've got one of my own."

CHAPTER 76

Bill called off the wedding. He said that he believed his fiancée might be disappointed with his ideas and he was afraid to move forward with the plan. Steven said he would make the necessary calls for cancellations.

• • •

Danny left a message asking Genie if they could have lunch. There was something he wanted to discuss. When he arrived at the deli, he gave Genie a kiss on the cheek, and sat down across from her.

Danny looked intently at Genie. "Kay wants to get married."

Genie felt something ripple through her core. It felt like some unidentified organ had detached and escaped from her body. She couldn't utter a word. Danny was quick with a follow up.

"But I told her there's no way I can make a commitment like that. I mean I'm just not there yet."

The organ returned back to her midsection, but the shock hadn't fully left her.

"What's happening with you and Jeff?"

"We haven't spoken since that big fight."

"But you're still in love with him?"

"I suppose I am. I just don't know anymore."

Danny shifted in his chair. Genie looked at him and saw something in his expression. For the first time in their friendship, Genie felt like she couldn't read him.

"What about you, Danny? Do you think you'll end up with Kay at some point?"

"Maybe."

The damn organ got out again! Danny *married?* She would have to make it through the rest of her life with a hole carved out of her middle. Genie became so uncomfortable at the table she wasn't sure what to do with it. She made an internal decision to get through the meal without spreading her feelings like jelly on toast. But it would be an impossible feat. The waitress walked up to the table. She was pretty but had an attitude that could scare a pencil into flipping its lead.

"Have you both decided?"

"Dan, how about we split a Cobb salad and a turkey burger?"

"You know, I think I'll just have the French dip."

THAT WAS IT! Now he'd crossed the line. Genie had taken about all the abuse she could for one day. Genie looked at the waitress who looked directly back at her. Genie spoke as she stared at Danny.

"That's just fine." She turned and faced the waitress. "I'll have the Cobb salad *and* a turkey burger."

The waitress looked at Genie.

"No *actually*... do you have banana pancakes?"

The waitress was clearly irritated. "Yes we do. Is that what you'd like instead?"

"Yes. I'll have the Cobb salad and banana pancakes. Full stack. Dressing on the side."

"Of the pancakes?"

"Of the salad."

The waitress turned from the table.

Genie's eyes, wide open, watched the waitress walk away. "Did you see her expression? What the *hell* did I do to her…"

Danny looked at Genie and said, "Genie, I do get to order what I like. I mean that is kind of a human privilege in restaurants. That's why *each* person gets a menu."

"You know what, Danny? I thought you were different. Turns out you're exactly like all the other guys."

Danny looked at Genie with total love and acceptance. She looked back at him. They stared at each other and finally they both laughed. And then Danny did what only Danny could do when Genie was being Genie. He stayed right there with her. He merely left the subject.

"So, how's work?"

Genie told him about Bill, the wedding, and the recent cancellation.

Danny seemed awkward. "You're telling me that the guy was planning a surprise wedding for his fiancée? What a weird thing to do."

"Well, I thought it was weird too. Now I think it's kind of romantic."

"So you would *like* that?"

"Well, I guess I would overlook whatever wasn't my taste because I'd be so… enchanted by the whole thing." With a hint of sarcasm she said, "Maybe you should plan one for Kay."

Danny looked suspiciously at Genie. "You don't want me to be with Kay, do you?"

"Oh Danny, that's ridiculous. I just don't like this attitude you're taking, that's all."

Danny laughed with affection. "And what attitude is that?"

"You're treating me like I'm leftover chicken."

"How would I accomplish that?"

"Well, before Kay came along you were different. Now you're ordering French dips."

"Genie, if anything, you got so caught up in Jeff that you ditched *me* on the side of the road."

"That is so not true! I love you and I hold on tight. You know I do."

"No, you hold *back* tight, Genie. You always have."

"Oh yeah? You hold back with me too, with everyone. Nobody gets all of you!"

"Well, everyone gets too much of you!"

Genie didn't know how to respond to that. So she didn't. Danny looked tenderly at her.

"Genes. I'm never going to leave you."

Genie welled up in tears. "I will never leave you either." She blew her nose in the napkin. "Just don't make me your best man, ok?"

"No, I could only make you the bride."

Genie stared back at him. "Danny, did you just propose to me?"

The waitress appeared with their food. She placed the French dip in front of Danny, put the salad in front of Genie and then tried to figure out where to put the pancakes.

"Well ma'am, I guess you can decide which one you want first."

And to that Danny said, "Amen."

CHAPTER 77

Jennifer looked at Genie as if she had seen a ghost. Well, in a sense she had. Genie had just given her a message delivered by her late husband.

"I know it sounds crazy, Mom. But he was in my room, sitting on my chair. He gave me the courage to go on that airplane. And he told me to tell you he was sorry."

Jennifer looked pensive and sad. Genie became sorry she had brought it up. But she felt like she owed her dad. He had *contacted* her.

"Genie. I want you to listen to me. I'm not saying I don't believe you because I don't rule out the possibility that these kinds of things happen. But I also think there could be other explanations."

"Like what?"

"Like Jeff."

"*Jeff.* What does he have to do with this?"

"Genie, Jeff is very much like your father."

"He is? How?"

"Your father was very charismatic. He was extremely friendly, funny, outgoing, and upbeat. He attracted people like a magnet. Women loved him and he always had his way with them. Men loved him too because he was a real guy's guy."

"Were you happy with each other?"

"We were very happy, at times. And we broke down at other times. Very much like you and Jeff. And for many of the same reasons."

"Was he a good husband?"

Jennifer smiled. She stared at Genie for what seemed like a full minute.

"Genie. Can I trust you?"

"Of course. I won't tell anyone."

"I'm not talking about that kind of trust. Can I trust you to hear about who your father was as a husband, but separate that from who he was as a father? Because those are two very different people. Otherwise, especially since he's not here, I would be wrong to talk openly with you. Do you understand what I'm asking you to do?"

"I think so. You want me to listen to something without judgment. And not to let it alter my memory of him as my dad."

"That's right. Because he loved you from the bottom of your toes to the highest hair on your head. You were his every wish come true."

"Are you about to tell me that he cheated on you? I already know. He said he was sorry, remember?"

Jennifer gently smiled.

"Sweetheart, when you love someone, and you really want it to work, sometimes you talk yourself out of the side of them that you don't want to see. You make apologies for them, defend them, try to understand them, or blame yourself, even justify being treated badly, thinking somehow you deserve it or have brought it on yourself. That's what they make you believe. So you keep trying harder and harder, never to get the outcome you keep hoping for. Does that sound familiar?"

Genie nodded and laughed. "Mom, Dad said the same thing."

Jennifer looked at Genie with confusion and raised eyebrows. Genie explained.

"When Dad appeared he pretty much told me to give Jeff the old heave ho."

"He said that?" Jennifer smiled. "They must teach some amazing classes up there."

Genie laughed.

"Honey, I fell in love with your dad because he had all of those wonderful qualities that people loved him for. But in a relationship, as a husband, he wasn't to be trusted. And he treated me badly. Very disrespectfully. Even though I know he loved me very much."

"I remember you guys fighting before he left town. I know you hated his traveling."

"We did fight. And this is where I'm asking you to see the man, not the father, I couldn't trust him when I wasn't with him."

"Did it happen more than once?"

"Lying was how he dealt with many aspects of our relationship and his life in general. It wasn't ever going to change. It just took me some time to see it and understand what was happening."

"Why were you so depressed when he died? I mean, if he was so bad?"

"Because he was also wonderful. I really loved him and I was very attached to him. And this is the part I want you to understand. While you're inside the relationship, and holding on to the love and hope, you don't fully experience the bad side. You won't let yourself. It's a fight to see the good so you can stay in the relationship. So when he died, and the good was over, I was left to sort through the bad. All the truths I didn't want to face. And of course, all the lies kept coming out through stories from other people. So I had to move through the pain of the loss, and of the discoveries of who he really was. And it was a very painful process."

"You think that's who Jeff is, don't you?"

"I don't know, Honey. But I know there are similarities. I think you fell in love with a replica of your father. And I think that may be why you saw him in your room."

"But the things he said. I wouldn't have known. It *had* to be him."

Jennifer smiled. "Well, like I said. He was a great dad. You were the love of his life and he was the type of father who would find a way to get here if it meant he could save you from harm. So, even though I don't necessarily believe in that kind of stuff, there's a part of me that believes it was him."

Genie's eyes welled up with tears.

"I'm so sorry you were hurt that way, Mom. I never really knew."

"It's ok, Baby. I got lucky and so did you. You were loved deeply by him and I'm grateful that was instilled in you. *You own that.* And I found Gregg. We've had some rough patches but see, here's the difference; when I work hard with him, I get somewhere. *We* get somewhere. And I *trust* him."

"Do you have the same attraction for him? I mean..."

Jennifer looked at Genie and smiled. She knew exactly what she was asking since she had asked the same question for years after Jimmy died.

"You know, when I was with Gregg in the beginning, I felt happy and calm. At the time I compared it to life with your dad since that was all I knew. I remember missing the highs. Then I realized that the reason the highs felt lower with Gregg was that we never hit the bottom." Jennifer looked at Genie who seemed deep in thought.

"Sweetie, I never thought I'd be attracted to anyone as much I was to your dad. I was alone a long time after he died and I had a lot to get through and past. When I met Gregg, I was ready. And the attraction I have with him is bigger. It's surrounded by so much that works. Do you understand what I'm saying, Genie? Gregg is..."

Genie interrupted. "I do get it, Mom." Then Genie spoke under her breath. *"Gregg is the twenty-fifth floor."*

CHAPTER 78

Genie and Lori were sitting at their favorite restaurant. The waiter came to clear their dinner plates. "Would you ladies like to see the dessert cart?"

Lori responded first. "Well, I know what she's having. The 'Out of Control Chocolate cake,' And I'll have the carrot cake."

"Ok, I'll have those out in a flash."

Genie sat upright in her chair.

"Lor, I'm going to break all contact with Jeff. I can't do it anymore. I get blamed for not trusting him, even though his stories are ones that anyone would doubt."

"Yeah, really. The 'young and beautiful' publicist. I bet it's *pubic* relations."

"She's married."

Lori laughed. *"Love it!* Don't you see? That would explain the night at the hotel, wouldn't it? Neither one could be in their homes. And they'd both need an alibi of getting sick in case they were spotted and it came up some day."

"Why would he go through all that? We're not married. He could be single and with as many women as he wants."

"Because he's totally in love with you and he doesn't want to lose you. She just makes a great side dish. You're the corned beef and she's the slaw. I bet she *loves* his pickle."

Genie gave Lori a disgusted look. Lori gave a devilish grin. "You know what he said the other day, Lor? He told me I will never be happy with another guy. With anyone."

"Really! And why is that?"

"Because other guys would give in to me and no one will challenge me like he does. And I'll be bored."

"Yeah, Genes, he's right. You'd long for the days you were whipped into your best behavior. Zero contact, Genie. It's the only way. Otherwise you're half in and that's not healthy for you. You'll never be able to live that way."

"Right."

"I just don't think you'll do it."

Genie laughed. "I probably won't."

The waiter brought over the desserts. Genie looked at her chocolate cake.

"Lor, what is it about this chocolate cake that's so damn good?" Genie took a bite, oohed and ahhed, held it in her mouth and suddenly made a connection. "Lor, this chocolate cake is *Jeff*."

"I know, that's what I'm afraid of. You'll just have to have him in bites. And he'll decide when those bites are offered."

Genie looked defeated. And suddenly, she got a look of determination.

"Oh, no he won't. I'm not a bites kind of girl. I get the whole piece, or none at all."

"But he's not going to give you the whole piece. So how are you going to give up something that you love that much? I know you.

You'll take the bites he offers knowing it gives you a crack at the whole piece in the future."

"No way. I won't do it. It doesn't feel good, Lor. It feels like I get fed if I'm a good girl. If I'm bad, I get sent to my room without dinner. He should be with me no matter what."

"That a girl! But how?"

Genie looked at Lori's carrot cake. Without saying a word, she switched the desserts so that she had the carrot cake and Lori had the chocolate.

"Genie, what are you doing?"

"I'm demoting Jeff."

"He's carrot cake now?" Genie nodded. "Do you even like carrot cake?"

Genie gave a brush-off shrug. With an arrogant expression, she took a bite of the carrot cake. She took the same flippant tone as she spoke. "I could take it or leave it. Certainly wouldn't miss it if it were gone."

Lori laughed with love and pride.

"So Gene. What if he comes back? What if he decides he can't live without you and he's ready to change his horrid ways by accepting your horrid ways?"

Genie reached over and switched their plates again.

"Oh, so good to have you again! Yummy yum yum."

Lori laughed. "And Genes? What if he never comes back?"

Genie looked at Lori. Her face grew more serious and determined. Genie picked up the chocolate cake and dropped it in the bus pan behind their table. She turned back, and looked Lori straight in the eye.

"Then no more chocolate cake."

"Not ever?"

"By that point, it won't even appeal to me."

Lori was riveted. *"Really."*

"It's a mindset, Lor. Chocolate cake is either something I'll love or it's something that makes me sick."

"Genie, you can flip it in your mind? Make chocolate cake *that* good or *that* bad?"

Genie looked at Lori with the intensity of a German soldier.

"In the fucking blink of an eye."

CHAPTER 79

The Break-Up Diet. The best weight loss plan on the market. Genie finally understood what she had learned over the last year. When you feel your feelings to the core you lose your appetite.

Genie kept replaying the end. Neither of them said, "I don't love you anymore" and nobody said it was over. But this last argument they were in, which was nothing they hadn't argued about hundreds of times before, had gone from ugly to toxic. These two people who had loved each other so deeply couldn't communicate anymore, other than destructive and biting accusations.

For two weeks, they obsessively fought by text. After a few horrible voicemails, Genie knew, without a doubt, they needed to be a wireless connection. She blocked Jeff from her phone and email. Jeff created new screen names to get through. Often his gestures were loving, but in no time flat, they'd become abusive again.

Genie had crying fits in the shower, and fetal position sobs on the floor. She couldn't eat foods they had eaten together. She couldn't wear clothes she had worn with him. Her mind was a movie on rewind. She pressed pause on dialogues. She blamed herself for everything. Then she went to blaming him. All she knew was that their relationship was on a gurney and she was trying to figure out how it got there.

She slept with his shirt, cried in the folds, and the next day she cut it up. She sewed it into a "blankie". After that she threw it away. She loved him and missed him. She hated and cursed him. She dipped him in sweetened memories. Then she sprinkled them with Cayenne pepper because loving him hurt too much. Every minute was a different emotion. Every hour he was a different man.

Some days she felt full of faith. This was just one of those silly break-ups that couples in love go through. She needed those days of hope because without them, the depression swallowed her whole. Whatever made her feel better was what she let herself have. *Healthy grieving.*

Other than work, Genie had cocooned. In the weeks that passed, she spent nearly all of her time alone. She felt unsettled when she ventured too far from home and her routine. She had trouble sleeping. She felt depressed and afraid for her life. She tried dating a couple of times but it only made her miss Jeff and cry. Nothing and no one felt good.

It had been three months since the break-up and she was sitting in Ellen's office.

"So Genie, how are you handling everything?"

"I'm obsessed."

"With what?"

"Jeff. I think about him all the time. The thoughts run around constantly. What I could have done differently. All the places I messed up. What he's thinking and feeling. Is he a monster or a good guy?"

"Genie, Jeff is not a monster. He has many outstanding qualities and that's why you fell in love with him. No one is all good, or all bad." Ellen paused at Genie's silence. "And how are you doing with the food?"

"I hardly notice it. I actually have to force myself to eat."

Ellen looked at Genie with pause. "Congratulations."

Genie looked like a lotto winner who hadn't ever purchased a ticket.

"Congratulations for what?"

"You're in terrible pain and the obsessing is part of your grieving, but it's healthy and honest. It's not hiding behind food. *It's good.*"

Genie looked over the winning ticket. "Wow."

Ellen looked at her with adoration.

"I want to call him so badly. But I know it wouldn't change anything. And until something would change, we don't have a chance."

"That's right."

"Ellen, he calls and hangs up every day. He blocks the call but I know it's him. A couple times he forgot to block it."

Ellen smiled a frown. "His hang-ups are just part of his pain. People do that during break-ups all the time."

"Sometimes when I think about him I hate him so much. And other times I wish I could just move in with him and never let go."

"Welcome to the complexities of feelings. They're all there. And as afraid as you were of losing Jeff, what have you learned?"

"That I can make it without him."

"That's right. And no matter what, you needed to know that."

CHAPTER 80

After a few too many, Genie finally understood why blind dates were called blind dates. You'd have to be blind to like them. You'd also have to be deaf and dumb. If she heard one more guy talk about himself, only to call her and ask if she'd like to go out again so she could hear more about himself, she would have to Google local convents.

Now that Genie had been given a taste of life after Jeff, despite everything Lori said, she kind of had to wonder. Which was worse? A bunch of blind dates with guys you don't care about, or a shit you just happen to love.

• • •

Genie was staring out the office window. The day was dark and raining and the buildings looked old and dirty. Genie thought about whether she had an umbrella and then remembered that Danny said he'd pick her up. Suddenly, as though she had totally missed this and it was the answer to everything, Genie turned to face Steven.

"Steven, Danny loves me."

Steven was thumbing through files, half listening.

"Of course he does. Did the Hanovers set a date yet?"

"No, they're waiting for… Steven, I mean he *loves* me loves me."

Steven looked up. "Let me guess. Are we about to have another conversation about you?"

Genie missed the dig. "I think he was too shy. You know, to be vulnerable emotionally."

"Maybe. But have you ever been in love with someone and been able to hold back?"

Genie thought about that one.

"Well, I've had crushes I've held back on. But being in love… no. It always ended up coming out." She stared out the window remembering.

"You know Steven, I can actually pinpoint the exact moment that I knew guys were in love with me. Or I was in love with them. Like, take Buns for example, my college boyfriend. I will never forget the day. We were standing…"

"Genie. If I wanted a romantic love story in the middle of the day, I'd order Netflix to the office, ok? Why don't you just call Bisky's and order our lunch."

Genie looked at Steven without expression, picked up the phone, and did what she was told.

"Yes, it's Genie Burns and I'd like to put in an order for delivery. I'll have a turkey sandwich on whole wheat bread but can you slice the turkey very thick, put some mustard on one piece of bread and some light mayo on the other piece? And I'll have sprouts on the side with the mayo. But please make sure they don't put it on the mustard side. Sprouts and mustard together are kind of a bad thing." Genie finished repeating the order back and hung up the phone.

"Uh, Genes. What am I eating? The delivery boy?"

"Oh! I'm so sorry!" Genie dialed the number back.

"This is Genie Burns, I need to add to my order. Just a turkey sandwich however you make it." She hung up the phone. Steven smiled and shook his head.

"Steven, maybe Danny and I are meant for each other and we just haven't been able to connect it up until now. Sometimes that happens, you know? Maybe we were both too scared."

"Maybe." Steven was trying to concentrate on his spreadsheet.

"Steven, so many people start out as friends. And then they fall in love later. It happens all the time!"

Steven looked up with the realization that work wasn't going to happen.

"Genie. If you have to analyze it that way, I don't think you're feeling it. If you were, you wouldn't be asking these questions."

Genie looked up at him with the eyes of a little girl.

"Hey, Genes, I know you love Danny. He's the perfect package and you could have a wonderful life with him. But if you want my opinion, you'd be settling."

"Settling! That's what I'd be doing with Jeff!"

"Well, you guys are stuck in a bad place. But I'm not sure he won't come back at some point with a different attitude. He's probably just hoping you come to him first."

"I'm not what he wants."

"Yeah you are. You're just both..."

"We're mustard on the sprouts side!"

Steven laughed. "Genie, listen to me. I have no doubt he will come back to you someday. He's in love with you and won't give up. But no matter how much you love him, you have to make smart decisions. *This is your life.*"

CHAPTER 81

The snow sat on branches like frosting. The buildings below looked like cookie structures, dusted with white powdered sugar. The light that poured into Genie's apartment was bright and unobstructed. Genie opened her eyes, not sure what had woken her up. She did remember though, regardless of the sound, that today was their anniversary.

Genie knew that part of the privilege of owning your own company was that you get to take first anniversaries off, with or without a partner to celebrate them. Just as she was trying to decide whether to work, or call in sad, the phone rang.

"Hey, Lor."

"Hey, Honey. You sound funny. Is something wrong?"

"Today's our anniversary."

"Oh. Sorry, Gene."

"I want to call him."

"Why?"

"Just to say…"

"Genie, there's nothing to say. It's not going to make you feel better. It's a really bad idea."

"Lor, I can't just pretend like I hate him. He's…"

"Seeing someone."

The words hit Genie so hard she wasn't sure she could hold on to the phone.

"What?"

"I didn't want to say anything, Gene. But if you're thinking of calling him..."

Genie was barely audible.

"No. I won't."

"Honey, I'm so sorry."

Genie couldn't ask any questions. Those three words were two more than she could handle.

"Lor, I gotta go."

"Genie, want me to come over?"

"No. I need to be alone."

Genie hung up the phone trying to figure out what to do with the pain. The confusion made her feel dizzy and sick. The images in her mind were unbearable. Suddenly, she felt total exhaustion as though her energy was sucked out through a hose.

She tried to lie down and take a nap but her thoughts wouldn't take a break. She got up, paced the apartment, trying to figure out how she was supposed to live through the rest of the day. She sat on the floor, against the wall, and stared across the room. The crying wouldn't stop. After what seemed like hours in that position, she tried to go to bed.

Genie's luxurious, beyond her budget sheets, suddenly felt cold and hard. The normally cozy, soft, warm bed felt huge and overwhelming. She had never before felt such a longing to be held, or to hold on to someone else. She grabbed a pillow, but it wasn't huggable and offered absolutely no help at all. Abruptly, Genie sat up with a plan.

She got out of bed and threw on sweats and Uggs. She put on some lip-gloss, got in the car, and headed for the only drugstore that was open until midnight. She walked into the toy aisle and looked over the stuffed animals. She picked up the larger ones and held them to her chest. After test driving the bears, she found a sizable brown and white dog, very squishy and fluffy, and its body conformed to her own when she hugged it. She went to the register and paid.

"Would you like a bag?"

"No thanks, I'll carry him." Genie figured she'd get to know this guy before taking him home to bed.

Genie went to her bedroom, turned on the computer, which was already on her bed and began typing the letter. She had no idea why this plan had formulated in her head, but it didn't feel like a choice. It felt more like a spiritual assignment, sent through the spiritual mail. It was as if the words typed themselves.

Dear My Answered Prayer,

Today is August 11th, 2011. I am lying on my bed without any hope that you really exist. A few days ago my mom said I just can't see you yet and that's why I don't believe you'll happen. And once you're in front of me, everything will feel different because there you will be.

I've been crying because I can't imagine there's any person that could actually make me feel safe, someone who I can trust, while still being the man I'm in love with. So far, I've proven that the two can't exist together. Not for me, anyway. I've begun to think I'll die an old lady without having anyone to love or be loved by. That I'm such a damaged and impossible person that if the right one comes along, I'll ruin it somehow. And that there is just a world of wrong ones anyway.

If this letter ever gets read, that will mean one of two things. One would be that I died and someone found this. If that's the case, I have to say that my beautiful family, my incredible friends, my work, my unconditionally loving, call-me-on-every-issue-I-have partner Steven, and Casey, have made me feel truly lucky. In some ways, I'd feel greedy asking for more. But if this letter is read and I'm alive, it's because you did the impossible. You loved me for exactly who I am.

You saw past the fears and craziness and by some miracle you don't resent me. You proved yourself to be someone who is so good and moral. You are sexy and I want to jump on you every second. And last but not least, you have convinced me that you're not going to leave me, or change your mind along the way. And because of who you are and how I feel about you, I won't leave you either.

I want so much to love someone, know he loves me back, and wants to spend time with me. I hope we have crushes on each other but with a friendship that backs it up. I know we'll have challenges but moving forward, all of that will be part of our history and that will build a foundation that wouldn't be easy to break. If it suffers some cracks, and I really do expect and even welcome those, our attraction and friendship will be so solid that we can just learn to step around them.

I already know what you'll be like. When we first meet you'll be warm and friendly. I'll see your sense of humor right away. I think you'll be very smart and I'll rely on that. I don't think you'll be overly emotional but your emotions will come out with me and that will be part of our deep connection. I think you'll be funny and clever and we will laugh a lot. I know you love to be around kids.

You're interested in many things, very active, definitely up for bike rides, nature, hikes, and spur of the moment fun. Maybe you'll get me to travel a ton because I'll know I'm safe with you. You love to cuddle with me. We love to kiss. We can't wait to see each other. We don't like being apart. We can't believe we found each other. We never thought it would happen.

I'm going to sleep with this dog until you come into my life. If it takes longer than I wish it would, I'm not going to give up. I am not going to look for a perfect person, just the person perfect for me. And I can't wait for the day I can look back and say that every painful thing I went through was just part of my training for you.

My last words to you as you're reading this are: Thank you for making me so happy, for making me half of a couple. Thanks for making me feel pretty. Thanks for making me feel wanted. Thanks for being enough of a challenge that I feel alive and excited, but not insecure and scared. I love you and when you're done reading this, I just want to hold and squeeze you instead of this fricking dog! *You're here.*

Thank you, My Answered Prayer.

Genie reread the letter and printed it. She rolled it like a scroll and taped it closed. She took a scissors and brought it to the stuffed dog. She turned him belly side up, cut the threads from the seam and opened him up just wide enough to fit the rolled up sheets of paper. She pushed them through to the middle of the stuffing so she wouldn't feel them crinkle when she squeezed the dog. She sewed him up, named him Teddy, and made a plan with a promise.

Genie would hold the dog tight in the wait. There would come a day when she would meet this special man and she'd know, *he's the Dog Opener!* On that very day she would put Teddy in a box with a bow. She would bring the box to this man. She would light two candles, put them on the floor, sit facing him, and hand over the box. She would watch him open it. Thinking he had received a worn out stuffed dog, she would hand him a scissors and tell him to look *inside.* And then she would watch as her Answered Prayer read the letter that brought him to her.

When the Teddy ceremony was over, he would look at her shaking his head in disbelief that a letter written before they met had described exactly who he is, what he does, and who they are together. This ceremony would seal the deal and whatever hard times they would face in the future, they would remember the words on the paper.

Genie turned off the lamp next to her bed and put her head on her pillow. She held Teddy close to her body. She could feel his soft fur against her stomach. His flouncy head, body, and limbs filled all the hollow places that had been there just an hour ago. Genie no longer felt empty. She cuddled him close, squeezing his head between her neck and chin. She allowed her eyelids to close for the night, putting an end to a difficult day. In seconds she was asleep.

CHAPTER 82

On Rosh Hashanah it is written. On Yom Kippur it is sealed. Who shall live, who shall die. Who shall be brought into this world, and who shall leave it. Who shall perish by water and who by fire. And as we move into the upcoming year, it's with repentance, kindness, and forgiveness.

Genie had been assigned a personal Kabbalah teacher named Leah. Genie was instructed to check in with her every few weeks by phone. This was free of charge, and an opportunity for students to discuss a particular situation in their lives that stands out as the most difficult. For Genie, it was the inner conflict between the love she felt for Jeff, and everything she knew to be true.

Genie spent about ten minutes giving an overview of her relationship with Jeff, the feelings they both had, and everything surrounding the break up. Leah's voice was quiet, confident, and had just a slight hint of an accent that Genie guessed to be European. "Do you still want to be with him?"

"I don't know. A part of me still hopes and I don't know why that is."

"It means you're not finished. And from what you've told me, he's not finished either."

"He has a girlfriend."

"My guess is that it's a rebound. I think you'll hear from him again, Genie."

"Are you saying I could still end up with him?"

"What I'm asking is that you're open to all possibilities in the future, no matter how remote or impossible they seem today. Because if someone pushes your buttons that way, there is a reason. You obviously push his too. So, if he comes back to you, and my guess is he will, you may have a decision to make. And if you choose to be with him, Genie, sometimes it means taking on someone's garbage."

Genie wondered, how stinky does garbage have to be before you give up on the person? And where do you pile the garbage as it starts to accumulate? Are you supposed to toss the load completely and forget everything in the past? Does the garbage truck come to take it away along with the pain it caused? Or are you supposed to use those memories to make smart decisions for your future?

Kabbalah brought another message. Think about what you want your life to look like in the upcoming year. Make a commitment to yourself, and to the light. Base it on your truth, *whatever* that truth is. When Yom Kippur arrives, at sundown, that decision is sealed for the year. And you'll pledge your energy to *that.*

* * *

A couple days later, when Genie opened her mailbox, she saw an oversized envelope and recognized the handwriting right away. As if a hand had just grabbed her neck, cutting off her breath, she stood frozen in her spot. Her stomach felt excitement, and then it felt tremendous fear. She grabbed the envelope, stared at the writing like it was an old camp friend, and slowly opened it up. Inside were a letter, and a DVD.

Gino,

I have tried to stay away but here's what I know for sure. No matter where I am, who I'm with, or what I'm doing, the biggest part of my heart is with you. I'll never be happy with anyone until I'm happy with you. You are the love of my life, Sweetheart. And right now, I just wish you were here. I'm so sorry about everything. I love you forever and would love nothing more than to have you here in my arms.

Love, Bear

Genie couldn't believe what she was reading. She felt a surge of happiness and hope. It felt like someone had walked in her gray shadowed room, opened up the curtains to reveal summer's bright light pouring in to proclaim, *"Of course you get to be happy!"* She ran upstairs, put the disc in her computer, and played the montage over and over.

The pictures of them he chose, the song he used, the fact that he took such emotional risk in sending it… To Genie, nothing that came before mattered anymore. She raced into her bathroom, opened her jewelry box, pulled out her ring and stared at it in disbelief, as though its sparkle had come back from the dead. She called him right away.

She heard his beautiful voice, not the Voicemail Lady! "Hello?"

"Jeff, that was so beautiful."

"Gino! Man, hearing your voice feels good. Is it really you?"

Genie smiled with excited tears. "The montage was perfect. And I miss you so much."

His voice was so sweet. She had thought she'd never hear it again.

"I'm so glad you like it. I miss you too, Sweetheart. Every day."

There was a pause. Even the silence was warm. Genie broke it anyway.

"So, what do we do now?"

"You tell me, Gino."

"What are you doing right now?"

"Honestly? Wondering why you're not here."

"Enough said, Bear! I'll be there in half an hour."

Genie had forgotten what *alive* felt like. As the tears ran down her face, she began visualizing what their relationship would now be. The time apart had obviously put things in perspective. Was Jeff really the dog opener? Was this the step back into dinners and walks, endless talking, cuddling in bed, and *laughing?* She had missed that part most of all.

• • •

Genie drove over to his place. When they saw each other, they hugged long and hard. They didn't move from the spot, just continued to hold on tight. Their hearts were beating rapidly, like drums in sync between them. Like everything bad that had ever happened was part of a past that was gone, they couldn't get enough of each other. Their passion was intense but full of warm affection. Genie began to cry in disbelief that they had finally found their way back.

"Jeff, I just can't believe this. I really started thinking that was it for good."

Jeff buried his head in Genie's neck. He spoke softly in her ear. "We'll never be done for good, Genes. No matter what, our feelings will always bring us back to each other. I'm resigned to that now."

Genie felt her stomach drop. She didn't move Jeff away from his position. But now it seemed like this was a terrible mistake and she didn't really belong there. "Why would we leave each other again? I mean, we know what we know. We're in love and we'll just always have to work it out."

"Genes, I love you to death, but you are a person who gets upset. I don't blame you, it's just who you are."

"Jeff, everyone gets upset sometimes." She began to cry. "It never means I don't love you."

"Genie, you can't tell me that it's ok for people to get upset. You got mad at me for ordering pancakes. For saying someone was attractive. You actually accused me of cheating. I can't be with anyone else, and I'll never really be able to move on. But how could I live that way?"

Genie was stunned and sick. She couldn't believe that he hadn't let any of that go. The tears came out with desperation to fix it, or at least to understand why she was here today, if he couldn't be with her tomorrow.

"Then why did you say all those things? Why did you send me the montage and letter?"

"I sent that stuff because those are my feelings. You always wanted me to share and be honest with them so I did."

Genie was crazed. "I don't want your feelings when we're broken up! How could you rope me in like that?"

Jeff was defensive. "I never *roped* you in. You were the one who came rushing over here. It was your idea, not mine."

Genie was hysterical. "Why would you tell me you love me and can't move on!"

"Because I do! And I can't!"

"Then we should get back together! I can't move on either! We are in love!"

"Look, Gene. I know that I will never be able to say no to you. We don't work in a relationship but we will always have the feelings. You know you can't deny or erase them. Neither can I. I could be married and living in France and I'd still go weak if I saw you. You're my Kryptonite! Whoever you and I are with, at any time in our future, I believe you never say never."

Genie cried. "That's not how I want to live, Jeff!"

"Genie, you can't just put things in a nice little box. Life is complicated."

Genie was sick. She was sad. Her vote was for the nice little box. She became a pleading child.

"Jeff, I won't get upset. I'll be very careful. I'll work very hard. I just want to be with you."

Jeff hugged and kissed her. He held on to her as tight as he could. He spoke with love and compassion.

"I love you more than anyone on this earth and you're the finest person I know. You're my baby, the love of my life. Sometimes you just fall in love with the wrong person."

Genie began to sob. Jeff held her and kissed her. The sobbing was so deep and the pain so intense, the crying wouldn't stop. She couldn't make sense of anything. He held her in a way that he never did, even when they were together.

"Genie, thank you. Really, thank you. You taught me everything I know. You made me a better person. I'll always have you to thank."

Genie sobbed. "You thank me by being with me and sharing your life with me."

"You know as well as I do, you'll just end up getting upset about something and we'll end up here again."

The tears turned to rage. "Don't you ever call me again! Don't you ever tell me you love me! Don't deceive me with words that you know won't go anywhere!" And then she screamed. *"I hate you!"*

Genie gathered her things and bolted out the door. Her phone rang and she didn't pick up. Jeff left a voicemail. With obsessive fear, Genie waited until she got home to gather the strength to listen. His voice was calm, controlled, and frighteningly still.

"You know, Genie. I really thought we had made a mistake breaking up. I had real hope for us. But your words were so full of hate that I now see who you are. I did nothing to warrant that attack but love you and give you the most vulnerable feelings I have. You think *you're* hurt? You are a sick and cruel woman. I actually think you need help. I'm so glad I got to see this part of you. I know I'll now be able to move on without doubt, that I did the best I could and you ruined us. You ruined the very best thing that two people can have. And one day you'll regret it."

Not as reportable as black eyes, bloody gashes, or cracked ribs. And since it masquerades as love, it's not punishable by law or judgment. But Genie had never felt more abused by anything or anyone. She took her phone, threw it against the wall and it crashed into pieces. She so missed the Jeff she had loved. She so hated this monster. She couldn't reconcile the feelings. All she could do was curl up in her closet and cry until her eyes swelled shut.

An hour later the phone rang. It was Lori. Genie picked up the phone and told her what had happened.

"Genie, I want you to listen very carefully."

"Ok. I am."

"I'm putting you on the AA one step plan."

"I'm not an alcoholic. And it's twelve steps."

"AA stands for Avoid Assholes. And it's one step. *You stay away from him.*"

Genie nodded with a sigh. "Ok."

Not convinced. "Genie, you are addicted to this man. You know he's toxic. You know he'll hurt you every time. He will never give you up, but he'll never give you what you need. You need to stop believing in this. You hear me?" Genie nodded in tears.

The next morning, Genie was in a dark haze. She felt cursed and tired and weak. She thought about the day, Yom Kippur, the upcoming year, and how she wanted to live. She thought about Jeff, what he had said, and how he was living his life. Without thought, she walked over to her dresser. She looked at the ring, realizing now that it had merely come back for a visit.

With tears and repulsion, with love and hate, with a love of it's beauty, and anger at its failure, Genie wondered what to do. Should she keep it as a reminder of the good? Was that good even part of a truth? Without more thought, she taped it to a piece of paper, put it in an envelope, addressed it to Jeff, then closed and licked the flap.

On Yom Kippur it is sealed.

CHAPTER 83

Genie walked into Starbucks for the first time since last seeing Jeff. She had avoided going anywhere they had been together. Maybe this was a sign that she was starting to get back to herself. As she approached the line, she saw her favorite client.

"Mrs. Finch!"

She rushed over and gave her a hug.

"Dear, how are you!" Genie must have looked how she felt, because Mrs. Finch added, "Uh oh. You look like I did many years ago. That's the face of a break up. Am I right?"

Genie nodded. She couldn't even speak.

"And you loved him very much?"

"Yes, more than I've ever loved anyone. But it ended very badly."

"Did he love you that much too? Honestly?"

"Yes. I know he did. He wanted a future together. He says he can't be in a relationship with me because I get upset with him about what he considers to be small things. He won't live that way. But he won't let go either. He's hurting me horribly."

Mrs. Finch frowned with warm, encouraging eyes. "Don't let him do that."

"I didn't mean to. He did and said things that made me believe he had changed his mind. I got close to him again and then he whacked me with his old self telling me why he can't be with me."

Mrs. Finch spoke with a voice that could cure osteoporosis.

"Dear, it's very hard to let go of someone you are in love with. It's hard to give up hope that he will change. Or that you will change! But if you don't let yourself detach and move on, you are held hostage. He will come and go as he pleases. You need to stay away until you are fully over him. The only thing you can respond to is a full commitment to exactly who you are, even if you are someone who gets upset about small things. Anything less than that kind of acceptance is torture."

"Did you have problems like that with Mr. Finch?"

"No. But the man I dated before him was very much like what you're describing. I got upset with him all the time and looking back, I had reason to. It took me a long time to let go. Once I did, that's when I met my husband. I never had to ask him for a thing. He loves me for exactly who I am. Even at my age, he makes me feel beautiful every single day."

Genie's eyes began to sting. It was a combination of marvel and envy. Part wish and part admiration.

"Mrs. Finch, I don't know if I'm ready to let go. I have to admit, I still have a small amount of hope."

"I understand." Mrs. Finch put her hand on Genie's arm. "You know, Dear, passionate love is not always the most comfortable love. At times, because the feelings run deep, it even feels abusive. But if it's the lasting kind, and if both people want it to work, it will sit in many uncomfortable chairs before it lands on that sofa I told you about."

Genie smiled through tears. "The one with the better view?"

Mrs. Finch smiled. "That's the one. And no matter how gone it is, love can come back in about twenty seconds flat. It just takes two people who let it."

"And if they don't let it?"

"Then it's a passionate love that is over."

CHAPTER 84

Genie walked in the office to see quite the annoying sight. Steven looked especially happy. Almost tickled in his expression. This could only mean trouble.

"What happened to you? Someone give you a gerbil for your birthday?"

"Cute, Gene. Just for that, I think I'll give you the message without preparation." Steven handed Genie a message slip.

"*Kay* called? Danny's Kay? What the heck does she want?"

"Love to tell you, but I gotta go feed my gerbil." Steven got up and went to pour himself a cup of coffee.

Genie put her things down, hung up her jacket, and sat down to dial the number. What a way to start the day.

"Kay? It's Genie."

"Oh Genie, I'm so glad you called! How *are* you?"

Genie rolled her eyes at Steven who was now sitting on her desk with his coffee. "I'm great, how are you?"

"I'm just fine. Listen, I want to hire you."

Genie panicked. She so did not need this. "Hire me for what?"

"I want to throw a surprise party for Danny and I want Surprise Enterprise to do it."

Genie couldn't imagine anything she'd like to do less. She looked up at Steven, who was totally eating this up.

"Oh, Kay… I'm so swamped right now, maybe Steven…"

With that, Steven lifted up one side of his rear end off of Genie's desk. He started squirming and pulling at the seat of his pants.

"Damn these rodents. Get back up there, Buddy!"

Genie hushed Steven, not at all amused.

"Kay, maybe Steven would be the best one to handle this…"

"Oh, Genie, you're the only one who could pull it off, seeing as how well you know him. Please do this for him. It would mean so much to both of us."

Genie choked on the thought. Working with Danny's *girlfriend?* Genie wanted to hang up the phone. But facing Steven's lectures about "business is business" seemed a worse fate at this point. "Ok, Kay, what did you have in mind?"

"Well, you're going to think I'm crazy but Danny's been talking a lot about getting married and…"

"Oh, Kay, can you hold on for a second. I have to get the other line."

Genie put the call on hold and shot up from her seat. She began walking quickly around the office, back and forth between the desks. "Oh my God, Oh my God, Oh my God… this can't be happening. Oh my God. Danny said he might marry Kay but I could tell he doesn't want to! What is it with these people!" Then she turned to look at Steven who was still obnoxiously pulling at the seat of his pants. He looked up at her with a smirk that said he was enjoying this way too much.

"DID YOU KNOW ABOUT THIS?"

"Know about what?" Steven, still sitting on the desk, jerked up in mocking pain. "Ouch!" Steven holds up a finger, "Mental note. Clip their nails."

"How can this be happening? They just met!"

"Genie, they've been together over a year. Sorry you gave up the guy?"

"I never had him to give up!"

"That's right. And that's 'cause you didn't want him. Now stop being so selfish, pick up the phone, and see what she wants from you."

"Why am I stuck with everything I can't FUCKING handle!"

Genie sat back down, gathered herself, took a deep breath, and picked up the phone. "Kay, I'm sorry. Now why don't you tell me what you've got in mind."

"Well, I know this sounds ridiculous, but here was my train of thought. I mean, I want you to know why I would come up with such an off-the-wall idea."

"Oh, not to worry. I've heard them all. But Danny's birthday isn't until January. Aren't you planning this pretty far in advance?"

"Well, it wouldn't be a surprise *birthday* party."

Genie laughed. "What then, surprise Secretary's Day?" She knew that was a bit on the mean side considering Kay was a secretary, but what the hell. Kay can take it. *She* has a great boyfriend.

Kay said, "Actually, believe it or not, I want to plan a surprise wedding." Genie didn't speak. She couldn't.

"Genie? Are you there?"

No answer. "Genie? Hello?"

Ever so gently, slowly, with very careful precision to make sure this was done correctly, Genie disconnected the call. The relief was immense. What she didn't know was that Steven was watching the whole thing.

"Genie Burns. Did you just hang up on her?"

Genie looked up at him in a misty gaze. "No, we were disconnected." The phone rang again. Steven glared at Genie. "Pick it up!"

"I can't."

"You have to!"

"I *can't!*"

"Why not?"

"Kay wants to plan a wedding to surprise Danny! Is this a fucking JOKE? Is someone up there having a really boring death and they need to mess up MY LIFE?"

"Genie. Danny deserves to be happy. Give that to him and stop thinking about yourself."

"Steven, can you just once cut me some slack? Can you ever say you know this is hard? Can you ever just be *kind?*"

"You know, Genes, I *was* kind once and I didn't like the way it felt."

Genie turned to face the phone on her desk.

"Hey Genes. Look at the bright side. Since you stopped pigging out, your ass is small again."

Genie perked up and looked at Steven. *"Really?"*

"Really. But so are your tits."

CHAPTER 85

Genie walked back into the office after lunch and saw Steven going through the files. He looked up at Genie when she walked in.

"Have you seen Bill's file?"

"Yeah, it's probably still on my desk. I was calling the vendors to see who was letting him out of contracts. Why?"

"The wedding is on."

"What do you mean the wedding's on?"

"I mean he's doing it."

"Why did he change his mind?"

"Well, now he says it was him. He just had cold feet. But there's something else."

"What? It's a different bride?"

"No, a different planner. He wants you involved this time."

Genie looked at him with a blank stare. And in the most cocky, told-ya-so fashion she could muster, she neatly stacked some papers and closed the open drawers. "Why does he want me to plan it?"

"Because he wants it perfect. He thinks whatever you love, she'll love."

"Well, it's about the first thing you've told me about him that I respect. Steven, I've decided there is no such thing as the man of your dreams."

Steven theatrically threw his elbows over his face and screamed, "SAY IT ISN'T SO! THE MAN OF OUR DREAMS *IS* OUT THERE. TAKE IT BACK OR I SHALL HAVE TO END MY LIFE NOW."

Genie laughed in appreciation, both for who Steven was, and what he was trying to do.

"Do you think I've already met him?"

"God, I hope so, I'd hate to have to go through all of this again. I just don't have the strength! Or the freezer space."

"Well then, who is it?"

"I don't know, Genie. Surprise me."

"I don't know either!"

"Well, then maybe he'll surprise *you*."

CHAPTER 86

Steven was hanging up the phone just as Genie walked out of the bathroom. He threw his hands up dramatically in the air and yelled "Surprise!"

Genie looked at him with question.

"Kay just cancelled."

"No way, Steven! Did she uninvite the guests too?"

"Not yet. Apparently there was some family dispute and her parents don't want to pay for a wedding that's a surprise. She can cover the cost of the deposits and that's all."

"Why are they backing out now?"

"I guess they didn't know it was a surprise. Kay isn't all that close to her family. She knew they wouldn't approve so she was waiting for the right time to tell them. And they thought she was a total idiot."

"Oh, she's got to be so upset. Even her dress is ready and paid for. Does Danny know?"

"No. And she doesn't want to tell him. She's really upset."

Genie perked up. "Steven. Why can't we have them get married at Bill's wedding?"

"Genie, have you been sniffing your highlights again? What are you talking about?"

"Well, all the stuff we're doing for Bill's wedding can be used again for Danny the next morning. Just like we did for the Ford party."

"Ok, and how are you going to explain to Danny and Kay that they are visiting the wedding of people they've never met? How do you get them down the aisle?"

Genie was on a roll. The plan was forming just as it bounced off her lips.

"We tell Danny and Kay the same thing we're telling Bill's fiancée. They get the chance to be extras at a big Hollywood filming of some clients of ours. Danny will take the free trip. He loves any scam or bargain."

Steven argued. "They'll figure out it's not a movie when Bill actually gets married! And then what?"

"They still won't know that theirs is the next one!"

"Then how do you explain to Danny that you flew them there for someone else's wedding that you were hired to do and 'Oh by the way, just kidding about Brad Pitt'?"

Genie finally looked defeated. Steven thought for a moment and then began to speak slowly. "Ok, Gene. You really want to make this work?"

Genie felt a lift of hope and listened.

"Ok, after Bill's wedding, you tell Danny and Kay that you invited them for the free trip but you weren't allowed to tell them the details. Company policy. And the next morning, we'll do their wedding day according to Kay's surprise plan. But I swear, I don't know why it's so important to you to do this."

"Because I love Danny. And I feel bad for Kay."

"Genes, have you thought about what it's going to feel like to see Danny and Kay get married? You're going to be a wreck."

"I know. I already am."

"Do you feel like you made a mistake?"

"Sometimes I feel that way. I just don't see them together."

"Genes, it's better not to judge people."

"Ok, Steven. What about that guy you met and said you wouldn't go out with because he said 'Oy vey.'"

"What about it?"

"You judged his whole personality based on two words."

"Those aren't words. That's a way of life."

"A Jewish life?"

"Right."

"Steven. You're *Jewish.*"

"Not that kind of Jewish."

"Ok, so it's alright for you to judge someone on a Jewish life, but you don't want to be judged on a gay life."

"That's right."

"Hypocrite!"

"Oh Genes, we're all hypocrites."

"Then stop defending yourself and attacking me. It's so hypocritical!"

"Oy vey, it is not."

CHAPTER 87

Genie came in to the office the next morning and put coffee and a scone on Steven's desk. And she knew the second he looked at her that she should have called in sick.

"Steven, what is that look?"

"Genes, I'm warning you right now, you're not going to like this at all."

"Oh no, Steven, please not today."

"Genes, there's one detail that you're going to need to take care of."

"Whatever it is, I swear you'll do a better job of it. I'm in a real bad place."

"Well, I don't think this is one for me, Babe. I'm too hairy, too tall. And I'm too flat-chested. Although…" Steven looked mockingly at Genie's chest. Genie shot him a look.

"Ok, but you're not too tall or hairy." He winced. *"Are you?"*

"Steven, WHAT!"

"You need to buy a dress," Steven said curtly.

"I have a dress. It doesn't really matter what I wear anyway."

"No, I don't mean the dress for you. I mean the dress for the bride."

"Are you out of your mind? I am not buying her dress!"

"Well, who is?"

"Bill was supposed to buy the dress!"

"He says he can't tell what they look like on. He sent me a photograph of her and he got her measurements from her modeling composite. She looks like she's exactly your size."

"Steven, there's no way I can get a dress in three weeks. It takes months for alterations."

"He's flying his fiancée's designer in. He wants to fit you tomorrow afternoon."

"Steven, this is hard enough. I lose two guys, have to plan two weddings and now I have to try on some gorgeous dress that someone else will wear? This is so not fair! Not now!"

"Genes, you started this business to make people happy. You're being paid to do this and you're being paid a lot. This isn't about your feelings. This is about the bride."

"CAN I EVER HAVE SOME FEELINGS!"

Steven pulled out a photograph and handed it to Genie.

"That's her. I don't know who this guy is, but whether you agree with his methods or not, what he's doing is exactly what you want him to do. He's planning something to make her happy. Now stop being such a selfish baby and don't make this personal."

"Why does everyone expect me to be so damn perfect! I'm tired of understanding everyone else and not getting anything I want."

"Ok, Genes. When this is all over we'll go to FAO Schwartz and buy you a new set of Legos. But right now we've got a job to do. What time do you want the fitting?"

Genie was curt. "Make it after lunch. Brides have to starve themselves before their fittings. The chumps like me get to eat."

"Ok, I'll order in. I'll even make the call, ok? What do you want?"

Genie felt a pull inside. It was an ache for the healthy side of Jeff. So she did the only thing she could think of to feel close to him in the moment.

"I'll have a brat. Ketchup and pickles. Make it rare."

"Uh Genes, they don't typically ask for temperatures on a brat."

"Well maybe it's time someone around here gets it exactly how they want it."

Steven smiled and nodded. "Maybe it is. So let's make sure it's well done."

CHAPTER 88

Genie and Hank stood to face the three-way mirror. He had just put the last pin in the wedding dress and neither of them could say a word. It was *spectacular.* Genie had seen several pictures of Bill's fiancée, who must have been a celebrity too because she definitely looked familiar. Genie imagined her in the dress, but even more magical, was to imagine how she'd feel.

Hank left the dressing room to grab some pins for the hemline. Just the two of them were left in the room, Genie and the dress. In her whole life she had never seen anything more beautiful. It was elegant, slinky, and somewhat sexy in a quiet and dignified way. It had a romantic nightgown feel with fabric so rich you could inhale it as a dessert. It was simple enough for the beach. It had a subtle sheen that Genie imagined reflecting the colors of the sea and the sunset.

She looked in the mirror, mesmerized by her own reflection. She stood for a moment and just stared. She turned to see the back. Thin satin strings were beaded with tiny white pearls, which tied loosely at the small of her back. The headpiece was a simple comb with pearls and white flowers with just a small spray of veiling.

The shoes were gold and strappy with large pearls that dangled over the top of her foot and rested on top of her toes.

She began to go over the details in her mind. She was concerned with keeping boundaries on the ethics. Bill may not want someone else using his wedding "stage". So Genie had to make sure that whatever they used would not be something that would have been Bill's to hold onto.

The chairs and platform, the vases and props; even the canopy would be considered rentals, therefore recyclable. The flowers *could* be used twice but that was where Genie drew the line. Kay and Danny deserved their own. Genie could use less expensive flowers and grasses. What Kay would have lost on deposits would afford that.

As for the food, it would be Genie's wedding present to the bride and groom. She knew Danny would cover the liquor and their hotel charges. She got wholesale prices anyway, so it was nothing they couldn't handle.

Genie took another look in the mirror. She was hit with a sadness that was hard to shake. When Hank came back in the room, he saw her face.

"It must be difficult. What you're doing."

"Oh no," she replied. "It's just a job."

Wedding white lies.

CHAPTER 89

Bill's wedding was six weeks away. The charter was scheduled to leave at nine o'clock in the morning on the day of the ceremony. That would put the "real" guests on the island by early afternoon with a few hours to get ready before the wedding. Since Bill wanted everyone surprised, guests included, Genie had hired "extras" to act as the extras. This just legitimized the making of the film. They would be flying down on the same flight as the rest of the guests.

The groom asked to pick the name of the supposed film. He titled it "Every Girl's Wish." A few of the guests were given some lines to recite. The set and flower designers, crewmembers, directors, and cameramen were on the plane as well. Genie spared no expense or detail in making sure that this looked authentic. Not even the hotel staff knew who the wedding was for.

Steven had booked Bill and the bride on a later flight so she wouldn't see any of the guests. She would, however, meet some of the extras on the set, in order to set the tone. She and Bill would be arriving just two hours before the wedding. The less time she had on the island, the less chance there was for a screw-up.

The ceremony, at Bill's request, would take place on the beach. So that the guests didn't have to walk in the sand, Genie arranged for a white wooden deck that would extend from the walkway to the altar. Four magnificent tall white logs, wrapped in Italian lights, would be staked into the ground at the end of the platform, closest to the shoreline. Sheer white fabric would drape over the logs acting as a makeshift canopy, tied down with vines and orchids.

White wooden beach chairs, each with a white cashmere throw for cool breezes, would make rows for the guests to be seated. Young white flowering trees would line the aisle, with mini spotlights underneath. Tall glass cylinder vases would be filled with floating island flowers, full of color, placed between candles that would flicker light, throwing hints of color up to the trees. The ceremony would take place during the peak of sundown. The venue was nature's ballroom.

The reception would take place by the pond. Votive candles would float on lily pads and swans would swim in the water. The food would be magnificent and plentiful. White sofas and white cushioned bamboo chairs made a few seating areas, with wood burning tables and fire pits to warm the chill in the air. Tall flowering trees would be brought in to surround three sides of the area, leaving an open view facing the ocean.

Most of Genie's days were calm now. Her mindset was more of a non-mindset. She thought about Jeff every day, but no longer attached any hope. That in itself was a death. Her work became a destination away from her pain and for now that was good enough.

CHAPTER 90

Glitches. They always come as the date gets closer. Kay was depressed and didn't want to go on a trip, especially to someone else's wedding. Genie could feel Kay's anger at Genie for being so insensitive as to suggest such a thing. Genie could relate.

Knowing that she might not give in, Genie called Danny. Since he knew nothing of Kay's heartache, he would go for the free vacation. That she was sure of. He agreed right away to the trip. He didn't sound all that surprised and seemed strangely distracted. He spoke with a trepidation that Genie hadn't heard before.

"So Genie, are you really done with Jeff?"

"Yeah. Why?"

"Well, what if he came back?"

"Well, if he came back not blaming me for everything, and not lying, I guess I'd feel differently. Why are you asking?"

"Just wondering. I gotta run to a meeting. I'll talk to you later."

Genie hung up and looked at Steven.

Steven, why is Danny acting so strangely?"

"I don't know, Gene. Maybe you just bring out the strange in people."

"No, I mean why would he ask about Jeff? What difference does it make to him?"

Steven looked at Genie. For a second, she sensed something odd in him.

"Steven! What! You're acting weird too! What's going on?"

Steven raised his eyebrows with the look that always made Genie crazy.

"Don't give me that look, Steven. Why does everyone want to make me look nuts?"

Steven looked at Genie with concern.

"You know, don't take this wrong. But I swear, Gene, I can't remember the last time you laughed. I mean really laughed. Every bit of life and spark that makes you *you,* is gone. And it left when you said goodbye to Jeff. I think you've died inside."

"I *have* died. I feel it. The pain…"

"I know it's painful. But you have a beautiful life ahead of you, with or without a man. And pain is a part of life that we all have to deal with one way or the other."

"So what am I supposed to do?"

"Give balance to both sides. Feel the bad but don't lose the good. Because wouldn't it be a tragedy, Genes, if the painful part won the battle?"

Those were the words that hit. She really didn't want to have anger. She didn't want to feel depression. She didn't want to give up on happy. She had been so focused on what she didn't have that she forgot about the word *certainty.*

Suddenly, Genie felt hope for *something.*

CHAPTER 91

The Christmas holidays were over. New Year's Eve had come and gone. And finally, the weddings were here. It was just one day before the momentous rite of passage. Suitcase packed, bed made, apartment clean and tidy. Tic-Tacs in the bag. Phone charger, passport, gum, People, and Us.

As Genie was checking her list, the phone rang. It was Danny.

Her best man. Someone else's groom.

"Hey Gene. You doing ok?"

"Yeah."

"Is Steven picking you up?"

"He said he's putting in for a seat change!"

Danny laughed. "Well, Kay and I will be there tomorrow. Just breathe. Oh Genes, my other line's ringing, hold on."

"Ok."

Genie imagined Danny walking down the aisle with Kay. Coming home a married couple. She pictured Danny as a partner, spending time with his wife. She pictured him holding a baby. Coming home to Kay at night. She felt a strange combination of happiness for Danny, and tremendous envy of Kay. Genie imagined waking up with Danny and starting every day with him. *Easy.* That would be a life and a man to trust.

Genie thought about Jeff. To think that flying was something she did to save them, and now she had to do it alone. Danny came back on the line.

"Danny?"

"Yes."

"Have I ruined my life?"

"No."

"How do you know?"

"Tell me what you're doing today."

Genie started to cry. "I'm *flying.*"

"That's right. You are flying to a beautiful place. Just relax and enjoy the ride."

Genie wanted to spill the whole truth. She wanted to ask Danny if he really wanted to marry Kay. She wanted to give it one more try; everything felt different now. She wanted to run to him, hold him tight, and take a new direction. But Genie the professional, kicked into gear, and talked the plan to her client.

"Ok, Dan. Well, you guys have a good flight. I heard there are other celebrities that will be there too." Genie felt so strange lying to Danny. It was the first time since her party for Gregg that she was planning a party for someone she knew. Someone who was about to walk down the aisle. Someone she might lose.

"Genes, I could care less about celebrities. I'm going for you."

"For *me?* You mean for *Kay.*"

"For *Kay?*"

Damn! How could she blow it like that?"

Genie stumbled on her words. "Well... she's the one who wants to see the stars. But what did you mean about doing it for me?"

Danny seemed abrupt. "I meant for you... for your client. To help you out with a client."

"Oh right. I knew that's what you meant."

After they hung up, Genie felt a strange pull inside. She felt an emptiness that made her feel hungry, but not a hunger for food. Then the phone rang. It was Steven, probably calling from downstairs. She knew he would be gentle, knowing this was such a tough spot for her to be in. Genie had known that his usual sarcasm would take a hiatus today. Comforting, sensitive, hand-holding Steven. It was almost worth the trip just to witness that side of him.

Genie sniffled as she answered, waiting for her first installment of kindness.

"Hi, Steven."

"Hey, Bitch. Get your ass down here. You're late."

Genie hung up the phone with a smile. That was exactly the fix she needed.

CHAPTER 92

The sky had surely rehearsed. The water digitally enhanced. The breeze must have had a climate control hidden beneath the surf and white sand. It was all so magnificent that even Genie never imagined it would look like this. She couldn't have. Life just didn't set up this way.

The guests had just one hour before they needed to be back downstairs for the take. No one had questioned not seeing the movie stars yet, but it was explained to them on the plane that they wouldn't see them until the actual filming.

Steven reported earlier that Bill and his fiancée had experienced some delays. They were due to fly out of New York and the weather had been too rough for private charters to take off. They'd be late, but they'd be there. Genie was getting anxious.

Thirty minutes later, the guests began to assemble on the platform. The camera and crew people were in place. The musicians were warming up. Steven was nowhere to be found. Danny and Kay were not around either. Genie had a sinking feeling that something was terribly wrong. Then she saw Steven in the distance. As he drew nearer, her worst fear was written all over his face.

"Genie, we're in trouble. Bill and his fiancée aren't coming."

"WHAT?" Genie felt her legs get weak and she thought she might throw up or faint.

"I swear I don't know what happened. I can't tell whether they got in a fight, or whether she found out, but he was acting really weird and wouldn't say much. I think he's really embarrassed."

"*Embarrassed?* That man ought to be shot!"

"Genie, it's his wedding. He has the right not to have it."

"Steven, I have all of these people here!"

"So, we'll tell them the truth. It's not a surprise anymore, Gene. The gig is up. He'll pay us anyway. He has to. The job is over."

"Are you crazy? What's the matter with you? All of these people flew here for nothing? Steven, I told you from the beginning this guy was a piece of garbage!"

"Ok, so he's garbage. Let's clean up and go."

"Steven, aren't you forgetting something?"

Steven looked at Genie as though he was trying to remember what he forgot.

"Kay and Danny! We need this wedding to happen or theirs gets ruined. Their wedding is the second shoot!"

"Oh *Man*, where's my head." He thought about the whole scenario. "Damn it, Genie, I told you that was a mistake. Now we're going to blow theirs too."

"No, we can't. We have to figure out a way to do this."

"There isn't a way. Once everyone knows the truth, there won't be a shoot tomorrow. There would be no reason for Danny and Kay to stay, let alone participate in a wedding. We need to call their guests and tell them not to come."

"No, Steven, we can't lose both weddings. We need to tell them that Bill couldn't come, but the film is still a go."

"Oh yeah? And where's Brad Pitt? Bad case of the runs?"

"Yes. *No!* We have the director act like the actors both got sick. Or lost. Or delayed or something. They only think that "Bill" is producing it, so they won't care if he doesn't show up. We'll say we need some volunteers to step in. Just to get the location shot with bodies and they'll plug the stars in at a later date."

"And who may I ask, are the volunteers?"

"Well... Kay and Danny! It's perfect."

"No, it's not perfect. They can't get married tonight. Some of their guests aren't coming until tomorrow, remember? Genie, it's not going to work. Give it up and let's just go home. Kay and Danny will never know the difference."

Genie felt horrible. She so wanted this for them. Otherwise it was all such a waste. There had to be a way.

"Steven, I've got it! You and I 'stand in' for the bride and groom. We have it filmed as planned. "Bill's" guests will be bummed that they don't meet any stars, but the worst is they got a free trip on a beautiful island and they'll think they're still in the film. They'll go home tomorrow night as planned. We only need to stick to the plan so that Kay and Danny stay. Tomorrow morning, their wedding goes as planned with their guests."

"Genie, I can't even *pretend* to marry you. I'm not kidding. I'll have post-traumatic stress for years. I'll start to..."

"Oh Steven, I love you so much. I owe you big. So big."

"Darlin', you have no idea."

CHAPTER 93

Genie and Steven rushed to take showers. The "director" explained the change in plans to the guests. Food and drinks were brought out to make the wait tolerable. Everything was nice and calm.

The suite that had been reserved for Bill's fiancée was magnificent. Genie thought how funny it was that she, herself, was going through the exact motions of the bride. She was having her nails, hair, and makeup done in a suite beyond her dreams. She was performing as a "stand-in" which is exactly what the bride would have done. She was calm and relaxed knowing that it wasn't her own wedding which is exactly how the bride would have felt. It was a fascinating peek into what it feels like to be surprised.

The people assisting Genie in the room were as nice as they could be. Kelly was there for makeup, and John was the hair stylist. They were fun, warm, and masterful. It was quite an experience living the life of her client. No wonder she was so successful. This was unbelievable! She felt sorry that the whole thing got wasted. It was by far the best team effort of Steven and Genie's career. And only she got to enjoy it.

There was something kind of twisted and depressing about it at the same time. She couldn't let Kelly or John know that it had been a surprise that was ruined since the secret was still in play. She couldn't talk to them about how sad it felt to wear her own dream, knowing it wouldn't be hers. As beautiful a moment this was, the pain inside tainted the fun.

Finally she was done. She looked in the mirror. She was beautiful. Genie began to feel weak in her stomach. Something was so unsettling to her. There was no one to talk to. She began to feel dizzy and faint. She felt like she couldn't breathe. She managed to excuse herself, grabbed her cell phone and walked out to the balcony. She dialed Ellen's cell, praying she'd have reception, and that the call would go through.

"Hello?"

"Ellen, I'm so sorry to call you. I'm in trouble."

"What's the matter? Aren't you on the island?"

"Yes. And I'm having a panic attack."

"Ok, talk to me. What's going on?"

"I can't see anything clearly. This wedding. Wearing this dress. All the feelings inside. Steven talking me into Jeff. Lori talking me out of Jeff. Danny... perfect Danny. It's all clogging my head and I can't work. When I talk to Steven and listen to my heart, I know I love Jeff even with his faults. Then Lori paints another side and I know loving Jeff is a mistake. He's not someone to trust. And I don't know who to listen to."

"Then stop listening to everyone else. Calm down. Breathe. Let's listen to you."

Genie stopped. She breathed.

"Genie. The question I always come back to is, how do you want to live?"

"I want to live comfortably. I don't want to be lied to. But I can't imagine letting go. I still feel him with me."

"Genie, he's going to be with you until either you two figure this out together, or you finally move past him. Either way, you're going to be just fine."

"I don't believe that, Ellen."

Genie dabbed her eyes with a tissue.

"Genie, I need you to listen. Are you familiar with Taoism?"

"The Chinese Tao?"

"Yes. They have a philosophy that instructs us to go the way of water. Since water always finds the easiest way to get around blockages, that's how we're to move through our lives. We are to act like water."

"How does that relate to me and Jeff? Are you saying I should believe we will be okay?"

"No, I'm saying that you should let *life* happen and *that's* what will be okay. I don't want you to give up hope, whether it's with Jeff or not. I want you to follow the flow."

Something about the combination of Ellen's voice and her words took the fever out of Genie's panic; to the point that she suddenly realized right there on the balcony, where she was and what she faced. *Water.* She immediately told Ellen where she was and the view from the balcony.

"Genie, that's perfect! Hang up the phone now and breathe. Just breathe."

Genie hung up the phone and closed her eyes. She faced up toward the sun and felt the rays land on her skin. She inhaled. She released the breath slowly. She put her hand on her stomach making sure she filled her belly with air. She imagined taking palm leaves and brushing bad thoughts to the side. She saw a clearing inside her head as she pushed the air out again.

Genie could feel the breeze building strength around her, sweeping her hair and the veil from her face. She could hear the sound of the ocean and the waves hitting rocks below her. She imagined the foam filling open spaces so that nothing could disturb this protected calm that nature had just handed her. She took a few more breaths. And then she opened her eyes.

The blue water that faced her was very possibly the most magnificent color she had ever seen. The sky had chosen a tone to offset it that could only be described as ingenious. Genie had never felt more grateful or honored to be a guest at such a performance. She closed her eyes again. She inhaled the experience.

Genie opened her eyes again. She took one last look. She smiled as a tear came to her eye. She smiled even bigger. She noticed her posture was upright and tall, but her balance was still a bit shaky. She turned around, put her hand on the glass door and reentered the hotel room.

As if Kelly and John sensed why she had left the room, they welcomed her back with warm smiles. They approached her, each grabbing one of her arms as they gently led her out of the room and down the corridor. They took an elevator down. As they walked toward the exit, she could hear the island musicians. She could see the color of the water again; the blue of the sky was now being joined by pinks and smoky grays. Suddenly, she stopped in her tracks.

Kelly and John gently took both of her arms. Kelly fixed Genie's veil with the gentleness of a dear friend. John took a stronger hold and placed his hand firmly on Genie's back. He turned her chin toward his face and stared right into her eyes.

"Genie, it's a dream. Step inside and enjoy it. We'll be right here when you wake up."

Something about John's words settled inside her. She felt an immediate shift. She nodded to him in understanding. She faced the exit and began to walk. In that moment she became... *The Bride.*

CHAPTER 94

Genie could see that the guests were seated, but large white umbrellas obstructed her view of them. She heard the music change to the most beautiful tune she had ever heard. It seemed to weave itself into the sounds of the tide, the birds, and the hugging breeze.

The colors of the sky blended together, casting lights like diluted rainbows. The sheer whites of the canopy hip-hopped in all directions, while the white, cashmere shawls draped over their shoulders made the guests appear uniformed.

Genie was just approaching the aisle. She felt like she was in a foggy dream. She was floating somewhere far away and even the people weren't part of her life. Until she saw a face that was. He came up and stood beside her. Genie felt like someone had turned her around three times fast, and then stopped her in position.

She couldn't make sense of anything she saw. She felt him take hold of her arm. She looked at his face but somehow it wasn't registering. She felt like she was hovering over but wasn't sure what stood below. Genie continued to stare at his face. He looked into her eyes, with such a warm smile, and it took her back to a memory. There she was, just a young girl, alive again in the moment. And then he handed her a daisy.

He put his face up to the side of hers. He wore an odd expression. He whispered one word in her ear.

"Surprise."

Genie looked at Gregg with wide eyes. Out of the corner of her eye, she began to see faces she knew. As if one by one, they took hold of her, and pulled her into the moment. Kay and Lori were next to each other, sending visual support. Steven was a couple rows up, with an expression of fun exhaustion. Friends and family members were interspersed among the rows. Genie looked to the other side. Luke looked ready to spring out of his seat. Jennifer and Aunt Dotty were teary eyed. In the row ahead, next to several of Genie's clients, was Hannah Bancroft and her mom.

Genie was trembling. Gregg handed her a bouquet of white flowers. She looked down to see they were daisies. Gregg spoke in her ear again.

"No matter what your decisions are, you're surrounded by people who love you. And that should be no surprise."

Her trust in the one man who had always been there for her propelled one foot to follow the other. She couldn't think to the next moment because she couldn't let go of this one. Somehow her feet moved forward. She felt all eyes upon her as Gregg's arm held her up. Then her eyes fixed on a sight up ahead that made her stop completely.

The two men stood close together, side by side. As her eyes met his, he stepped away from the spot he was in and walked toward Genie. His eyes called her with calm intensity, yet raging in their command. She felt a force pull her toward him. Once her eyes had found his, there was nowhere else to look. Nowhere else to go.

Genie saw his eyes leave her face and travel up and down her body. He looked like he couldn't grasp the moment any more than she could. She saw him weaken in his own emotion. Genie could see his senses leave him and that brought her back to her own. The little girl inside of her calmly went off to the side. Genie, the woman, taking full control, walked up to the man she loved.

When she reached the spot where Jeff was standing, they looked at each other and smiled. Jeff spoke softly.

"To the right one."

Genie smiled in a haze. "With a chaser." She couldn't catch up to the moment. It was all happening way too fast. It was like stepping into a magical place that erases bad history. She was amazed that she could drop a whole past, just by holding his hand.

"Jeff, I don't… I mean all of this. It's so beautiful. I just can't believe you came up with this crazy idea."

"I didn't, Honey."

"You *didn't?* Who did?"

Jeff turned to face the chairs. And his eyes pointed to Casey.

"Casey?"

Casey focused on Genie with the innocence of a little girl dreaming. Genie whispered in disbelief.

"Oh my Gosh. I don't know what to say."

Jeff looked at Genie with the most humbled expression. He smiled.

"It's been one crazy ride. But I think we just say 'I do.'"

CHAPTER 95

Funny thing about dreams coming true, they get damaged on the way to your doorstep. By the time you open the delivered package, it's not only missing some parts. It's got other parts that don't belong there. Do you sign your name and accept the package because no dream in life is perfect? Or are dreams called dreams for a reason?

Genie was so focused on Jeff's face, and how much she still loved the good parts of him, that she lost sight of what stood around them. The shock wasn't wearing off. No answers were appearing. So Genie did the only thing that seemed genuine and not confusing. She reached up and she hugged him.

There was no question that these two bodies knew a home together. Everything that was wrong went away. Every doubt turned to gratitude. But Genie knew it was only for a moment. Similar to looking at a cloud and seeing a figure, it's so vivid you can point it out. But soon thereafter, the cloud moves on and the picture disappears.

Genie let go of Jeff and looked at his face. There he was, so familiar. As if no time had passed, no trouble existed, no other women, no lies told, and a life force with a mind of its own. Why was seeing him so impactful? How could it erase so much bad?

"Jeff, I always said I do. All you said was 'I can't.'"

"Well, now I know *I can't* live without you. After you left that day, the words we said..."

"But you know what comes after '*I do?*'"

Jeff got his cute Jeff look. "Well, the bill. But I know the boss. I think we'll get a good discount." Jeff looked at Genie and smiled.

"Jeff, what about the rest? I feel, I express, I vent—and you don't like that."

"You can do and feel and say anything you want. I have no problem with that at all. Just as long as it's not about me or what I'm doing. And so long as it's not said with distrust."

Genie looked into his eyes. "And if I think what you're doing isn't right or fair? Or even healthy for us as a couple?"

"Benefit of the doubt."

"Happy with you no matter what?"

"No reason not to be. Knowing I'm doing my best."

"And the past? Everything we've been through? All the craziness?"

"Clean slate. No discussion of the past. It's our only chance to survive."

Genie paused. Was he rational and right or were they both being conned by his dark side?

Genie looked at Casey. She was watching the whole thing, waiting for a wedding. Their eyes locked; hearts connected. A conversation traveled between them. Genie gave her a look that said 'I love you'. Casey mouthed the same words back. Genie put up a finger signaling, 'Give me a moment'. Casey mouthed 'Okay'.

Genie stood in a trance. She was trying to feel something but her body and mind had gone numb. Her navigation was broken. Suddenly, out of the corner of her eye, she saw something that pulled her in. *The fricking wedding cake.*

All eyes upon her, E.T. in full wedding drag, began to take steps to phone home. She touched Jeff's arm and gave him a kiss on the cheek.

"I need a minute, ok?"

Jeff smiled. "No rush, Sweetheart."

Genie sped toward the wedding cake as if it had been programmed to summon her. And when she finally got there, she heard a voice behind her.

"Half chocolate cake, half carrot cake. My wedding gift to you."

"Lori!"

"Genes. You learned to stop feeding your gut. Now you need to trust it."

They stood next to the cake and looked at each other. There was no conversation to have. Only the unspoken confirmation of what they already knew. Genie slowly walked back to the seated guests. She hugged and kissed her mom and Aunt Dotty. They exchanged some private words. She gave warm hugs to friends and clients and thanked them for their efforts to be there. She took Casey by the hand and walked up to Jeff who was still at the end of the aisle. Then she took his hand.

"This little girl wants us to be together. And I understand how little girls think because it wasn't that long ago that I had the same thoughts she did."

Jeff spoke gently. "It took a little girl to convince me that I like the way they think."

"Jeff. I love you. I don't want anyone else. But what has changed?"

"Maybe nothing. But I don't want to live without you."

Those words would have been more than enough had they been delivered six months ago. But Genie was a different person now. She wasn't afraid anymore.

"I don't want to live without me either. And if I don't have a voice with you, I can't live with you."

"Gino, we'll have to compromise. No more drama. You'll just need to pick your battles."

Genie spoke with confidence. "I have. I'm battling for my voice." Genie looked at Casey. She grabbed her hand and began to walk away.

"Genie! Tell me what you want."

"I want a partner who communicates truth no matter what it is. I'd rather see an ugly truth than live a pretty lie. I want someone who is loyal to me and wouldn't dream of risking what we have by going to another woman or telling me a lie. I want my feelings to be heard, even if they're about you and something you're doing. And I don't want you leaving them. Or me."

"Genie, you have more feelings than anyone I know!"

"Casey? Shall we?" As Genie and Casey approached the cake, Casey pulled on Genie's dress. She whispered up at Genie.

"Genie, can I have a piece of cake now?"

Genie figured what the heck. This was her wedding. "Sure." She took the spatula and cut a piece of carrot cake.

Casey whispered again. "Can I have the chocolate side instead?"

"Not yet!"

Jeff called out. "Genie! You can get mad or hurt twice a year."

Genie shrugged. "You know, we'll call you."

Jeff looked pained.

"Ok Genie, once every other month. I think that's unreasonable but it's my final compromise."

"Thanks. We're just going to shop this one a bit more. There are men who actually expect women to get hurt. Even act crazy sometimes. And they don't shut them out of their lives."

Casey whispered loudly. "Genie, you *are* crazy! That's a good deal! You said you don't even let yourself get that hurt anymore!"

"I know that. But sometimes he pulls crap that he won't admit to. He's a guy, Case! Guys get mean! Especially if they're in love with you. He knows my weak spots and he comes in for the kill!"

"Oh Genie, the boys at school do it on the playground! It gets really bad in the fourth grade. They're nice to the ones they don't like. Or they ignore them. But the girls they like? They're sooooo mean!"

Genie laughed. "Exactly! Jeff is a boy on the playground. He's going to trip me. Even if he doesn't mean to, he will because he has the sensitivity of cement. I'm going to say ouch. And then he'll leave me with my scraped knees to cry."

Casey begged. "Can't you ignore him?"

Genie looked at Casey. Suddenly the fog and self-doubt cleared. Everything she hadn't wanted to see was dangling in bold memories.

"You know, Case. Not anymore."

Casey was desperate. "Do you think he'll budge?"

Genie whispered. "Nope. Maybe with some other girl. But something about me…"

"Oh Genie. Don't give up!"

Genie smiled. She paused. "Ok, Case. We haven't gotten the walk away deal yet. Who knows, maybe he's still got some room."

CHAPTER 96

Genie took Casey's hand and walked out toward the beach. Genie took her shoes off and put them under an end table that sat next to a chaise. Casey took hers off and put them next to Genie's. They were now in the sand, walking along the shore. They heard Jeff, out of breath, running up behind them.

"Ok Genie, once a month."

"That's better, Jeff. I love you. Not quite where we need to be. I might have PMS and be in a bad mood two days in a row. And then the next week you might be stressed out, say something mean, and if I react to you I've exceeded my monthly allotment!"

Jeff stood where he was, out of breath, shaking his head in exhaustion.

Casey spoke in a desperate tone.

"Genie, what are you doing? There's only so far he can go!"

"Case, this is not the kind of prenuptial agreement that people typically fight over, ok?"

Casey looked up in thought. "I think I get it. It's just like Freddy and his frogs."

Genie looked at Casey with surprise.

"All the girls love him. But he only wants this girl, Maggie. Once she opened his lunchbox not knowing that he keeps his frogs in there. She started screaming. *And he liked it.* So, now he puts the frogs in other places like her locker and even her gym shoes. He loves it when she gets all crazy."

Genie nodded. "Whoever invented boys, had to be a boy!"

"Genie!" Casey panicked as she saw Jeff had turned around. "He's doing the walk out deal on you!"

Genie turned around and saw Jeff walking away. She called out to him.

"Jeff, don't judge me by how you handle things. Accept me as I am."

Jeff's voice was loud since it had to compete with the wind. "If I accept it you'll do it all the time."

"No. If you accept me, I won't need to."

"Genie, all I want is to know you're not going to get upset with me for being who I am and doing what I like to do. I want to get up in the morning and not have to worry about how you feel, about what I do or when I do it. If I'm around other women, you'll give me the benefit of the doubt. I want to know that if I come home late and you can't reach me, you won't jump to me fooling around."

Genie took pause. Would Danny wake up in the morning without interest in Genie's plans? If she couldn't reach him would she think he was with a woman? Would Kay suspect him of that? No. Danny didn't live in a way that led people not to trust him. Genie knew without a doubt that her gut was worth listening to.

"Jeff, trust doesn't come from demanding it. Trust comes when it's earned. And I'm sorry, but trust goes away when someone blows it. It might have to be earned again."

"You've got my offer, Gene. I love you but I can't give you any more."

And there it was. A whole relationship reduced to two recipes. One separates the yolk from the egg whites and one whips them together. One includes vinegar and one is vinegar free. One includes unlimited ladyfingers, and one wants them rationed.

No different than I want Chicago; I want New York. I want Jewish; I want Catholic. I want two kids; I want seven. Half the nation would agree with one side; half would agree with the other. Two sides that are right; just on different sides. It's what you call an impasse. A wedding without a marriage. Half of a heart with half of its beats, and a soul without its mate.

Jeff smiled and shook his head. He looked at Genie. He walked up to her and wrapped his arms around her tight. She folded into him. They didn't let go for a long time. He hugged Casey and kissed her on top of her head. Then, he walked back up to toward the guests. Casey looked like a little girl who had just lost her puppy.

"I can't believe you did that, Genie. He came all the way here. *We had him.*"

"We had his love. But I want more."

"But Genie, he would do anything to have you."

"I want more than to be had. I want a full relationship with someone I trust and if I can't have that, I'm better off alone." Genie looked at Casey with soft eyes. "It hurts less, Honey."

Casey looked down at the sand, making patterns dragging her shoes. Genie held Casey's chin and directed her face up to Genie's.

"Case, you did something nobody has ever done. *You surprised me.* It's the best gift I've ever gotten from anybody! It came from your heart and I know that. The wedding wasn't the gift, and it's not the forever, don't you see? *You are.*"

Casey looked down at the sand again. Genie looked at the top of her head in thought. Then she gently pulled her chin back up.

"You are my little girl. That's a commitment I can make and there is no doubt. You understand what I'm saying?"

Casey smiled. Genie could see something calculating inside Casey's head. She had a feeling she knew what it was. And then Casey confirmed it.

"So this was OUR wedding!"

Genie laughed. "Yep. We planned the whole thing *together* didn't we?" Genie grabbed Casey's hand. "Shall we walk?"

Casey took Genie's hand. "Yep."

Genie and Casey walked along the shore; white dresses flowing, hands interlocked.

After a few minutes, Casey spoke. "Do you think we'll get him back?"

Genie walked a few steps before responding. "I think there is someone out there for Jeff who he will be more comfortable with. We aren't a good fit, Case." Genie looked down at Casey's face. She could see her disappointment.

"I'm sorry, Honey. I know how much you adore him."

"How will we get over it?"

Genie smiled. "We'll cry a lot. We'll laugh. We'll cry some more. And then we'll see a movie. Maybe one day we'll make one!"

"Who do I get to play?"

Genie smiled and patted her daughter on the head. "You get to play *yourself*."

CHAPTER 97

The best part of a surprise party isn't the surprise. It's the stories and plans of the lead up. The secret phone calls, missed innuendo, the cover-ups, sneak-ups and mishaps. In this case, there was no happy event to retrace. And one little brother knew that. He came up to Genie as she was talking to Lori and Hannah at the reception party.

"Hey Genie Butt."

"Hey Lukey Slut."

"Knock knock."

Genie smiled. "Who's there?"

"Don't marry up!"

Genie laughed and hugged him.

Just then, Steven came up to Genie. In all of the craziness, she hadn't even spoken to him. They looked at each other and smiled. They both shook their heads. There was so much to say neither of them knew where to start. So Steven took the lead.

"Nice duds."

"Gee, thanks."

"Got any questions for me, Partner?"

"Just one, Steven. What the *fuck?*"

"What was I supposed to do? Casey called as a client. And Danny foot the bill so I…"

"*What?* Danny was in on this?"

"No, Genes. I did a credit check on Casey and put the tab on her Visa."

"I don't understand! Danny wanted me to marry Jeff?"

"Honestly? I don't think so. But I think he thought it was what you wanted. It was Casey's idea to make a surprise wedding. But Jeff knew about it too."

"He *knew?* But we were broken up! He had a girlfriend. Or a few."

"He did. But in between them, I think even during, he never gave up hope. He thought you'd change or see things differently while you were apart. He went along with the wedding, backed out, came back in… kind of building and losing hope like you did."

"What about Kay?"

"Set up."

Genie's eyes doubled in size. "*She didn't want a wedding?* She and Danny aren't getting married?"

"Nope. Danny got her to call you."

Genie's head was spinning.

"You were doing this wedding to make Danny happy, and Danny was doing it for you. It was enough sweetness to rot my teeth. I'm adding the cost of my root canal to the bill."

"Hold on. Who was the picture of Bill's fiancée? She looked so familiar."

"My sister."

"Steven! That's right! I knew I'd seen her before. She lost weight!"

"Yeah." Steven laughed. "I sent her to Ellen."

"What about the dress, the plans, the cancellations, the changes, *and standing in for Bill's bride…* holy shit! I walked right into it all!

I planned my *entire* wedding! You just kept setting up problems and I kept figuring them out. I got myself down the aisle!" Genie paused in thought. "Wait. My mom and Aunt Dotty. Gregg... Lori, Hannah... did everyone know?"

"They didn't know until they got here. Nobody except for Danny, Casey and Jeff knew about the wedding."

"How did you get everyone here?"

"Jeff pitched in an airplane."

"Wow. But I mean, what did they think they were coming here for?"

"We planned it for now because your birthday is next week so we made it about that. They got a free trip out of it so for them, it was just all fun."

"Steven! I can't believe you didn't tell me! Even when Jeff and I were broken up, you let me suffer that way!"

"Client confidentiality, Gene. I knew you'd be pissed about that! Even though I did it for you. But come on. I know you can find a way to turn it."

He was right. She *was* mad. "This is the same fight we always have. You put business before our friendship!"

"Aha! I did not. This time, I put our friendship first!"

"How!"

"I couldn't share business with you because I wanted my friend surprised."

Genie looked like a cash register waiting for the total. She looked at him with suspicion. He looked at her with an evil grin. She smiled and then they both laughed.

"What about all the guests I met before? Bill's guests?"

"People staying in the hotel. They got guests to sign up and help out."

"How did they get them to do that?"

"Offered them a free breakfast tomorrow."

"Who's paying for that?"

"The hotel, if we promise them a gig here in the next year. And now that you *travel,* I figure we can make good on that."

It was all catching up. Genie's eyes filled up with tears. "Steven, I don't know what to say. I don't know who to say it to."

Steven got quiet. He looked down at the ground.

"Genie, listen. *I* have something to say." He paused again. "I pushed hard for you to be with Jeff. But I got to know him through planning this thing, and you know what I think?"

"That I made a mistake? I should marry him?"

"No, more that I finally saw what you saw. I mean, Casey had this crazy notion. No one in the world would have taken this on. But I guess Danny was of the opinion that if Jeff wanted to marry you, you'd want to marry Jeff. So Danny called him and asked how he felt about Casey's idea."

"What did Jeff say?"

"He said that he had been totally obsessed and unhappy living without you. He felt you had both learned a lot being apart. So as crazy as the whole thing was, he was in."

"Wow."

Steven nodded and looked down at the floor. "You know, Danny worked really hard to make this happen for you. And he wasn't even marrying you. So for him, there was nothing to gain from giving. But there wasn't one day that Jeff called or asked what would feel good to you. I guess what I'm saying is, I didn't see any effort to make you happy. Just the effort to make sure you were there for *him.*"

Genie nodded her head. Finally, the validation.

Just then, Lori walked up. She whispered to Genie and Steven. "Genie, I may have misjudged Jeff."

"What are you *talking* about?" Genie passed hard glances between Steven and Lori. "What is *with* you guys?" But Lori was genuine in her tone.

"I think he really loves you. I just saw him, and Genie, he's heartbroken."

Steven nodded his head side to side. "He just wants what he can't have."

Lori broke in. *"I don't think so.* I think for the first time, he really knows what he wants."

Steven spoke sarcastically. "Trust me. He loves many women and that is what he wants."

Lori shook her head. "No, Steven. You know what he told me? Every night, before he goes to bed, no matter who he's ever been with, he says *Goodnight Gene, I love you.* If he's not with Genie, he'll end up living a lie. He wants to be with her!"

Lori looked at Steven. She shrugged her shoulders at Genie. "I voted against him all along. And I think he's made a ton of mistakes and hurt a lot of women but it was because he was in love with you. Maybe the monster wasn't Jeff. Maybe it was both of your fears. So, I'm changing parties, Gene. I'm voting Jeffocrat."

CHAPTER 98

If Genie had written a four hundred page novel, studied and researched every detail, tied it up in her conclusion, printed it out, and set the stack of pages on the table, listening to Steven and Lori was like aiming a leaf blower right to the pages and daring the book to make sense.

Had fear told her a story and disguised itself as the truth? Or had Jeff been lying to everyone, disguised as a rational man? Had all her senses fooled her? Or had they been sharp, in tune, and protective? Does anyone know who anyone is? On what basis do we judge truth, feelings, or actions? And for that matter, on what basis do we judge love? It was in that moment of so many questions, she found her universal answer. Her judgment would exist inside her own comfort and she would make all decisions from there.

Genie stayed downstairs with her family and friends. When everyone was engaged in talking and eating, and Casey was in Luke's lap, Genie took a walk toward the shore. She looked back at the wedding platform. The canopy that dripped in white satin, and the candles whose flames had gone home.

She took off her shoes to feel the cool sand. Her dress felt heavy as it dragged and caught up with her feet. The sound of the ocean was a mother's voice as the breeze gently stroked her hair. Suddenly, she heard someone behind her.

"Did somebody around here order a pizza?"

Genie turned around. Danny gave a quiet smile. Genie smiled back. She looked at his face. She could feel the tears making their way up, but she made the decision to block them. She turned those tears into the deepest gratitude for the person who stood before her.

Danny spoke softly. "Are you ok?"

The tears kept trying to come, trying to bring along pain. But Genie wouldn't let them. She smiled at Danny, and just for a moment, felt a pull to run to him. But something inside quieted the instinct, and told her to stay where she was. Instead, she simply reflected.

She thought about every year, every walk, every bike ride, each conversation and phone call, the pizzas he ate without the cheese and the banana pancakes he ordered for *her.* His loyalty to their friendship, his patience with her confusion, and his flexibility. Every ounce of trust and consistency sat witness to the moment. Genie smiled as she spoke.

"Thank you for being my friend. My ever so loyal friend."

Danny paused before he responded. He looked at her with eyes she had never seen before; certainly not in Danny. He spoke so genuinely.

"*You are welcome.* Do you want to take a walk? I know you need to talk."

As much as she wanted to run to Danny, Genie made another choice.

"You go back to Kay. She doesn't really know anyone here. And I won't be gone long."

Genie gave Danny a hug. They took each other's hands and squeezed.

"Ok. But if you need anything at all, you know where to find me."

Genie nodded and smiled. In that small exchange, she felt a sense of peace. She no longer felt confused or torn. Instead, she just felt lucky. Danny turned to walk back toward the hotel, and Genie faced the opposite direction. The wedding platform got further behind her, every step she took away.

As Genie kept walking, she looked up and saw an airplane, silvery and shimmering, reflecting the setting sun. Tears began to run down her face but she kept the pace of her steps. She looked out over the ocean. She looked back at the distance she'd covered. She thought about her life, her family, and her friends. She thought about the office, Steven, and the clients with celebrations, then Lori's and Steven's words that presented themselves in debate. And then she thought about Jeff, and going home without him.

In the recent past, especially with the ugly encounters of the break up, her thoughts of him were dark. There was relief in getting away. The problem was, and still would be, that loving him had made her so happy. Being loved by him filled her up. To lose all that seemed equivalent with losing her happiest self. But holding on to something so unsure, so damaging and unhealthy—what to do with this?

Genie noticed a pelican hovering over the water. Instantly, he dove straight down. A nose-dive crash landing with an almost immediate return toward the sky. She thought about Mrs. Finch, that all it takes is twenty seconds for love to come back if both people let it in. Maybe Genie could do that all by herself. Not for

Jeff and not to be with him. Not for their relationship, but for her, because even after a diving crash, feeling the love feels better.

Without the safety belt of bitterness, she dove straight into the memory of the first day they met. She remembered the first glance, the first kiss, the first time they said I love you, the belly laughs and long talks where they learned and discovered each other.

She thought about his belief and insistence that she rise past her fears, her insistence that he listen to her, the knowledge that before she came along, he had never really loved, and had never wanted to. In a sense, she had given birth to his heart. Did a break-up take that from her? Could it take that away from Jeff?

Genie came up for air and took another dive in; the long and luxurious cuddles, inhaling each other's breath and making pretzels out of their limbs, the way he held her so tight and wouldn't let her go, the words, the days, the experience, looking into each other's eyes and making that unspoken trade. This was the man, after all, who taught her how to *breathe.*

Genie pictured the Jeff look, the terrible fights, the rage, and all the pain. *The stories and suspicions around them.* Separate from that though, she thought about how hard he tried to keep her, to hold on and stretch himself to be better for her, and better for everyone else.

Genie thought about all the good things that made up who he is even though it was easier to see the bad. Because there had been love, Genie made a decision. Regardless of wherever they ended up, she would pass by the bad view from time to time, but not place the sofa there.

Genie turned around and looked back toward the hotel. It would be the last time for a while, maybe forever, that all the people she loved in her life would be gathered in one place: her mom, Gregg,

Luke, Casey, and Aunt Dotty, Danny and her closest friends. And for tonight, Jeff was still there in body; her dad so close in spirit. Not exactly perfect people. Not in their actions or in events. But somehow, in spite of it all, Genie felt *embraced.*

As the sand refreshed her toes, she inhaled the cleansing breeze. The little girl inside of her pulled the covers up tight, and rested her face on the pillow. Her face sank into that soft warm place with the smile that comes when we're safe. She closed her eyes and waited for sleep. Finally, she was home.

ONE YEAR LATER

Genie was walking across the street just as her cell phone rang. She picked it up on the second ring, glanced at the screen to see who was calling, *hah!* As if she didn't know.

"Dan, I'm almost there. I got stuck behind a..."

"Just tell me what you're wearing so he recognizes who you are."

"Navy blue strapless."

"Perfect. You look hot in that one."

"Thanks! Is Kay with you now?"

"She just walked into the bathroom."

"Well, tell her I said thank you for setting this up. But you know how I loathe blind dates."

"Genes, you never know. Blind dates are the best way to meet people these days. It worked for Kay and me."

"Geez Dan, do you have to rub it in?"

Danny laughed.

"Dan. What if you were the right guy and I lost you?"

"If I was the right guy, you couldn't lose me. I'm the right friend though. *Right?*"

Genie smiled. "Right, *Guy!*"

Danny laughed at the pun.

"Why do I have to meet him at a *wine tasting?* And I never got the chance to get details from Kay. We kept leaving messages but never got a hold of each other. And I don't know anything about wine, you know that! Couldn't we have met up at a buffet? Now that I'm not bingeing anymore, I can go to all those fine places!"

Danny laughed. "Genes, you can't drink Manischewitz the rest of your life. You need to get educated. Anyway, that's where he is tonight so it works."

"What's the matter with Manischewitz?"

"Nothing if it's Passover and your name is Uncle Irving!"

"Yeah, well I'd like to *pass over* this whole night. You guys make me feel like a loser. You're so damn cute together. It's *really* annoying. I'm about to give up hope, Danny. I'll never meet anyone!"

"Genie, hold on. Kay wants to talk to you."

"Okay, put her on."

"Genie?"

"Hi, Kay. I'm really not..."

"I promise you'll like him. Women go nuts over him."

"Kay, I'm really picky."

Kay laughed. "Ya *think?*"

Genie rolled her eyes but she couldn't ever hate Kay. She still allowed Danny and Genie their Saturday morning bike rides.

"So, how do you know him?"

"We grew up together. He broke up with someone about a month ago but I just ran into him Sunday. It's *fate.*"

"It's *rebound.*"

"Not at all, Genie. Long story. Trust me on this, ok?"

"Ok, I'm walking in now." Genie walked up the marble stairs of this grand old building. She entered through the white-paned beveled glass double doors, framed with crimson drapes. It was somewhat tired in décor, but still elegant and lovely. The high ceilings and magnificent crown moldings looked regal, historic, and proud.

Genie began to scan the room. There were three long tables, all filled with wine bottles and people assembled around them. Behind each of the tables were people pouring wines and talking to the guests. Genie didn't see anyone that fit the bill of the ultimate blind date.

"Which one is he?"

"Look for a white shirt, black pants, and thick dark hair combed back."

"Kay, I don't see anyone like that. And anyway, Jeff put the curse on me. He said I'll never find anyone who I'll..."

Just then, Genie felt a tap on her shoulder. She turned around to see who it was. *It had to be him, holy shit!*

"Are you Genie?"

With the phone still on her ear she answered, *"Matt?"*

Genie heard Kay in her ear. "Oh my God, he's there! What do you *think?* Don't be obvious! Genie, if you think he's cute, just say the name of an animal or a car or something. If he's not cute, just say goodbye and I'll know."

Genie stayed on the phone as she looked at Matt. There it was. The dark, thick hair that was combed straight back. A few strands had unleashed themselves, curling down toward his forehead, which had the some of the smoothest skin she had ever seen on a man. His complexion was clear and slightly tanned. There was just a touch of gray at his temples.

His features were simple, his eyes were warm, and his jaw line was wide and strong. He had beautiful lines running down from his cheekbone and when he smiled, the lines were deeper and more pronounced. But most of all, he looked gentle.

"Uh... Jaguar, Kay! Gotta go." She took the phone down from her ear and slipped it into her purse.

Matt raised his eyebrows, looking curious. The lines that formed above his brow looked like a design drawn on an etch-a-sketch, unexpected and perfectly spaced. This man's face was *art.*

Genie extended her hand formally.

"Nice to meet you, Matt."

Matt nodded. "Likewise." He raised his eyebrows again. "Do you drive a Jaguar?"

Suddenly, Genie panicked. How the *hell* was she supposed to explain this one?"

"Uh, no. I don't drive a Jaguar, no."

Matt smiled with even more curiosity. "Does Kay?"

"Uh, no. I believe she drives a Prius."

Matt spoke with a polished yet kind-hearted tone. "Do you have a *pet* Jaguar?"

Genie could see where this was going. "No pets, no."

He smiled bigger. *Much bigger.* "I see. So that was *code?*"

Genie laughed with embarrassment. She nervously tucked her hair behind her ear. She smiled sheepishly, looking down at the floor.

"Uh, yeah. It was code."

He looked at her with adoring warmth. "Do I get to crack it?"

Genie looked up at him and rolled her eyes. Matt began to laugh. Genie laughed with him. They looked at each other with the kind of smiles that normally come *after* the wine. She felt sweaty under her shirt. It was exactly the sweat that begins to build up when you meet a blind date that works.

Genie cocked her head to the side. "Can I have some wine first?"

Matt nodded with confidence. "*Absolutely!* Care to walk around?"

"Absolutely!"

As if they'd known each for much longer than sixty seconds, Matt took Genie's hand. He led her to a table. They stood among the others and began listening to the man who was describing a bottle of Chardonnay. Matt looked at Genie and smiled. He leaned toward her just a tad. This connection didn't seem forced or unnatural. It actually felt strangely organic. Genie was hit with a feeling that was so clean and joyful, her insides began to applaud.

Matt reached toward the table and grabbed two wine glasses. He held them up to the man pouring wine and watched him fill each glass. He handed one of the glasses to Genie, held his glass up to hers, and spoke quietly with a slight smile.

"To breaking each other's codes."

Genie smiled. She spoke with warm flirtation. "Don't you have to trust someone before you give it out?"

Matt raised his eyebrows and nodded. He gestured with a glance around the room. "You know, there aren't any wines in this room that happened quickly. If they did, they wouldn't be here."

Genie nodded. "What about someone who wants the perfect wine right now? There's a lot of that going around, you know."

"Then they buy a cheaper bottle, I guess. They'll still get the alcohol rush, if that's what they're looking for."

Genie laughed. "And what are you looking for?"

Matt smiled. He looked Genie straight in the eye. "Well, I'm not looking for a rush. But, I also don't mind when good things happen quickly."

"Would you trust that?"

"I trust it can happen."

Genie felt shy, but not too shy to ask. Something about Matt allowed it. "Has that ever happened to you?"

Matt's expression was soft. He spoke slowly. "Not really. Not yet. But who knows..." His face lit up with the most adorable smile. "Maybe I just met a Jaguar."

Genie's insides felt like they had just been poured a warm dose of cocoa on a cold winter Sunday. She touched her glass to Matt's glass. She looked into his eyes, to his broadening smile and took a sip of the wine. Matt took a sip from his glass. Just as he was about to comment on the taste, a man came up to them and patted Matt on the back. They said their hellos, Matt introduced Genie, and she half listened as the two men chatted.

Genie looked around the room and took another sip of the wine, which wasn't all that bad considering it wasn't the good old holiday stuff. As she brought the glass halfway down from her face she saw something in the distant corner. She did a double take. There he was, sitting in a chair, holding his own glass of wine.

He sat casually with his legs crossed. He looked peaceful and confident, exactly the same as he had that morning she woke up to see him sitting in the corner of her bedroom. The light was better in this room than it was that day. She could make out his face more clearly. He looked exactly as she remembered. And for the first time in her life, she realized she looked just like him.

He took the glass, raised it as if to toast her, smiled proudly, and nodded his head just once. He took his other hand, held it close to his chest, gestured with his head toward Matt, and gave her a thumbs up. Genie stared at him, and then looked over to Matt.

She faced his profile and watched him speak to his friend. She noticed his gestures, his smile, and the gentleness of his tone. Suddenly, he turned to face her and caught her staring at him. His eyes were warm and accepting. He smiled and held the glance. As awkward as it would seem, since their history was all of five minutes, he reached his hand for Genie and pulled her closer to him.

Genie glanced back at her father. She raised her glass to her dad and nodded in understanding. She mouthed the words I love you. She felt a light glaze of a tear in each eye, just enough to make the room twinkle. She wasn't afraid to look away from her dad because she knew she would see him again. Genie returned to the conversation that Matt was having with his buddy. He gently put his arm around the small of her back and stood very close to her. When she looked toward the corner to find her dad, he wasn't there anymore. He was too busy orchestrating.

The lights of the opulent chandeliers reminded all of the crystal glasses, every piece of sterling silver, and each grape still on its vine, that they were there for a celebration. Their assignment was to reveal the light. Each glass was instructed to shine and sparkle, the ice cubes would sing in harmony, and the building that stood for over one hundred years, set a foundation of strength and survival. A beautiful new couple was in their midst. Hope had indeed won its battle.

THE END